PENGUIN BOOKS

DEAR DOCTOR LILY

Monica Dickens, great-granddaughter of Charles Dickens, has written over forty novels, autobiographical books and children's books, and her works have been adapted for television and film. Her first book, *One Pair of Hands*, came out of her experience as a cook-general – the only work for which her upper-class education had fitted her. It made her a best-seller at twenty-two, and is still in great demand.

Although her books arise out of the varied experiences of her life, she has not taken jobs just in order to write about them: working in an aircraft factory and a hospital was her war work, not research. When she joined the Samaritans, it was the work of befriending distressed fellow human beings which she found compelling, although her novel *The Listeners* came from that experience.

She set up the first American branch of the Samaritans in Boston, Massachusetts, and lived near by on Cape Cod for many years with her husband, Commander Roy Stratton, retired from the U.S. Navy, and her horses, dogs and cats. She now lives in England, in an old thatched cottage on the Berkshire Downs. She has two daughters.

Her autobiography, *An Open Book*, appeared in 1978.

D0307791

MONICA DICKENS

Dear
Doctor
Lily

PENGUIN BOOKS

PENGUIN BOOKS

Published by the Penguin Group
27 Wrights Lane, London w8 5tz, England
Viking Penguin Inc., 40 West 23rd Street, New York, New York 10010, USA
Penguin Books Australia Ltd, Ringwood, Victoria, Australia
Penguin Books Canada Ltd, 2801 John Street, Markham, Ontario, Canada l3r 1b4
Penguin Books (NZ) Ltd, 182–190 Wairau Road, Auckland 10, New Zealand

Penguin Books Ltd, Registered Offices: Harmondsworth, Middlesex, England

First published by Viking 1988
Published in Penguin Books 1989
1 3 5 7 9 10 8 6 4 2

The extract on p. 249 is from 'My Word, You Do Look Queer', copyright 1923 by
Francis Day & Hunter Ltd., London wc2h 0ld. Reproduced by permission

The extract on p. 448 is from 'As kingfishers catch fire, dragonflies draw flame' by
Gerard Manley Hopkins

Filmset in Monophoto Bembo
Printed and bound in Great Britain by
Richard Clay Ltd, Bungay, Suffolk

One

When she was eighteen, Lily went to the United States. In the early sixties, London Airport was still a fairly romantic muddle of small buildings and temporary wooden sheds left over from the war. People wandered about in a leisurely way, carefully dressed for travelling, because flying was still an event, instead of a trauma to be survived in old clothes and flat shoes. There was room and time for everybody. You could arrive late if you wanted, and hop on your plane at the last minute, as if you were catching a bus.

Lily, a naïve, passionate adventurer, with smooth brown hair fastened back from her innocent round forehead and the frame of her glasses loose, was anxious to shake off her parents and go forth alone, to be whoever she wanted to be. But James and Nora stuck to her closely, as you could in those days when there was no formal security, breathing behind her neck while she stood at the counter, walking down corridors where she wanted to run, strolling with her across the tarmac, her father carrying her bag and hoping people would think he was a passenger.

'Hurry.' Other people were ahead of Lily, climbing on to the plane. 'It might go without me.'

'Knock it off, you've paid for your ticket.' Her father slowed, his huge hand dragging at her arm. 'My ankle's acting up.'

Lily shook him off, dragged the bag from his shoulder, kissed them both quickly and ran, the bag bumping against her leg.

At the top of the steps, on her own at last, she looked down at them from a world away. The little people of England, un-ambitious, safe. Daddy in the Post Office. Mum a State-enrolled nurse. Neither of them had ever dreamed of doing any of the amazing things that Lily was going to do in the remarkable life ahead of her.

She waved, turned away, put up a practised middle finger to push her glasses back on to her nose and stepped into the plane.

7

It smelled of cooking, electricity, rubbery fabric and manu-factured air. Up front, three men in white shirtsleeves were gods in the cockpit. When one of them turned to reach for something behind his narrow seat, Lily quickly looked away, as if a lavatory door had been left open.

'Seat 23B.'

'Yes, I know.' Lily gave the hostess a breathy smile. Had known, as soon as they gave her the number that in the seat next to her would sit a person of excitement and promise.

Half-way down the plane, she put her coat and bag on the rack, sat down and dared to look. By the window, the person of promise was only a pallid girl with dry curly hair and a mouth painted on like a rose, with small crooked teeth inside.

Oh well. Lily could not have coped with a man anyway, let alone an exciting one.

'I'm glad you've come.' The narrow starved-looking face, which made Lily's cheeks feel as wide as pillows, turned to her eagerly. 'I thought I'd sit alone. I couldn't have stood that for seventeen hours. My name's Ida Lott. Do you want to say yours? It's quite exciting isn't it, this big plane and everyone so matter of fact as if it happened every day. Well, it does of course, but not to me.' Her rosebud mouth closed carefully over the crooked front teeth. Her watchful eyes were set far back in shadows.

'Nor to me.'

'I'm too nervous.' Ida was a good bit older than Lily and the shadowed eyes were not born yesterday, but now Lily felt re-sponsible. 'It's my first flight too,' she reassured her. 'I'm going across for a wedding.'

'Don't be daft. So am I.'

'A friend of mine from school is getting married. Is yours family or a friend?'

'Well.' Ida looked down at her hands. The ring! It blazed like a tiny headlight on her thin finger. 'Me.'

'Oh, how romantic.'

'Yes.' Ida kept her head down and raised her eyes sideways. 'I suppose it is, really.'

'It's the most romantic thing I ever heard of.'

8

Ida giggled, and put her left hand over her mouth. To show the ring? To hide her teeth?

Lily bought Ida a gin and lime, and they had an intriguing meal of small unsuitable dishes, and Lily got gravy on her skirt and mayonnaise on the floppy bow of her grey and white dress. Afterwards, people got up and milled about, lining up for the lavatories as if the drinks and food had gone straight through them. When most of the passengers had settled down to read or sleep, Ida got her pictures out of a new shiny black handbag and told Lily about Bernard Legge, who was Airman Second Class at Watkins Air Force Base in Massachusetts.

'Well, everyone calls him Buddy, and I do too. "I, Ida, take thee, Buddy." ' She giggled. 'What do you think of that?'

'I think it's marvellous.' Lily imagined herself stepping off the plane into the arms of a man in uniform with whom she would walk away, leaving everything behind. She thought about going home in five days' time, different because she had been to America, and finding everyone the same. Daddy going to work on his bike, Mum still on the night shift, same old back and forth about when to have supper, and no one at college even remembering that she had been away, until she asked to copy their lecture notes. 'What's he like?'

'He's very nice, really. It's a new life.'

Because of the gin, Ida told Lily a few things about the grim life in Staple Street, Stafford, from which she had been rescued by going to an Air Force dance and meeting Buddy.

His picture in uniform showed a babydoll face unsuitably garnished by a bar of dark eyebrows that met over his inconsiderable little snout of a nose.

'Do you love him?' Lily liked to risk direct questions.

'Yes, thank you,' Ida said politely. 'And he says he loves me. "You're kinda cute," he says, "I guess I love ya." Though I don't see why he should really, because I'm not much of a –'

'Don't fish,' Lily said sternly.

'Excuse *me*.' Ida lowered her long mauve lids and went to sleep.

Leaning sideways against the window, she was very slight and exhausted looking in her new pink suit with the bon voyage carnation slewed sideways on the lapel. Her tightly curled wedding hair had risen too high. With a narrow bony forehead like that, she would have looked less vulnerable with a fringe. In spite of Buddy Legge and Staple Street, Stafford, Lily still felt protective, enclosed with Ida in the private pocket of their seats, cut off by the high backs in front and behind. Beyond the window the curved grey edge of the plane's wing, with frost on the rivets, was the only reminder that they were divorced from the earth. The circular blurs of the two propellers bore them faithfully through icy space, while Lily watched over Ida palely sleeping, and speculated on whether she needed help – a commodity Lily was always poised to hand out. She was training to be a social worker. While she was waiting to save the world, she could start with Ida Lott.

She slept and woke after what seemed only a few minutes of dreams that hustled her with sharp instructing voices, but her watch had gone ahead two hours. Ida was still asleep. Lily leaned forwards to look at the sturdy wing and the propellers. The circular blur nearest the window was gone. Blades were there, three of them, standing still in the moving air that vibrated their curved tips slightly.

Lily woke Ida. 'Don't look now,' she muttered, 'but look out there.'

Ida's heavy eyelids, curved like mauve shells, lifted slowly. She turned her head to the window without moving her head.

'They give it a rest now and again, I daresay,' she said and closed her eyes.

Lily shook her again and whispered, 'Something's wrong. It's not supposed to be like that.' She watched the blade outside the window to see if it started up again, or dropped off. 'Do you suppose they know?' She leaned away to look down the aisle. Passengers all in their seats, not a stewardess in sight. 'What shall we do?'

'Don't ask me. I've never flown before.'

'Nor have I.'

'Are you upset?' Ida took hold of Lily's arm. Her finger nails were painted to match the pink suit, but bitten.

'No,' Lily lied, because she was the leader, and if she was upset, Ida would be upset.

The boy on the other side of the aisle had his painful adolescent face bent into a magazine, scowling. Lily stretched a hand across to him.

'I say.'

The boy's face flared, but he hunched his shoulders and pretended not to hear. Beyond him, a man with his jacket off was reading a book. Lily leaned behind the youth's back and said, 'I'm sorry to bother you.'

The man had thick fair hair and narrow blue eyes whose colour was intensified by his cornflower-blue pullover. A woman must have bought it for him. 'One of the propellers isn't going round.'

'My God.'

'Do you think they know?'

'Hope so.' He was American.

He got up to look, then stepped over the boy's legs and started forwards along the plane. Something about him made Lily and Ida feel as relieved as if he had gone to start up the propeller.

Now things were happening. The stewardess with hair like clipped straw came very fast down the plane, and the dumpy one with the eternal smile went very fast up it.

'No cause for alarm.' The Captain's deep, folksy voice over the intercom began to alarm the passengers. 'We're experiencing a small bit of trouble with one engine. Still got three others, ha ha.'

Some passengers got up and came to stare at the propeller, like motorists gaping at an accident.

'Please be seated and fasten your belts. Everything is fine. But we're gonna make a little detour, folks, and get this baby fixed. No big problem, but just for extra security, we're gonna turn back and make a landing at Reykjavik, Iceland.'

Iceland! A buzz of talk swarmed through the plane.

'Repeat – no problem. We regret the delay and we'll take care of all you good folks with free beverages.'

Who wanted free beverages? They wanted to get to Boston. Some of those on the aisle reached out to catch the dumpy stewardess on her way to the galley, with questions, complaints, anxieties. She smiled and nodded and reassured. The straw blonde went watchfully down the other side, like a nurse going round the ward at night.

'You okay?' Back in his seat the blue-eyed American leaned across to Lily.

'How long will we have to stop there?'

'Who knows?'

'Is it dangerous?'

'No, just a bore. Stay calm. I don't want you to be scared.'

The boy with the erupting skin was nervous, but too shy to join in. He pretended to be still looking at his magazine, but his hands were shaky and his raw face on fire.

'Take it easy, son,' the man told him.

'Take it easy,' Lily passed on to Ida.

'I feel dead queer.'

'No, you don't. This is an adventure.'

'Buddy will be waiting.' Ida twisted her small sparkly ring. 'He'll think I've crashed.'

'Oh, rubbish, no he won't. If he's in the Air Force, he'll have the sense to find out what's going on.'

'He might,' Ida said unhopefully.

Over Iceland the sun was knocking sparks off the sea. Craning with Ida to see this small rock in the northern waters, Lily saw an unwelcoming grey moonscape. Hardly anything green or growing, an inadequate landing strip carved like a narrow step out of the rocks at the base of bare cliffs. Ida's small hand reached for Lily's large one, and they hung on to each other, fiercely crushing, clammy.

The first take-off had been frightening enough. The first landing, and in a place like this, was terror of death. As the plane rushed down past the cliff so fast that it must cannon into the jagged bluff at the end, Lily saw that the cliffs were broken rocks and fissures among which small groups of square hairy ponies like goats grazed on nothing.

The plane landed, bumped, hit the ground again, shuddered and braked smoothly. Lily let go of Ida's hand to join in the short applause, genuine or ironic, which greeted this miraculous feat.

'Okay?' The man across the aisle looked over and smiled with his eyebrows raised. He had put on his jacket, a tweed the same colour as his hair. Lily nodded, but she could not smile yet.

'Vellee sollee for bumpee landing.' The Captain over the

intercom. 'We'll offload here, folks, while they get some spanners out and wind up the clockwork again. See you later. Take your hand luggage with you.'

That should have warned them. In the seedy airport café, which smelled of cigarettes and wet rags, fifty-odd passengers were given coffee. Lily and Ida sat crushed at a slopped table with several people, including a Canadian couple like a pair of bison who itemized everything that had been wrong with this flight since they bought their tickets. When an airline official came into the doorway with a false smile, they said, 'About time,' and got up, collecting their bags.

'No hurry.' The official had grown a small clipped beard to make his chin look stronger, without success. 'We'll take care of everyone. We apologize for this unfortunate delay, but the mechanics are going to need a little longer.'

'Well hell, how long?' the Canadian asked for all of them.

The official coughed and ducked his head and said, 'We're going to put you up overnight in the United States Air Force base at Flekjavik.'

Groan, groan. Anger, protest. But the passengers were too tired to give the man more than a token hard time. They trooped out fairly meekly to the buses. Ida was anxious, and bringing up hot wind from the coffee, which she always did when she was upset, she said, dragging on Lily's arm while Lily carried her flight bag over the other shoulder with her own.

Lily was alert and expectant. This was much more exciting than just flying the Atlantic like everyone else, and Pam's wedding was not for another two days.

'Brace up, Ida. Not everyone goes to Iceland.'

'Not everyone wants to.'

The bus passed sturdy white houses with painted shutters and fences, one-storey shops with steeply pitched roofs, stone farms low to the ground, open moorland with sheep grazing on grey-green grass, no trees or hedges to be seen in the light twilight that did not grow darker.

Inside the wire fence of the Air Force base, they were given sandwiches and ice-cream in the mess hall, and then there was nowhere to sit and nothing to do but go to bed.

Lily and Ida had a room together. Ida took off her pink suit and lay down with a great sigh. The ice-cream had made her teeth ache. Lily roamed, looking out of the window at the bare ground and the functional buildings, inspecting empty drawers, opening the door to listen to the corridor of closed rooms, where someone coughed, voices rumbled without emphasis, water ran, a child cried.

'Go to bed. Aren't you tired?'

'I feel charged up. Must be the Arctic twilight.' Lily's body felt electric. Her skin felt smoother, creamier, her hair thicker. 'I wish . . .'

'I wish we had a cup of tea,' Ida said with her eyes shut.

'So do I.'

'Very strong.' Flat on the bed, Ida's slight body disappeared into the mattress, only her curled hair rising like a bush in the desert.

'I wish you hadn't thought of it.' At the mirror, Lily was examining her skin with her glasses off, which improved it. 'Now we've got to have one. Let's go and prowl.'

'We can't.'

'We can.'

Lily waited while Ida tried to struggle into the pointed shiny black shoes with very high heels in which she was to totter towards Buddy on the Boston tarmac.

'They're too small for you.'

'No.' Ida changed her mouth of pain to the closed smile which hid her teeth. She stood up, then sat down again on the bed and took off the shoes. 'I don't want to put my suit on again anyway.'

Annoyed with her, Lily went out of the room and down the concrete stairs. She found her way back to the mess hall, where men were now sitting at the tables with food and bottles and paper cups, playing cards and dominoes or reading or smoking or just sitting. Lily spoke to one of the men, who leaned back in his chair and looked up at her, tongue in the corner of his mouth, dark Mediterranean eyes boldly amused.

'A cup of tea?' he mimicked. 'Oh, veddy, veddy Bwitish.'

A wolf whistle from another table, and someone called out something that Lily was glad she could not hear.

'Give her a break.' A woman in Air Force uniform looked up from a letter. 'Try the vending machines.'

The machines were in a corner space off the mess hall. Coca-Cola and pictures of other fizzy things, ice-cold and condensing. No tea in the hot machine, but tomato soup, hot chocolate, coffee, coffee regular, coffee extra cream, coffee extra sugar. Insert two dimes.

Lily had no American money. Did she dare ask?

A warm bitter smell of coffee came from the machine. In the pictures over the knobs, the tomato soup was bright orange, the chocolate had a foam of cream on the top, the coffee had bubbles swirling and a spiral of steam rising.

Ida would like it. It might keep her awake to talk about Buddy, which Lily wouldn't mind, because if she was really going to end up as a counsellor, she had got to learn what made people cleave together, as well as what split them apart.

'Having a hard time choosing?' A man's voice behind her. 'They probably all taste equally foul.'

It was the man from the seat across the aisle. He had taken off the blue pullover, so the colour of his eyes had calmed down. He had a good nose. Lily liked a good nose. No one in the family had one, only splodgy common things.

She pushed her glasses back on hers. 'I haven't got any American money.'

'Let me.' He fished a handful of coins out of his pocket. 'What'll it be?'

'Oh, thanks. Two coffees with milk and sugar. Where does it say that?'

'Coffee regular.' He put in two coins. The machine digested them, then with a whirr and a clunk, a paper cup descended and a spout plopped the right amount of coffee into it.

'How marvellous.'

'Don't they have these in England?'

'Not like this.' They did, but Lily wanted to admire America. 'Were you there long?'

'Just a quick business trip.'

Another cup arrived and was filled. Lily waited for him to get his black coffee, so that she could walk back through the mess hall with him, but he waited, starting to drink his coffee.

'Your first flight?'

To lie, or to sound inexperienced? Lily took a sip of coffee, then put down Ida's cup and pushed back her glasses to see him better, and said, 'May be my last.'

'I don't blame you. Why do you do that all the time with your glasses?'

He'd noticed her. 'The frame is loose.'

'Take them off.'

'I can't see.'

'You don't need to see to drink coffee.'

Without her glasses the small corner space was less dingy, the garish vending machines muted, the man less real. Seeing only soft blurs of colour increased the feeling of being part of a dream. 'I must . . .' Her voice was blurred too. 'I must take Ida's coffee up to her.'

She put on her glasses to follow him through the mess hall. The bold airman said, 'Quick work, baby,' and some of the others laughed.

The man with blue eyes said, 'Hey, fellas,' placidly. He did not spill his coffee on the stairs, but Lily did. On the next floor she turned to go on up and he said, 'This is where I leave you.'

'Thanks so much.'

'You're entirely welcome.' For such a relaxed man, he was exceedingly polite.

'I say.' Lily stopped with her feet on the bottom step of the next flight. 'When I – you know, noticed the propeller standing still and all that, and I told you and you went up, I mean, did they *know*?'

'Oh, I don't think so.' His eyes narrowed when he smiled. 'If you hadn't been so quick on the ball, we might have crashed.'

'Honest?' But he was smiling more to himself than to her. 'Oh, come on. The pilot must know whether an engine's running or not.'

'Let's say you saved us.'

Lily wanted to say, 'If you're making fun of me, please don't.' He was at an age when he would probably think that childish, so she said, 'Oh, well,' and went on up.

'Have a nice night.' He had not gone through the swing door.

He was looking at her back view. Damn. She was plodding up with her legs apart so as not to spill any more coffee.

In the bedroom, Ida was unhappy.

'Why have you been so long? The coffee's cold.'

'Want me to go down again?'

'No. I'm all blown up as it is. I'll never get to Boston. Why did this have to happen to me?'

'I told you. It's adventure.'

Lily took off her flowered dress and hung it up carefully, shaking out the bow, trying to smooth the skirt. At a knock on the door, Ida got back into bed and pulled up the sheet. It was the man from the coffee machine. Lily was in her petticoat, with bare feet, which made her a little shorter than him.

'You forgot your magazine.'

'I didn't . . .'

He had one in his hand. 'Gee, you have a better room than I do.' He looked round, his clear blue eyes passing over Lily as if she were his sister. 'Goodnight,' he said quietly and went out.

'You didn't have a magazine,' Ida said. 'Who's he?'

'He gave me change for the coffee.'

'So now he wants to see you in your slip.'

'Pity I'm so fat.'

'Better than me.' Ida sat up and looked down at her flat chest. 'I've always been too thin.'

'Does Buddy like that?'

'Oh, yes. He says — well he don't say much.'

'Doesn't he tell you you're beautiful?' Lily felt beautiful from the coffee-machine man's eyes, even though they had been brotherly.

'Well, you've got to know Buddy. He's not like that. I don't mind. I'm not romantic, like you are. There's more to marriage than romance, you'll find that out one day. There's having your own home and nice things and people giving you attention, because you're Mrs Someone.'

Lily sat on the end of the hard institutional bed. Although Ida was talking as if she were her big sister, Lily still felt older.

'At Watkins Air Force Base, see, we're going to have married quarters of our own, half a house, made of wood, with a bit of garden and a covered-over place to put your car. Buddy has a Plymouth, they call it, two-tone blue. We'll have a television and a machine to wash clothes.'

'He must be very rich.'

'He has good pay, but everyone has those things, and I will too.'

She looked up at Lily with a tired defiance in her violet-shadowed eyes, her closed mouth nondescript without the bright pink lipstick.

'Ida,' Lily leaned forwards. She could feel it coming on. She had to ask, 'Are you sure you love him?'

'Oh . . . love.' One side of Ida's mouth went up in an ugly little sneer. 'What's love got to do with it? There, I've shocked you, haven't I? But in my situation you don't pin all your hopes on love.'

'Has it been tough, then?'

'Bit rough in spots.' Ida pushed back the sheet and got out of bed. Her small blunt feet were still swollen from the plane, with red dents across them from her new shoes. She went to the mirror to fiddle with her tightly permed hair, pushing it up, pulling bits of it down. It always sprang back to the same shape, like a wig above her pale bony forehead.

'Tell me.' People needed to get stuff off their chests, and Lily was ready to listen. 'Dear Doctor Lily . . .' One of her many ambitions was that one day she would have an advice column in a women's magazine. 'Dear Doctor Lily, I have never told this to anyone before . . .'

'What was it like, Eye?'

'No worse than most, I suppose.' Ida shrugged.

'Bad enough to make you glad to get away, though.' A statement rather than a probing question. They had done that in Preparation for Interview Techniques, Session II.

'Knock it off, dear.' Ida's eyes met hers knowingly in the mirror. 'I'm not a case history at your college.'

They had pancakes and maple syrup for breakfast. The coffee blew Ida out again into delicate little belches behind her fingers.

18

'If you didn't say "Excuse me" every time and put your hand up,' Lily muttered, 'no one would notice.'

The two teachers from Rhode Island who sat with them did not notice anyway. They were on the edge of their chairs, wearing coats and checking their cameras and tickets and passports, their minds already ahead to arriving in Boston. The man Lily had met by the coffee machine did not even look at her. Had seeing her in her slip been too much for him? Another chance lost.

The airport was a springboard, the rocks less sinister, the ponies less deprived. In their seats by the wing, Ida and Lily held hands again as they taxied past the broken cliffs. At the end, the plane stopped for a long time before it turned and moved forwards to take off. The runway was so short, it would have to spring up like a pheasant. Ida's ring cut into Lily's fingers. The boy across the aisle clutched the arms of his seat. The coffee-machine man stared fixedly out of the window as if he would never see land again. All four propellers were going, but where was the engine's roar of power, where the speed? They would never make it.

They weren't even trying. The plane was merely trundling back along the runway, and the passengers sat back in dismay, the energy they had used to urge it off the ground wasted.

Back in the airport building, the man with the blue pullover came over and moved someone's coat and sat next to Lily. Electricity charged up through her body into the roots of her hair. Her hands trembled, so she put them in her pockets. When he spoke to her, she answered without looking at him.

Sourly the passengers watched their Captain walking back from the plane.

'Sorry, folks.' He came into the lounge, tanned, thickening, prematurely grey (with the uncertainty of flying the Atlantic?). 'We're gonna get you outa here, but not yet. See the agent about cables or phone calls. On us, of course. Relax. Take it easy.'

'We don't want to relax,' the bald businessman said. 'We want to get to the United States.'

'So do I,' said the Captain. 'I have a brand new baby to see.'

Nobody cared about his rotten baby. They were offended by it, but he went away pleased with himself.

Back to the buses. Back to the Air Force base.

They sat apathetically in the mess hall, drinking eternal coffee and reading old newspapers. Children ran wild and their parents ignored them. An earthy girl with long, fine cobwebby hair and loose cotton clothes unbuttoned her man's shirt and fed her baby. No one looked, or looked away.

The agent came in, looking bruised. 'We're getting a plane from France,' he said gloomily.

'When?'

'Tomorrow.'

Cries of anger. Wails of protest.

'Listen here, Bud.' The bald man in the heavy black jacket moved forwards threateningly. 'It's not good enough.'

'Look,' Lily's blue-eyed man spoke up in a pleasant conciliatory way. 'Apparently it's the best they can do.'

'And I'd appreciate it,' the agent added with more spirit, 'if you didn't call me Bud. My name is Mortimer.' He put back his shoulders and jutted his neat beard.

'Fair enough. Okay, Mort.'

After that the agent was Mort to everyone, and the passengers began to be names and characters.

Ida and Lily. Ida the GI bride. Jokes and sentiment. The bald business man became Wally, who had a bottle in his bag. The coffee-machine man was Paul.

He worked for a big luggage and saddlery shop in Boston.

The bus drivers took them on a tour. Paul and Lily did not say much. Once when they were walking in a small grove of stunted birches behind the hot-spring greenhouses, he put his hand in her pocket and threaded his fingers into hers. Lily had the sensation of walking lightly upwards, as if her feet had left the earth.

Back at the base, the airmen were in the mess hall, so people wandered in and out of each other's rooms. Wally had another bottle of whisky and some paper cups. Paul brought doughnuts and hot chocolate up to Lily and Ida's room, and they sat on the beds because there were no chairs.

'I like this,' Ida said. 'In a funny way, I don't want it to end.'

'But we've got to get you married,' Paul said. 'You've got to be Mrs Bernard Legge.'

'Ida Legge,' Lily said. 'Can she stop being Ida Lott and be Ida Legge? People will want to know, "What happened to it?"'

They laughed and were easy together, and Paul sat very close to Lily on the bed, with his jacket off and his skin magnetic under his shirt. His quiet, amused voice, close to her, was overwhelming. She could hardly breathe. The chocolate threatened to rise up from her stomach.

'Ida Payne,' Ida giggled. 'You know what? Perhaps my mother was right. She looked angry when my cousin came to take me to the airport and brought me that flower.' The white carnation was browning in a paper cup. 'I thought she was going to say, "Don't go," but she said, "You're a bigger fool than I thought."'

'Don't you want to get married?' Lily swallowed down the mutinous cocoa.

'Well, I had to escape.'

'What from?' Paul leaned towards Lily and rested his hand on the bed behind her, so that her arm was against his chest.

'You wouldn't want to know. Jackson, who's coming out of prison. My family who hates me. Well – my mother does worse than my Dad, for obvious reasons. With incest, if you'll pardon the word, the mother always pretends it's the child's fault.'

'My God, Eye.' Her heart competing with the cocoa in her throat, Lily leaned forwards away from Paul. 'You poor –'

'Don't give me no more case-worker talk. I've heard all that. Forget it anyway. It's only because I let Wally give me that whisky.'

'He fancies you.' Lily managed to say it lightly, although her mind and body and spirit were fainting towards Paul.

'Knock it off. Let's go to bed. We've got to get up early if that plane's really coming.'

When Ida went out to the bathroom, Paul turned Lily quickly, and before she could take off her glasses, kissed her long and searchingly, with his eyes open, watching hers.

She had never known this with anyone. Clumsy slobbers, bony adolescent bodies, grabs in the wrong places, drunken lunges. A sliver of her mind went wandering off with those memories while the rest was submerged, with her body, in Paul. How long could you go without taking a proper breath? Dear God, if you let my stomach rumble first chance it gets with a grown-up man, I'll never . . . never what? She had never done anything worth mentioning for God yet, and now there was no future. Only this spinning swirl with thoughts flying off at the edge and her body dissolving at the centre. Time stopped.

She jumped up when Ida's heels hobbled along the passage outside, pushed back her glasses and stood by the window, looking agitatedly out at the colourless light night. When Ida came in, Paul got up and said goodnight to her and went out.

'Think I'll use the bathroom too,' Lily said feebly. She took a towel, but she didn't really care what Ida thought.

Paul was waiting for her by the swing door at the end of the corridor. He pulled her through the door.

'Take off your damn glasses.'

Even if there had been someone on the stairs, they would have gone on kissing and holding each other and fusing together, as close as people can be without actually – oh, what will happen to me now? This has never, I've never – Paul's murmurs to her were gentle and surprised and admiring. Hers were gasps, a sort of choking madness.

'Oh, I love, I love you,' she had to say.

'Ssh, quiet now. No, you don't.'

'I do, I love you.'

Her youth's search was over. I've found you! she shouted inside.

When he lifted his head again, she felt so happy and sure of him that it was fun to ask, 'Have you got a girl?', knowing it did not matter.

'Do I have a *girl*?' He pulled back and held her away, his arms stiff. 'Lily, I thought you knew. I have a wife.'

Fool. You've made a fool of yourself again. Heavy as lead. Wish I was dead. She put on the glasses which had been imperilled in the crushed pocket of her dress, and picked up the grey Air Force towel off the floor.

'No, look, Lily. I'm married, sure, but we're in the middle of nowhere, not attached to anything we know.'

Lily turned away and put the towel up to her face.

'Don't go back to your room.'

'I must.' She was going to cry. She ran away from him and went into the bathroom and made faces at the plain child's face in the mirror, glasses blurring, skin reddening, the ill-bred nose splodging.

In the bedroom, she took off her dress and got into bed without looking at Ida. Lily willed her not to say anything, although she herself probably would have asked, 'Want to tell me what happened?' or some such damn fool Lily question.

When Ida turned out the light and soon began her little snores, like a thin old snuffly dog, Lily lay with her arms wrapped round her disintegrating body and stared into the half darkness where furniture and bags and coats on hooks were still discernible in the monotonous twilight outside the window. Soon she got up, put on her poor creased dress that had started out so new and fresh to captivate Pam's brother at Boston airport, and went downstairs to the coffee machine.

He didn't say, 'I knew you'd come,' so she didn't either. She had not known that anyway, only that she had to be there.

He was wearing the cornflower pullover that made his eyes intensely blue. He got their coffee and they leaned against the dull-green wall to drink it, looking at each other over the paper cups. One or two men came into the little corner space, said, 'Hi', or didn't say, 'Hi', and put their money into the slot and thumped a button.

How will I ever be able to bear the sound of coins rattling through the works of a machine? I will never forget the sticky red Coca-Cola dispenser with WHERE'S SHIRLEY? scrawled across it, and the OUT OF ORDER sign amended to KICK ME. The smell of the stewed coffee will break my heart.

Paul did not say anything. It was a self-assured trick he had, waiting for someone else to speak first. Not fair.

'I suppose,' said Lily huffily, because she had decided to be huffy, 'your wife bought that jersey for you?'

'No.' He smiled at her as if he knew her right through and out at the back.

'Do you know what it does to your eyes?'

'Yes.'

'Are you vain?'

23

'Isn't everyone?'

'If I was,' Lily said peevishly, 'you cured that.'

'I tell you I'm married, and you translate that into, "You're ugly." Look, what the hell, it makes no difference now. We're on an island the size of Kentucky in the middle of the North Atlantic, helpless and frustrated because we can't get to Boston, and trying to make life easier for each other.'

Was that all?

'I love you,' Lily said miserably.

He had strong shoulders and a small waist, worn higher up than English waists, long legs, rubber-soled shoes that didn't lace, trodden over at the sides, funny comfortable things to wear with that decent grey suit. His face was on the same design as his body: broad at the top and narrowing. His thick hair was the colour of wet sand, buff envelopes, dun horses, the dark side of blown barley. His nose was unremarkable, as noses should be. He smiled with his mouth closed, the corners going out and up, the wide cheeks pushing up the lower eyelids. His skin had a warm woody colour, as if he spent a lot of time out of doors, even in the winter. The lines at the outer end of his agonizingly blue eyes had been put there by smiling and the sun.

He moved easily and was naturally polite to people. He was lovely, thrilling, a man in a dream, the kind of man that other women had – and another woman did.

'I love you.' Lily had never said that to any man, and now she could not stop.

'Come up to my room.'

Oh my God, what am I doing? I know what I'm doing. I want to. He'll think I'm a child if I don't. The men in the hall know, although Paul says, 'Hi there,' casually, as if I were his sister. I'll never get up the stairs. Thank God he's in front. He can't see me hanging on to the banister, with liquid knees. Faint with desire is what I am.

Outside his door, Lily put up a hand to push back her glasses, then took them off instead, and walked blindly into the bedroom. He took off her coat and stood looking at her, smiling.

What do I do now? He is so much older and more sophisticated. Why doesn't he tell me what to do?

'What shall I do?' she had to ask.

'Let's lie on the bed. Do you want to take off your dress?' he asked politely, not a bit sophisticated.

'Yes.' She wanted to tear off everything and stand there, naked and lusting and too fat. She took off everything except her slip. He took off everything except his shorts. When his head emerged from the dangerous blue pullover, she saw that he was watching her and smiling.

In bed, Lily became wild, desperate. Her flaming body ached. She was a screaming void. She wanted to shout, 'Do it! Do it!' But not in this rabbit warren of thin walls and many people; and he didn't want to do it anyway. He wanted to stroke and touch and lie together peacefully, and Lily didn't know whether to climb on top of him, or pull him on top of her, or what to do with her hands.

'*Please*,' she whispered, 'I'm not a baby. I've never done it before, but I want to, with you. Please, you must.' It was not like with the bumbling, lunging boys, fighting them off. Paul was holding *her* off. 'Don't you want to?'

'Look, I'm ten years older than you. You're a virgin. I'm not going to – '

'Someone's got to.'

'Not me. We'll never see each other again after we get to Boston, and you'd hate me.'

'No, I love you.'

'Don't keep saying that. Let's just be close. Here, it's nice like this. Lie quiet. Let's hold each other. You're lovely.'

'One day, then.'

'There isn't going to be a one day. I'm sorry, Lily, I have to say that, if you're hoping I'm going to leave Barbara.'

'I'm not.' She was.

'You've got to understand. I have a small son.'

Oh, you can't have. You can't. You can't be caught up in all that. Hurrying home from work and bending over a cot, smiling and babbling and matching the blue of your eyes to the round, staring ones with their spotless whites. 'He's the image of Paul,' everyone says.

'I'd never do anything to hurt him . . . or Barbara. Hush now, quiet,' he whispered, as tears sprang out of Lily's eyes and flooded both their faces. 'It's lovely together. Don't spoil it.'

Lily wept a little more and shuddered, and looked bleakly at the pain of eternity without him, her body grown cold and empty of desire.

Still for now, he held her, and she slept.

When she woke in grey light, he was asleep on his face, his back a graceful landscape of bone and muscle and beautifully designed long curves that she did not dare to touch. Better not wake him anyway, if her face looked as it felt after crying puffily and sleeping.

At the door, with her coat over her hastily buttoned dress, she turned to look at the small transient room, green walls, metal cupboard and chair, hinged table flap with briefcase, a razor, the vague blue lump of the pullover, the sleeping man on the narrow rumpled bed. Other beds, other men – whatever was ahead of her, she would never forget anything about this.

'I'm not scared to stand before you this morning.' Mort's voice was unusually loud. His little beard waggled. 'Ladies and gentlemen, your plane is on the runway.'

Cheers and excitement, and in the stampede out of the mess hall, Paul and Lily came together out of sight in the corner by the dispensing machines, and he kissed her once, gravely.

'My heart is broken,' Lily said.

'No, it isn't,' he said kindly.

'Will you come to London again?'

'I doubt it. I was only there for the trade fair.'

'And even if you did . . .?'

'Yeah. Even if.'

He let her go and stood back so she could walk out. She looked round. I will never forget this place, never. She bent down and picked up a plastic spoon off the floor and put it in her pocket. The dream was over.

The engines started, all four of them, with not even a ragged cheer from the passengers, because it wasn't funny or frightening any more.

Lily took Ida's hand and ran her finger over the courageous little ring. 'Look, Eye,' she said, under cover of the engines revving up at the end of the runway. 'You know, perhaps you shouldn't marry him, if you're not really sure.'

'Who *says*?' Ida pulled her hand away.

'Well – *you* did. I mean, last night.'

Fool, fool. Put your foot in it again. Dear Doctor Lily and her advice column, forgot one of the basic rules – don't remind people what they said. Yesterday's leftovers are not today's hot lunch.

'But I mean.' She had to plod on, to make sure she had done everything she could to rescue Ida from possible disaster, willing or not. 'Marriage is the rest of your life (*I'd never do anything to hurt Barbara*). You haven't got to go through with it, if you –'

'Leave me alone.' Ida set her pink mouth in a sucked-in grimace that looked as if she had no teeth. 'I didn't tell you not to make a sketch of yourself with that fellow all over the Air Force building.'

'I didn't.' Having started this wretched conversation feeling like Ida's grandmother, Lily felt absurdly young again. 'I'm sorry, Eye, I was only trying to help.'

'I know.' Ida turned and gave Lily her crooked smile. 'But you got to learn to leave people alone.'

'That won't get me far as a social worker.'

They both laughed, and Paul looked across at them, and then away.

'Good thing too,' Ida said.

The plane roared to a crescendo. The broken cliffs approached, slid by, sped past, the black buff ahead menaced them and then gave up and dropped out of sight as they soared.

Paul got off the plane ahead of Lily, who could not get up until Ida finally managed to squash her feet into the new shoes. She saw him in the baggage hall, going through customs, and followed him through the narrow exit where the crowd waited, forcing herself to look for his wife. Barbara would be small and chic, with tiny feet and hands and short crisp hair in overlapping leaves. The child would toddle forwards, and his father would put down his bag and briefcase and bend to pick him up.

Paul walked out through the glass outer door alone, and disappeared among the crowd of taxis and cars. He had not looked behind him.

'Lily!' It was Pam's brother, looking different in America, wearing a loose old jersey and torn grey tennis shoes. 'Where the hell have you been? Don't bother to tell me. We kept calling the airline and telling them for God's sake, you'd got to be here for the great day tomorrow. C'mon.' He took Lily's suitcase. 'We'll just make it to Pam's last supper if we drive fast.'

Two

*B*y the time Ida had got through customs with her two suitcases, she had lost Lily and was on her own in the crowd of passengers and greeters. She had to have a porter, but she had no money to pay him until she found Buddy. Suppose he wasn't here? Suppose he had given her up and gone back to Watkins A.F. Base, Mass?

'See your party, miss?' The friendly black porter stopped his trolley.

Ida looked everywhere, moving this way and that to see past groups of people gathered round passengers, talking noisily, small children clamouring at ground level. No Buddy. No patch of grey-blue, moving rather stiffly, as he did when he was in uniform.

'He'll be here, I know he will.' Did the porter think she had been ditched?

'Sure he will.' The porter took her bags off the trolley. 'I have to go help another party.'

'But I can't pay you till I –'

'Don't worry about it. I'll be back. Just look for me on your way out. You'll be okay.'

He was huge and kind and dignified and safe, like Jarvis Murray at the bottom of Staple Street, whose daughter had taught Ida to jive. When he had gone, Ida stood by her luggage as if she were on a tiny desert island, and wondered if she would recognize Buddy, even if he were here. They hadn't seen each other all that many times, and people didn't look the same over here anyway. Mrs Bison had put on dark glasses and crimson lipstick. Wally, talking to a man in a black suit by the phones, didn't look so jovial.

Where was Lily? She had wanted to meet Buddy. Why hadn't she waited? Ida's feet were in agony. She kicked off her shoes and stood with them in her hand, searching, waiting, not knowing where to go if she moved from this spot.

A shortish man was walking down the main hall, frowning as he came towards her. She looked him right in the face before she recognized the heavy eyebrows that ran into each other over his short nose and made his eyes look close together. Buddy out of uniform, in a plaid wool jacket over neat dark green trousers.

Too late, she lifted her face into her closed-mouth smile and held out her arms with her shoes in one hand. He knew she had not recognized him.

He looked not like himself. A stranger. Her heart battered against her flat chest in a panic to escape.

'Ida,' he said, in that way he said it, half-way between Ahda and Eyeda, putting two slurred syllables into the *I*.

'Hullo.'

'Where the hell have you been? I've been out of my mind. When I didn't get no call from you, I thought, hell, what's going on here?'

'I did send a cable.'

'Where to?'

'The Air Force base.'

'So how could I be there if I was here, waiting for you? What the hell. Put your shoes on.'

'They hurt. Aren't you going to say hullo?'

Ida stepped over the box and he put his arms round her, and now he did feel familiar, his arms like iron bands, his body pushing at her. He smelled of beer. He only kissed her very briefly because he was angry. His round childish face was petulant, the lips pushed out, the frown a dark roof over his aggrieved brown eyes.

'I know, I know, but I'm here, aren't I? And it wasn't my fault.'

'Well, shit,' he said. 'It's a hell of a way to start our life.'

'Oh, shut up, stupid. It's all right now. I'm here. Everything's all right.'

His frown softened. His pouting mouth relaxed into his smile for her, teasing, head on one side, wanting favours. Not a giving smile, it wasn't, though. An asking one.

Ida struggled into her shoes and the porter came back and

wheeled her luggage outside. Buddy didn't tip him enough, and the porter said, 'That'll be two bucks more, mac,' quite happily. In England the porter wouldn't say, 'Give me another two quid, mate.' He would just walk away and hate you.

While Buddy went to get the car, Ida stood with her bags, loosening first one shoe, then the other, and panicked again. What if he never came back? What if he was so browned off that he got into the two-tone blue Plymouth and drove away and left her in a foreign land? She couldn't just turn round and take the plane back to England, as if it were the tube.

In England, she had thought she was quite tough, fighting for survival, fending off her family, getting that job in the hotel, chucking Jackson when it was obvious he was going to be nailed for the car theft. Here, she felt like a beginner. Buddy seemed to need her. That was surprising. She needed him, and until she'd found her feet here, she would have to get used to that. A dependant, she would be, as an Air Force wife, and that was how she felt, as cars and taxis and buses crowded past, three abreast, or stopped and picked up passengers, until finally she would be alone on this bit of pavement with her borrowed suitcases, which looked revoltingly shabby compared to other people's luggage.

'Walked out on you, has he, Ida?' Wally grabbed her arm and squeezed it. He was a great one for grabbing and touching and moving his foot about under the table. 'Come on with me, then, ho ho.' He wagged his head roguishly, and winked at the man in the black suit, who looked Ida up and down very coolly and said, 'C'mon, Wal, better get a cab right away if we're going to make that meeting.'

'Can't leave this little lady alone.'

'My friend is fetching the car.' Fiancé was a stupid word. Ida had not been able to say it, even at work, when she had shown her ring at the tea-break in the housekeeper's room.

'This is my girlfriend,' Wally kept on. 'We've been bundling with the Eskimos, haven't we, Idaho?'

He had his arm round her shoulders when a huge blue car slid up to the kerb, and Buddy sprang out and bounced over the pavement like a frenzied ape.

'Get in the car,' he told Ida curtly. 'I'll get the bags.'

'You must be whatsisname,' Wally said genially. 'Put it there. You've got a wonderful little —'

'What's it to you, mister?' Buddy pushed between Wally and Ida and shoved her towards the car. She started to get into the passenger seat, but the steering wheel was there and she had to go round. Buddy threw her stuff into the back and got in, seething. She had never seen him like this, except once in a pub, when someone made a feeble joke about America, and he had raised his fists and shaken them in a ridiculous way, and the joker had laughed and pushed them down and bought him a pint.

They drove off among the traffic sweeping away from the airport.

'This car's huge,' Ida said.

'Bigger than those toys in your country, maybe. Small for here.'

So it was. Some of the other cars were enormous. A long black job, with hatchet-faced men in the back, took about five minutes to pass them.

'Mafia,' Buddy said.

'They've got a crucifix hanging in the back window.'

'Natch.'

Like water going into a drain, twelve lines of cars crowded two abreast into an endless tunnel, where a man walked moodily along a raised walk, deafened by noise and choked with fumes. Ida said nothing. There was nothing to say. Her eyes closed, but Buddy wouldn't like it if she went to sleep yet. He did not speak. His right hand, the one with the big service ring, which Ida's mother had said was sissy, tapped on the wheel. Out of the tunnel, they went up on to a road on stilts that stalked across the city on a level with the roofs of houses and the middle of office buildings.

'Is this Boston, then?'

'Where else? Real hick town,' Buddy said.

Ida thought it looked exciting. 'Lily says it's the next best to New York,' Ida said.

'Who's Lily?' He had nothing but contempt for the name.

'She and I shared a room at Flekjavik.' Ida pronounced it glibly. 'She's ever so nice. I wanted you to meet her.'

34

'And I suppose old knucklehead with the wandering hands was in the room too, was he?'

'Oh, shut up. What do you think I am?'

'I don't know. I don't trust you. I don't trust any woman.' Buddy had a built-in saga about what women were like.

'But I'm going to marry you.'

'Yeah.' He sighed. 'I'll be glad when it's over and we'll be on our own at Watkins.'

Driving north, they passed a sign that said Peabody. That was where Lily was going, somewhere near there, she had said. When they said goodbye, they had told each other, 'See you again some time, somehow, somewhere.' She ought to have waited for Ida. 'I want to see Airman Second Class B. Legge,' she had declared, and then forgotten. Perhaps just as well, since B. Legge had been so angry. Lily would have tried to make the best of him, and said something embarrassing like, 'I know you two will make each other very happy.'

Dream days. You make your own happiness in this world. Or not, as the case may be.

'Peabody,' Ida said. 'That's where Lily was going.'

'So what's so great about this Lily?' Buddy asked without interest. 'You and she have a good time?'

Although she knew so little about Buddy, Ida knew enough not to say, 'It was fun.' She said, 'I was worried about you.'

Buddy's driving profile looked self-satisfied, which was how he looked when he was pleased.

'Love me?' Ida risked.

'I guess so. I tell you, kid, I've got the hots for you.'

He took her hand and put it in his lap. That was different, though, that wasn't love, the sort Lily talked about, but it would do for now.

They drove endlessly to reach New Hampshire. America was too big. Ida slept, waking two or three times to see towns, villages, then hills, and a sunset like a picture postcard. Then darkness the next time she woke, the headlights tracking the road, hundreds of pairs of other headlights approaching, passing, the wireless drumming out a perpetual beat, without any tune. Stupefied, half awake, half asleep, she felt the car going up a hill, swinging round a lot of bends. It stopped with a soft crunch, and she had to open her eyes.

In the black night, a small house stood by itself at the side of the road, yellow light coming out of the windows on to a veranda with wooden pillars and some wooden steps. Buddy got out and came round to Ida's side, to pull her out of the car.

'Come on in and meet my folks.'

'I'm scared.' This was the worst part so far.

'Nah, it's okay. They're probably scared of *you*.' He laughed his Buddy laugh, rather high and giggly, and ran up the steps to bang on the door.

The starless night smelled of fir trees. The air was very sharp and still, colder than Boston had been when they got out of the plane. At the back of the house, dogs barked, children shouted, a woman yelled, something smashed. A car passed on the road behind Ida, swinging its lights on tall tree trunks and a sharp hill bend, otherwise it seemed very quiet and isolated up here. What would there be for Ida to do, when Buddy had to go back to Watkins?

It was not quiet inside the house. A bolt crashed. The door flew open and an enormously fat woman put short arms like bolsters round Buddy and shouted at him, and at the two dogs who squeezed out between their legs and leaped on to Ida, so that she was pushed against the post at the edge of the porch and nearly fell down the steps.

Ida screamed, and Buddy's mother shouted, 'They won't hurt you – Mick, Walker, come off it, damn you!'

Buddy got one dog by the scruff of its neck so that it yelped, and a boy with porcupine hair lunged across the porch and got his arms round the smaller of the two dogs, which wore no collars.

'Well, come on in, come on in.'

Buddy had described his mother as 'a real homey lady, you won't need to feel strange with her'. But he had not said that she was huge and powerful and very noisy. Bad things had gone on in Ida's house, but quietly: insults hissed, warnings whispered, a secret bitterness lurking in the passages and cold small rooms like rat poison behind the wainscot. Whatever went on here was at full belt. Everyone shouted, including Buddy. The wood-stove was bashed at with a giant poker. Huge logs were hurled into it. Plates were crashed on to the table and into the sink, and even through the air when the dog, Walker, a bristly ginger criminal, put its paws on the kitchen counter and got a tin plate from across the room into its ribs.

The only quiet person in the family was Buddy's father, Henry Legge, who greeted Ida in a long-sleeved vest and blue trousers too baggy for his lean frame, and said she was very welcome, and must be tired out.

'Cut it out, Henry, she's as fit as a fiddle,' Verna Legge yelled from another room. 'Don't mind him, Ida.' She filled the doorway, cradling tins of beer. 'He'll say the first thing that comes into his head, amazing it is sometimes, how the old man carries on, though most of the time he don't say much, thank God, but it's all up here.' She put down all the beer cans except one, which she tapped against her head. 'He's very deep, is this one.'

She sat Ida and Buddy down at the table with mugs of coffee and plates of food. Billy, the porcupine boy, and a plump, bossy girl called Phyllis and a sticky toddler in a sleeping suit crowded round, asking questions, hitting each other, grabbing at the cake, while their mother's arms swept about like a flail and her voice bounced off them unheeded.

When she spoke to Buddy, the flesh of her wide face creased into a soppy smile and her chins wobbled as she shook her head fondly at him, her small eyes, dark brown, like his, soft as velvet. She put food in front of him in a doting way that he accepted as his accustomed right. She put two sugars in his coffee and stirred it for him.

'Tough luck, Buddy boy,' Ida thought, 'if you expect that from me.'

What did his mother think of her? The father was polite, but how could Ida ever be found good enough for Mrs Legge's little darling?

There were no spare beds in the house, so Ida was to sleep outside in a sort of caravan parked at the back, until Buddy came home next week for the wedding. For tonight, he would sleep on the sofa in the front-room, crammed with battered toys and bicycles and broken furniture and old boots and car tyres. The rooms were bigger than the neat, pinched rooms where Ida's parents lived in Staple Street, but there was less space to move about in them.

Buddy and his parents were drinking beer, and Verna Legge was shocked because Ida wouldn't.

'I thought Limeys invented beer. Well, she'll learn our ways.'

But Ida's insides were not much good with drink at the best of times, and now she felt sick and exhausted.

'I need to go to bed,' she whispered to Buddy.

'Need to go to bed, do you honey?' One of Verna's eyes disappeared among folds of rubbery flesh. 'I've heard *that* before.'

'I'll take her out, Ma.' Buddy got up. In this house he had hardly talked directly to Ida.

'Turn on the yard light, then, one of you kids.' Their mother shouted at Billy and Phyllis, although they were leaning on the table, eating potato crisps and taking sips out of the beer cans. 'And you come back in, Buddy, you hear me? You're sleeping on that front-room sofa. I don't want no funny stuff. This here is an English girl.' The eye disappeared again. 'And we're going to have a decent and proper wedding, done right just like everything else in this family. That right, Henry?'

'I'll say that's right,' he echoed firmly, as if it had not already been said.

A glaring yellow light outside the back door showed Ida a small caravan nesting in weeds among tilting sheds and piles of wood, two cars without wheels, and assorted rubbish which spread up the hillside.

Verna Legge shouted from the back door, 'The old man's hooked up some lights,' at the same time as Buddy and Ida ran into a sagging wire running from the corner of the house to the caravan.

A car mechanic's lamp hung on a hook from the caravan's low ceiling, and by its naked light, Ida saw two seats and a flap table and some old clothes and bedding stuffed into plastic bags. A wire led from the light fitting to a rusted electric heater fixed to the wall.

Ida's suitcases were on one seat, and Buddy showed her how to pull out the other one to make a bunk bed, and they put grey sheets on it and blankets which smelled of dog. When it was down, there was no more standing space. Ida had to climb over a pile of plastic bags and over the end of the bunk. Sitting there, she watched Buddy's face, pasty and critical, as he looked at her.

In the car she had looked forward to being in bed with him. They had never had a chance at anything, except the back of a small car he had borrowed from an airman at the base in England. Now she felt drained, and her nerves were on edge from the clamouring children and restless dogs and the noise which Buddy's mother broadcast generally around herself, giving no clue as to where Ida stood with her.

'What have you done to your hair?' Buddy chewed on his rounded lips which were always wet, sometimes with spittle in the corner of his mouth.

'I had it permed. Do you like it?'

'It's okay.'

'For the wedding. Are you excited?'

'I guess so.' He stared at the front of her blouse for a while, the bar of his eyebrows lowered, and then he said, 'Turn off that heater before you go to sleep. Pop's a mechanic, but nothing he fixes works right.' He nodded and went out.

When he banged the door, the small caravan trembled like a cardboard box. He moved more violently here than he had in England. If the heater fell down on the bed, that would be it. Sad to come all this way and then be immolated.

She put on a nightdress with a jersey over it, and a pair of socks, switched off the light and heater together and hurried to crouch under the bedclothes, shivering not only from cold, but from strangeness and loneliness. You couldn't call it homesickness, because what had England or Stafford or her family or anyone she knew ever done for her?

But as she huddled in the small flimsy space, curtained with

39

torn lace, the bad and boring and miserable old scenes which had so powerfully propelled her into this daring venture would not stay inside in her head. Instead, the things she thought about and the pictures she saw were the ones she missed, and would never know again. Tea after school with her grandmother in the ground-floor flat where the cat came in and out of the window and threaded through the windowsill plants like a native through the jungle. Secret games with her friend Lizzie in the grounds of the old asylum, with code words and a funny language, and a shrieking dash out of the bushes when the boys found them, to climb the fence the same way they got in. The sea, the sea, the sea, in Wales, very fierce and mysterious. It would suck you in and drown you, but you could skitter along the edge of it, veering up into the sand when a wave broke, and dashing back when it retreated, to dare it to come at you again.

Ida had only ever been to the sea once, but it was the best day of her childhood, about the only one she remembered in full detail.

She thought about the other women and girls at the hotel. They had been suspicious of her at first. When they dumped some of their own work on her, she did it for one day, and on the next, she told them where they could put it. After that they liked her better. She and Linda would giggle, making beds together, and make up wild stories about the people who slept in them. Linda had a mind like a sewer.

When Ida left, the girls gave her a cosmetic-bag with rosebuds on it and a rubber lining and a slot for your toothbrush. If she had stayed at the hotel, she could have worked her way up to being housekeeper.

Sleep, Ida ordered. She was usually able to drop off like an underfed dog, wherever she was, whatever was going on. She had slept away half her childhood when her mother let her stay up in her dog-kennel room with the sloping ceiling and low rounded door. From twelve on, she was late for school almost every day, and asleep again after supper over homework in the corner, especially when Dad had some of the Faithful in and they were going at it, their bullying commands to the God they owned – 'Scatter our foes by the wayside' – bouncing off the ochre walls.

Sleep, Ah–eye–da. She gave a few light snores, to fool her body into thinking it was asleep.

The noises of the Legge night assaulted her caravan. Dogs barked, doors banged, shouts, whistling, a hundred tin cans thrown out against an iron fence. The whistler fell over something in the yard and cursed thickly.

Ida knelt on the seat and saw the last light go out upstairs. Window groaned up. Cat yowled. Window croaked down. Silence. The wind rose and took over. Ida went back to her maggot's hole, alone with the night.

Here I am. What the hell have I done? Have I made a horrible mistake? Curled under the covers as she must have been inside her mother, if you could imagine that woman's stingy frame expanded to accommodate a baby, Ida cried in a lonely, unsatisfying way. She thought about Lily: 'Are you sure you ought to marry him?', and how kind she was and anxious to say the right thing, and got her head snapped off for her trouble.

If we were still in Iceland, I'd be nicer. Lily was a good kid, with her open, round face that hadn't yet been written on, and her clean brown hair and her jokes and big clumsy feet. The fat would drop off her once she found out what life was all about. Ida was homesick for Lily.

She was still awake when a movement of cold air told her that the door at the end of the trailer had opened.

'Who's that?' Ida sat up. In the doorway, a darker shape blocked the darkness of the night.

Buddy's light laugh, excited. 'Who do you think?'

'Oh, Buddy, no. You know we said.'

'What?' He had shut the door and was taking his shoes off, thump, thud.

'We'll be married in a week. We said we'd wait.'

'You did.' He was taking off clothes.

'Suppose your mother – ?'

'Shit on her.' He launched himself over the plastic bags like a diver and was on her, outside the covers at first, grinding her into the hard mattress, then tearing away the blankets and wrenching up her nightdress like a man just out of prison.

It wasn't like what it was in the back of the borrowed Ford.

That had been quite nice. He'd been nervous, anxious, needing her help. Now he was a mad bull, stinking of beer, his mouth all slimy with saliva, gasping out words Ida had never heard, even from Jackson at his worst, splitting her apart with a brutality that made Ida cry out, 'No!' in the remembered desolation of that child who had cried out, 'No, Pa, no!' and got a pillow stuffed over her head, so that she was dying at both ends at once.

One thing about Buddy: he didn't take very long. Pa had gone on and on, praying over her in that disgusting way, asking his God, that madman, to cleanse her, whispering, so no one would hear, bits of the Bible, frenzied calls to the prophets.

Buddy ravaged her and was done. Couldn't hold it.

'Agh!' he yelled with his head thrown back, and one of the dogs barked in the backyard, hoarse on its chain. A window banged open and Mrs Legge screamed, 'Cut that out, Walker!' and banged down the window.

'You liked it, you liked it.' Buddy started to bite at Ida, not teasing, but painfully. He lay on her like a spent stone, so she could hardly breathe.

'If you think I liked that, you can't know much about women,' she said with what breath she could get. 'Get off me and out of here.'

He went backwards on all fours to the end of the bunk, groped for his clothes, opened the door on the cold night, giggled conceitedly and was gone. Ida lay battered, and let the pain slowly seep away. At least she didn't have Pa kneeling by the bed, the bald spot at the top of his thinning hair thrust into her face as he muttered prayers for forgiveness into the eiderdown.

Buddy was gone before Ida woke up. She lay and moved bits of her body to check if it all worked, then got up and put on her plaid skirt and a high-necked jersey. She climbed carefully down the steps of the trailer and picked her way across the yard, feeling straddle-legged.

The kitchen was the only warm room. Everyone was in there. Mr Legge in his dark-blue working overalls, with 'Henry' woven on the pocket, was eating coloured cornflakes like a child. Phyllis was dressed for school, with petticoats under her skirt. Billy shovelled food into his mouth and around it. The baby was on the floor, wearing only a wet nappy. Mrs Legge was at the sink, crooning to a song on the radio.

'Sleep good?' she asked Ida over the radio and other noises. 'Coffee's on the stove.'

Ida had planned to ask for tea, but lost her nerve. She picked up the pot to pour coffee into a mottled enamel mug. Mrs Legge shot a look sideways at the high-necked jersey, which did not hide the red grazes on the side of Ida's chin from Buddy's beard stubble.

Would she be angry? Let her. Curiously, now that she knew about the boozing monster side of Buddy, Ida felt more confident, more in charge. America was a treacherous jungle, but this was a situation she could cope with. She knew where she was now. She had Lily's address in England. She would write to her when she had the chance to buy postcards and say, 'Iceland was nothing – this is really an adventure, Lil, but I'm surviving.'

Mr Legge went off up the hill on a motor-bike. Billy and Phyllis went off to school down the hill in a long yellow bus filled with children fighting and waving their arms and legs about behind the elderly driver who ignored them. Ida would have liked to unpack some of her clothes and hang them up, but there was nowhere, so she refolded some of the stuff in the suitcases, put her short white wedding dress on a wire hanger she found in the yard and hung it over the trailer door. When the yellow bus ground up the hill in the afternoon, Phyllis came flouncing into Ida's caravan and knocked the dress to the floor and trod over it in boots.

Ida snatched it up and held it, furious.

'What's that?' Phyllis made a face at it.

'What I'm going to get married in. What's it to you?'

'When Sis got married she had a long white gown and white veil.' When Phyllis stood with her stomach out under the stiff petticoats, there wasn't much room for her in the small space at the end of the trailer.

'Well, I haven't.'

Ida had not even wanted to wear white, but her mother had set her face. 'We're not having those people over there think we

43

don't know how it's done,' and bought this dress in a sale for her. It turned out the sale had ended the day before, so Ida had had to make up the difference in price.

'Lemme see what all else you got in your bags.'

'No.' This one had to be stopped before she started.

'Hey, not fair! Mom!' She threw her shrill voice over her shoulder towards the house.

'C'mon back in!' Her mother threw the shout back.

'You're a pig,' Phyllis told Ida.

'Ditto.'

When Phyllis had jumped out, shrieking, Ida shut the door and hung the dress up again. There was no lock on the door, so Billy knocked the dress down when he came to say 'Hullo,' blinking shyly and jerking his mouth, and Mr Legge knocked it down again when he came to call Ida for supper.

'Settled in okay?'

He looked hollow under his overalls. His long jaw was dark blue.

'I'm all right, thanks.'

'Is that so?'

Whatever you told him, he answered, 'Is that so?' and sometimes 'Could have knocked me down,' or 'Could have fooled me.'

Life at the Legges' was hardly worth flying the Atlantic for, let alone a detour to Iceland, but the wedding was only a week away, and then Ida would be able to hang out her clothes in the semi-detached at Watkins Air Force Base and lock the doors and wash herself in a bathroom where the bath wasn't full of old newspapers and potatoes, and no dogs shouldered in to have a go at the broken bag of biscuits. She could have a pee without someone pounding on the door, and cook sausages and pies and custards in a kitchen she would keep clean as her mother's. Here in Leggeland, the stove was too far gone to tackle, and she was not allowed to scrub out the sink on the grounds that it was going to be used again before she could turn around. Verna Legge produced mostly frozen food from a huge freezer chest in an outside shed, thawing it out at full power, so that the outside was burned and the inside ice-cold.

Ida helped as much as she could with the children and the baby Vernon and the washing-up and throwing away – cartons and tins went out of the back door in the vague direction of some old oil drums – and there didn't seem to be any sweeping, nor a broom to do it with.

She went shopping with Mrs Legge. 'Downtown,' Verna said. She was stuffing dirty clothes into a heavy cotton bag that was stencilled USAF.

'I could clear out the sink and wash some of those,' Ida offered. 'I have some things of my own to do.'

'By hand?' Verna was alarmed. 'This is America, girl. We don't wash our own clothes here.'

Her own outfit could have done with a soak and a scrub. Vast grey knitted trousers, as wide as they were long. A purple T-shirt over bellying breasts that fell to where her waist might be. Hairy black cardigan that rode her gross shoulders like an animal of prey, its loaded pockets swinging at the front, the back ending half-way up her back in a ragged arch, the T-shirt ending soon below that, and half a yard of bumpy flesh before you came to the stretched elastic of the elephantine trousers. When Verna moved about the small house, knocking things over or aside, she created a disturbance in the air, and the wind of it was sour.

On the way downtown where the shops and launderette were, Verna's great rustic car, whose back window was taped up with plastic, coughed up the hill and rattled down the other side into a valley of superb pine trees and scattered white or red farmhouses, swinging from side to side round the corners, kept on the road by Verna's powerful arms at the helm. Ida had to hold Vernon tightly on her lap to prevent his head bashing against the window. He was a passive little boy. Born to hubbub, he had decided not to compete.

At the foot of the hill the car crossed a wide river and slewed to a stop behind the grain mill, where Henry Legge worked.

'Henry!' His wife leaned an arm and a squashed bosom out of the window. 'C'mon out here!'

'Shaker!' A man doing something outside called into a shed. Henry was called Shaker at work.

He hurried out, flapping long hands at his wife. 'You'll like to get me fired. This place is full of visitors.'

'Bunch of snots.' Verna put her finger under her spread nose, and pushed it into a pig's snout. 'Why can't they buy their flour at Lefty's?'

The mill ground and sold earthy grains and cereals and special flour of all kinds from coarse to silky. Ida, yearning to the rustic like all city people, was entranced by the old waterwheel turning slowly in the swift river. Lunchers in the glass-walled restaurant above watched the great wheel dip and raise and spill the water as it had done for a hundred years, wet green whiskers dangling and dropping silver pearls, and floating soaked again to rise dripping.

Henry could not take her into the milling shed or the barn or the mill store, or anywhere the visitors went. The old waterwheel was believed to power the grinding, so Henry must be invisible in his oily overalls in which he ran the machinery that actually turned the grindstones.

Lefty's Market was a grocer's in a town no bigger than a large English village, but with many more shops. The shelves of the low-ceilinged market were crammed with things that Ida had never seen. She wanted to stay and explore, but Verna careered through the place like a lava flow, throwing tins and packets on top of Vernon in the trolley, criticizing, swearing at prices, smelling the pork chops.

'This here is Ida that Buddy brought over from England to marry,' she told Lefty at the paying counter.

'American girls not good enough for him?'

Ida was to hear this a lot until she lost her accent. It was an insult disguised as a joke.

'So you're from jolly old England,' Lefty said, with a blue-lipped grin, and some shoppers turned to have a look. 'How about a spot of tea?'

That was another joke Ida was to hear many times. Sometimes she tried saying, 'We say "cup of tea",' but the joker knew better.

There was a rack of dud-looking postcards at the front of the shop. *I'll get fat here*, she would write to Lily. *Jam doughnuts and everything is giant size, and six different kinds of tomato soup*, but

Verna pushed her past the cards and on to the No-name Laundromat, where Ida saw her pink nylon blouse going into the machine with the baby's dirty nappies. Mrs Legge sagged on to a chair to wait. Ida wanted to go back to Lefty's, but Verna pulled her down next to her and gave her a lecture on how to take care of Buddy.

'Very sensitive boy, you can't cross him. It upsets his system. He's a free spirit, like I say, a free spirit. He shouldn't marry, really.'

Oh, thanks very much. Ida put her hand over her mouth. The hot dog she had eaten at lunch was getting back at her. 'If you didn't put your hand over your mouth, no one would notice,' she heard Lily saying. Mrs Legge didn't notice anyway. You could die of a burst ulcer before she paid any attention.

Folding the pile of torn grey nappies, Mrs Legge sighed and said, 'Isn't it always the way? I'll just get this one trained to do his jobs in the toilet like God meant him to do, and it'll be time to start all over again with the next.'

'What?' Ida stood with a sock in each hand and stared at her among the tumbling washers, the soap and hot air, the waiting women with their feet planted parallel.

'Didn't you know? Lookit.' Verna showed her profile.

'It doesn't show.'

Where was the baby under all those layers of fat? How did Shaker ever find his way in? Ida had seen enough pregnant women, God knows, including herself before Jackson was sent down, but she was shocked.

Hot from the No-name, Verna smelled very bad. She put one bag of laundry over her shoulder and pulled up Vernon from among the fluff balls on the floor. Ida took the other bag and followed her out.

During the next days while Ida was waiting for Buddy to come back and marry her, a few women neighbours dropped into Legge Manor, to inspect the new recruit to the family. They talked a lot, so Ida didn't have to say much. They seemed quite pleasant, but almost before Verna Legge had shut the door behind them with a thud that brought a nervous 'ting' from the wall clock, she had started to find fault.

'What did *she* come for? I know what she came for. Looking around. You see how she looked around? Three cups of coffee she drunk on me. Then I make a fresh pot and she takes but one sip. Well, they got a good look at you, so I hope it was worth it.'

'They made me feel welcome,' Ida said. 'They're very nice, your friends.'

'They're not *friends*, they're neighbours,' Mrs Legge said firmly. 'Shut up in there!' She slapped at her mounded stomach. 'Lookit,' she laughed gleefully. 'See the rascal? See him poundin' about?'

But the baby could no more make itself known to the world than if it had been inside a two-foot thick igloo.

The day before the wedding, they went downtown to buy a white hat. Ida had planned to pin a flower in her hair, but Mrs Legge said she had to wear a proper hat, like it or not. On the way back, they would 'swing by' Buddy's married sister, 'since she hasn't chosen to behave like a Christian woman and stop around and tell you hello. Put on them shiny spike heels, Hilda.' She sometimes called Ida that.

'I thought she lived at a farm. I'll wear my flats. She won't mind.'

'She's supposed to mind.' Verna made her frog face. 'She's jealous of Buddy, see. Thinks she's something now because her husband went to college before he dropped out to farm a few ratty sheep. I want her to see my Buddy's done it again.'

'Done what?' Had he been married before? One more surprise along with all the rest.

'Gone one better than her.' Verna pulled out her gum, squinted at it, passed it as fit and sucked it back inside.

'Can I have some gum?'

'Help yourself.' Mrs Legge waved at the jar full of gum packets on the windowsill among the dirty mugs and dust-snagged cactus plants. 'English people are so polite. It gets me down how they talk so polite.' She was getting sick of having Ida there.

The hat was a white felt with a wavy brim turned down all round. It rode rather high because of Ida's stiff hair, but Mrs Legge paid for it while Ida was still trying to come to terms with it, and carried it out in a bag. Ida took it out in the car and turned it round on her fist, wondering about a bit of ribbon to hide the join where crown met brim.

'Leave the price tag on.' Verna smiled, driving with straight arms to give herself room behind the wheel. 'I want Sis to see it.'

Sis lived over another hill in a small farmhouse that sat comfortably by a stream in a valley, with a sheep pasture sloping up to a dark magnificent wood. In front of the house was a garden with flower-beds and a low uneven wall, and across the unpaved road, a big barn and some smaller sheds, old and weathered. There was a fenced yard with two cows in it and some speckled chickens. Ducks sat in wet grass at the edge of a muddy pond. Ida's heart rose.

A collie ran out barking, and a healthy-looking girl in a long skirt and boots came out of the house. The afternoon sun, shining low along the road, put coppery lights into the thick bush of hair that stood out round her head.

'There she is,' Mrs Legge said gloomily.

A wiry little girl with a streamer of long fair hair ran out behind her mother and charged into her grandmother, who bent to pick her up with some fond pride, although she told Sis, 'Looks as if she didn't have a square meal in weeks.'

Ida and Sis took to each other, which annoyed Mrs Legge. She had talked about Sis and Jeff as if they were on their beam ends, but they seemed to be living a fine life among animals and growing things in an airy, uncluttered house, warmed by a huge ornate wood stove.

Sis took Ida out to see the farm. You could hear the movement of the water in the stream behind the house. The wind came down the valley from the hill and rushed about in the trees. The smell of cow manure was sharp and oddly clean.

Behind the barn Ida met Jeff in a fringed leather waistcoat and corduroys, filling a small truck with logs he sold to help support them in the winter. He was shy and so was Sis, but Ida felt less shy with them than she had with anyone, including Lily, who wasn't exactly critical, but who knew how she wanted you to be. This slow, hard-working, outdoor life was different from anything she had ever known, but it called to her.

'Do you think Buddy would leave the Air Force and become a farmer?' she asked.

Sis and Jeff laughed heartily. No comment, so Ida laughed too.

At the car Verna Legge showed the wedding-hat.

'I was going to find some sort of flower to wear,' Ida said, disclaiming the hat.

'Put it on, Hilda.'

'No.'

Sis was laughing inside herself. Ida was not going to be made a fool of.

'Don't make her, mother. She – well look, it might be bad luck for me to see it before the wedding.'

'Oh, you are coming, then?'

'Sure.' Sis began to laugh inside herself again. 'Wasn't I invited?'

Mrs Legge backed the car without looking to see if the dog or child were behind it, and hauled it round like a battleship.

'See what I mean,' she stated triumphantly as she lurched off, scattering stones.

Ida had turned round to see Sis and the little girl holding hands, with their hair and their long skirts blowing. She fought the stiff window to roll it down far enough to lean out and wave.

Buddy did not turn up until early the next morning.

'They screwed up my pass,' he said. 'Been driving through the night.'

As Ida understood it, Watkins base wasn't all that far away, but he needed a grievance to present to his mother, like a bunch of flowers.

He looked better in his uniform. He always did, and when he had had a shower and a shave and a stack of Verna's pancakes, with floods of maple syrup and oily butter that clung round his mouth, he was quite a dashing bridegroom.

My wedding day. Who would have believed it? Eighty-five per cent of English women get married at least once, but each one is shocked when it happens. The electric heater in the trailer had set fire to itself and burned a hole in the wall that smelled of scorching rubber, so Ida was allowed to get ready in the bathroom, and to have it to herself for one whole half hour. She soaked with a highly scented bath cube given her by Phyllis, who was in a romantic mood, thrilled with herself in a new dress the colour of cough syrup.

What the hell am I doing? Ida lay in the fragrant scummy water, keeping the back of her hair dry. Do I love him? Lily shouldn't have talked like that. Secretly, it had shaken Ida a bit. Does he love me? In his way, I suppose. We can make a go of it. Because it was her wedding day and therefore quite unreal, Ida let herself drift away into lying fantasies of low, cushioned rooms and log fires and flaxen-haired children and cow manure.

When she came out of the bathroom in her white dress and silver shoes, with her new silver eye make-up and pancake foundation over the wretched shadows below them, and the best pink mouth she had ever drawn, glossy as satin, Buddy looked up from the kitchen table and passed the back of his hand over his lips.

'Not bad,' he said in a wet throaty voice, which meant emotion with him. 'Bit like they wear for tennis, but not bad.' He looked her slowly up and down and up (she had a padded bra). Then he wiped his mouth again and gave a low whistle.

Mrs Legge had the white hat over a lampshade near the door, so it could not be avoided, but after Buddy had driven off with his friend Malc who was going to stand up for him as his best man, and the rest of them were all ready to leave for the church, Sis hurried in wearing a long Indian kind of dress and gave Ida a big white carnation made of silk that she had bought for her hair.

Ida was in a spot. Not really. Mrs Legge could stuff herself with the hat. Sis pinned the flower on to one side of her curls. Since Verna Legge was raging, Ida went off to the church in Jeff's truck.

After the wedding – my God, I've gone and done it! – they had coffee and cakes and beer and sweet wine in the hall at the side of the church. It was nice. There was a doddery old grandmother on a walking frame and a few cousins and local people, and Buddy stayed next to Ida all the time, holding her hand in his hot sticky one, or stroking her arm and telling people, 'This is my wife.'

'Never thought they'd get ya, Buddy boy.' 'Nor did I. Feels good though.' 'Atta boy.' 'Sure feels good.' And other comfortable remarks that made Ida feel glad about the whole thing.

Henry Legge, in a suit, said to her quite formally that he was proud to welcome her into the family. Mrs Legge did not say a word to anyone the entire time. She sat by the wall with her knees apart, and when Buddy and Ida came to say goodbye to her before they left, she turned her head away, so Buddy's kiss landed nowhere.

'You better kiss her goodbye,' he whispered, but Ida merely gave her a victor's smile and drew him away.

At the gates into the Air Force base, there was some fuss because Ida did not yet have a Dependant's identity card, and the guard, who was as brusque and suspicious as a gaoler, would not believe she was Mrs Legge.

'Look, this is my wedding dress,' she leaned forwards shyly to tell him. She had taken the white flower out of her hair and put it carefully away in a paper napkin with silver bells on it that one of Verna's despised neighbours had brought, but she was still wearing the white dress.

Buddy put out an elbow and pushed her back. Women didn't talk to guards. Although he lived here, Buddy was quite nervous, because the man in the white helmet was a military police sergeant and out for trouble. He finally had to unpack a bag at the back of the car, scattering things on the floor, to find the marriage certificate.

'Welcome to Watkins,' the sergeant said dismissively.

Their house was Number 1009 Pershing Street, which did not mean that there were one thousand and eight other houses there, but they were in the tenth block. Although Buddy had already been to the house after the last couple moved out, and moved in a few bits of furniture, the sergeant had humiliated him and he was too nervous to find the street in the dark. The officers' houses were bungalows spaced apart, with gardens like a suburb, but the huge enlisted family area had dozens of streets with identical, square, two-storey wooden houses, almost all with a bright light outside.

'Electricity must be cheap over here,' Ida observed, to ease the tension.

Buddy was too rattled to answer. At last, when they found themselves at the crossroads of Otis and School Streets, he had to ask a group of boys discussing a motor-bike on the corner, which he hated to do. By the time they found the house and pulled into the covered car park alongside, he was cursing under his breath and his hands were shaking.

'He gets easily upset,' Verna Legge had told Ida in the No-name Laundromat

Too right, he did. When he had unlocked the front door, he forgot to pick up Ida and carry her over the sill, as he had promised. He walked into the house, switching on all the lights, and went right through into the kitchen at the back to run water and sluice his face.

'Come back here!' Ida stood on the wooden front step in her good coat with the Peter Pan velvet collar over the white dress.

Her shout brought him. He looked hastily to right and left to see if any neighbours had heard Ida and come out to look, then scooped her up and carried her easily into the bare house, kicking the door shut behind him. When he bent to put her down, Ida clung round his neck and giggled. He squeezed her tightly and kissed her with his wet face, and she made him carry her into the kitchen, kicking off her silver shoes as they went.

There was a stove and a sink and a refrigerator and a washing-machine, but they only had two chairs and a card table in the living-room, and a bed upstairs.

There was some beer in the fridge. Ida didn't drink much of hers because she didn't want it to repeat on her in bed. Buddy drank quite a lot, stopped being jittery and became sentimental. He even mooed to her, 'Don't ever leave me, Ah-eye-da.'

He carried her up the stairs, because that had gone well for both of them downstairs, had a quick but satisfactory bash at her, and went to sleep.

That was all right. When Ida was twelve, sex had turned out to be less exhilarating than the magazines made out, and nothing that had happened to her since Pa had changed her mind.

Buddy woke in a foul mood and went off to work, hardly speaking to her. That was all right too. Best thing about playing house was having it to yourself all day. Ida stood in the kitchen in her nightgown and bare feet. The house was warm. The re-frigerator made a responsible whirring sound. My own home! She stroked counters and door frames, and furnished the house in her mind with flowered wallpaper and bright-coloured chairs and carpets. She had bread and grape jelly and tea without milk. Among the few groceries Buddy had got in, he had remembered tea. She thought of him fondly.

He came home in his lunch-break and they went to the huge dazzling Commissary and the Base Exchange and bought masses of everything, and Ida bought a postcard of a jet fighter going like a dagger over Washington DC. That evening they went to a late-night discount store to look at couches and tables. They bought a television set. Buddy seemed to have plenty of money.

Ida would write to Lily: *All okay. Marriage is wonderful. I like it here.*

Next day Buddy came home for supper and a quick bash on top of the bed upstairs, and went out again, because the boys wanted to celebrate his wedding.

In the following days Ida made friends with some of the other wives in this settlement of white wooden houses. They thought she was cute, and invited her in for coffee to astonishingly immaculate interiors, considering they had two or three children and sometimes a dog. They took her shopping in their cars, because the base was so huge, you couldn't walk anywhere.

At the end of the week, Buddy came home from his work in the supply warehouse to change his green fatigues, went out without eating the supper Ida had prepared, and didn't come back at all until he woke her by kicking open the bedroom door at seven a.m. and changing into uniform without a word or a look at her.

'Where have you . . . Buddy, I . . . Pardon me asking, but . . .'

He was a man of stone. Soft fleshy stone, but stone.

That day she finally wrote the card to Lily, and Sandy from two blocks down took her to the base post office.

All okay, she wrote to Lily. *You okay?*

Three

*A*bout six years after the side trip to Iceland, Paul Stephens went to England again to promote a new type of waterproof horse blanket manufactured by the firm for which he was now chief buyer.

The store near Boston Common sold bags and belts and suitcases and boots and wallets and everything made of leather, including jackets and camel saddle stools. They also sold everything for horses and their riders and slaves. They had small subsidiary tack shops in two of the horsier towns outside Boston, displays at all the big shows and cross-country events, and a small workshop which made their own lines of equipment.

Paul had started out with them on the floor, and graduated to buying and marketing. After high school, he had served two years in the United States Navy and come out of it knowing how to cook and splice a rope, but knowing nothing about what he wanted to do, except that he did not want to be a lawyer.

'You're breaking your Dad's heart,' his mother said, but his father, an overworked attorney, was tougher than that.

'You'd never make it, anyway,' he told Paul plainly. 'You're too easy-going. You like everybody.'

'He gets that from you.' Paul's mother never gave up trying to sentimentalize her prosaic, private-souled husband.

'Not guilty. That's not the way I got to be successful.'

Paul went to business college and came out to discover that finding a job took longer than he expected. He cooked fast-food in a highway service-stop for a while, and tended bar in a restaurant that was dark at lunchtime, and shared an apartment with two friends from college.

Walking in Boston on his day off, he stopped in at Turnbull's to buy a belt that was in the window, with a buckle like a snaffle bit. Horses were an old love from childhood riding days.

The salesgirl had an eager, confiding way with her. She was not busy, so they talked, and Paul found out there was a job going, and applied for it on impulse.

Two weeks after he started work, the eager girl left to go to Canada with her boyfriend, but Paul stayed.

He had met his wife, Barbara, at a horse show in which she was riding, and his connection with her family, who were in the North Shore hunting world, helped him in his job. Barbara taught him to ride all over again, her way, but after Terry was born she became very depressed, and was not helped by the doctor saying it was physical not psychological, because she wanted it to be psychological.

Her body eventually recovered of its own accord, but the marriage never got back to the way it was. Paul's native patience was wearing away on the grindstone of her stifling moods. The two horses had gone, because they cost too much, and she couldn't be bothered anyway. Paul was successful, with good contacts, but his job compared unfavourably with the husbands of most of Barbara's friends. A salesman was a salesman. Some of the North Shore women had taken up with trainers or opportunist show jumpers, but the man who sells you the saddle is in a different class to the man who teaches you how to sit in it.

'Where did our youth and rapture go?' Barbara mourned.

Paul still felt young at twenty-nine, and vulnerable to rapture from the open air, the sun, the snow, horses, summer beaches, and his son, his son, his beautiful son who had been mostly his until Barbara began to pull out of the depression, unwillingly back into life.

'Trouble with you,' she would say, 'is you're too happy. Why are you always smiling?' She had adored his cheerful face at first. Now she disgruntled it into a weapon against her. She began to wonder whether she was going to fall into depression again.

It was at this point that Lily fell in love with Paul in Flekjavik. But that was only a dream. Crazy too. You didn't throw away two people's security for what was an illusory kind of cruise-liner romance with a girl only fourteen years older than your son.

However, when Terry started school, Barbara got a job with a man who was making expensive dressy sweaters in Wellesley, had a loveless affair with him, then a more involved and open one with somebody sleazier, and through a high-priced lawyer hired by her father, got custody of their son when she and Paul were divorced.

58

'I might just as well have slept with that girl I met in Iceland,' Paul told Barbara at one point during all the nastiness.

'Like all the others?'

'What others?'

'You can lay off pretending now. You and your standards. If there's one thing I despise, it's a hypocrite.'

I would never do anything to hurt Barbara, Paul heard himself telling Lily pompously on the cement staircase, a stifling funnel for the Air Force's hot-spring heating system.

Alone in London, Paul managed to get a ticket for a musical about travelling in time.

From the circle, he watched the tops of people's heads coming into the seats below. A man and a woman walked sideways along the third row. Broad shoulders in a low black dress. A swath of glossy brown hair, shining under the high chandelier, caught back with a wide clasp and falling squarely to the exact level of the cut ends at the back.

Is it? Isn't it? It was six years, after all. She wouldn't be doing her hair the same way.

In the interval, he went looking for her in the crowded bar. Not a hope. He manoeuvred round two expansive men and a gesturing woman, and came face to face with Lily. She was leaning against striped satin wallpaper, staring at him with her mouth open, the same but different.

'Is it? It is, isn't it?'

'Paul.'

She still had the same high colouring, but her face seemed narrower, her neck more slender on the wide shoulders that carried the low-cut black dress, very different from the bunchy thing she had worn. It had been a child's face then, the features unformed, soft and round. Now it was strong and very alive and glowing.

In six years she had grown away from him. He wouldn't have a chance with her now, a battered old divorcé of thirty-four. The young man she was with in those good orchestra seats was probably one of many, unless the swine was her husband. She was out of Paul's reach.

'Lily – what happened to you? You were such a kid. What happened to those God-awful glasses that kept falling off?'

She relaxed into a smile. 'Sorry about them.' She poked the middle finger of her right hand towards the bridge of her nose. 'I've got contact lenses now.'

'You're lovely.' He shook his head slightly as he said it, regret in his voice.

'Oh, rubbish.' That brisk denial had not changed.

A man with hair longish and curling at the sides materialized alongside. 'You stay here, Lil. I'll get the drinks.'

'Your Husband?' Paul nodded towards the curly sideburns trying to get the barman's attention.

She laughed. Although her face was no longer plump, when she laughed her cheeks still went out sideways in a rounded chubby way. 'You're the one who's married, remember?'

'That's just it.' Paul dropped his voice like a stone between them. 'I'm not any more.'

Her mouth fell open again. She searched his face. Then she recovered and muttered things like, 'I'm sorry . . . hard for you.'

When the other man fought his way back with two drinks, Lily introduced him.

'I'm Paul Stephens.' He knew Lily did not remember his last name, if she had ever known it. He did not know her name.

The man asked Paul where he was from and what his business was, and said some things about the play, and how he hoped it wouldn't start up all that popular nonsense about reincarnation again.

'Why not?' Paul asked. 'We've all lived before. That explains a lot of things, like *déjà vu* and instant attraction.'

'I can't agree. You get one stab at life and that's it. If you make a mess of it, you don't get another chance. Right, Lil?'

'I don't think so,' she said softly, hard to hear in the hubbub. 'I think you can recognize someone from another life.'

Not hearing, the man turned away, as someone called his name. Paul and Lily looked and looked at each other.

Paul stayed an extra day in London and changed his appointment with a racing stable. Lily came to his hotel at nine o'clock. 'I'm not going to work,' she said. 'Can we have all day?'

'Till I have to drive to the country this evening.'

'I'll come with you.'

They were having breakfast. It wasn't a very nice hotel, since Turnbull's were tight with expenses. The dining-room was drab and the waitress discouraged, with a nasty bulge in her shoe. They were not eating, but drinking coffee and staring. Lily stirred her coffee with the plastic spoon she had picked up from the floor by the coffee machine in Iceland.

'You're still sentimental, Lily. You haven't changed.'

'Nor have you. I love you. Now say it, go on.'

'What?'

'"No, you don't. Hush now." You were so edgy and cautious.'

'Well, Lily, I was married, for God's sake.'

'You're so proper. If we got married, would you still be like that with another woman who tried anything on?'

Back in America, as soon as he had told Terry, Paul telephoned Barbara to say he was going to marry again. There was a pause. Then Barbara said, 'Oh, English. She rides, then?'

'No, she doesn't know anything about horses, as a matter of fact.'

'Good. Then you can teach her. You'll like that, being better at something.'

'Barb, don't be like that.'

'No, I shouldn't, should I?' She had been more mellow towards him of late. There had not been so much trouble over Terry's visits. 'Seriously, Paul, I really am glad for you. As long as it doesn't mean –'

'It won't mean anything, if that's what you mean.'

Paul was paying her only for his son's support. Her lawyer had been clever about the custody, but not as crafy as Paul's lawyer about the settlement. The process had been squalid and villainous. Paul and Barbara both hated it so much that they had even briefly discussed staying married. The happiness they had shared – the small house outside Boston her father bought her, the early rapture, the horses, the meals Paul cooked her, her serene pregnancy, the miracle of a perfect baby boy being suddenly among them – all brought to nothing, and the memories of them violated and strangled by delays and greed and the horrible warfare process of the court.

At one point, Paul had been ready to say, 'I'll give her everything I have, what does it matter?' Now it did.

'I wondered.' He called Barbara again tentatively. She could be quite friendly and rational, but she could still be triggered off. 'I thought, I mean, after all, this is very important to Terry too. I wondered whether he would like to come to England for my wedding. My parents could take him over.'

'Your wedding.' Barbara did not go in for exclamation marks. She said it flatly, as a statement. 'You must be crazy.'

'I was going to ask him myself, but I thought I'd better check with you first.'

'I'm amazed you even thought of it.'

'Let me talk to him. What time will he be home? Why don't we let him make up his own mind?'

'He's only ten years old. You don't lay those kind of choices on a child, Paul. In any case, he shouldn't even be offered the choice right now. He's not been acting in the kind of way that deserves a trip to England.'

'Oh God, not again? Why didn't you tell me? You know we agreed I'd always be involved when there was any problem.'

'Well, you don't want to be bothered every time he screams at me, or tears the place apart. I can't call you eight times a day.'

'Barbara – what's wrong with him? He was into a much easier phase.'

'He was. Until you presented him with your joyful gift of a wicked stepmother. Happy Columbus Day.'

'Listen, if you'll let me say this. He'll get along fine with Lily, I know he will.'

'Why don't we let him make up his own mind?' One of her ploys: quoting you back at yourself. 'But let's at least try to make it a little easier for him, huh?'

Getting married to Paul was splendid enough. Going off with him to live in the United States was an incredible adventure for which Lily was eagerly ready at twenty-four. Her life had already been threatening to get into a rut. Train, work, train home to Wimbledon, try to be at least half as fair to her parents as they were to her. Fight with her sister Blanche, make it up. Meet men, get rid of them or be dropped, meet new men with persistent hope, hang on to one or two drearies so as not to be at home too many evenings.

With the usual good luck in which she believed, as some people believe themselves dogged by ill fortune, here was salvation, before it all got boring and she lost zest and hardened towards her thirties. Now she would be a married woman during that dread decade, a mother perhaps, with Paul in America, the bird who flew the coop, the daughter who would always be prized because she wasn't there, the sister who would seem glamorous, the friend who was envied.

In Boston, she would lose weight, become witty, magically develop a clothes sense, be gracefully domesticated, stop bossing people about.

Telling her parents had been more difficult than she had foreseen. When she took Paul home, her father put on an act, jovial and very British, and her mother came out of the kitchen and realized she had forgotten to take off her apron, which set her back in the conversation. Blanche looked unhappy. But you could tell they liked Paul. He was agonizingly polite, and very considerate. He laughed at Daddy's jokes and laid on a bit too thick his admiration of the supper, the house, the garden, the photographs, and made too big a deal of being friendly with the dog, who would make friends with anyone. No need to make the family suspicious.

But they liked him. They did. They were glad for Lily. Even if they had not been, she would have gone roaring ahead with the enterprise, and they would have had to take their chances.

In the Family Centre, the helping agency where she worked, it was exciting to break the news, and show a photograph. When

Joan said, very sincerely, 'I don't know what we're going to do without you,' Lily did feel a pang of guilt and regret strike through her armour of self-centred excitement.

Three years ago, she had left college without completing the social work course, because after a summer typing job with the Family Centre, they had offered her a permanent post as a secretary. She talked to the clients a lot. There were always people in the waiting-room, and Lily's ear was useful to them as a preliminary to the person they had come to see, or sometimes instead of, if Joan or Jane or Bill or Tina or Mrs Levy never got round to them. The budget did not allow any more case workers, but Joan began to train Lily, and to let her go out on calls with the others, and write reports, and eventually have clients of her own. She had got in at the back door to just where she wanted to be.

Although the rest of the staff were happy about Lily's marriage, Joan, unmarried, a middle-aged sane saint in stretched cardigans, did not want to understand how Lily could give all this up. As Director, she had been wonderfully encouraging and helpful to Lily, and now she was hurt, and looked suddenly vulnerable and a bit older.

She rallied to resume her tower-of-strength behaviour. In the weeks before Lily left, Joan treated her as if nothing had happened, and continued to trust her with almost as many sad and difficult and frustrating cases as the others.

On the afternoon of a day of disaster, when someone had swallowed pills in the lavatory, and a drunk and abusive husband had to be fetched off the premises by the police, and the Hutchinsons had been evicted from the new flat, and five people in crisis came in without appointments, and Bill had to dash away to the juvenile court when magistrates decided to hear the twins' case at the last minute, Joan had said mildly to Lily, nodding her untidy grey head towards the door of the teeming waiting-room, reeking of sour baby by now, awash with spilt tea and knee-deep in crumbs and chocolate wrappers, 'I wonder how you can be so ecstatic about marriage when you see what it does to people.'

That was all. When Lily left, Joan gave her a brooch made like a fleur-de-lis, and Lily promised to find herself the same kind of work in a Boston agency, and send for Joan to come over and sort them out.

'I'll always be grateful to you,' Lily said. *You've taught me everything I know*, she wanted to say, but that would sound conceited, as if she really did know something now. In any case, someone burst into Joan's office, crying, 'Where are the files on the Mulcahys?'

Saying goodbye to the clients was far worse. A temporary worker had already started to take them over, but Lily kept on as long as possible with Sidney and the McKnights and Mrs Daley, and spastic George who was about to leave the day centre and go to his job-training school.

The trouble was, Lily had made it too easy for them to get too dependent. Joan had warned her about this a dozen times.

'Don't worry, don't worry,' Lily always said. 'I'm helping them to use *their* strength, not mine, such as it is.'

'Don't woo them, then,' Joan said.

'What do you mean?'

'If they need you too much, you'll end up needing them.'

I do though. It's time I went. I need Paul more.

Sidney was resigned, because everybody in his life disappeared sooner or later. Mrs Daley was angry, because Lily had promised to take her on an outing, and there had never been time. The McKnights were so nice about it that she could tell them why she was leaving, and show them Paul's picture. She had taken it on the common when he came to Wimbledon to meet her family, wearing another blue pullover she had bought for him the day they had breakfast together.

The McKnights had an old, sick mother living with them in two rooms, with no proper heat or water supply. Lily had been the only person who could get anywhere with the landlord. Could Lily speak to him *just* once more before she . . .

'Oh dear, I haven't got time. I'm sure Theresa will help.'

'But if you could just talk to him once more about the electricity. When are you leaving?'

'Tomorrow,' Lily lied. She had to escape.

Family, girlfriends, old boyfriends waxing or waning, the job, the beloved clients, her whole twenty-four years of life. How lucky she had been to be able to throw herself into it all, and then before it got stale, jump out of it and start again somewhere else.

'I'll come back, I'll come back,' she told everybody, and this was what made it possible to go, in the end. She was escaping to be somebody different with Paul, but the old solid love and knowledge would still be here, to come back to.

Lily's father thought Paul seemed a decent sort of chap, although a good bit too old for Lily, childish as she still seemed to be, in spite of getting the job in the counselling agency and coming home with all kinds of unnerving expressions like 'single parent syndrome' and 'anger turned inwards'.

Paul was a step up for this family, with his dad a judge, and certainly a cut above some of the con men and misfits Lily had brought home, let alone the ones she hadn't brought home, for reasons that would have been obvious, James Spooner supposed, if he could have laid eyes on them. Paul had called James 'sir' and laughed at his jokes, which, when James got to know him better, he would have to explain wasn't expected in this family. James would make the jokes because he liked to, whether anyone laughed or not, just as he would continue to act up a bit if he felt like it in the tea-break, to keep his mind and wit supple, even when the Post Office staff were surly from the shock of Monday or the toll of Friday.

But how would he get to know his son-in-law better, with Paul and Lily Stephens, as he must write to her now, gone off to Massachusetts with indecent haste right after the wedding, and how would he struggle through the tedious backwaters of life without his bright, kaleidoscopic daughter?

His best daughter. James allowed himself to admit that, after she was gone. Blanche the Good, his Bianca, had always been Daddy's girl, and Lily the one with whom you never quite knew where you were. Big sentimental dramas about 'I love my ugly old Daddy', one minute, and storms of protest the next if he suggested any improvement in her style of dress or behaviour.

Now she was gone, a married woman. After all the years of kidding himself that Lily wasn't *really* having it off with any of the buffoons or delinquents, James had to abandon his fantasy of Lily as an unsullied child.

When he tried to put this into words to Nora, she had surprised him by saying, 'Well, I certainly never kidded myself. When she asked me for information about contraception, I told her.'

'She asked you – her mother? That's depraved.'

'Well, I am a nurse, when all's said and done. You've got to keep up with the times, Jamie. Things have changed since our day. Now the young think they invented sex.'

'How did they get here, then?'

'They don't want to know. They don't want to think about their parents doing anything in bed.'

'Nor do you, most of the time.'

'I've as much right as you to say when and when not.' Since she had started working at the hospital as a State-enrolled nurse, Nora had taken some alarming turns towards independent thought.

'Since when?' James grabbed her by the front of her thick healthy hair and bent her backwards over the kitchen table, snarling like a gorilla.

'Let me up, there's a dear,' she said, his fangs at her soft white throat. 'I've got something on the stove.'

'And about time.'

When Nora was on night duty, she slept in the afternoons, and usually did not get up in time to have supper ready before James's gastric juices started eating into his stomach wall. When she was on the seven-to-three shift, life was normal, but when the hospital, which knocked staff around like snooker balls and didn't care a fish's eye for family life, put her on three to eleven, she left something on the stove for Blanche to heat up, and James came home and went to bed wifeless.

Those nights, he went down to the Three Horseshoes, or up the hill to the George, if he needed an audience. He could usually find someone to give him a laugh for one of his imitations. Harold Wilson making a speech at the opening of a brothel was a current favourite. James had a nice throaty baritone voice for the evenings that turned musical, when someone was in the pub who could jangle the old upright, like playing on a skeleton with spoons.

Tonight, he popped down to the George while Nora was finishing supper and putting on her uniform.

'Well, here he is!' Nigel called from the bar. It was warming to be welcomed like that, so that heads turned. 'James Spooner, the man who sold his daughter to the Yanks.'

James enjoyed the teasing, and the chance to make a story out of Lily's wedding; how she had practically pulled him up the aisle at a trot, what the clergyman had on his breath from lunch, and how the whole thing had ruined him, and Blanche would have to elope, in the unlikely event she fell out of love with dogs for long enough to find a man.

Someone bought him another pint, and he said some sturdy, hand-across-the-sea things about Paul, and boasted that Lily had looked a knockout.

It would have been nice to be able to tell her about the expansive things he said about her and her husband in the George. When he had something to tell, Lily used to put her arms on to the table and open wide at him the eyes that had become so beautiful since she got rid of the goggles. Used to? She wasn't dead, for God's sake.

He raised his mug. 'Here's to her happiness,' he said cheerily. But the thought that she wasn't there made him feel very low and aged. New aches and twinges darted in and out among the old predictable ones.

Terry was ten. He had been eight when his father and mother split apart, and then started to get divorced from each other.

He knew they had been fighting. You couldn't not know, living in that house with them, not because of the noise and screaming, like in Warren's house, or Jason's apartment where the glass ornaments trembled, but because of the deadly cold silences.

Sometimes at supper, Terry had been the only one who talked. It was tough, trying to keep things going, telling a few stories – 'Don't play with your food, Terry' – putting on funny voices, dropping things to get attention. 'Pick it up.'

'It's got germs on it now.'

'The floor's clean. And anyhow, your system is immune to household germs.'

'At school, if you drop something, they won't let you –'

'Go and wash it.'

'You do it, Mom, if you're going to the kitchen.'

'Do it yourself.'

'No!'

'Don't shout at me. You see the way he is, Paul, he's like a savage.'

'No, he's not. Come on, Terry, go get another fork.'

'You can't make me. I don't want to eat anyway. I hate pork. I hate everything – I hate you! Don't – no, Dad, no! Let me go – I hate you!'

Mild stuff really, just routine, to liven up the boredom of mealtimes. Terry got away with it most of the time, because his mother was all talk and his father was patient and wanted to be gentle. When he started going round to Eddie Waite's house, he began to find out how much farther you could go without getting butchered.

Eddie had a few brothers and sisters and his mother was sort of whacked out most of the time, drunk or sober, so Eddie got away with all kinds of things she never knew anything about.

Like slipping candy and small stuff off the store shelves into your pocket, and then going with a big grin through the checkout with the detergent or whatever it was you'd been sent to buy. Easy.

'You mean, you never done it before?' Eddie asked as they walked away from Art's Super Store. Walk, don't run, even if you're peeing your pants with fright. 'Stick around, kid. I'll show you a lot of fun things.'

Like breaking off car antennas, snap, snap, snap, all along the line in a parking lot. Like running a nail along the paintwork of a fancy new Mercury. Like taking coins out of your mother's purse when she was in the bathroom, dimes and quarters here and there, so she wouldn't notice and make a big scene.

The first time Terry took two nickels from the mug where his mother collected coins to pay the newspaper boy, he thought the kitchen walls would crash in on him. He heard her feet on the stairs and almost put the coins back, but he had promised Eddie, so he kept them. The next time Eddie asked him to get money, he said he couldn't do it.

'You always do what I say.' Eddie was not a tyrant, but he was older and he was the leader. Terry admired him and desperately wanted to keep his friendship.

'She's locked the money away,' Terry invented. He had reached up his hand once or twice to the mug on the shelf over the stove, but it became paralysed on the way up.

'Okay, dummy, do this, then.' Eddie was always testing Terry, to see if he was worthy of his friendship. 'Come into Kale's Market and knock down that pile of tomato soup cans they got there.'

'Sure, Eddie. Easy.'

'Hey, you!' A man caught Terry's jacket sleeve as he was running out of the store. 'I been watching you kids. I don't want no trouble. I don't want that Waite kid in here, and I don't want you neither. Now get on home.'

When Terry got home, he sat outside until he saw his father's car, the beloved little red car that he could steer, sitting on his father's knee, but pretended to despise, because it was three years old, with a lousy radio.

'Hi there.' His beloved father got out quickly with an extra-large smile. 'Waiting for me?'

'I guess so.'

'Want to do something outside while it's still light? Get some more boards up on the shed, or something?'

'Sure.'

As Terry followed him through the side door that led into the house from the garage, his mother called from the living-room in her flat, monotonous voice.

'Paul, please go right back out –' she always said please when she was upset – 'please go back out and look for Terry. He's off somewhere.'

70

'He's here. He was waiting outside.'

'Hello, Terry. Couldn't bother to come in and let me know you were home?'

In the living-room, his mother looked quite ordinary and peaceful, sitting by the coffee-table with a drink, filing her nails. So Terry made a sound like 'Hunhnyah', and shrugged his shoulders and spread his arms.

'Mr Kale called,' his mother told his father. 'One of the men who works there caught Terry making trouble in the store.'

'It was an accident.'

'Was it? And I suppose it was an accident that you put a chocolate bar in your pocket?'

'Terry – what's this?' His father pounced round as if he was going to spring on him.

'Him and Eddie Waite.' His mother chewed on Eddie's name with grim satisfaction.

'I told you I didn't think you ought to hang around so much with that kid.'

'I don't, Dad. I don't even like him.' Eddie was Terry's best friend. He loved him, but he would say anything to stop his father getting angry.

'He's lying, Paul,' his mother said, without looking up from her nails.

'I'm not, I'm not! What's the good of telling the truth? Nobody ever believes me.'

'Terry, calm down.'

When his father took hold of him, Terry bent his head, quick as a cat, and bit him in the fleshy part of his hand. His father swung him around and pushed him up the stairs to his room and shut the door.

Terry listened for a moment to see what they were saying. He opened the door and heard his mother cross the hall in hard heels. She said, 'Lay off me, Paul, just this once, will you, please.'

'For ever, if you like.'

Terry took two books from the shelf and hurled them down the stairs. Then he pulled one of the small drawers out of the top of the bureau, opened the window and emptied the socks and underpants outside on to the side path. He followed them with a holy picture Grandma Stephens had given him last year, to ward off nightmares. Crash, tinkle.

'Come down at once and pick all this up!' His mother's voice from the garden, a bit later. He kept the window shut, and did not answer.

'I thought we were going to work on the shed.' His father was out there now. Terry turned up his radio. 'Too bad. Well, come down and pick this stuff up before supper. It's going to rain.'

Much later, after the kitchen sounds told Terry that they had had supper, the dog next door began to bark. Terry looked out of the window and saw his father kneeling in the dusk, picking up bits of glass from the brick path. In the light from the lower window, the top of his thick hair glistened in the rain like early morning cobwebs.

Every part of Terry's being wanted to run down and help him. Who wouldn't let him? It was like a separate person holding him back. He pulled down the blind, stealthily, so his father would not hear the roller, and look up.

After his father went away to live in an apartment, and then they got divorced, Terry began to see that it must have been partly his fault for behaving so badly, and being in trouble all the time.

His mother's explanation was, 'Your father didn't love us enough.'

His father did not try to explain. He just told Terry, 'We'll be together a lot of the time, and we'll still always be the most important people in the world to each other.'

So if that was truly so, what Terry had to do was to act decently, and Dad would one day come back and live at home, and there would be another dog, even Buster back, why not? His father's terrier had gone to a new home, because he could not be kept in the apartment, and Terry's mother had never liked him.

Terry began to behave quite well. No screaming or throwing things. Enough homework to get by. The garbage taken out. 'You're the man of the house now, Ter.' His mother thought that would flatter him. He explained to Eddie that he had got to lie low for a while, and Eddie understood, true friend that he was, and did not involve him in the riskier adventures. Terry did not see his father often enough, but it was great when they were together. No arguments. No testing Dad to see how much he would stand. They did things his mother would not approve of, like going to a wrestling match and staying up late to watch a horror movie propped up side by side on the sofa-bed in Dad's apartment, eating Chinese food with chopsticks.

His father usually dropped him off at the house, had a few calm, reasonable words with his mother on the doorstep, and then drove away.

One time, to get him used to the idea of coming back, Terry said casually, 'Why not come in?'

'Oh – I don't know that I have time.'

'Cup of coffee, maybe? A drink?'

'All right, then. Why not?'

His mother, who was dressed to go out with one of her boyfriends, was annoyed. So Terry made the coffee and his father sat in his usual chair, the one he had wanted to move to the apartment, but it was too wide for the doorway, quite at home. Terry fussed around him, bringing him a cushion, a plate of cookies, lighting the table lamp, showing some new photographs.

'You want a Polar Bar? We have some in the freezer. Still eat Polar Bars, Dad?'

'Not without you, I don't.'

'Let's have one now. Can we, Mom?' he remembered to ask, being virtuous. He brought the ice-cream, unwrapped in saucers, with spoons and paper napkins, and sat on a stool near his father.

'Gee, this is cosy, isn't it, Dad?'

'Sure is.'

Terry's mother had not sat down, and was walking about in high heels, the calves of her legs tight and her hair polished like a metal cap.

'You'll have to go, Paul. I have theatre tickets, and Terry's going to sleep over with a friend.'

'I don't have to, Mom. I can stay here, if Dad could stay till you get back.'

His mother frowned. 'I don't think that's a good idea. Your father has to go anyway. How about dropping Terry off at the

Waites', Paul?' When she was telling you to do something, she often put it as a question.

'Eddie Waite? You still seeing him?'

'Yeah. He's my friend. Why?'

'Nothing,' his father said carefully. 'Just watch it, though.'

At school, Terry and Eddie still had fun beating the system wherever they could, using their secret code to each other in spelling tests, pushing vile notes through the ventilation holes of enemies' lockers. But it was hidden stuff. No open warfare with teachers, who began to suspect that Terry Stephens might make something of himself after all.

When he showed his father his report card, with three Bs, his father was so thrilled with him that Terry almost jumped in and said, 'So will you come back home, then?' Only somehow he couldn't say the words.

'Missed your big chance,' Eddie grumbled at him. Although he did not personally agree with Terry's new image, he was involved in this campaign. His own father would never come back. 'If he did, I'd walk out,' he boasted.

'There'll be lots more chances.' Terry was hopeful. People could get undivorced any time. His parents were just being divorced for a bit, like a vacation.

He had never earned any money, except for the odd quarters his father had paid him for doing jobs his mother said he should do for nothing; but when Randy Sparke got fed up with his newspaper route, Terry took over his job.

Three days a week, the van from the local paper dropped bundles at the drug store. Terry counted out his copies after school, slung them over his shoulder in a big orange bag, and bicycled around several streets. It was tedious work, and often wet and cold. In old movies, newspaper boys hurled rolled-up newspapers from a great distance on to porches and front paths without getting off their bikes. The *Clarion* prided itself on personal delivery. Terry had to get off his bike, trudge to whichever door the customer wanted him to use, ring the bell or knock, wait, sometimes for ever, until somebody opened the door, and hand over the paper with the celebrated '*Clarion* smile'. If nobody was home, you tucked the paper behind the storm door, and if there was no storm door, you put it in a plastic bag and left it on the step.

It took a long time for not much money, but secretly Terry quite enjoyed the routine and the serious purpose of it. He would not admit that to Eddie, who knew easier ways to get money.

He had to keep accounts, and have the right amount ready for the *Clarion*'s Mr Frazier, who called every week, counted the money with a face as if he were going to sneeze, and gave Terry his small share, which he often took round to Eddie, to see what they should do with it.

He had a lot of trouble with Mrs Jukes. She lived with ailing Mr Jukes, who was imprisoned somewhere within and could be heard calling for her feebly and without hope. Their violet-coloured house was fronted by a painfully neat garden, where the stiff bushes stood to even height, like soldiers, and the two square flower-beds had shiny metal edges round them.

For some reason, Mrs Jukes hated Terry. The first time he rang her bell, she stuck her big ugly purple head out of the back door and snarled, 'Where's Randy?'

'I'm on his route now, ma'am.'

'Why didn't the paper tell me?'

Terry shrugged. 'How should I know?'

'Don't be fresh. And don't ring the bell again, do you hear? Never. There's sickness here, whether you care or not. Put the paper in the mailbox.'

'Suits me.'

Her mailbox was on a rustic post near the sidewalk. It was made like a little wooden model of her violet home, with her number on the hinged front door. On Friday, there was no money in it. Mr Frazier gave you a hard time if you didn't collect from everybody, so Terry rang the bell.

Mrs Jukes raged and stormed. 'I *told* you,' etc., etc. Mr Jukes's voice called very faintly, as if he were bricked up between the walls.

Terry swallowed and looked at his boots. 'The money, ma'am.' He kept his head down. It was raining. Water dripped off the hood of his rubber poncho. 'I have to collect the money.'

'Tell the *Clarion* to send me a bill. That's what they did before.'

'I don't know nothing about that. Randy told me you paid him direct.' 'But it's like blood out of a stone,' Randy had added, 'and she don't tip.'

One Friday, the door of the little mailbox house was swinging on one hinge, and Mrs Jukes swore that Terry had wrecked it. She would get him fired. She'd sue the newspaper. She despised the *Clarion*'s politics anyway. She was going to call Terry's mother. He was the worst boy she'd ever seen around here. She didn't want to see his frizzy hair again (rain made Terry's hair curlier) or his ugly grinning face (he was trying to calm her with the *Clarion* smile). She was cancelling the paper.

'Suits me,' Terry said, and ran off without collecting her week's money.

When Mr Frazier told him he would have to go back, or pay it himself, Terry folded his arms sullenly and said, 'No way,' which upset Mr Frazier, tired, fussed, always in a stew about the paper carriers and their money.

'Leave her to me,' Eddie said, when Terry reported all this. 'I'll fix Mrs Pukes. Meet me at the corner around seven.'

When it was dark, Eddie stuffed paper soaked in kerosene into Mrs Jukes's empty mailbox and set fire to it. Terry watched from the corner. It looked marvellous. Even the varnished rustic post burned up, right down to the ground.

Eddie was caught, because a neighbour saw him. A man in a car saw Terry running away from the corner, and a policeman came to his mother's house. His father was in England, but when he came back, the whole fuss started up again.

'I told you about Eddie,' he said. 'I told you to watch it. You've been doing so well, Terry. Why did you have to blow it?'

'I didn't do nothing.'

'Anything. You're old enough to speak properly.'

'Didn't do anything, Dad.'

'Maybe not this time.' His father brooded at him, his narrowed eyes alarmingly blue.

'I'm sorry.' Terry dragged that out of himself. It was no fun apologizing for nothing, but maybe it would help.

'Just watch it, that's all.'

'Lay off him, Paul. He's not a criminal.' Terry's mother had been giving him a hard time, until his father started.

'You don't keep an eye on him. You don't know where he goes. What was he doing out there after dark anyway?'

'Really, Paul, he's not a baby.'

'You've spoiled him enough to make him into one.'

'*I* spoiled him! You're out of your mind . . .' And on and on in the front hall, until his father banged out of the house without calling goodbye to Terry, listening from the top of the stairs.

Things were desperate. After everything he'd done, working, boring himself with being good and not getting into rages, the rotten newspaper route and putting up with shit from stinkers like Mrs Jukes . . . His father was further away from him than ever.

There was only one thing to do. He would make the supreme sacrifice. 'I did it for you,' he would say, and his father would melt and smile again, and come back home. How could he resist such nobility?

Terry went to see Eddie. He was in the cellar, doing dangerous things with his chemistry set.

'Hi!' He looked up and grinned as Terry came slowly down the stairs. 'C'mon and help. I'm making dynamite.'

'You're not.' Terry began to back up the cellar stairs again.

'Wish I could. We could put a bomb under Mrs Pukes's window.'

'The bathroom window.'

'Inside, back of the toilet.'

'In the toilet.'

They giggled and worked each other up as they always could together.

Then Terry stopped abruptly. 'Look.' He half turned away. ' I didn't come to fool around. I have to tell you. We can't be friends any more.' He had rehearsed how he would say it, strong and noble, but it came out in a rush, squeaky and feeble.

Eddie's grin stayed on his cheeky, funny monkey face. 'Oh, yeah?' He grinned at Terry, waiting for the joke.

'I mean it, Ed. This is it.'

'Your mother said?'

'No. I said.'

Eddie dropped the grin into a stuck-out lower lip.

'Okay.' He shrugged and turned back to the bench where he was mixing little piles of different coloured powder on squares of paper.

If he had raged or cursed or argued . . . Terry looked at the shoulders of Eddie's torn sweater, raised towards his cup-handle ears.

'Listen.' Terry's voice reached out like a groping hand. 'I made almost three bucks last week. You can have it all, if you –'

Eddie's thin brown fingers moved busily, mixing the powders. Terry's head exploded into black despair. He gave a gasp and stumbled up the stairs, dodged one of Eddie's younger brothers and ran out of the back door and through the gap in the hedge that led towards his own street, blindly sobbing.

It was mid-term vacation, so he didn't have to see Eddie at school. Not yet anyway. Terry hung around with some other boys, because if he stayed at home, his mother would say, 'Given up on Eddie Waite at last. If you have nothing to do, my friend and helper, I have a hundred jobs for you.'

'Your father called,' she told him at supper, using that quotation-mark voice, as if Dad were not really his father, but only called himself that. 'He wants you to call him.'

'He still mad?'

'He didn't want to talk to *me*. He wants to talk to you.'

Terry made the call. From the depths of his unhappiness, he managed quite a sprightly, 'What's up, Dad?'

'I'd like to see you. Want to come round for supper tomorrow night? I've got a piece of steak.'

If he was offering steak, he couldn't be mad, so it was safe to ask, 'Are you still mad at me?'

'Of course not. I just want to talk to you.'

'What about?'

'Oh – things. My trip to England. Stuff like that.'

'Did Mom say I could?' The Law said that he was only supposed to be with his father one weekend in three.

'I didn't ask her. Get her to come to the phone.'

But she wouldn't. 'Go back and see what he wants, lover boy.'

'He wants me to go round for supper tomorrow.'

'Oh, you know? He's supposed to check with me before he asks you.'

'But you won't go to the phone.'

'But he asked you before he knew I wouldn't.'

'Cut it out, Mom!' Terry screamed and stamped at her.

'Oh, you and I understand each other, don't we, honey?' His mother tipped her chair backwards to put an arm round him, but he retreated to the doorway.

'Yes or no?' At this point he wasn't even sure which he wanted.

'I don't see why not.'

'What took so long?' his father asked when he picked up the phone.

Terry did not say, 'She wouldn't talk to you.' He would never tell either of them anything against the other, especially now when he was about to break the righteous news that was going to make everything all right again for all of them.

'She says okay.'

He waited outside the house for his father to fetch him. He did not say anything about Eddie until they were upstairs in the apartment. It was at the top of an old bulbous-fronted yellow sandstone building at the outer end of a long avenue, that wandered through half a dozen jumbled neighbourhoods on its way into Boston.

His father's apartment had odd-shaped rooms with funny angles and windows at the end of walls instead of in the middle, because it had been cut up from a larger one. There was not much furniture, but a lot of light and a jungle of plants clamouring to get out of the big rounded bay window. Across the broad avenue were the high brick buildings of a small college, where students went up and down the wide red steps, and hung about in groups. Between, endless traffic and the green trolley-cars sliding by below.

Terry liked the apartment and this busy view. A good place to break his sensational news. He turned indoors, and with his back to the plant forest, he called to his father.

'By the way, Dad, I want to tell you something.'

'What's that?' His father came through from the small kitchen, wiping his hands on a towel.

'I'm not seeing Eddie now.' Terry had his hands behind him on the edge of the windowsill, propping him up, because it was hard to say.

'Why?' His father came forward and sat on the arm of the sofa.

'Oh – I don't know. I guess I don't like him any more.'

'But he's your best friend. You can't suddenly not like him.'

'Well, I don't,' Terry lied, 'so you don't have nothing to worry about no more.' He deliberately said it that way, as a secret tribute to Eddie, but his father let it go.

'I worry about you dropping him, just like that.' He was not beaming and pleased, as Terry had planned. He was leaning forward crumpling the towel in his hands and looking serious. 'A friend's a friend, and Eddie's been through a hard time, because he tried to get back at that Jukes woman for you. Okay, it was dumb and wrong, but you could say it was loyalty, I suppose. Where's your loyalty to him?'

'I thought you didn't like Eddie.'

The conversation was going wildly wrong. Terry felt as if he'd been hit on the head.

'Whether I do or I don't is not the point. I don't want you to be one of those fair-weather friends who takes people up and gets their trust, and then gets bored with them and skips off to the next person who beckons. Friendship is solid and real. You don't turn it on and off like tap water.'

A lecture was the last thing Terry had expected. How could he say, 'I did it for you! I did it so you'd see I want you to come home'? He couldn't say anything.

He ate his steak and salad without tasting it, jaws, teeth, swallowing mechanism working by themselves, since the person who normally operated them had died. His father talked on about England, and the stuff he had bought for the store and the people he'd met and the horses he had seen, and didn't seem to notice that Terry was a mute who could hardly hear either.

At the end, he pushed his plate away and finished his beer.

Then he looked across the table at Terry and said determinedly, with a funny excited smile, not one of his wide amiable ones, 'Now I have something important to tell you.'

'Yeah?' Terry did not look at him, but out of the window, at the bookshelf, at the blank television.

'I'm going to marry again.' Terry could feel his father watching his face. 'Someone I met in England. Well, I'd met her before, some time ago. I'm sure this must be a shock to you, but you'll like her, I know.'

Terry looked down. He should not have eaten the ice-cream right on top of the steak. If he threw up now, all over the rough pine table, what good would that do?

'It won't make any difference to you and me.' His father reached out a hand across the table, palm curved up, and left it there, in case. 'We'll see just as much of each other. We'll go off on our own and fish and walk up hills and explore and go to the movies, maybe start some riding lessons for you, how about that? And you'll also have someone else here to have fun with. She's longing to meet you. Her name's Lily.'

'Big deal.' Of all the things Terry might have said, that was the only one he could manage.

In the car on the way home, he said two things. 'I don't want to have fun with her,' and, 'Does Mom know?'

'Not yet. I wanted to ask you about it first, of course.'

But he had not asked. He had told.

He would never come home again.

Up in his room, Terry dropped the framed photograph of his father on the floor, put an undershirt over it to muffle the sound, and smashed into it with his baseball bat.

Never make me look at you. In the intense pain of the betrayal, Terry was as ashamed of his father as he was of himself, for betraying Eddie.

He gave up his paper route. He threw all Friday's newspapers into Lion's pond on a raw day when no one was about, and watched them soggily rising, like dead, bloated corpses. He stopped trying to behave well, although he had no heart for dangerous exploits, and no one to do them with, and no one to think up the great ideas, since Eddie, his leader, now had a bunch of other kids in tow at school, and was lost to him for ever.

Life was flat and shrivelled, like a burst balloon. His mother threatened to go into cyclical depression, and did. She gave up her part-time job and lay around a lot, or moved slowly about the house with a tan blanket over her shoulders, like a camel. Depression made her feel cold.

She hardly ever went out. She did not do her face or cook regular meals. That was okay. She gave Terry money to buy frozen dinners and french fries, but it wasn't okay that she expected him to do more around the house, because she was 'sick'.

Whether she ordered him irritably to run the vacuum, or wheedled him, it was just as bad.

'Come on, lover boy. Help me out. Poor Mommy's so sick.'

'You're not sick. You just need to get off your dead ass.'

It was surprising what he could get away with when she was in a camel-blanket phase.

Terry was not invited to go to England for the wedding.

'Why didn't he invite me?'

'Well . . .' His mother put on that small cup-shaped smile with the lips sucked in that she used for thinking about Lily. 'I suppose he didn't think you'd want to be asked. You wouldn't have gone anyway, would you?'

'Maybe.' The actual wedding would be nothing, a lot of people in a church, dressed up, and Gramma mopping at her pale eyes. But he wanted to go to England. Everything he had heard about it attracted him; pictures he saw, old houses, greenness, weird-looking young people owning the streets of London.

'Really, Ter? I thought you felt so terrible about it.'

'Hunhnyah . . .' Now that she was out of the depression, al-though she kept it by for future use, Terry felt quite close to his mother at this time, as you would with anyone with whom you were abandoned on a desert island; but he never discussed any-thing about his father.

What with school, and his mother taking him away at Christmas to her aunt in New York state, and then sticking rigidly to what she now called the Statutory Visiting Times, Terry did not meet Lily for quite a long time.

The apartment looked a bit different. All the plants were there, and Dad's pictures of horses and the cartoon sketch of Buster that Terry had drawn from memory a year ago, but it wasn't the same. There was more furniture and a rug in the living-room and some new ornaments and photographs of people Terry didn't know, and women's clothes hanging in the hall and on the back of the bathroom door. The bathroom smelled unfamiliar, and the whole place was much more untidy. His father's neat kitchen was a wreck. Sweaters and books lay about at random and phono-graph records slid off each other on the floor. His father picked some things up automatically as he passed them, and rinsed out the coffee mugs, but he did not seem to mind. His smile was there all the time. His eyes were narrow and crinkly, always a sign of good times.

'This is Terry,' he said quickly, when they came in. 'Terry, this is Lily.'

Terry had imagined someone the size of his mother. A much taller woman unfolded herself from the low sofa, not fat, but quite large and solid. She was smiling widely, excited, a bit overpowering. Shaking her strong hand, Terry was aware that he was shorter than she expected. That had been one of the great things about Eddie. Although he was older, he was shorter than Terry.

People like his Dedham grandmother said comfortably, 'You'll shoot up in your own time.' But now was now, and meanwhile he was small for his age, and Lily was as tall as his father.

She tried hard, and laughed a lot in a clear, English sort of way. Once Terry saw her reach to put her arms round his father, and then drop them self-consciously, and step back and stumble over a stool. She had brought Terry a set of carved wooden boxes from England. One fitted into another, and the smallest was about as big as a stamp.

She watched him take all the boxes out and range them on the coffee-table. He felt he had to do that. When he said nothing, she could not help asking, 'Do you like them?'

'Sure. Yeah.' He began to put the boxes inside each other again, which filled in some more time. They were all on their best behaviour. His father waited, but in the end he reminded Terry to say thank you.

'I'm glad you like it. I had a lovely time choosing it. Look.' Lily squatted down to the low table. 'I bought it because I like buying presents, not because I'm trying to bribe you to like me, all right?'

She knew what he was thinking. Some people's stepmothers bought them so much stuff, it was pathetic.

Terry could not play checkers with his father, or put on records, or talk back and forth as they usually did, because Lily was there, slopping his orange soda as she carried it in, hunting for potato chips, making coffee, making conversation, filling the apartment spaces. They were both watching her: Terry to see what her game was, his father because he wanted her to feel comfortable.

None of them could think what to do, so they went across the avenue to the park behind the college, and walked fast, because it was cold. Lily galloped about in new furry boots like a giant kid, because she was not used to so much snow. Terry galloped off with somebody's bounding dog, so he would not have to throw snowballs with her.

'He liked you,' she said when the owner called away the dog, and Terry came back. 'Have you got a dog at home?'

'Not any more.' Terry and his father looked at each other.

'Sorry, have I said the wrong thing?' Lily banged the snow off her mittens.

'Buster was more my dog,' his father said, to avoid it being known that Barbara would not let Terry keep the dog.

'Yeah. He'd never sleep on my bed or pay attention to me when Dad was home.'

When Dad was home. Why did he have to say that? The words hung in the still cold air. The bright-coloured children on the sled slope stopped shrieking. Saturday traffic sounded miles away.

His father put an arm around him, but Terry jumped away. Playing with the dog had reminded him that he was still angry with his mother about Buster, so to hide that, he muttered to Lily, 'We didn't want to keep him,' stamping about in his own snow footsteps.

'Come on.' His father brushed snow off Lily's face. 'Let's go get something to eat.'

They had lunch at a more expensive place than his father usually took him. Lily – he was to call her that, but he did not use her name – ate in a peculiar clumsy way, with two hands, and Dad reminded her to put the fork in her right hand, as if she were a child.

'Oh, yes, sorry.' She changed over the fork and put the knife on the edge of the plate so that it fell on to the tablecloth. 'I want to do everything the American way, Terry. You'll have to teach me words to use. They don't know what I mean in shops when I say things like cotton wool and tiss-yew.' She gave one of her loud spontaneous laughs.

Terry kept silent. He did not know what she was talking about.

They tried to get him going by making plans. 'At Easter, let's do such and such . . . On your next weekend, why don't we . . .' Grown-ups did that to work you up into being pleased, and when it did not come off, they had some more plans to promise.

'Lily and I are going down to the Cape pretty soon. Maybe look for a cottage to rent for a week this summer.'

'Would you come and stay with us?' Lily asked.

'I guess so.'

'So could I, Mom?'

'Cape Cod?' His mother raised her eyebrows, which were pencilled in again since she had stopped being depressed. 'Your family and friends are on the North Shore.'

'Dad likes the Cape better.'

'I know.'

She was not going to say yes or no, so it would have to wait. She wanted Terry to talk about Lily, even though someone was there, a new guy called Silas.

'What's she like, Ter?'

'I don't know.'

'Didn't you look at her?'

'Not much.'

'Tall? Short? Young and girlish? Funny accent?'

Terry shook his head. All that Saturday, he had been watching out for attacks on his mother. Now he felt he had to defend Lily.

'She was okay.'

'You liked her?'

'Hunhnyah.'

'Not easy is it, feller, all these new things to deal with.' Silas got up. 'Come on, I'll take you round the block in my new Corvette. See how you like it.'

Uh-oh. Was this the new boyfriend, then, muscling his way into favour? He was quite old. His hair was going grey. His knowing face had a rogue's smile, with a sticking-out lower lip, very sure of himself.

'Leave me alone.' Terry hunched his shoulders forward and scowled.

'You see the way he is?' his mother said, as he headed for upstairs. 'Don't take it personally, Silas. That's just the way he is.'

'See you again, some time, somewhere,' they had promised each other at Boston airport, but Ida did not believe they ever would. After a couple of postcards each way, and a Christmas card from Lily with a scrawled message Ida could not read, that was it.

When Bernie was born, Ida wanted to write to Lily, 'Now I've got everything I wanted,' but Buddy, in a whirlwind mood, had been through the kitchen drawer where she kept papers, and Lily's address had been lost.

When Buddy brought home Lily's letter from the base post office, Ida was surprised. She turned it over a couple of times, fascinated by the huge colourful stamp, for she hardly ever got a letter from England. When she opened it, she was amazed.

'Guess what?' she called to Buddy, who was upstairs changing out of his uniform fatigues. 'I'm amazed.'

'Guess what?' Bernie echoed. He could talk perfectly well, but he often parroted what she said. He copied what she did too, putting on her apron like a long skirt, and standing on a chair to wipe off the counter.

'What the hell?' Buddy muttered. The walls were so thin that you could talk from one end of the house to the other, as if you were in the same room. You could also hear more than you wanted from the duplex next door.

'This girl I know. Lily, you know, who I met on the aeroplane.'

'Airplane.' Bernie started up the stairs to his father. 'Puppa, kin I have . . .' the whine he put on for Buddy.

'She's getting married to an American.'

'Like you did.'

'Yeah, like I did.'

Sort of. Lily was marrying the nice friendly man she had gone crazy about in Iceland. 'All my romantic dreams come true,' she wrote to Ida. 'Can you believe such luck? Secretly, Eye, I never forgot him in all those years.'

'She's going to be married and live in Boston,' Ida told Buddy when he came silently downstairs in his sneakers, and tried to scare her by putting his hands suddenly on her hips from behind. She *was* scared, but she always pretended she was not, controlling the jump of nerves and keeping her voice calm.

'Where are you going, Buddy?'

'Down to the Fisherman.'

'Working or drinking?'

'Working, you cow.'

'Cow,' Bernie said thoughtfully, through the candy bar his father had given him. He wasn't allowed candy before supper.

'Get your ass in the kitchen, Ah–eye–da, and get me sump'n to eat.'

'We got dogs and beans, that okay?'

'What's Bernie going to have?' Buddy's plump face screwed up into an anxious concern he never showed for Ida or Maggie. 'You know he don't like wieners.'

Taking his cue, Bernie went, 'Yuck,' watching both of them with his bright brown eyes.

'Well, it's what we've got, and he'll eat it or go hungry,' Ida said manfully. What a hope.

'Come on, little boy, Puppa will fix you a peanut-butter and jelly sandwich.' Buddy ambled towards the kitchen.

'He can't live on peanut-butter.'

'Why not? I did.'

'And look at you.'

'Li'l boy gets what he wants when Poppa's home.'

'You spoil him, just like your mother spoiled you.'

'Sure.' Buddy picked up his five-year-old son and looked into the child's alert, inquiring face, his dark eyes liquid with a soppy love he never showed to anyone else.

They ate at the small table, messily. Ida was up and down all the time – 'You'd think I'd lose weight at meals, not gain' – mopping up, fetching things her males wanted, picking up food the little girl scattered around her sticky high-chair.

'I thought we were going to the club tonight,' she said, when Buddy found his car keys where Bernie had hidden them, and went to the door.

'You shouldn't complain. I make money for you, babe. You shall have it all, clubs, champagne, furs, jewels, what is it they have – caviare.'

'All I want is to see the money coming in, not going out to lay bets on the track.'

'Shut your face,' Buddy said amiably. He was usually in a good mood when he was going out, whether it was to work (if he did go to work), or God knows where.

'Bed, Maggie.' Ida extracted the three-year-old from the high-chair. Maggie's hands clung to her like rubber crabs. She nodded her head and made silly gobbling sounds. 'Talk properly,' Ida said severely. She never let up on her. 'Bed, Bernie.'

'Not yet.'

Oh, well. She would carry him up when he fell asleep on the couch. Maybe he would be too tired to wake when Buddy came noisily home. If he woke, Buddy might get him up and bring him downstairs and play with him, exciting him past sleep.

Ida sat down in front of the television, which had been going all this time, and read Lily's letter again.

'. . . going to marry my one and only love.'

'You could knock me down,' Ida said to Bernie.

'Down.' Bernie rolled off the couch, to make her laugh.

In the six years since she had lived in the United States, Ida had become quite Americanized. She had always been quick, and she picked up the accent and the sayings like a monkey. She had copied 'you could knock me down' from Buddy's father, during the time she had to stay with Henry Legge and take care of the children while the hospital tried to find Verna's baby under all the layers of fat.

Ida and Henry had enjoyed quite a good time, playing cribbage and chatting about nothing very much on old wicker chairs, when the evening sun slanted on to the porch. Billy had fed the dogs and cats and chickens for Ida, but Phyllis had been jealous and lazy, although when her mother came home with Laverne, she complained to Verna that Ida had made her work her guts out. She was also jealous of Laverne, who was an amazingly pretty baby with fluffy silver hair, delicate as a moth in Verna's vast embrace.

Ida had to stay on to help for a few days, until Buddy came roaring up the hill in his car to demand the return of his wife.

'I was never so glad to see you.' Ida ran out to the car, carrying the demoted baby Vernon, who had been having a hard time, raising his arms at his mother and crying, 'Up! Up!' when she was holding Laverne.

'That's my girl.' Buddy pulled her and Vernon into the car across his lap. He was so pleased, that she did not tell him she was glad because she was sick of Legge Manor.

'Where's my fella?' Verna came shouting out on to the porch. 'Come on in and say hullo to your new baby sister!'

Laverne was in the scarred old swinging crib in which they had all rocked as babies. Buddy was so tickled by her that he put his hand on Ida's thin waist and started pinching, trying to find a fingerful of fat.

They had agreed not to have any children yet, but when Verna bent her great bosoms over the crib like a ceiling caving in, to pick up the baby, and asked with a wink, 'You gonna put one of these in there, Buddy boy?' he licked his soft lips and crowed, 'You bet,' as if it would be totally his achievement if Ida had a baby.

When she did, the following year, Verna did not come to help her, thank God. Sis came. She took Ellen out of school and stayed at Watkins for a week when Ida came home from the hospital with Bernie. Two and a half years later, she came back to take care of him while Ida was going through the terrible experience that she thought would kill her, when Maggie was born. Although it was lambing season, Jeff let Sis stay on the base until Ida was back on her feet, and later, Buddy took Ida and the children to the farm for two summer weeks of quiet hills and animal sounds and smells and hay and walks in the green woods.

They picked vegetables and salads from the garden, and Sis taught Ida how to make wholemeal bread.

'Wish you hadn't.' Ida smeared a crust with honey from Jeff's bees. 'I'll never get rid of the birth fat. If I have any more kids, I'm going to end up like Verna.'

They laughed, since Buddy was out fishing with Jeff, and could not hear. Sis would rather laugh about her mother than hate her. Ida wished she could do the same about her own mother, but if she tried to think about Clara Lott as comic, the dour figure, with 'nothing under her apron', as they said in Staple Street, would not shape into a clown, and the old bitterness and spite spilled over the picture and washed it out.

All Ida's clothes were too tight, except the maternity things, and she had sold those, sick of them, at the Women's Exchange. Sis, who was larger than her, gave her a loose top and one of her long cotton skirts. Ida wore it with bare legs and feet and took off her bra, like Sis. Would Buddy admire this new image? Although he wanted her to be well-dressed at the Enlisted Men's Club, it didn't make much difference with him how she looked. He either fell on her or not, according to the urges of his moods.

Although he had leave, he did not stay in New Hampshire the whole time, because he got bored in the country. There was country around Watkins Base, but they did not go out to it much, beyond driving to some place along the highway to eat.

Ida and Sis became quite close, more like sisters. They told each other things about their lives, and Ida felt good, because Sis admired her and said she had guts and was a survivor.

It was while she was at the farm, that Ida first began to notice that Maggie was slower to do things than Bernie had been.

'Don't worry,' Sis said comfortably. 'Bernie was quick, like you. She'll come to it when she's ready.'

'You think I should take her back to the doctor?'

'Not until her next check-up. What can a doctor do that you can't do, Ida honey, with your love and patience? Why, Ellen here wasn't turning over by herself or taking the strained food when the book said she should.' Sis shook her thick hair, which had gold as well as red in it in the summer. 'So I threw away the book.'

Ida had written to Lily that there was no way she could come to Boston, so when Lily had got used to driving in America, she dropped Paul off at the shop and then drove his red car up through unknown northern Massachusetts.

Watkins Base sprawled over a large tract of countryside. When Lily had got a pass from the sentry and some directions, she drove down a long straight road with no sign of any planes or hangars, and then turned past barrack buildings and a school and two wooden churches and rows of hospital huts and a high gaol fence marked, 'Confinement Facility'. It was a city in itself: filled car parks round the Commissary buildings, and beyond, dozens of streets and hundreds of houses: white wooden boxes with flat roofs and two front paths to each. Some had fences enclosing a space at the back. Some had toys and bikes lying about on rough grass that sloped up to a low scrubby woodland, penetrated with children's pathways, like rabbit tracks.

1009 Pershing Street had a few daffodils and a flowering bush braving the general landscape of coarse grass and scrub oaks, hanging on to their brown leaves as if they did not trust green buds to ripen. Ida's laundry was neatly pegged on a carousel washing-line, big things, little things, nappies.

Lily parked under the carport between this house and the next, and went to the back door. She was suddenly self-conscious, and did not want to be seen walking round to the front, if Ida was watching behind the muslin curtains to see how much she had changed.

A little boy opened the door. He had Buddy's baby face that Lily had seen in the photograph, but without the heavy brows. Bernie's eyebrows were a delicate line, arched over bright, wide-open eyes. He looked Lily up and down with intelligent interest, and called out, 'She's here, Ma!'

Lily went into the kitchen. Through the opening into the living-room she saw Ida turn round from something she was doing at the table, and push back her chair with a cry of surprise, as if she had not seen Lily's red car and heard her at the back door.

They had not kissed goodbye at the airport years ago, but now they went towards each other with open arms, and embraced. Lily had to bend down. Ida was even shorter than she remembered, but there was more of her, much more.

'You've put on weight, Eye.' She had to say something, since it was so obvious.

'Aren't I disgusting?' Ida patted bits of herself. 'It was having the kids. You wait.'

'I'm too big already.'

'No. You've lost. You look great, Lil. Remember how fat you were when he saw you in your slip?'

'Was I so awful? I thought I was alluring.'

'Uh-*uh*.' Ida shook her head. The springy curls had gone. She had cut a wide fringe, and her straight no-colour hair was pulled back behind her ears and tied with a thin piece of ribbon. 'But you sure were romantic.'

She smiled with an open mouth, and Lily saw that her crooked front teeth had been straightened. 'They fixed my dyspepsia too, here at the base. It's amazing what they can do in this country. I can eat all kinds of fried stuff, and I don't upset Buddy by not being able to drink.'

Her face was not so frail and bony, although the skin round her pale eyes still looked bruised. Her rose lipstick had become red. She carried her head with a bolder tilt above a new and considerable bosom. She looked well: coarser, but with a lot more confidence.

'I say, Ida.' Lily hugged her again. 'America has done wonders for you.'

'I was a mess, wasn't I?'

'Don't fish.'

They both had more confidence, but otherwise, it was just the same between them. Ida made coffee and brought out a swiss roll, because she thought Lily might be homesick, and although they had only been together those two strange days in Iceland, they felt they had been friends for a long time.

In Iceland, Lily had felt like the leader. Now Ida was the old hand. Her varying grades of british accent, from broad to refined, were gone. She sounded quite American, except for occasional throwbacks, like 'Don't be duft'. She called her son·'Bernie', sounding the r, and the funny little fat girl 'Myaggie'.

'It slays me, you sound so English,' she told Lily.

'I am English. So are you.'

'Not any more. I got me naturalized. You'll lose it, hon, like I did.'

'I don't want to. Paul says I should stay the way I am.' Lily was still at the stage where she needed to drag Paul into every conversation, but Ida was thinking about herself, so she interrupted by calling Myaggie away from a china ornament, and did not hear.

Although she was more earthy and carnal now, she did not shout at the children. She had become one of those fat-bodied people who have a surprisingly soft voice, and move lightly on small feet, like a balloon. If you met her first on the telephone, you would visualize a little weightless woman, as she used to be.

Maggie was three-and-a-half. She moved about rather clumsily and did not say much, and when Lily went down on hands and knees to give her some close attention, the child's light-brown eyes would not look into hers. They wandered away, not looking at anything in particular. She had a beautiful pristine face, unmarked by much movement of expression.

'Having a hard time training her?' Lily had seen all the nappies on the line.

'Of course not,' Ida said quickly. 'She wears diapers at night, is all.'

But the child was padded. Why the defensive lie?

'Come and see what I've got for you.' Lily was fishing in her bag. Bernie came over, his eager face ready to be pleased, but Maggie wandered away to pick at the back fur of the cat stretched out on the sunny windowsill.

'See what Lily has for you!' Ida took her hand, and she came back passively. 'She's a little slow right now. Well, poor kid, her birth was so difficult. She like to killed me. They even said at the time she might have minimal brain damage, but she's a hundred per cent, aren't you, Myags?'

Dangling Lily's cuddly animal by its foot, the child nodded her head violently, like a doll with a spring neck, and said, 'Mam-amamamamama.'

'Sure, she don't talk so good yet, but Bernie's such a yacker, he talks for her, and she'll come to it when she's ready.'

'Are you going to have another child?' Ida seemed prepared to make her life round the house and the children, so she might as well have one or two more.

'I'd never go through that again.' Ida gave Lily some fearful details. 'Buddy don't care either way. He signed on for another four years, because of the kids, but who knows what he'll do after that? This suits him okay. The work's not hard in the stores, or riding the mowers, like he'll be this summer. He's moon-lighting too, tending bar some evenings, and the base is a good place for his other business. He sells a bit of stuff for a firm that makes jewellery. "Elite", you've heard of it.' Lily shook her head. 'See these.' Ida swung one of the glittery earrings that were too fancy for her plain tent of a dress. 'I help him by showing the stuff around, among the women.'

'He sounds very ambitious.'

'He spends a lot. Very high requirements. Well, I have to say this, Lil. He bets on the horses.'

'Oh dear.'

'No, it's okay. He'll get his big break, and then we'll get out of here into some nice house in the suburbs.'

'Paul says we'll have a house on Cape Cod some day. That's

his dream. His first wife didn't like it there, so they never went. I'm not saying anything against her, because I've never met her and don't want to, but I think she was pretty selfish. She didn't know her luck, having Paul, so now she hasn't got him. I ought to be sorry for her.'

'I cut "ought" out of my language long ago,' Ida said. 'There's no ought and should. You do what you do.'

'What you do,' Bernie, on the floor, told the miniature car Lily had brought him.

'Too right, kiddo. That's all a person can do.'

Since her schoolfriend Pam had gone off to the West Coast with her husband, Lily had no close friend in America to talk to. She had looked forward to confiding in Ida, but Ida did not really want to hear about Paul. Lily told her anyway.

'You always used to laugh at me for carrying on about love.' Their brief companionship six years ago had become 'always used to ...' 'I think I never really thought I'd find it, after Iceland, and knowing he was married. I was like a zombie for weeks after I got home. Pain, as if someone were squeezing my ribs against my heart.'

'Go on?' Ida said in her old Midlands accent.

'Why am I so lucky, Eye? Starting marriage is weird, isn't it, because you're so set in your spinster ways, and starting in a new country could be incredibly difficult, but Paul makes it so easy.

'I talk funny. I don't dress quite right. Boston women don't go downtown in sweaters and slacks. I'm not organized like they are. I spill things. When we have people to dinner, I forget to cook the veg if I've had a couple of drinks. But he goes on thinking I'm marvellous. I suppose it helps, having followed poor old Barbara. She – well, anyway. But Paul is the kindest, funniest, most exciting man anyone ever met. When I go out, whatever they think of me, I feel that other women envy me, because what they've got is so ... sort of, nothing. They should never have settled for it.'

'Still trying to straighten people out,' Ida said. 'Did you ever get to be a social worker in the end?'

'Sort of.' Lily told her about the family centre. 'Joan gave me a wonderful reference, so I'm going to try and get another job like

95

that over here. Paul is doing very well and he's just got a raise, and he's invented something marvellous that his firm is going to market. But I need to earn some money of my own, and I need to be working.'

'Then you can come here with a clipboard and ask me, "Did you make a mistake?" ' Ida looked at her challengingly.

'All right, did you?'

'Still like to ask 'em, don't you? I told you about marriage, long ago. You get kids. You got a home, a bank account. Once in a while, you have good times together. That's about as good as you can hope for, in the long run.'

'I suppose so,' Lily had to say, although her happiness was crying, no, no, you can have it all, the love and the trust and the excitement. I've got it all.

Ida got up and pulled down the short tent dress, and picked up Maggie. 'If we're going out to eat, we'd better stop yacking and go.'

'Of course.' Lily jumped up and looked for her jacket.

Ida's friend Cora came in through the back door, a savvy-looking woman in startling colours, with flat black hair that looked dyed. She wanted to talk, rapidly, about the jewellery sales in which her husband was involved with Buddy. 'Don't let me hold you up,' she said, and kept on talking.

In the general confusion of Ida trying to get the children ready and Cora following about, talking with much stabbing gesticulation of hands, Bernie wild with enthusiasm and Lily trying to find where Maggie had hidden her bag, Lily knocked over the china ornament. It broke, a simpering woman in a ballet dress, lying on the floor in half a dozen coloured pieces. Maggie screamed.

'Oh, my God, Ida, I'm sorry. I'm so clumsy, I –'

'Don't give it a thought, love.' Ida picked up the pieces and threw them into a wastebasket. 'I don't care.'

'Isn't that the statuette Buddy's mother gave you?' Cora asked.

'So what?' Ida made a face. 'She never comes here anyway.'

They had lunch near the Air Force base at a new snack bar disguised as an old railway carriage converted to a snack bar, which Lily had learned to call a diner.

When they got back, Buddy's car was under the carport.

'What are you home for?' Ida greeted him, on her way to the bathroom with Maggie.

'Looking for you.' He was sitting in front of the television in a reclining plastic leather chair with the foot-rest raised, a thick sandwich and a can of beer held on his stomach. 'I had to make myself a sandwich.'

'So I see. Aren't you going back to work?'

'Sure.'

'Why the beer, then?'

'Because I'm having my lunch.'

'They'll smell it on you.'

'So? Just for that, get me another can, Bernie my best boy.'

'Buddy, this is my friend Lily.'

He was not going to get up, so Lily went to stand alongside the television set, where he could see her.

'Hi,' he said with his eyes on the screen. 'Seems I've heard about you.'

'I've heard about you.'

He looked the same as the photograph, no older, a plumpish, pettish, immature man, with bits of bread and liver sausage on the front of his green shirt, and an unfriendly glance at Lily before his eyes went back to the blathering game show on the screen.

Bernie brought the beer. 'Puppa, kin I have a popsicle?'

'No,' Ida said. 'You just had lunch.'

'Sure you can, little man,' Buddy said through her voice.

'You spoil him,' Lily said. Shut up, you fool, it's none of your business.

Buddy frowned. His mouth pushed a chunk of sandwich about petulantly.

'Well, the kid's a little saint,' Ida said. 'He don't take advantage.'

Buddy finished the second beer. He stood up, rebuckled the belt of his fatigues, and aimed the beer can at the wastebasket. 'What the hell?' He bent down and picked out a piece of china. 'My Ma's beautiful gift. Who done that?' His fist clenched round the broken china. His face reddened. His eyes glared under the dark roof of eyebrow.

'The kid.' Behind his back, Ida winked at Lily and muttered against her hand, 'He can do no wrong.'

'Little Bernie?' Buddy's face cleared. He opened his fist and threw the piece of china back into the basket.

'What, Puppa?' Bernie came from the kitchen, sucking a bar of coloured ice on a stick.

'I know you didn't mean to do it, son,' Buddy said soppily.

'Do what?'

'Of course he didn't,' Lily said, 'because he didn't break it. I did.'

'You broke my mother's wedding gift?'

Buddy was furious. From a thick soft man with a petulant baby mouth and an early paunch, he turned into a human gorilla, arms squared, heavy body leaning towards Lily on short legs, lower jaw out, sprouting dark prickles.

'I'm sorry.' Lily was taller, but she backed towards the door. 'I'll replace it. I'll find out where she got it. I know it won't be the same, but – '

'Sure as hell it won't be the same.'

What would he have done if Ida had not grabbed Lily's arm and pulled her out of the front door?

'My God,' Lily said on the path. 'Does he often get like that?'

'No, no, he don't mean no harm.' Ida laughed, but the old anxious shadowed look had come back into her eyes. 'But his mother's kind of a sacred object, and beer takes him bad, is all. He'll forget it.' She opened the car door. 'Lucky you, being able to drive.'

'Can't you?' Lily got into the driver's seat and put down the window.

'Not yet, but I will. You can do anything in this country.' Ida put her arm on the edge of the door. Her hand shook a little. Her nails were still bitten, but now they had no bright rose polish. The loose sleeve of her dress showed a greenish-yellow bruise on the white skin inside her arm.

'Buddy?' Lily laid her fingers on it.

'No. Maggie pinched me. She holds on real tight. But lots of the women here do get beaten up. Cora and me's going to start a battered Watkins Wives' Club.'

'As bad as that?' Lily's ideas of American servicemen had been based on old wartime pictures of French girls kissing GI heroes.

But the man who came out of the house next to Ida looked mild, with spectacles. Another, with a narrow sandy head, driving by with his wife, beamed, 'Hi there!' to Ida. Buddy came out of the side door to get into his car and called out pleasantly, 'Come on in, honey. Maggie peed herself.'

'Bye, Eye.' Lily drove off quickly.

Four

*W*hen she was first married, with an enthusiastic reference from Joan at the Family Centre, Lily had started to look for work quite confidently, but finding any kind of social service job in Boston turned out to be difficult. She answered advertisements, made phone calls and was never called back, wrote letters that were never answered.

When she finally got an interview for a counselling job in the teenage unit of a psychiatric hospital, the harried man who interviewed her in his lunch-break told her, through a sandwich and a glass of milk which frosted his fleecy moustache, that she was not only unqualified, she was illegal. Even if she had stayed at college to get a degree, it would not count in Massachusetts, and until she was accepted as a permanent immigrant, she could not work anywhere in the United States.

'But you're so busy. You told me that yourself. You're terribly understaffed, you said. Couldn't you just, sort of, slip me in?'

'Mrs Stephens.' It still brought a little swell of pleasure to her diaphragm to be called that, instead of Miss Spooner. 'It isn't, sort of, possible.' He finally wiped his mouth. 'I'd be glad to have you with us, but you have to look good on paper, as well as in the flesh.'

She travelled with Paul to a big indoor horse show in another city, where he was in charge of Turnbull's stand. Lily wore a gold shirt, which was the firm's colour, and her denim overalls with the big studs and buckles, which made her look American. She helped Paul and his young assistant, Lionel, to set up the display of weatherproof Turnbull blankets, and the boots and whips and bags and wallets, and the belts and sheepskin pads and riding hats with plastic rain covers, and the mangers and the bandages and the brushes and the name plates for stable doors, and the everything else that went with horses.

The saddles and bridles and halters were displayed on units of Paul's new Tack Rack, which attracted as much attention as anything on the stand, and a number of orders, which was exciting, since Paul was getting a royalty.

When he went off to buy hot dogs and beer and Lionel was busy among the boots and exercise jackets, Lily talked up the Tack Rack to anyone who paused while walking by, or even turned their eyes sideways.

'Have you seen our newest product? An adjustable modular racking system for your tack, just on the market, and it will revolutionize your barn.' She had learned not to call it a stable. 'You buy it in units, like this, you see. You can assemble it in any way to fit any wall space. A place for everything, no space wasted, and you can adapt or expand it any way you want. It comes in your choice of four colours, red, green, brown and our Turnbull gold. As well as the basic set you see here, you can add to it with all kinds of extras. Hooks for pails.' She had learned not to say buckets. 'A rail for your horses' blankets. Have you seen our weatherproof blanket, by the way? Slots on the rack here, see for their names.'

'You're British.' A knowing smile from a man in tight breeches and skinny boots and a clinging polo-neck that gave him bosoms.

Sales conscious, Lily discarded, 'Thanks for telling me, I'd never have known,' in favour of, 'Yes,' and one of her breathy smiles, outdoorsy, made up bright and shiny, with no powder and a lot of glossy lipstick.

'They sell so much English stuff, I guess they got you over to go with it.'

Lily was torn between, 'That's right,' which would look good for Turnbull's, and 'I'm married to an American,' which sounded good to her.

She chose that, but the man leered his smile up at one side and leaned towards her on the narrow balls of his boots. 'So would you personally bring the kit out to the customer and set it up?'

Lily had never been the type for leers and propositions. The speculative eyes of sales reps and middle-aged desperadoes with brown finger nails had passed on to her smaller and saucier friends. But in America it seemed she was more desirable, because Paul desired her; or else there were more men here on the make.

'You place your order,' she said. 'We'll see.'

The man said, 'That thing costs a hell of a lot of money.'

'Isn't it worth it, for your horse?'

'I don't have a horse, sweetheart.'

By the time Paul returned in his gold sweater with the motif of an Ayrshire bull's head and his brown corduroys with the Turnbull belt and buckle, Lily was dealing seriously with a woman who owned a big riding school in White Plains, New York, and wanted to revolutionize her barn.

Paul had brought back a friend from his old horse days, when Barbara used to ride in some of the shows.

'Harry wouldn't believe how marvellous you were,' he told Lily when the riding-school woman had gone to fetch her husband. 'Now he can see for himself. I think you made a sale, darling. She'll place a big order.'

'Good for you, Lily.' Harry was admiring and impressed.

'Oh, I don't really know anything about it.' Lily was trying to teach herself to say, 'Thank you,' to a compliment, but the old blush-and-scrape-your-toe instinct died hard.

They ate hot dogs behind the hanging blankets, and then Harry took Lily to see a jumping class. He was a thoughtful, dark-skinned man with slightly mongolian eyes, attractive and attentive, the sort of man to have an affair with if you had married the wrong person.

'I'm glad about you and Paul,' he said.

'But you were Barbara's friend too, weren't you?'

'Still am, but I'm still glad about you and Paul. He deserves you.'

'What a nice thing to say.'

'You're okay, Lily.'

'So are you.' She laughed, going up the steps of the stand. 'I love it in this country, being able to make instant friends. It takes longer in England, walking round each other, like dogs.'

She leaned forwards and watched the horses closely.

'You like it, don't you?'

She was aware of Harry watching her.

'I don't know much about it.'

'You will. Get Paul back on a horse again,' Harry said. 'When Barbara quit, he had to quit, because she had the money.'

'Wish *I* did. I'm going to get a job, though, when I – oh, look at that beautiful white horse.'

'Grey.'

'Grey. I love this. I'll watch a bit, and then go down to the stand so Paul can come up.'

She had seen horse shows and the Olympics on British television, but now she watched with a more personal interest. Through Paul, she was beginning to be drawn to the sounds and smells and the powerful animal beauty, not detracted from by the rider, as she used to think when she saw the hard-bitten faces close up on screen, but guided into controlled grace, an amazing communion of flying horse and earthbound man that she wanted to share.

She saw herself on that horse which snorted ardently with each reach and thud of his oiled feet, leaning forwards with an intensely set jaw, her hands up behind the keen curved ears of the great bay as he sailed over the wall. Paul was going to teach her to ride. One day they would have a horse. Horses. Ponies for all the children. A barn with a de luxe custom-made Tack Rack, cornflower blue, their lucky colour.

While she was waiting for the Government's green card, coveted talisman, which would make her a resident alien, almost as unattractive a word as immigrant, Lily took up a series of under-the-counter jobs. She looked after an unruly child for a woman in one of the other apartments. She worked the cash register at one of the small local markets, getting the drawer stuck and panicking over the change if there were people waiting in line. She distributed leaflets and samples of soap powder door to door. She did some typing. She stood with a clipboard on a windy corner of Copley Square, taking a survey for a tourist bureau. She made telephone calls to resentful strangers, asking them to vote for a local politician.

She got that job through a girl from the college across the avenue from the apartment. One morning, between baby-sitting and cashiering, temporarily with no immediate purpose in life, Lily was looking out of the window over the plants which flourished with casual attention from Paul, but hesitated and dropped leaves when Lily sloshed water over them. Students were going up and down the stone steps, hurrying because it was cold, tops bundled up and bottom halves exposed in shrunken jeans. One girl had been standing at the edge of the street for quite a long time. She stood with her arm round a street light, her head hanging forwards as if she were going to be sick. Then she would throw back her head and put her hair behind her ear in that age-old gesture of young women with long thin straight hair. Then she leaned her cheek against the cold metal post. Then she dropped her head again and kicked the heel of her boot against the edge of the kerb.

She was not waiting for a street car, because they stopped in the middle of the road. Lily watched to see if a boyfriend would come ambling along at last with his coat flapping open, or whether he would be in a car, leaning over to open the passenger door, or whether someone would run down the college steps and claim this forlorn figure.

Nobody came, so Lily went down in the elevator and crossed to the middle of the road, over the street-car lines and across the heavy traffic going into Boston. The girl was wearing a dark loden coat, worn threadbare in places like a family carpet. She was in one of her head-down phases, the hood of the coat bundled on top of her shoulders.

Lily plunged in. 'I saw you from my window up there. It's cold and you've waited so long.'

'Any law against it?' The girl lifted her head. She did look wretched, grey and tense and shivering.

'Are you waiting for someone?'

She shook her head.

'Then why . . .?'

'I came out here to throw myself under a truck.' She turned her head to see how Lily would take this. 'Better than a street car, because they go too slow. Crunch. Crunch. I don't want to die by inches.'

'Why die at all?' Lily put out a hand, but the girl stepped away, still on the edge of the kerb with trucks and vans and commuting cars roaring past, too close. Lily wanted to grab her, but that was probably wrong, so she put her hands in her coat pockets.

'It's not why at this point,' the girl said flatly. 'It's how. I thought it would be kind of elegant to do it outside the college, so they'd all know. I didn't know it would be so difficult.'

Lily took her up to the apartment to get warm. Anna had two mugs of coffee and a stale Danish pastry, and after a nap on the sofa-bed, put her hair behind her ear and took Lily to the politician's office to make 'Hi there' calls, because they needed extra help.

Two dollars an hour. 'Hi there! I'm calling from the headquarters of Sloane Donahue?' Voice up like a New Zealander, implying, 'You've heard of him, surely?' 'Just want to make sure you're planning to get to the polls next week and give him your vote. You know what he's done for this city, I'm sure, and we want to be able to count on your support. Sloane Donahue's the name to rely on, for a cleaner, crime-free Boston. Family values, a fair deal for the small businessman . . . Well, wait a minute. Look at the alternatives. Do you want to see property taxes go sky high?'

If they argued, Lily argued back at them. If they hung up, she hung up and dialled the next number.

When it was time to go home, dry of mouth and of enthusiasm for Sloane Donahue, she unfolded from her crouch over a desk to find that Anna had gone. She did not come back the next day, and Lily did not see her again on the other side of the avenue.

Oh, hell. Job only half done. Dear Doctor Lily falls down on follow-up. When she worried to Paul, he said, 'She knows where you live. She'll find you if she wants you.'

'What's it like to be so rational? I can't *be* like that. I keep thinking she might be dead.'

Lily asked one or two of the students, and even went into the college to leave a message. But Anna Heiderman was not known and not registered there.

Lily did not go back to Donahue headquarters, after another woman there told her about Gloria's answering service, which needed people to fill in at odd times.

'Dr Madison's line. Allied Cleaning. 232-4968. No, Mrs Beggs, no messages. Concrete City. Capital Oil. I can take your order, but the trucks won't go out till tomorrow. I'm sorry, I don't know. This is the answering service. Day-Nite Answering Service. Okay, dear, I'll plug your jack. Let me know when you go for lunch.'

The switchboard and its jacks and plugs and crossed wires and blinking lights drove Lily insane at first. But the pay was the best she'd had yet, and the two students and the knitting woman and the man in the wheelchair handled the calls and messages quite easily, and they were not geniuses, so Lily hung on, and learned from them, and from Gloria when she was not off running one of her other businesses.

Phil in his motorized chair rescued her many times when she had lost a call, or got a message wrong or forgot to punch it into the time clock, or lost one of the endless slips of paper which crowded the pigeonholes – blue for messages in, pink for basic client info, green for new temporary info, yellow for 'if' calls: 'If so-and-so wants me.' In return, Lily did shopping for him and fetched his laundry from the Washeteria.

Dr Madison was a hectic children's doctor, always out of breath when she called in for messages, as if her office was on the fifth floor with no elevator, always besieged by desperate mothers.

'Mrs Hanney? Oh, my God, not again. How high is the child's temperature? . . . Well, please always ask. Three times she called? Help. Who else? Good (pant). Okay. Not good. Are you the new operator? Don't worry, I don't suppose she minded, but ask Phil about her for next time. I've got to go. If Nurse Baxter calls, I want you to tell her – no, forget it. Tell her I'll call. What's the time? Oh, my God.'

You could build up quite an acquaintance with the faceless voices. You knew their business. You knew who they wanted to talk to and who they didn't. You knew if they were lying when they said they were in Baltimore. 'You must never tell anybody anything outside,' Gloria had said, but Lily told Paul, because he wasn't anybody, and he understood about monotone Miss Arnold who kept calling, calling, with less and less hope.

'No messages from *anybody*?', when all she wanted was a word from Lootenant Connolly of the State Police, the rat.

Once when Paul was in Oklahoma buying Western saddles, which Turnbull's deigned to keep in stock in an amused, derogatory way, Lily had spent all night at the switchboard. An eye-opener about how many people called other people in the small hours, and were aggrieved when they did not answer themselves – '*Answering service?*' they repeated, as if it were an incomprehensible phrase – and how many people wanted to talk to an anonymous operator, rather than talk to nobody in the middle of the night.

Asleep in the defunct armchair, she was woken by the rich deep voice of Martha Mackenzie, who ran some kind of mental health agency. 'Yes, yes, yes. He leave a number?' Martha was as brisk and on top of things as if she weren't in her kitchen at six-thirty a.m., in a new scarlet bathrobe, watching the street lights go out and the office lights go on, which she had told Lily she was. They had made friends after a bungled message, when Martha had yelled and Lily had blown up and yelled back, 'I wasn't even here!'

'If you stop shouting and call the man back,' Lily told Martha severely, 'he might not have left for the bus station.'

'Good idea.' Martha swooped down to earth through two octaves.

After several weeks of Dr Davidson and Miss Arnold and Concrete City and Martha Mackenzie, Gloria discovered that Lily was not legal, so she went back to Fidelio's Super Store and baby-sitting, and typing at home, and took a rich old lady from Beacon Hill to Filene's basement to pick over marked-down underwear with jewelled talons.

By the time she finally received the green card which entitled her to work, she had year-old baby Isobel, and was four months pregnant with Cathy. They had left the apartment with the partition walls that cut across the pattern of the moulded plaster ceiling, and moved all the plants into a small pleasant house in the suburb of Newton, with Paul's easy-chair from Barbara's house, and his piano, since Terry refused to practise or take any more lessons.

On Easter Saturday, during the time when Lily was working for the Day-Nite Answering Service, Paul took her to Cape Cod to look for a cottage to rent for two weeks in the summer.

They would have liked to take Terry with them for the day, but Barbara said, 'I thought he was supposed to go with you to your parents' on Sunday, for the great ham dinner with all the fixin's.'

'Everybody has ham at Easter,' Paul said. 'Don't jeer. If Terry came on Saturday, he could sleep over and come to Dedham next day.'

'It's not even his statutory weekend,' Barbara said. 'Sunday was a concession.'

'Thanks.' Paul made fierce doodles on his desk, stabbing at the paper so he wouldn't stab at her. He had learned long ago when they lived together to pretend to be cheerful when Barbara dragged him into moroseness, and to keep quiet when she tried to stir him to anger. If she railed at him, he did not answer, a technique known in the navy as dumb insolence, which infuriated her.

'Look, Paul.' Barbara suddenly sounded quite warm and sympathetic. 'I know you like to give Terry a good time, but why don't you and Lily go to the Cape by yourselves, hunh? This first time. I know what it means to you.'

'She's up to something,' was Lily's opinion.

'No, she can be really nice and understanding, like that, she always used to be, when we were first married.'

Lily did not want to hear. She did try to be fair about Barbara, but, being a wholesale sort of person, it was hard for her to see all sides. She really only wanted to hear the rotten things, to reassure herself: 'He never loved her like he loves me.'

The sun was as warm as early summer. The sky was a clear primeval blue. The green haze that had been softening the trees for the last two weeks had uncurled into the beginning of leaves. Slender white birches were bent this way and that from the winter's snow. The oaks were still brown, but the pines were tipped with fresh bright needles. A Plymouth motel had a newly painted sign. Children making gross faces in the back windows of station-wagons wore shorts and summer tops. Everyone was heading to the Cape.

Closer to the canal, which made the peninsula of Cape Cod an island, the air warmed to a soft breeze, carrying the scents of salt and seaweed.

'Roll your window down, Lily. Smell it, do you smell it? Put your head out.'

Paul slowed down, and dozens of cars swept past them, obliterating the seacoast fragrance.

Paul desperately wanted Lily to love the Cape, as he did. His dream was, as it had been with Barbara, only she dismissed it, to belong to this enchanted sandbar, and not be just a visitor. One day, if things went well, he and Lily would have a small cottage, near a beach, by a marsh, on a village street, in the woods, anywhere, with coloured beach stones and broken shells hanging about on the sandy porch from summer to summer. One day. A dream closer to reality now, if his lucky Tack Rack went on selling as it had begun.

During the hell of the divorce, work had been the only thing that kept him in one piece. The long hours on the road or in the store, in his office or out on the floor with customers, being friendly Mr Stephens, made sense. Heating frozen chicken pies in the apartment, and calling up the few friends who had not been friends of both of them to see if they would come and have a stir-fry, did not.

One day, an impatient woman who was hard to please came into Turnbull's and bought some bridle hangers made of burnished horseshoes, very elegant, very expensive, then changed her mind after they were wrapped, because they were the wrong size. She was a top rider and a good customer, so friendly Mr Stephens came out to see if he could order something for her.

'I don't know what I want.' She complained about the inconvenience of her tack room, how there was never enough room for everything, and nobody made the right kind of equipment any more.

Back at the apartment, Paul was putting up units of adjustable book shelves and cabinets, when a great idea hit him. Without telling anyone at Turnbull's, he roughed out the modular Tack Rack on paper and got a friend who was a talented woodworker to make a prototype. His employer bought the Tack Rack for a few thousand dollars and ten per cent of all sales to Paul. Turnbull's had it manufactured in blow-moulded plastic and sold it expensively, since rich or poor, horse people don't want bargains. If the Tack Rack became *the* gadget that everybody wouldn't be seen dead without, then one day . . . maybe.

On a rising tide of excited pleasure, he drove his darling Lily along the landward side of the Cape Cod canal, which, where the road rose above a steep, wooded slope, looked for an illusory moment like the Rhine, and over the arched bridge that soared high enough across the water to let the big ships pass underneath. On the seaward side, the railroad drawbridge was hoisted up between its elegant Victorian iron towers. Paul had thrummed over that lowered bridge as a boy, but there were hardly any trains now. All cars and trucks and vans and campers. Too many of them. The Cape was getting ruined, visitors said, as they poured across the two canal bridges to add to the ruin.

But off the road, the little villages of the unfashionable Upper Cape pottered along more or less undisturbed in a peaceful dapple of sunshine and shade, and not all the elms had been accused of disease and executed. Roomy white houses with black shutters, low shingled cottages with steep roofs, an archaic post office, ponies in a field, haphazardly fenced, grey weathered houses with curly gingerbread trim under the roof and pillared porches looking to the west above short curving beaches.

Paul showed Lily the house his parents used to rent when he was a boy. The same woman was in the real estate office, still pretending to be at her wits' end, still off-handedly efficient.

'Two weeks in July? For that money? What's this craziness? Look, there's going to be dozens of clients coming in and out of here all weekend, and I don't have a thing to show them. What am I supposed to do? Wait now, you only want one bedroom and a rollaway, so let's see.'

She sent them off with a cheerful young woman, who showed them two possible houses and one perfect one.

It was tiny, not much more than an elaborate whitewashed shed, off the road down a sandy track that ended in a hump of rough grass and a broken fence crushed down by clambering rose briars. Through a miniature kitchen, they stepped up into an odd-shaped living-room, barely furnished, and full of light. Lily made for the big window that was the end wall, and cried out when she saw the marsh which lay like a carpet below the sandy mound on to which the house had been fitted. Paul stood close behind, holding her.

The marsh, half land, half water, stirred in the breeze, the grass and bog plants all shades through grey to green, an insignificant stream glinting yellow where its curves emerged. A flock of geese headed over the flat wet expanse to where, between two distant houses on the low dunes, shone the sea.

'Can we live here for ever?' Lily's face was vulnerable with delight. She had grown up a lot since Iceland, but sometimes she still looked like that eager child who had cast herself, with such reckless joy, headlong towards disappointment.

'For a coupla weeks anyway, Saturday to Saturday,' the agent said.

She took them back to her office, and then they drove to the long sweep of Old Silver beach, which had a big hotel at its edge. Although it was colder here than in Boston, quite a few people were lying in the sun or picnicking or walking or wading, as Paul and Lily did with their pants rolled up, far out in the low tide water towards the blurred line of the New Bedford shore across the bay.

'In July, we'll hardly find a space to sit on this beach,' Paul said. 'Terry and I came last year, and everybody else had come too. When I was a kid with a pail and shovel, there was almost nobody. We were outraged if another family sat down within fifty yards. In the good old days.'

'Don't talk as if you're middle-aged.'

'I'm thirty-five.'

'Rubbish, that's nothing.' Lily would never talk about the difference in their ages.

They raced each other down the long beach to the line of breakwater rocks, scrambled over them and fell into the soft sand of a private beach below a sturdy shuttered house, where no one could see them.

Before going into Falmouth for lunch, they went back to their shed house to glory in the view again and look in through the windows. Still barefoot, they explored down one of the other narrow tracks which branched off to other houses. It turned back through some trees and wound about, soft with old pine needles, until it came out on a small road of sand and sea-grass tufts that ran along the edge of an inlet. At the inner end, the tiled roof of a big house showed above thick trees. At the outer end, they found a steep mound of smooth sand at the inlet's opening, and across the road where the trees ended in coarse grass and thorny bushes, a narrow beach backed by a groin of huge stones that ran out and fell into the sea. The edges of the sheltered water lapped quietly at glossy pebbles, more like a lake than an ocean. It was a bay within a bay within the broad horseshoe of Buzzard's Bay, secret, untrodden. The distant Massachusetts shore and a nearer headland dotted with houses were worlds away. Five dark cormorants stood motionless on a lone rock, waiting for the tide to turn.

'I never saw this,' Paul said. 'I don't remember this beach being here.'

'You invented it for me.'

'You love it all, don't you?'

'You know I do. Especially because today . . . well, specially because.'

It wasn't worth asking, 'What?' When Lily stopped in the middle of a sentence and her eyes stilled and looked inward, she did not want to be probed or coaxed. She wanted to be left alone.

After lunch, they went into a greenhouse store to buy an Easter lily for Paul's mother. There were dozens of them, white madonna lilies, flaunting their loud sweet scent. Lily said it looked like a funeral.

'Everybody has to have lilies on Easter,' Paul explained. 'Like the ham with all the fixin's.'

'Dead right.' A square, crew-cut man was waiting at the counter with them to get their lilies wrapped. 'Why do we do it? It's a heck of a bore.'

'Oh, no.' Lily, ardent immigrant, was shocked. 'I'm fairly new here – oh, this is my husband.' She always introduced Paul to everybody she talked to in stores, restaurants, the subway, waiting in line to get into the movie theatre. 'I love all of it. Thanksgiving, Christmas, Easter. It's so – so, sort of, *sumptuous*.'

'And unnecessary.'

'Oh, don't feel like that.'

She looked so concerned that the man told her, 'It's senseless this year, because there's one less of us.'

'Far away?'

'My young son was burned to death two months ago. In a play hut he had in the woods. The other boy got out.'

Paul could say nothing. He could not even look at the man. Lily put her hand on his arm and said, 'Oh, my *God*, I'm so sorry.'

'Oh well.' The woman in the green overall was putting stiff paper round the man's plant. He gave a small snort, between a laugh and a moan. 'C'est la vie.' He put some money on the counter, picked up his funeral lily and went out.

In the car, Lily cried, not so much for the man, as for her own guilt at having said too much, not enough, the wrong things.

'I should have run after him.'

'What would you have said?'

'I don't know. Anything. Asked him to bring the rest of his family to have Easter with us.'

'All the way to Dedham?'

'Oh, *I* don't know, but I should have done something.'

'What could you do? You couldn't bring his boy back. Don't lash yourself, darling. It's like with that girl, Anna. You couldn't bring her boyfriend back or make her parents suddenly dote on her.'

'I couldn't even find her. And now that man . . . how can he bear it? C'est *not* la vie.'

'He told you. That's something.'

'Not enough.'

'Don't cry, Lily. Don't spoil our lovely day.'

'I'm a mess.' Paul's mother's favourite statement when she met you, fussing at her hair and clothes, straightening ornaments, bashing a cushion.

'I didn't want to tell you till I'd had a test, because it's bad luck, but now I've got to. Because I really do feel . . .'

Paul stopped the car on grass at the side of the road. Lily shed a few more tears, and dug back into the self-indulgent guilt.

'Me with a child, and that man without one. Do you suppose he tried to get the boy out? Suppose he couldn't get into the hut, and heard him screaming.'

'Hush, Lily. Stop that.'

'I'm homesick, Paul. I want my mum.'

'That proves it,' he said. 'It can take women that way. Barbara never liked her mother, but when she was carrying Terry –' He shut up. Luckily, Lily had her head buried in his arms and could not hear.

'I'm a mess, Lily dear.' Paul's mother opened the door of her house, a Dedham miniature baronial Tudor, in her apron, pushing at her soft, faded yellow hair. 'Oh, a lily from Lily! Aren't you a doll?'

'Paul bought it,' Lily said honestly.

'He always buys me an Easter lily. Hello there, Terry, come on in. Your Grandpa can't wait to see you.'

Terry walked in wordlessly, with his shoulders hunched. He and the Judge greeted each other soberly. Lily never knew whether to kiss her father-in-law, or what to call him. Paul had told her, 'Kiss him and call him Steven. He'll like that.'

But Lily imagined he was rather grand and intellectual. He wasn't. Steven Stephens had been a scrupulous attorney, and now he was a very fair and humane judge, popularly known as Even Steven. Paul's mother, Muriel, from small-town Indiana, was more like Lily's family. His father had come from the same town, but, in working his way eastward through his law career, he had shed whatever folksiness he might have had, while his wife had hung on to hers, like an heirloom. When the Spooners came over to visit, Muriel and Lily's mother would get along fine together.

Paul's cousin Joanne came for Easter dinner with her husband and two daughters, self-conscious in fancy new dresses and white straw hats.

'Does everybody get new clothes at Easter?' Lily asked in her bright, interested way.

'Sure, honey,' Muriel said. 'To knock 'em dead in church.'

'Did you go to church?' Lily asked one of the girls.

'No.'

The Judge carved the huge glazed ham, and Paul's mother was happy with 'a lovely crowd of folk around my table'.

'You almost had a few more.' Paul told them about the man in

117

the flower store, and Lily, who was still distressed about it, added some elaborations about the father running up and down outside the burning shed and hearing his son screaming.

The children stopped eating, fascinated. Muriel put her fingers to her lips and shook her head.

'Who started the fire?' Terry asked. Paul wished he hadn't. The family were beginning to forget about Eddie Waite and the mailbox.

'I don't know. The poor man just told me, and then went out.'

When the children had gone into the garden – 'Watch out for those new white dresses' – and they were having coffee, Muriel said to Lily, 'You don't look so well, honey. Are you okay?'

'I always look puffy for ages if I've been crying. I can't get that man out of my mind.'

She was genuinely upset, yet, because he already knew her so well, Paul could hear her listening to herself. He loved and admired her desperately, but he knew when her full-blooded participation in life was enhanced by being an audience for her own drama, like everyone who lives in the present.

This is me in my new red dress at a big oval table with the best white cloth, laying my feelings on the line for my new family. Lily's letters to him before they were married had been present-tense autobiographical narrative: 'There I am, rushing for the train, my God, I'm late! My bag's open and my wallet falls on to the line. I'm paralyzed – help! Do I climb down, miss the train? I'm shouting and people are staring,' etc., etc.

'I should have gone after him,' she said.

'You can't take on everyone else's troubles,' the Judge told her. 'I know I've lost sleep at night over some terrible story I've heard in court, but I've learned to do the job and not get involved. It's too destructive.'

'But you've got to be involved!' Lily leaned forwards to him across the table. 'That's the whole point of life. You can't just stand back and watch what happens to people. You've got to be a part of it.'

'True up to a point,' Even Steven said. 'I've pronounced a man guilty and then had the verdict overturned on Appeal, and felt pretty guilty myself. I've wanted to write to people sometimes, who've stood in front of me in court, and say, "I'm sorry." '

'Did you?'

He shook his head. 'One has to learn not to plunge in up to the neck. That could, if you'll forgive the mixed metaphor, sow the seeds of ruin.'

His face was too serious. Paul looked at Lily. The words were too chilling. But if they had affected her, she did not show it. She was leaning forwards, impatient to make her point again, when Muriel cut in.

'Lily's all right,' she said comfortably. 'She's not a cold-hearted old buzzard like you, are you, honey? Maybe you're so upset because you're – you know.' She nodded at the table edge in front of Lily's stomach. 'We're so happy that you and Paul are going to give us a grandchild.'

Her indulgent OB-GYN face made Paul want to protest, 'That's not why people have children.' But it was more important to say, 'You've got Terry.'

'That's not the same,' Muriel said in a half whisper, although Terry was at the end of the garden. She had not cared much for Barbara, with whom she had never felt at ease.

'That's a perfectly rotten thing to say.' The Judge was angry with her.

'Oh, you know me, Steven, I don't mean a thing. I'll just make another pot of coffee,' she said to get herself out of the room.

'Don't bother for us,' Paul said. 'We have to go.'

'I thought you were going to stay and watch the football game.'

'We have to get Terry back.'

They took him to a movie and then for pizza, and got him home quite late. Lily stayed in the car. Paul got out to go to the door and explain why they were late, but the chrome of a black Corvette was glittering in the driveway.

'Shit,' Terry said. 'Silas.' So Paul let him go in alone.

The house that Terry's father rented for two weeks that July was not much more than a shack on the edge of a bog.

'My father has rented a Cape house for the summer,' Terry had said at school. The people who talked a lot about 'my father' were those whose fathers did not live at home.

During the drive from the Sagamore bridge bus stop, Lily yacked away like a maniac, because Terry was silent, building up the house as something so beautiful and special, that when they rounded the last bend of the sandy road, he had to say, 'This is *it*?'

'Don't you love it?'

'Isn't it great?'

Lily and Paul had obviously plotted to deal with any sulks by turning sour to sweet.

Terry was fed up with being dealt with by various grown-ups at home and at school, and the hints his mother had leaked out about the whole situation had made him almost not want to come to the Cape at all. But she had gone to Maine in the Corvette with Silas, so he had to come.

When he saw the narrow white house standing sentinel over the marsh and the slow stream that meandered away to the sea, his heart raced, but he was not going to show them that he was dazzled.

'Take off your jacket,' his father said. 'It's hot.'

'Maybe.' Terry shifted his light jacket back on his shoulders. Taking it off was an admission he wasn't ready to make yet.

He took off his sneakers and jumped off the bank into squelching mud, and waded along the stream. The water pushed gently at the back of his ankles. Farther down, two boys were fishing, and another was digging something out of the mud bank. Terry said, 'Hi,' but they didn't. He kept to the side as the stream broadened and deepened. His shorts were wet, but he wasn't going to plunge in wearing clothes among the whole mess of kids in bathing suits, large and small, who were shrieking and wrestling and letting themselves be carried out by the quickening water into the shallow sea.

Terry walked across the sand between groups of people, and felt their eyes on his back as he stood at the edge of the water. A clamour of gulls with wicked curved beaks and silly feet tucked up under their bodies flew sideways along the beach and veered out to sea. Staring after them to the far shore of the bay, Terry emptied his mind of thought and feeling. He had got quite good at this. You could just *be*, which passed the time pretty well, with no effort.

His father and Lily came to the beach another way and turned up with a picnic lunch in a cooler. They had brought Terry's swimming trunks.

'Put them on under a towel,' Lily said, but Terry would not take them.

Lily added that he shouldn't wander off without saying where he was going, and Terry snapped, 'You found me, didn't you?'

'That's no way to talk to Lily,' his father said.

Terry kicked up sand. If they were going to gang up on him . . . He saw Lily make an 'Oh dear' face at Paul. Was this kid going to ruin the vacation for them?

Was he? He had not decided. He could give them hell and have a lousy time, or he could enjoy it and let them think they'd won. It wasn't up to him anyway. It depended on the system of weights and balances inside him. He could be light one minute, free and feeling great and expecting marvels. Then someone said or did something, or he remembered something, and the weight dropped, plummeting him down with it into a murk of rage and disgust where nothing good could happen.

Later when they had gone to their room, Terry knelt on the rollaway bed under the living-room window with his arms on the sill, and stuck his head out to breathe in the moon and stars and the dinosaur smell of the silvery marsh. This was the best place he had ever slept, the most fantastic house, like a dwarf's home, with a kitchen like a closet and patchy white walls and old cane furniture with floppy cushions.

He woke early and went outside to poke about. When he smelled bacon and came in, Lily was making coffee in her nightgown, which was different from seeing his mother in her nightgown, because there was more of Lily.

'I like it here.' Terry made wet tracks toward her over the speckled green painted floor.

'Oh, I *am* glad!' She turned with a mug in one hand and her arms out as if she was going to embrace him.

Terry kept a safe distance, but he said, 'Yeah, it's okay. What are we going to do today?'

They did everything. They went to different beaches. They crossed Sandwich marsh by the boardwalk and climbed over the beach rocks to plunge into the icy sea on the north side of Cape Cod. They bought lobsters and cooked them in sea water with seaweed on the top. They ate fried clams. They rode bikes. Terry's father rented two horses to ride through the woods.

'Lily's not coming?'

'I don't know how to ride properly.'

'Oh.' Terry had thought it was because his father wanted to ride alone with him.

'And to tell you the truth, Terry,' Lily said, looking at him uncertainly, 'I'm going to have a baby.'

'Oh.'

'Do you mind?'

'Why should I?'

He did mind, so he insisted on a Western saddle, to annoy his father. But Paul was so determined to give Terry a good time that he let him ride like a half-baked cowboy, with his feet stuck forward and his hands in the air, although he cared desperately about that kind of horsy thing, and doing it right.

When Paul went to see a customer in Osterville, Lily took Terry to the secret beach she had found, a lagoon full of clams and mussels on one side and a small horseshoe of empty sand on the other.

'Where is everybody?' The other beaches were crowded.

'They don't know about it, so let's not tell them.'

'Is it private?' A swimming raft was anchored some yards out.

'Beaches belong to everyone. It's our special, secret place.'

Before she could start blabbering about fairies and mermaids, Terry ran into the sea and swam out to the raft.

That evening, Paul's friend Harry came down, and they went to a small summer theatre and saw a musical. In the interval, a glamorous woman with sparkling silver eyelids and a cloud of colourless hair like cotton candy swept through the crowd to them with cries of rapture. She was in charge of the theatre, but she was also in the horse world, and knew Harry quite well. Her name was Paige, which was no kind of name for a woman, or a man either, come to that.

'Poll Stephens!' Holy shit, she knew Terry's father too. He had sold her a saddle she adored to death. She kissed him theatrically.

'My dear,' she told Lily, standing far back to allow room for her huge spangled boobs. 'You've no idea what this adorable guy of yours has done for my seat!'

People were looking at them. Paige shone out in the crowd as if she were on stage in her own spotlight.

'Don't you adore the show, dahling?' She swooped on Terry.

He nodded without bringing his head up again, and ducked away to pretend to look at the old theatre posters which papered the walls.

She invited them to stay in the bar after the show and meet the cast. Terry thought he would fall through the floor, but off the stage the actors were just ordinary people in jeans and sweat shirts. The one who had been the bald comic uncle, who was now young with hair, showed Terry tricks with coins and glasses. Paige and Harry and some of the actors sang, and Terry's father played the piano. Terry expected to die of shame, seeing him up there banging away, with his foot thumping the pedals and his hair disordered and a wild light in his blue eyes, laughing when he hit a wrong note or muffed a chord. But everybody thought he was great.

Harry pulled Lily on to the little stage and made her sing a cockney song with him, which she did quite well, in an odd deep voice, in the same octave as Harry. Terry stayed firmly at the table, with his arm hooked through the back of the chair for safety. He would not sing, but he told the comic uncle his story about the German policeman.

During a break in the singing, the uncle called out, 'Listen, everyone, you've got to hear this! Tell it again, Terence.'

The blood rushed up into Terry's head and out at the top, but he told it. They all roared, including Lily, who had already heard it six times in different accents. His father was so proud that for a moment of incredible surging lightness, Terry wanted to die for him.

When would real life come relentlessly back? When would the weight drop down?

Because there was only one bedroom in the dwarf house, Harry had to sleep on the rollaway bed in the living-room and Terry slept on the floor in a sleeping-bag. Or tried to. Harry turned on the light to make himself a drink, and wanted to tell Terry at some length how wonderful his mother was and that he must always remember she was the most wonderful mother in the world, although he had been making up to Lily all evening, and telling Paul how wonderful *she* was.

Next morning, Terry did not want to get up, but he had to, because after Harry left, they were going to Provincetown on the tip of the Cape to see the old fishing village gone arty, where men wore jewellery and make-up, and then to picnic on the great outer beach. Terry was edgy in the car. He practised whining. Pity to lose that useful small-fry skill. Provincetown was too crowded and the only man with jewellery was a fake pirate with a ring in his ear selling nets and plastic fish. On Newcome Hollow beach, Lily had forgotten the Coca-Cola. There were ham and cheese sandwiches, but no peanut-butter.

Terry left them to climb on all fours up the high dunes. Poised on top of the cliff above the Atlantic ocean, with nothing between him and Spain, he could have taken off like a bird. Some kids behind pushed him, and he dropped over the sheer edge on to the steep slope, stumbled up and ran and slid on his heels with his arms out, and across the beach to dive into a breaking wave, which knocked him back to shore.

He ran out with the sucking tide that drew the shingle out, and stayed in the surf for a long time. His father, wearing his shorts and shirt, came down to the edge of the sea and called that it was time to go home.

Terry wanted one more wave, and then one more, and another. He hit a soaring wave at the wrong angle. It tipped him up and knocked him under where it was black for ever, with the weight of the whole ocean on top of him, sucking him out over the shingle, flaying him alive, blinding and suffocating him.

Someone grabbed him painfully and hauled him out. His father threw him up on to the sand like a dead fish, and Terry choked up some water and sat up. He was amazed to see the sea and the sky and the afternoon sun in place, and the kids still toiling up the dune and flying down with their arms out.

'You all right?'

Terry nodded. He coughed and blinked and wiped back his curly hair which was full of sand, and saw his father's face. It was terrible, white and stricken, with his smiling eyes staring and his smiling mouth dropped and jittering over his soaked shirt. Lily was standing just behind him, looking scared and helpless.

'I'm okay.' Terry got up. 'No big deal.'

Lily made a small sound, like Buster when he wanted to jump on to your bed. She put her arms round Paul and hugged him, as if she could dry him off and warm him with the closeness of her body.

She got at him, Terry's mother had said. 'She's taken him from us.' He remembered everything again. The weight sank down and took him with it. I should have drowned, he thought.

Sunscorched and waterlogged, his knees and arms grazed, his wrist aching where his father had grabbed it, Terry fell asleep in the back of the car. He woke and got out grumpy, as he used to when he was a little kid tired after a treat. The tiny house looked like a pink dog kennel, painted by the sunset. Plumes of cloud raced down the sky to follow the descending sun.

'Look, Terry, how beautiful it is!' Lily called, as he trudged up the grass slope to the house.

She could never just look at something, or just do something. Everybody else had to see or do it with her. 'Walk to the post office with me.' 'Quick, come out here – the gulls are dropping clams on the rocks.' 'Who wants to help me find my contact lens?'

His father called him back to the car to carry something, but Terry went on into the house.

While his father was in the shower, Lily said she would make him supper, so he could get to bed early. As if he were a baby.

'Hamburger well-done or rare?' She used to ask, 'Over or under-done?' Now she aped the natives.

The frozen fries were limp and pale and only warm. The meat wasn't cooked in the middle, mushy-red, like a turned-back eyelid.

'What's the matter with it?' Lily saw that Terry had pushed his plate away.

'It's not cooked.'

Lily sighed, and took the plate away, making a patient face, which included turning her eyes up to the ceiling. When she brought it back, a few of the french fries fell on the floor. She picked them up and put them on the plate, and Terry pushed them off on to the table. He sneaked a look at her. Her eyes had gone mean and her big full mouth was shut tight. Ignoring the potatoes, she picked up the plate and thumped it down again on the table, and waited, questioningly.

Terry took up his fork and reached for the ketchup bottle. Lily picked up the plate again as he was going to pour ketchup.

'Hey!' he said.

She banged the plate down and asked angrily, 'Did no one ever teach you to say thank you?'

Terry pushed back his chair and stood up. The ketchup bottle fell over into the plate and went glug, glug over the food.

'Don't you tell me what to do!'

He and Lily stared at each other. Her face was too far above him. He had to tilt his head.

'Don't talk to me like that, Terry.' His father came into the room, so she added, 'Please.'

The weight inside him exploded into a rage that set his body on fire. His sunburned cheeks and lips burned painfully. His throat was choked.

He threw the fork at her and ran. As he banged out of the screen door and jumped the three steps, he heard Lily yell out something, and his father said, in that infuriatingly calm voice when he was taking control, 'Let him go.'

Terry ran blindly down the curving track. At the end, he stopped to see if they were coming after him, then turned down the road to the other houses, turned off at random, and plunged into the woods. He scrambled through, hopping over briars, zigzagging round the sharp trunks of the pines, trying to run where their soft needles had fallen. If he'd known he was going to split, he would have put his sneakers on.

How far was he going to run? To the sea and swim far out. To the Cape Cod canal and hitch a ride to Boston and call his mother. He had cut the bottom of one foot, and bruised the other. The shingle scrapes on his knees were beginning to bleed. He made for a place where the trees cleared, and came out on to a path with a narrow strip of water beyond.

Which way? He heard a car away to the right, and headed toward the road. Then he recognized the tiled roof of the house above the trees on the other side of the water, and the place where he and Lily had gone in to look for razor clams.

Terry stopped and listened again for sounds of someone crashing through the trees. Then he turned away from the road and ran alongside the lagoon to the beach at the far end. 'Our special place.'

No one was there. On the other side of the small bay within a bay, a few windows were lit in the houses on the headland. The tide was out. The sun had gone down. Terry walked out on the breakwater, climbing the sloping chunks of rock, jumping over gaps between the flat ones. It would be hard to come back this way in the dark. Almost at the end, he sat down. The cormorant rock was high out of the water. Three birds hunched darkly, motionless as hangmen.

The rage was gone. This was a vacuum of time and place. No need to think or feel. It must be like this up in weightless space.

'Hey there!' Someone shouted at him from the inlet side of the rocks. When he paid no attention, they shouted again, in voices that were clear and young and arrogant.

Terry turned away from them. He jumped down into the shallow water and headed back to the beach, with the rock barrier between him and the arrogant shouts. Underwater rocks slippery with seaweed trapped him. He would step on a crab. He stumbled over a round boulder and one leg went up to the thigh in a hole. When he got to the beach, they were waiting for him, two smart-ass boys carrying a pail and clam rakes.

'Get off the beach,' one of them said, the tall skinny one with the flop of fair hair that he didn't bother to push out of his eye to see Terry.

'Why?' Terry tripped on the last treacherous slimy rock and stepped on to the sand.

'It's a private beach.'

'My —' Lily had said it belonged to everyone. 'My —' step-mother, father's wife? He felt like a toad, but he could only say, 'My mother comes here all the time.'

'Well, you tell her to lay off, or my grandfather will get after her. What's her name? What's your name, punk?'

Terry shook his head. As he ran past them, they took lazy swipes at him with the clam rakes, and laughed as he ploughed up through the soft sand to the road, turned right and kept on running.

When at last he got back to the house, he was sobbing, not messily, but a dry, steady sob with every indrawn breath.

Lily rushed out of the screen door and called, 'Paul! It's all right, he's back!'

Presently Terry's father came out of the trees, where he must have been searching, with a flashlight, for God's sake.

'Where the hell have you been?' With all grown-ups, if they got anxious over you, they were so mad when you did turn up that you wished you hadn't.

'I went to that beach.' Terry stood with his sore arms wrapped round him, trying to get his breath, still shaken by sobs like hiccups. 'It belongs to everyone, *she* said.' He would not look at Lily. 'Stupid Limey. What does *she* know?'

'What are you talking about?' His father came up close and grabbed him by both clenched upper arms.

'I got kicked off, that's what. They may come after her and I hope they do, because she . . . because she . . .' Terry collapsed on the grass in a passion of weeping, with his head butting against the wooden back of the bottom step, beating his fist on the top one.

His father picked him up and carried him in like a sack, and dropped him down on the rollaway which was ready for him under the window. He cried until he had no more breath. His father thumped him gently on the back and waited. Finally Terry turned over and lay flat, looking up at their faces through his wet lashes. A few surplus tears rolled lazily out of the corners of his flooded eyes and burned their way down his scorching cheeks.

'I think I have a fever,' he said calmly. His mother was a great

128

one with the thermometer. If he bit it and rolled it around, sometimes he could push it up a notch or two and miss school.

'You had too much sun.' Lily sat on the end of the bed. His father was sitting beside him, smiling again, his closed-mouth smile which spread curves into his cheeks.

'Too much of everything, I guess,' Terry said.

'Like what?'

'You know.'

'You still upset about the divorce, old son? I thought you felt okay now about Lily.'

Terry moved his head from side to side on the flat summer cottage pillow that felt as if it were filled with sand. 'She loused up everything. We were okay before she came along and – and –' *She took him from us*, his mother had said, one day when she was brooding and fed up.

'Terry, I don't think I want to hear this.' His father stood up.

'Paul – Let him. Let him say what's on his mind.'

'I don't want to hear it.' His father went outside.

Lily stayed at the end of the bed. She did not try to move up. She said, 'Tell me, then,' and Terry told her. It was surprisingly easy.

After a bit, she said, 'You've got it wrong. You've forgotten I didn't meet your Dad till after the divorce. I mean, except that time in Iceland centuries ago.'

'But if you hadn't, then in the end, he would have –'

'He would have come back home? No, listen, Terry. Your Mum and Dad wouldn't have come back together even if he'd never married again.'

'I don't believe you. My mother says . . .' He tried to tell her some of the stuff his mother said, but it was hard to explain it, because she never exactly *said* anything you could grab on to. You never knew where you were. Shit, he was going to cry again. He turned over and told the hard sand pillow, 'He shouldn't have married a foreign person. She thinks you're too young and too silly to cope with anything. She didn't want me to come here.'

'I know, but you did, thank goodness, and now it can be all right. Can't it?'

She wanted it to be, so he turned his hot face sideways and said, 'I guess.'

Lily turned off the lamp on the table. She sat there with him in silence. Out on the marsh, one of the night birds made a harsh, lonely noise.

'Where's Dad?'

'Outside. He'll come in.'

'What will happen to me?'

'You'll be all right. What are you afraid of?'

'Well, the money, and all that stuff. We haven't got enough.'

Lily explained about the money. His mother was earning now, in the design centre. Her father helped her. Dad gave her enough money for everything she and Terry needed.

'I hate to ask you this.' Lily coughed and looked toward the door. 'But what does your mother tell you about the money?'

'Nothing.' Nothing he could tell Lily. She said things like, 'You ought to go to a better school, Ter, but who's going to pay?' Sometimes she said things about his father that weren't true. Or were they? Once, to Silas, she had called him Paul the Prick.

'Enough, then.' Lily got up. 'We're going to have supper soon. Your first was a flop, so why not have a second one with us? Paul!' she shouted. She usually yelled from a distance, instead of going to where the person was.

His father came in and made drinks.

'All right now?'

'I guess.'

'I'm sorry.' Terry and his father said together, and laughed.

'What for?'

'I don't know.' Terry didn't. His head had cleared now. It was sore with crying, as if he'd been battered around, but all right on the inside.

'Nor do I.'

Things were better. Terry was still confused. Okay, so he had got some of it wrong, but he wasn't sure yet what the truth was.

At supper, when Lily let something burn in the flimsy rented pan, she said she was a young and foolish foreigner, which wasn't really fair, but she and Terry giggled, and it became a private joke between them.

Even without the burned pieces, she had fried too much chicken, so they would take a picnic supper tomorrow to Brewster when the tide was out and they could walk half a mile out to sea on the hard flat sands.

Next morning, Terry's mother called. He was to come home.

'Can't I stay, Mom? One more day? We're –'

'They've been getting at you,' she said crisply.

'No, but we have stuff planned to do.'

'So do I. Your grandparents want to see you. We're going up there for lunch tomorrow, so get the noon bus and I'll meet you at Park Square and we'll have time to get your hair cut and buy you some new sneakers.'

His old ones were ragged, with holes at the big toes. Lily had bought him a new pair at Woolworth's, but his mother did not like them. She bought him another pair, more expensive, which didn't make sense, if what she said about the money was true. She didn't like it that Lily had washed some of his clothes. They were a bit damp, because of having to catch the bus (which had meant Dad and Lily couldn't go to Brewster). His mother shoved everything into the washing-machine, clean or dirty.

'Did you have a good time?' she finally asked. 'What did you do?'

'Everything. Beaches, ferry to the Vineyard, fried clams, riding, theatre.'

'I'm glad, Ter. But I'm glad you're home.' She was so nice to him, and so easy and jokey that he was glad too. She let him ask Spike Clay to supper, whom she didn't usually like, and they all went to the movies.

Lunch at his North Shore grandparents was as boring as expected. They sat inside the screened porch, instead of out on the lawn, and ate in the dining-room. After lunch, everyone went to look at the horses, or swam in the pool, which Terry didn't want to do, because his grazes and gravel burns hurt.

He wanted them to hurt. They brought him a picture of the dunes and the flying children and the huge wave knocking him into the blackness, and the strong man in the soaked shirt and shorts carrying the boy through the surf on to the sand. It was a good picture to summon up. Terry hoped he wouldn't lose it.

'Got nothing to do?'

His Uncle Robert, who had come back to live at home after his wife walked out, took him upstairs to play with the elaborate train set he had kept in the attic since he was a boy.

With Uncle Robert, it wasn't play, it was work. He timed the trains with a stopwatch. You had to get the signals right to the fraction of a second. He wrote out a schedule, and each train had to arrive and leave dead on time. If Terry bungled it, he had to start the train again on its complicated journey around the snaking tracks on the attic floor, through the tunnels and road crossings, past the lever that dropped a mail bag, and a child who waved, and a dog that came out of a kennel and lifted its leg on a fire plug. Terry's knees on the bare floor were sore from the shingle under the powerful wave.

Although Uncle Robert was in the family firm, he was a bit childish: long-faced, with a jaw that dropped and a heavy under-lip, and slow of speech. If he was hustled along, he stuttered. He played practical jokes on people, and giggled.

Downstairs, someone had talked about his wife possibly coming back.

'I don't know that I want her to,' he told Terry, over the whirr and clacking of the two forty-six to Deerfield Corner.

'Don't worry. She won't. Once you split, that's it.'

Terry knew that now.

In the years after their elder daughter took herself off to the United States, James and Nora Spooner found themselves getting a bit restless.

Granada Avenue was no longer the flowering haven it had once seemed when they moved into it with Lily and Blanche. There was more room now at Number 127 without Lily, who had always seemed to take up more space than she actually did; but the house was shabby and the neighbourhood was going downhill. Some of the brick and stucco houses had two or three bells beside the front door. Gardens had grown rough, or were ironed out with concrete to park a second car beside the garage, or an egg-shaped caravan. Traffic at the top of the hill was so thick, you had to wait to cross to the bus stop. Down at the bottom of the road, where the church school used to be, some of the houses and shops and the red-brick school buildings were being demolished to put up a block of flats.

'Noise and dust for years.' James flapped his hands round his face and head to illustrate. 'And then a lifetime of council tenants.'

'Like my mother.'

'Oops.' James ducked from a non-existent blow. 'She's different.'

'*Vive la différence*,' Nora said comfortably. She had a fund of apt remarks. Her mother *was* different, with her righteous ways and her lavatory window thrown open to the Hounslow gales. She was worse.

They often talked about moving out to the country, 'before we hit fifty'. The Chilterns, perhaps. Somewhere with hills and village life. James could transfer to a sub post office or take over a sweetshop with a miniature post office in one corner, counting out stamps over the sausage rolls, being kind to pensioners and kiddies stopping in for suckers on their way home from school, and so on. Nora could nurse anywhere. Blanche loved dogs and country walks. James would grow scarlet runner-beans and giant marrows.

They talked a lot about it, because talking meant you could enjoy the thought of it all without having to do anything. When Lily and Paul came over to visit with fierce little Isobel and the new baby Cathy, they told them what was in the wind.

'Look at it this way,' Nora said. 'I could probably get a job anywhere, a nursing-home, if all else fails. I like the old ones.'

'But to work in a place where people only leave for one reason,' Lily said. 'How awful.'

'Someone's got to take care of those poor old dears.'

James saw his son-in-law – funny to call someone that when you hardly knew them – look up from the floor where he was changing the baby's nappy – these modern fathers were beyond all belief – to smile because Nora was so kind and motherly.

'Insurance for my old age.' She smiled back at Paul. 'Want Granny to help? No? Aren't you marvellous.' She was dotty about the fellow already. 'Do unto others, I say, as you would be done by. Will you "do by" me, Jamie, when my time comes?'

'I'll die long before you. Look at me. I'm falling to pieces.'

'What's wrong, sir?' Paul fastened the baby's playsuit and picked her up.

'You've just said it. My son-in-law, who's only fourteen years younger than me, calls me sir. I'm all in, podner. I'm beat. Want to feel my heart? Cardiac fibrillation.'

'Rubbish,' Nora said. 'It's hypochondria.'

'Don't ever live with a nurse, Paul,' James grumbled. 'You never get any attention.'

'You do from me, Jam.' With Isobel on her knee, Lily reached up to pull his head down and kiss him. Isobel's short arms went up too, and she kissed him passionately and wetly on the mouth.

'What happened to "Daddy"?' Lily had started to call him James or Jam in her letters almost as soon as she got married.

'I'm finally grown up. I'm an equal.'

With a black bow behind her head where her hair was pulled back, and a bit of extra plumpness from the last baby, she did not look very different to James from the girl whose hockey stick had always fallen across the bottom of the cellar stairs when he went down to change a fuse.

Paul had been at the Equestrian Trade Fair all day, flogging his brainchild, a new kind of adjustable rack to hang up saddles and bridles. After supper, he wanted to take Lily to the West End, since Nora would listen for the children.

'Well now, wait a minute.' Was the man trying to treat James's house as a hotel? Bed and breakfast, suppers, baby-sitting, and claiming expenses from his firm, no doubt. Polish off a steak-and-kidney pie and rhubarb crumble and then off into the night with Lily, who was supposed to be visiting her dear old Dad and Mum. 'I thought you and I were going up to the George.'

Lily started to protest, but Paul looked at her, and then turned to James with one of his great disarming smiles that looked as if he were in love with all the world, and said, 'Sure, James, I'd love to.'

Paul was a hit at the pub. A Yank. Dennis, who liked to take a dig where he could, had a go at President Johnson and Viet Nam, and complained that America wanted to run the world, but Paul turned it aside. If James and Nora ever visited America, as Lily said they must, when they had settled into their new house, and someone attacked England, Jam would floor them. But Paul turned Dennis off with an amiable, 'I guess we shouldn't be there.'

Everyone liked him. James had talked about him enough, and now here he was, Jam's Yank. Paul liked the look of the old upright, and was going to ask if he could play, but when Jonesey left the girl he had in his corner and came towards the piano, Paul stepped back, as if he had been a George regular for years, and knew about Jonesey's touchy temper.

James did the verses of 'The Parson's Lady', and Paul joined in the chorus with the rest of them, once he got the hang of it. Later, Paul got James and that chap with the beard whose name no one ever knew to do 'Lida Rose' with him in barbershop harmony. James, who was taller than Paul, had to bend over, so they could put their heads together and feel the sound vibrating. The smell of the man's skin and the feel of his thick hair against his temple gave James funny thoughts about Lily, his grown-up equal, who now belonged to this hair and this smell.

Keep it clean, Jamspoon. But Lily had once been a gullible wriggly cuddler like Isobel, only the other day, so soon they grew away from you . . .

'So soon,' James got Jonesey to play after the barbershop. 'So soon, the bird of love has flown,' in melancholy mood, with an elbow among the glasses on top of the upright, and the other hand over his heart.

'That was great,' Paul told him, as they dropped, loose-jointed and mellow, down the hill. 'You were great, Jam.'

'Bit of fun, that's all.'

'When the Brits throw a compliment back in your face, do they mean to insult you, or does it just happen?'

Paul had been putting questions about the pub, to Nigel, behind the bar. Being American, he always wanted to know how things worked.

'You could do something like that, you and Nora,' he told James as they went down Granada Road, falling into a snatch of close harmony opposite the haunted house with the pinnacles. 'If you really want to get out of town, you could buy a pub somewhere, or manage one.'

James's imagination took flight immediately. Why mess about with a post office sweetshop? 'I could be a jovial landlord. Mein Host. Nora could do bar snacks. Free beer for you any time.'

At home, Lily and Nora were in the sitting-room, in dressing-gowns. Lily was bottle-feeding Cathy. James saw Paul's eyes light up as he went quickly across to her, and she put up her face contentedly to be kissed. It was still odd to see clumsy, impulsive Lily with her large gestures and know-all opinions, scaled down to this gentle woman, beloved, bending in a curve over the sleepy baby.

Blanche's black and white dog was asleep on Nora's foot. Paul picked him up and took him into his lap, massaging the knuckle of his ear with a practised hand.

'He was the hit of the George.' James put his huge hand on his son-in-law's shoulder. Son-in-law came more easily to the tongue of the mind after the camaraderie of the smoky, malty saloon bar. 'Your dad and I and a rather hairy character did some close harmony.'

'Oh, Paul, not that awful barbershop quartet stuff.'

'What else?'

'In the pub? That's so – so American.'

'I am American.' Paul remained mild.

James knew that face on Lily. 'Are you angry because you couldn't go dancing up West?' he asked her.

'Yes.' Lily always said what she thought. 'I felt left out.'

Oi, what's this? She used to be sent upstairs for that pout when she was little. In years but not in size, because she had grown early. Better knock that off, ducky. Can't interfere with a man going off to the pub. James was going to chide her, but then there passed between his daughter and her husband a look of such naked devotion as he had never seen, much less felt.

Number one first. Never offer up your sanity to the god Eros. Keep 'em guessing, etc., etc. The safe principles he had proudly

followed shook like blancmange. There was something here –
Lily of all people – that was selfless and abiding.

'And you know what, Lil?' James broke into the union of the
look. 'Your husband has settled our future. I'm going to run a
country pub.'

'Pigs might fly,' Nora said. 'Too much work for you.'

'Oh, you'll help, of course. You can learn to pull beer and do
the ordering. Big cheeses in damp cloths in the larder. Hard-
boiled eggs from your own chickens. I'll carve the ham. Oak
beams. Darts. Jangly old piano with dripping candles. Log fires.
Beer garden in the summer. Everyone in the neighbourhood
drops in.' James leaned on his hands on the back of the sofa as if
he were behind a bar, and passed an imaginary damp cloth along
it. 'Drink up, Sir Percy, Reverend Sid, old Tom, me lad. This
one's on the house. Grand, eh?'

'New audience to show off to, Jam,' Lily said. 'Give them a
break at the George.'

'They'll miss me,' James warned.

'Like a hole in the head.' Nora had learned some new phrases
from Paul, popping them primly from her practical mouth.

Upstairs, James was still full of the plan.

'We'd be together all the time, me old dear. No more me off
to the post office salt mines and you off to that pest house at all
brutal hours of the day and night.'

'But you know what they say,' Nora was comfortably in bed.
'I married you for better or worse, but not for lunch.'

'I get so lonely for you, dear.' Before he turned out the light,
he saw himself in the dressing-table mirror, lugubrious in his
broad-striped pyjamas, big crooked nose, mouth and eyes pulled
down like a basset-hound.

'It's all right,' Nora said. 'I'm here. There now.'

When he climbed into her twin bed (she had used the excuse of
his imaginary bad back to sell their soft old double, genesis of
Lily and Blanche), she took him to her in a motherly fashion.
'There now, lovey.'

'It's awful that I never see you,' Lily said to Ida on the phone. 'I've had you on my mind.'

'Too bad there's nothing better on it.'

Lily sounded guilty, poor old Lil, with her incurable passion for taking people on and doing right by them.

'I need to see you, Eye,' she said, but did she really, with her successful husband and her two children and her house in Newton and probably a lot of new friends? She doesn't need me, Ida thought, without bitterness, just as a statement of fact.

Although Ida could drive now and had a bashed-in grey Chevrolet with rust-chewed flanks and a low seat from which she could hardly see over the wheel, she would not go to Newton. She did not want Lily to come up to Watkins, with Buddy the way he could be, so they met at a Howard Johnson's restaurant on the highway.

Lily's two little girls were beautiful. The four-year-old was dark and intense, staring with shiny round eyes and not saying much, while the younger child was fair and fairylike and never stopped chattering nonsense.

Lily said Ida's children were beautiful too. She could not get over what a saint Bernie still was at ten years old.

'Paul's son was so mixed up and difficult at that age. I thought he came round to our side that first summer on the Cape, but his mother's still so possessive and difficult. She tells him, "Your father abandoned us." I try to straighten things out, but I can't say, "Your mother was the one who was sleeping around." And he's so unpredictable. One minute he's calling to say he wants to come to us, but then Barbara won't let him. The next, she's agreed to him staying with us, and he'll be all over the girls, playing with them and being very responsible, and then start shouting because we can't go to the movies since there's no baby-sitter, and calling his mother to come and fetch him home.'

'Well, he's fifteen.' Ida did not want any more of Lily agonizing over her stepson. 'When Bernie's a teenager, he'll probably be just as bad.'

'I don't see why, Ma,' Bernie said, eating salad. What kid his age chose salad in a restaurant?

'You can't go on being perfect for ever.'

He worried Ida sometimes, he really did. He ought to be a mess, seeing the way Buddy was with him, either yelling at him or indulging him, or coming home pig drunk and smashing things. Last time, he had hauled Bernie out of bed to come downstairs and listen to him raving, and when he threw up on the new couch-cover, Bernie, pale and skimpy in his shrunk pyjamas, had cleaned it up.

Lily was careful also to praise Maggie, and not to notice that she made gaping faces and did not finish words. At seven, she had grown pretty homely, with thick-lensed glasses in the passionate pink frames she loved, and a short pug nose like Verna Legge's side of the family. This bad luck made Ida love her more.

'She's just a bit slow, is all.'

Maggie never minded what she heard said about her.

Ida saw Lily take a breath before she risked asking, 'How does she get on at school?'

'Bit slow.' Ida put some pieces of hamburger bun back on Maggie's plate and mopped at the spilled juice. 'But it's a rotten school, on the base. Everyone knows that. If she can't read too good, that's the teacher's fault, not hers.'

'You don't think she should be tested?'

Four-year-old Isobel stared with those eyes like wet damsons. Maggie paid no attention.

'There's a place in Boston,' Lily began, smiling with her head on one side to cover her nosiness.

'Shut up,' Ida said. 'You leave us alone, eh?'

'All right, all right. My God, Eye, what's the matter with you?'

Lily raised her voice, which was still so English that people at neighbouring tables looked around. Cathy began to wail in her high-chair, and Bernie gave her one of his french fries.

'Gi' a fren' fry.' Maggie scowled, and Bernie gave her the biggest one he had been saving to eat last.

'There's so much help children can get,' Lily ploughed on. 'You haven't got the right to –'

'Just lay off of me,' Ida said. 'Just lay off.'

The doctor at the base, and the school, and other mothers, some of whom were just as nosy as Lily, had finally forced Ida to accept the truth about Maggie, but she was not going to let Lily feel sorry for her.

Buddy said Maggie was an idiot, which did not help, but there was nothing much Ida could do about Buddy. They lived pretty well, with enough food, and the Air Force paying for the furnace to roar all day and all night in the wicked New England winters, which somebody should have told Ida about before she left home to be a GI bride in her pink suit and crippling shoes.

'Remember those high heels I was going to cut a dash in, and I couldn't get them on when the plane landed?' Ida brought Lily back to the far-away adventure, which they never tired of remembering, because it carried their lost youth. Or was it because their lives were so different now, that it was the only shared topic? 'And now here we are in Hojo's, with a couple of kids each and my figure gone, even if yours is still more or less okay.'

'Just a couple of mums.' It was ice-cream time, and Lily was wiping sticky fingers with a wet paper napkin. 'You seem so good at it, but I don't think I am. I scream sometimes, don't I girls?'

'And hit,' Isobel said.

'You rat, I don't, not hard anyway, and only when you ask for it.' Lily came up red in the face from bending down to find a spoon on the floor. 'Paul's so patient with them, but then he doesn't have them all day. Here we are, those giddy girls from Iceland. Remember Wally following you about with a paper cup of Scotch? Here we are, talking about our children like every other mother you meet.'

'Who'd have thought it?' Ida said obligingly, although one of her reasons for marrying Buddy, aside from needing to escape, had been to have her own children and be like everybody else. 'You and your career. You were going to become this great social-worker person.'

'I still want to. I'm going to try to start working part time, when the girls go to school.'

'I want to go to school *now*,' Isobel said, folding her mouth in her determined way.

'Won' li' it.' Maggie shook her head exaggeratedly, making her thick, wiry Legge hair fly out.

'I will too. I know all about it,' said Isobel, who went to play-school twice a week.

'Will nah.'

'Will so.'

'Wi'nah. Hit her, Bern.'

'Cool it, Mags, or I'll take you outside.' Bernie was the best person to deal with Maggie when she got agitated.

'No no no I wanna don't wanna Mumma Mumma no no no,' from Cathy.

'I love all this,' Lily said, ignoring it, with her chin on her strong hand and her eyes focused inwards on herself. 'I thought it was all I'd ever want, with Paul, but I really do want to get back to work some day and do something that matters. I mean, make a small dent in the world. Don't you, Ida? Do you think about that?'

'Not much.'

When Lily got into her blessed saviour bit, Ida felt like an ant person left behind on earth by someone who soars away in a balloon. 'I don't know what I'll do.'

Right now, when she finally got back to 1009 Pershing, after getting a flat tyre outside Billerica and changing the wheel with Bernie's help and limping home on the leaky spare, she had Buddy to cope with.

He was on the swing shift in the warehouses, four to twelve, but he didn't come home till long after midnight, reasonably sober, but very jumpy and active in a rubbery sort of way that meant no more sleep for Ida.

She got up, to stop him waking Bernie, and came down in the fancy pink robe he had bought for her birthday. Depending on the jewellery and horse-racing situation, Buddy either had money in his pocket or he didn't. When he was flush, he would woo Ida with unpractical luxuries, and buy expansively for the children – overpriced dolls that Maggie broke or lost, a ten-speed bike that Bernie was not ready for.

Ida made him something to eat, and sat with him while he grumbled about the Air Force, and the Tech Sergeant he was going to kill, and the late movie on the television, which he always snapped on as soon as he came into the house, and his digestive system, which he was sure had cancer somewhere in it.

He was terrified of cancer and terrified of death. Where did he get that from? Nobody in his immediate family had had cancer, and Verna, from whom he had absorbed a lot of his whacky ideas, did not think about dying, because she was not going to do the world that favour.

'It's got me worried, Ay-eye-da.' He burped on the last chunk of boloney sandwich. He had grown a moustache like a small blackthorn hedge this year, to match his eyebrows. When he ate or talked or did both together, it went up and down. 'There's something there, I know there is. Like it was some kind of obstruction, so I can't get anything down.'

'Except three square meals a day, and snacks in between.'

'Don't get smart with me, doll. I'm a sick man.'

When he looked at her with his eyes turned up like that, and his rubbery body deflated, he was her pitiful child, which he loved to be, and Ida could not help melting into tenderness, as she did when Bernie or Maggie were sick. She left her puzzle book and sat on the couch by his chair and reached forward to take his hand and stroke it.

'Open it up,' he said. He was not her pitiful child any more. His brow came down and the round ball of his chin went out and the jumpy energy tightened his body. 'Open up the robe.' His moustache was wet at the corners of his mouth.

'No.' Ida pulled it closer over the astoundingly large breasts, which she would have liked when she was young, but were too heavy now, and drooping.

'Open the goddam robe.' He lunged at her and tore it open to get his hands inside.

'Don't, Buddy, that hurts.'

'That's what you like.'

She had never been able to rid him of that myth. Had Verna told him that too, about women? Is that what she required of poor old Shaker Legge?

When Buddy kissed her, she turned her head away, because she hated the feel and smell of the moustache. He sat on her lap and put an arm behind her head to hold her mouth hard against his, scrubbing the moustache around, so that when she finally pulled away, she felt as if she had been dragged face down along a dirt road.

'Good, huh? I grew it for you, babe. I know what women like.'

Poor fellow, he had only had a couple of women before Ida, except possibly his mother, which Ida wouldn't put past either of them. She didn't think he'd had anyone else since, because when he came home late, he was usually too pissed to function, although he talked as if he were the stud of all time.

'Get up the stairs.' He made his soft brown eyes go glinty, which he thought was lecherous. When she pushed him off her lap and stood up, he pulled the robe off her shoulders and tore the neck of her nightgown.

'No, Buddy, I told you. I've got my period.'

'That's a lie.'

It wasn't this time. That was probably why she had felt stupid and out of touch with Lily and her rapt ideals.

'Goddam lie.'

'Want me to prove it?'

'You're disgusting.' Buddy hated anything that happened below the waist, except sex. He had never changed a baby's diaper in his life.

'I'm tired. I'm going to bed.'

He grabbed her. 'If it's no, you stay here. We'll put on some records, live it up. Open a bottle of wine, kid.'

'Oh, God. Okay, then, come on.'

Ida turned off the television, took his hand, and led him like a child, giggling and poking at her, up the stairs. He dropped his fatigues on the floor and got heavily into bed.

'No tricks now, or I'll kill you, you stupid fat woman.'

'That'll be the day.' Ida went to the bathroom and took out her Tampax.

What Buddy thought was good sex was falling on you like a gibbering baboon and hurting you as much as was possible with a quick in-and-out method which was all he could ever manage. Women at the base talked about foreplay and female orgasm, and Cora and Duane Ellis kept a book by the bed, and tried things. But if Ida ever attempted to educate Airman Second Class Bernard Legge, he took it as a criticism, and became angrier and rougher.

Afterwards he rolled over and gave her his fat little bottom. Sometimes Ida still thought back to the narrow cold bedroom in Staple Street, and her father's trembling hands. The worst thing about him had been that occasionally she had almost liked it, at the same time as she hated it. Which was worse, George with his prayers and complicated rituals, or Buddy with his childishly brutal onslaughts?

'If my boyfriend Jackson hadn't got sent down all those years ago in Stafford,' Ida said aloud, to annoy Buddy, who was falling asleep, 'my life would have been different.'

'Yeah.' Buddy kicked a foot backwards. 'Worse.'

Coming back from the bathroom, Ida picked up Buddy's clothes from the floor. She checked the pockets and put his money in the mug on the bureau. At the bottom of the pants pocket she found a brooch in a tightly folded envelope, and took it to the window to look at it in the light of the street lamp.

Beautiful. The Elite Jewelry Company made some pretty gaudy stuff, hard to sell at the price they wanted, but this was a gorgeous gold pin with two hearts entwined, and what looked like diamonds, but must be zircons, set round the edges.

'I'm going to Margie's coffee,' she told Buddy next day. 'I'll take along the good-looking gold brooch as well as the earrings and charm bracelets. There's always women there looking for something special they want their husbands to buy for them.'

'What brewch?'

'It was in your pocket.'

'You silly cow, I told you to leave my things alone.'

'And let them go through the washer and drier? Oh, fine, fine. I'll know next time.'

'Where is it?'

'In the drawer with the rest of the Elite stuff.'

'Oh, Jesus.' Buddy ran up the stairs in his socks, with Maggie after him like a puppy. She had not gone to school today. When she cried and put two fingers in her mouth, upside down with the elbow stuck out, Ida usually let her miss the bus. What difference did it make? Ida could teach her as much at home.

During the week, a few more pieces appeared which Ida was not to show, because they were for special buyers. Cora and Duane came round to fetch a couple of rings with large blue stones.

'They look almost like sapphires.' Ida put on one of the rings. It was too big for her. Her fingers had remained small and fine. She twirled it around under the lamp to sparkle for Maggie, who had a nice eye for things of good taste. 'Marvellous what they can do.'

'Sure is.' Cora took the ring off Ida with her long curved nails that were coloured like jewels themselves. 'It's a new line. Keep it under your hat. They're not to be marketed until the price is right.'

'Are they stolen, then?' Ida asked for a joke.

'What kind of talk is that?' Cora looked at her sharply. 'In front of the kid.'

'That dummy don't know if it's Christmas or Easter,' Buddy said.

Unless you spoke directly to her, Maggie did not listen, like Bernie did, to what grown-ups were saying, or look at them; but why did he let her down to other people? He liked to cuddle Maggie when he was in a good mood, or roll with her on the floor until she giggled and shrieked from the tickling. On the road, he would sometimes repeat names of towns and makes of cars to her, as if he were trying to teach a parrot, so why couldn't he be loyal? Instead of trying to impress Duane and winking at Cora, who was supposed to be Ida's friend anyway.

'Don't knock it,' Cora said. 'Better than living with a genius like our Harvey.'

Cora and Duane, who was a flashy dresser, always had everything the best: kids, cars, stereo. Duane had one stripe on Buddy now.

Ida took Maggie to the kitchen to work on her reading book. If the others knew something she didn't know, she didn't want to know it anyway. She gave Maggie a piece of candy.

'Make the best of it, eh, Mags?'

That was how she had coped with this marriage, in this country. Millions of GI brides had given up and gone home. Ida had done well, making the best of it.

The next thing Buddy brought back from the bar was a small brown dog with a Ho Chi Minh beard, and a white patch over one eye.

'This guy gave it me to pay off a debt.' Buddy brought it in on a short piece of rope, and it gave Ida a short, squeaky bark and went under the table.

'You've gone soft,' Ida said.

'Give the kids a treat.'

The bark had woken Bernie. He hurtled down the stairs, and then up again to wake Maggie. Stupefied with sleep, and half blind without her glasses, she lay under the table, her arm over the watchful dog, her mouth curved up in a clownish slice-of-melon smile.

The dog's name was Abraham. 'A-ham.' Too difficult for Maggie, so Bernie shortened it to Adam.

'First man in the world, first dog at Ten-oh-nine Pershing.'

He adored the dog. He was the one who fed him, and ran out with him as soon as he came home from school, but Adam, an apologetic, insecure mutt, forever looking in corners and under furniture for something that wasn't there, attached himself to Maggie. He slept on her bed and padded about after her on long-haired feet that were too big, as if he were wearing someone else's socks. She pulled at his hair and his wispy beard, and tied scarves over his frayed ears, and patted him as if she were beating a carpet, but he stuck by her.

Maggie had always been given to wandering off. When she was little, Ida sometimes tied her to a small tree with a long piece of clothes line around her waist. One of the neighbours complained.

'She's to be shut indoors away from the sun, then?' Ida squared up to the neighbour. She was not afraid of any of these women, including a couple of English wives from Surrey, who fancied they would not have spoken to Ida, back in England.

'Put up a fence around your backyard.'

'My husband's going to.'

They had priced the lengths of fencing and the posts, and he was going to borrow Franklin's pick-up to fetch it; but he never did.

Now when Maggie wandered off on one of her dreamy walks, along the paths among the pines and scrub oaks, or across the backs of the houses toward the baseball park, from which she sometimes had to be brought back by Ida or Bernie, the dog went with her. Just about the time when Ida began to worry, she would hear the high single bark, which sounded like 'Yuck!' Adam would be scratching anxiously at the back door, his lamb's tail, which he never wagged, between his legs, and Maggie sitting on the bottom step with her back to the house, as if she were starting out rather than coming home.

Buddy had been scared, when he brought the dog from the bar, that Ida would be angry with him and throw it out. He was pleased to find himself a success. He had done something for the kids. He was a good father. He and Ida told anecdotes about Adam at the Enlisted Men's Club. For a while there, they were kind of a happy family. It was cute to see Bernie out back with his friends and their dogs, throwing sticks for them, and taking them off into the woods to look for squirrels.

Ida showed Maggie how to write the dog's name, ADAM, and told her some bits of natural history: how dogs were once wild, like wolves, and how they lived by their noses. When Adam went smelling from tree to tree and checked the fire hydrants and the wheels of parked cars to find out which other dogs had been around, 'He's reading the paper,' Ida told Maggie, 'to see what the local news is.'

Buddy either screamed ferociously at Adam or worked him up to excitement, or fed him chocolate, the way he did with the powerful unruly dogs at Leggeland. Bernie had a special tender face for Adam, his bright eyes softened with love. When his father forgot to give him his allowance and then gave him too much, he put some of it away for his old age, and bought dog biscuits with the rest, instead of candy.

Ida made up stories about the brown dog, which had become the central focus of the family, pulling them together.

'Adam used to be a queen's lap-dog; he wore a jewelled collar. Adam was a spy in his former life. That's why he grew a beard and patched out one eye. When it snowed in Moscow, he wore a fur coat and ski boots, four of them.'

'You're crazy, Ah-eye-da.' Buddy enjoyed it too.

'He had an electric tail warmer, he says. Once it shorted. That's why he only has half a tail.'

'Adam says' was a way to get Maggie's attention. 'Adam says to go back upstairs and make yourself decent. You brush his hair, he says, so why can't you brush yours?'

Maybe Lily was right. Maybe Ida might go back to some kind of work one day. She could be a teacher.

Adam still searched uneasily in empty corners, and spent a lot of time poking about in the cellar, as if he had buried bones there.

One Saturday morning, he suddenly rushed through the kitchen, slipping on Ida's waxed floor, and sat by the door with his head on one side, white patch up, one ear cocked, one dangling.

'Adda!' Maggie shouted at him.

'He wants to go out. Let him out, honey.'

Maggie opened the door and went out with the dog.

Half an hour later, they had not come back. Almost an hour. No frenzied scratching at the door, as if wild beasts were after him. Ida went outside and called the dog, and whistled her special whistle for Maggie, the first three notes of 'There was I, Waiting at the Church'.

'Don't pee your pants,' Buddy said. 'She'll turn up, she always does.'

'Adam will bring her home,' Bernie said.

'She went out without her jacket.'

'So what, it's warm, and she's got her sweater on, ain't she?'

'She'll be tired.'

'Nah.' Buddy was doing his push-ups on the living-room floor, with Bernie beside him, thin arms collapsing. 'She's like me.'

Maggie was solid and rubbery. Bernie was slight, like Ida had been, and light on his feet as she still was, as if her extra bulk was air.

Buddy let himself down and lay prone. Bernie jumped on his back. 'Let's you and I go fish in the pond.'

'I'm too busy.'

'Puppa. I wanna go fishing, Puppa.' The infantile whine was obnoxious at ten years old, but it still worked with his father. They went off to buy worms at the bait shop.

Ida walked along to the baseball field, where some fathers were chucking balls for sons to catch in the enormous leather mitts which still made Ida smile, although she was so Americanized. When she used to go with Jackson to the county ground, naked hands were all that grabbed the hurtling cricket ball out of the air.

No one had seen Maggie. Ida walked down the path that crossed empty land to the Commissary. It was closed now. Nothing in the parking lot. No Maggie. She'll be home, time I get back, wondering where I am.

No Maggie on the step, too lazy or too oblivious to open the door.

Ida went to the clearing in the straggly woods behind her house and asked some of the children who were playing there on the bike bumps and in the tottering forts. She went to all the nearby houses, including that of the Englishwoman who had hung out the Union Jack on Independence Day.

'Worried?' Cora asked.

'Not really. She always comes home.'

'I'd be worried sick,' Cora said unhelpfully. 'Here, I'll help.' She drove Ida around the streets in her car, making wider and wider circles.

'Let's go back,' Ida said. 'I know she'll be there.'

Buddy and Bernie were there. They had not been able to buy bait. At noon, Buddy called the base police. Two men in white helmets and leggings came round in a jeep and talked to them calmly in deep voices, as if their anxiety were the only problem. After lunch – Buddy could always eat – Adam turned up, dusty-pawed and drooping as if he were tired, or guilty.

'Where have you been? Where's Maggie?' They took him out on a leash, and encouraged him: 'Come on, Adam, find Maggie. Good dog, take us to Maggie. Maggie! Maggie!'

Ida's lips were dry from repeating the sad little whistle.

Adam would go along with them, but he would not lead ahead in any direction.

'Useless mutt.' Buddy aimed a kick at him.

'Don't, Puppa.' Bernie went down on his knees to put his arms round the dog.

'He leads her off somewhere and then comes crawling back with his belly on the ground. I'd never oughta brought him home.'

'It's not your fault.' Ida was making herself stay calm.

'Who says it is? Goddam dog.' Buddy jerked the leash, and the dog choked and coughed up foam.

Adam did not find the glasses. Bernie did. At the corner of their street, Maggie's bright pink glasses lay in a crack in the sidewalk.

'She don't see so good without them,' Ida told the police when they came back. 'I guess she's lost.'

Dusk fell. Night crept in to separate Maggie from her like a wall. Dozens of people were out with flashlights. The military police drove around in jeeps and trucks with spotlight beams. Walkie-talkies appeared. The alarm was out to the town police and the cruiser cars, in case Maggie had wandered off the base, although she never went that far.

The search was stopped briefly after midnight, and started again at dawn.

For some reason, Lily called Ida early on Sunday morning to see how she was. When Ida heard her voice, she began to cry noisily, like a howl. Gasping and sobbing, she trembled out the words of crisis, and Lily felt a void open up within her, transposing Isobel or Cathy for Maggie.

'There's people come from all around, Lil. Hundreds of them, out searching.'

'I'm coming,' Lily said.

'No, you can't.'

'I'll be there.'

Lily left the children with their grandmother Muriel, and she and Paul drove north. Along the road from the main gate of Watkins to the housing area, they saw groups of people, some with dogs, some men in uniform, going in and out of the trees and bushes, beating at the brushwood with long sticks, and calling. There was a crowd round Ida's duplex. She was inside with some of the women, getting soup and coffee ready. A brown dog was tied to an outside drainpipe. It sat leaning against the wall of the house, as if it were eavesdropping.

As Lily got out of the car, she saw Buddy coming down the road with his son, tired, with a black moustache and a sooty stubble of beard. He walked on without looking at her.

'I'm Ida's friend Lily.' She went to them and put an arm round Bernie's shoulders.

'Oh, yeah.'

'This is my husband, Paul Stephens.'

'Yeah? Well, you come at a bad time.'

'That's why I've come.'

'You shouldn't have,' Buddy muttered, meaning, 'I don't want you,' not, 'How nice of you.'

'I couldn't stay away. I'm so sorry, I –'

'Come on, son.' Buddy took Bernie's arm and pulled him away from Lily. 'Let's go get us something to eat.'

'He's a pig.' Lily made a face at his back, as he went through the people outside the house, paying no attention to anyone.

'He's going through hell.'

'He's a pig anyway. Do we dare go in?'

Ida saw them in the road and rushed out, short and wide and frenzied in jeans and a black jersey top that were too tight. She clung to Lily, and then Paul put his arms round her and kissed her. He had kissed her goodbye that last morning on the plane from Iceland, and called her Ida No, because she was so uncertain about her marriage.

Ida clung to him too, standing on tiptoe in small coloured sneakers.

'Sorry.' She righted herself, and pushed loose ends of hair behind her ears and took another turn on the childish pony-tail fastener with bobbles that held back her long straight hair. 'Oh, Lil, what'll I do?'

'It'll be all right, Eye. Someone will find her.'

'She's a wanderer. You don't know. Maggie's not like a normal seven-year-old. She's retarded. A bit. I don't know if you –'

'Sort of. I'm sorry I bullied you at Hojo's.'

'I'm sorry I was stubborn. I didn't want you to know.'

'Of course. I'd be the same.'

'Why am I always afraid you won't understand? Oh, Lil, they think now someone might have taken her. Her picture's in the papers this morning. It's going out on TV. Hundreds of people are searching, not just Air Force, but civilians too from off base. They're so great, all these people, but suppose she –' she looked up, her eyes fixed steadily on Lily's – 'she could be dead.'

Buddy shouted for her from the house.

'But she's not.' Ida nodded and squared back her shoulders. 'We'll find her.'

'You've got guts,' Paul said.

'Hope so.' She hurried into the house, with her elbows working.

Paul and Lily went with a truckload of men and women and teenagers who were going to walk in line through the woods on the other side of the hangars and landing field.

'This is ghastly, but it's exciting.' Paul sat with his arm round Lily, very close on the floor of the truck. 'I'm scared for Ida, and the poor little girl, but I'm glad we're part of it. I never went on a rescue before, did you?'

Lily thought about the Family Centre and taking away the Warrens' battered son, and the time Mrs Daley's daughter had driven her in the lop-sided van down a one-way street and up on the pavement to pass double-parked cars, because they thought Mrs Daley had taken an overdose; but she said, 'No,' because this was their first adventure together.

In the woods, she stayed close to Paul, needing him, not knowing how to look in the undergrowth, where anything might be hidden, not knowing what it would be like to see a hand, a foot, a child's dead face.

'Spread out!' Their leader was a large man in a plaid shirt and heavy boots. 'Cover as much ground as you can, about thirty yards each. Scan in front, each side and behind you. Gently with the poles.'

They moved slowly through the woods in a long ragged line. Paul was at the end. His red jacket moved farther out and disappeared behind pine trees into a hollow. The man on Lily's other side had stopped to turn over a mound of dead leaves.

She was alone. Ahead of her, the trees thinned and the ground rose, sandy, with pine needles and angled broken branches and trailing brambles. She walked to the top of the rise, above small oaks crowded into a dip where she could hear Paul moving on her left, and could see the young girl in the yellow slicker up ahead. The man on her right caught up and went on down, bent over, poking his long branch everywhere, stopping, turning over dead branches with his foot.

What does he think he'll find? What's the good of this? It's something you do when a child disappears, hundreds of people like me and Paul, not able to sit at home and do nothing. But Ida's child may be across several borders in a distant state by now. Soon she'll be a picture on a notice in post offices: 'Have you seen this child?'

Let me find her. Lily clenched her stick in both hands. Let *me*, she prayed to the God within herself, which was the only one she knew. Let her be found, but let it be me who finds her.

They gathered with the leader at the far edge of the wood, by a cindery road which led dry and flat to abandoned concrete workshops.

'We're off base now, folks. Let's comb back through the woods again, and check with some of the other groups at the meeting point. By the water tower.'

'Let's not.' Lily took hold of Paul's arm. 'Let's go and have a quick look in those buildings before the others do.'

'Too far away?'

'Not from the houses. The road curves round.'

'They must have looked there.'

'*We* haven't. I want to be the one who finds her.'

'So do I. So does everyone who's out looking.'

'I'm hungry.'

He gave her half a chocolate bar: He always had everything.

Lily found Maggie in a hidden angle behind two walls. She was sitting in a deep concrete drain with her knees drawn up, picking at her bare feet and looking at nothing, looking right through Lily, as she stumbled over rusted pipes in the grass towards her, shouting for Paul.

Let it be me who finds her. Once that was satisfied, Lily wanted to be only part of the team effort. Paul carried Maggie down the long road on his back, dirty bare feet dangling, and set her down to wave both his arms at a camouflaged truck, crossing up ahead. When the excitement started, Lily found that she wanted it to be everyone's triumph.

'Hop up in back,' the man holding Maggie in the cab of the truck told them.

'Let's walk, Paul.'

'Don't you want to see Ida's face?'

Lily shook her head. It didn't matter now. A great warm wash of light had flooded through her. The trunk and branches and twigs of all her veins were lit with a golden glow.

When they reached the house, they stood on the edge of the crowd. People and cars and photographers and television cameras. Buddy and Bernie on the front step, having their pictures taken.

'There they are!' One of the men from the truck saw Paul's red jacket. Attention swung to them.

'It was my wife, not me. She got the hunch about the buildings.'

'It was luck.' Lily could hear the purr of the television camera. 'Anyone could have found her. What's it matter? She was found.'

Lily and Paul were famous for ten minutes. A weakened Buddy, pale and at a loss, took Paul into the house for a beer. An Air Force officer stopped the press from getting inside.

Lily went upstairs. Bernie was in his room, lying on his bed with the dog. Maggie was in the bath, solidly fleshed, thick-legged, playing boisterously with boats. Ida knelt on the wet floor, not crying, not smiling, just looking at her, her face pinched, as it used to be, with bruised shadows, as if she had been hit across the eyes. She looked quite old, with a dead sort of passive resignation.

Lily was the one who cried.

Sis and Jeff had come down from New Hampshire to help with the search. Henry could not get away from the grain mill, but Verna came on Monday with Vernon and Laverne, who had grown to be like Phyllis at her age, very bossy and demanding.

'How did you lose Maggie?' Laverne bounced in, wanting to know.

'I didn't,' Ida snapped. 'She got herself lost. And you get lost too.'

'Cut that out, Hilda.' Mrs Legge followed Laverne into the house. 'Where do you get the nerve to speak to the kid that way, after what you done?'

She had come to comfort Buddy, who had been given two days' leave after his ordeal. Bernie had been allowed to stay home from school. He and secret, silent Vernon went out with Adam, and Laverne went upstairs to look through Ida's clothes closet, Ida suspected. The Elite Jewelry drawer was locked, or she would have been into that.

Buddy and Ida had not talked much about what they had been through. It was over. They were no longer in the news, and Maggie was just the same as she had been before, neutral in her own world, neither contented nor disgruntled. It had not brought Ida and Buddy closer, but it had not pushed them apart.

Verna had come not only to comfort her favourite fella, but to scold Ida for being a bad mother. Nothing Ida said made any difference, and Buddy did not stand up for her. He kept his eyes on his mother, who was gross in a green top as wide as a baseball field, and chumped his moustache up and down, and said, 'Hey, yeah,' when called on to agree that it was Ida's fault.

Ida said, 'Thanks a bunch,' and went out with Maggie to the Commissary to get some things to make spaghetti sauce. When she returned, Bernie was back, and Verna had started on the dog. It was true that Adam might have led Maggie astray, but equally, he might have just been following her faithfully in her wandering.

'Takes her off and then abandons her. What kind of a dog is that?' Verna demanded to be told. 'Got the devil in him, anyway. I never liked his looks.'

'He's a good dog, Grandma,' Bernie said in his clear, confiding voice. 'He did come back and try to tell us something. It's not his fault that we were too dumb to understand.'

'Humph.' Verna looked at her grandson with a face that would terrify a more timid child.

'You can't blame him for not leading us to Mags.' Bernie stood in front of her with the dog by his side, his hand on Adam's head. 'He's not Lassie, after all.'

'He's not fit to be around kids,' declared Verna, whose own dogs nipped and snarled and killed neighbours' chickens, and the fluffy barn kitten that Jeff had given Vernon last Christmas. 'How can you keep him here after what he did?'

'We like him,' Ida said.

'Buddy don't. I can see that. That dog will take that poor child off again, you watch, and next time you won't be so lucky.'

'Hey, yeah,' Buddy said. 'Goddam dog.'

But Adam had been a good friend to all of them.

By the time Verna left, having allowed Ida to make a whole pan of spaghetti sauce and then said they wouldn't stay to eat, Buddy had gone from beer to vodka, and was belligerent. When his mother drove off with his brother and sister, he went down the road to Duane, and borrowed his 38-revolver. He came back and took Adam behind the house and shot the dog, in front of Bernie.

That's it, Ida thought. I've had it with him. There was nothing she could do about it, but the knowledge – that's it – lay with her like a reprieve, although she went through all the familiar motions in the house, where no one told stories, and there was nothing to hold them all together any more.

The war in Viet Nam had dragged on and on, and most people wished they would put something else on the television news for a change. Watkins had lost some of its personnel. Memorial services were quite frequent in the chapels, and Bob Grainger, whose boys had been in the same class as Bernie at school, came out of hospital in a wheelchair, addicted to pain-killing drugs. Ida had never thought they would send Buddy to Nam, because what use would he be to them? But they ran out of people, and

Buddy had to go. His CO promised him a promotion when he came back.

'*If* I come back, Ah-eye-da.' He was doleful. He thought he was going to die. Ida was almost sorry for him.

He went up to New Hampshire to say his last farewell to his mother, who would have written to her congressman to protest, if she had known his name and had a bit of writing paper. When he came back, he stopped off at the Fisherman and got drunk, side-swiped a parked car at the corner of Lemay Street and Pershing, and charged up the stairs to have a last bash at Ida.

'Buddy, shut the door.' Bernie might be awake. He had slept with his door open since Adam had gone. 'Get up and shut the *door*!'

He slobbered over her, giggling. His moustache stank of liquor. Ida slid out and shut the door of the room, and he was up, crouched like an orang-outang, and he swung her back on to the bed, wrenching her arm, and pounced on top of her.

She gasped, winded. 'Don't get me pregnant.' She was even more scared of that since Maggie's wandering. Another child would kill her. She thought he had dislocated her shoulder. 'Buddy, for God's sake –'

She was nothing to him. He might as well have been screwing the mattress.

Ida had thought that Bernie would be upset about Buddy leaving. But the morning after the bedroom door had been open, the poor boy told his father, 'I'll kill you if you kill my Mom.'

Buddy, who was hung over, eating chocolate-frosted cornflakes like a child, petulant, swung back a hand and clipped him.

'That does it,' Ida said. 'That's it.'

Some time after Buddy left for overseas, one tall man and one short one rang Ida's front doorbell. It played chimes. Buddy had put it in for her last Christmas, then had to move it higher, because Maggie played with it all the time.

'Mrs Legge?' the short man asked.

'That's me.'

'Legal wife of Airman Second Class Bernard Wyvern Legge?'

'At the moment.'

Ida was feeling jaunty. It was a golden fall day, and she was going to the shopping mall with her funny friend Shirley, who didn't give a damn for anybody, and it was good to be married with children, and without a husband.

'Detective Sergeant Nutting.' The short man opened a wallet and showed her his badge. The tall one did the same, without saying his name.

Ida took them inside. The new woman at Number 1006 opposite was cleaning her front windows.

Detective Sergeant Nutting had reason to suspect that Airman Legge had received and passed on stolen jewellery.

'No way.'

'But you knew about it, ma'am.'

'Don't drag me into it.' Ida was furious. She had heard no more about the brooch and rings, and she had given Buddy credit for staying clear of any funny business. 'My husband is in Viet Nam. He's a war hero.'

'We understand.' If Nutting had worn a hat, he would have removed it.

'I don't know nothing about anything.'

'Fine. I believe you are friendly with a certain Mrs Ellis, on the base.'

Ida found herself telling them about Duane and Cora. Why not? They had got Buddy into the Elite Jewelry business, and they had trapped him into this. As a receiver of stolen goods, he wouldn't have been smart enough to operate on his own.

They already knew about Duane and Cora. It was Cora who had put them on to Buddy. So Ida could have kept her mouth shut and not made herself feel like a louse for playing the same cheap rotten game as Cora.

But she hadn't exactly grassed on her. She had just answered questions truthfully, like she had about Jackson all those years ago, when the oily CID man stated, 'You know where he is, don't you.'

'We're getting out,' she told Bernie and Maggie when they came home from school.

'Ow?' Maggie went back to the door. It was what she used to ask Adam.

'We're not going to stay here.'

The housing office always needed quarters. Ida told them she was giving up the house, and they offered her a rental and cost-of-living allowance. She sold the Chevvy for ninety-three dollars, sent the stuff from the house to storage, put the first month's allowance towards air fares, and went to England to see her family.

George and Clara Lott, in Christmas cards and very rare letters, had suggested in a lukewarm fashion, 'We ought to see our grandchildren.' Well, they should. It was time now.

Five

$\mathcal{W}$hen James and Nora Spooner had been landlords of the Duke's Head for about five years, they left it for a three-week holiday with Lily in Massachusetts. James wanted to do this long before, but Nora, who was so serious about the pub that she would have taken all the fun out of it if he had let her, would not risk leaving it.

'We're establishing ourselves. We've got to be here in person. Slow and steady wins the race, you know. The first five years is the worst.'

'I thought that was marriage, Nor.' Jam did a fake duck.

'No, that's the second five, and then the third, and the fourth.'

'You hear how she talks to me?'

They were having this conversation in the bar, where the customers enjoyed the double act of Nora being so brisk and sensible, and Jam the eternal little boy in trouble, playing games to please everyone and always getting it in the neck. If Nora had a bladder on a stick, they could have done a nice Punch and Judy turn.

The Duke's Head was in a built-up village on the border of Bucks. and Oxfordshire. Too near the motorway, said new commuter residents who would not have been able to come here and put plumbing and sun porches into old cottages and joined all the local activities that the villagers avoided, if it had not been for the motorway.

Jam had been forty-nine when they moved in, so he remained officially in the neighbourhood of fifty, mature enough to cast sage sayings over the bar, but in his prime as far as jokes and easy talk went, and meeting the customers on their own level, which was what you had to do.

He did his mein Host act, but not as a jolly beaming landlord. It was better to be lovably eccentric and a bit quirky, so that new people craved for him to remember their name. The subtle impression he liked to foster, which made the Duke the success it was growing to be, even though the Lamb still had the cricket club, was that the customers were not doing him a favour, but the other way round.

Everybody wanted to have their name given to them, to feel they belonged: 'They know me here.'

Nora greeted them quietly with the tight little smile that still dented the dimple that had driven Jam mad when he courted her in the crankcase shed at the fighter aircraft factory.

'The usual?'

But if James did not care for them, and they had brought a guest they hoped to impress with the quaintness of the pub and their own acceptance here, he might make them suffer, until he chose to come round from behind the bar and start telling the tale, which would have any tricky customer eating out of his hand with gratitude.

Nora had mastered the ordering and the accounts and the occasional part-time help they employed. James had learned how to take care of the beer, and had brought the social side to a fine art.

'It caters to the ham in Jam,' he told Lily. 'You were right. It's a God-given audience.'

But enough was enough. A West End star wouldn't stand for being on stage matinées and evenings seven days a week, even though earning far more than James, whose profits, after meeting the expenses of the house behind the pub, were ploughed back by Nora into the business. They needed a break. Jenny Dobson, who had been at the Duke's Head before they came, could manage the bar food and the serving and cleaning up, and muttonchop Melvyn, who helped at weekends, could handle the bar in his fluffy sideboards, and shifting the barrels round in the cellar at night, as long as he kept the contents outside himself, and not within. Blanche, living nearby with that weedy young husband to whom she wouldn't give kennel-room if he were one of the terriers she bred, would come in and do Nora's office stuff.

Boston was wild. Jam travelled everywhere on buses and the archaic subway, talking to strangers and telling them about the London Underground. He could imagine some English tourists being shy and lost amid the noisy bustle of hurrying people who knew where they were going, but not James Spooner. He had learned long ago to make the best of looks that were more comic than handsome. Now that his receding hair accentuated his big crooked nose, and the fat that used to fill out the skin of his face had fallen into his paunch, he exploited himself as an amusing devil you'd not be afraid to get to know.

When Nora was with him, she fussed. 'I'm sure people in Boston don't talk to strangers in lifts.'

Lily told him, 'It's easier to get arrested over here, or shot. I'm not going to drive you around if you're going to make signs at women out of the back window.'

Out with the children, if he stopped to chat with another family on the Common or the harbour excursion boat, or in the Aquarium, Isobel called fiercely, 'Gramps, come 'eer!' and slapped her thigh as if he were a dog.

James did not want to leave Newton, which was only a short subway ride from the stimulating city of Boston, but Lily and Paul had rented a house on Cape Cod, and that was where everyone else wanted to go.

The journey took two cars, crammed with suitcases, the dog, Isobel's friend Rose Mary, and more cartons of food and washing powder than they could possibly need in two weeks, unless Cape Cod was the outback, in which case, why leave Boston?

The way down was a bit glum. Monotonous fir trees on either side of the long, straight, featureless road, few houses, a flat land with glimpses of sea and marsh. James was cheered by the accumulating lines of cars among which they travelled, and, as they approached the canal bridge, there began to be gift shops, restaurants, ice-cream stands, motels and supermarkets.

'Don't mind the Strip,' Paul apologized, as they climbed the high arc of the bridge, with the swift tidal water swirling far below. 'The Cape's not like that, although a lot of it is beginning to be ruined by too many people and too much building.'

'The march of progress.' James was quite keen on progress, as long as he didn't have to make it himself. The new bright brick houses in their village at home were better looking than the old dingy council houses with their propped-up gates and narrow back-compounds of chickens and Brussels sprouts. The village shop was now a mini-market, which stocked almost everything you could want, at shocking prices, but the council tenants seemed to be rolling in money, on or off the dole, and poured in and out of the mini-market as if it were going out of style.

Paul and Lily had found a low house made of grey wood, with sheds and a leaning barn, set back from the main street of the village in small rough fields with broken walls and fallen fences.

'Originally a farmhouse when this end of the village was all open land,' Paul said. 'Built in 1880.'

'Gee,' Jam obliged. Part of the Duke's Head had been built about 1650.

Lily and Paul thought it was perfect. Two of the bedrooms were under the roof, with steeply sloped ceilings and a smell of damp. The long living-room had scrappy wicker furniture and rag rugs over the silt of last summer's sand. The kitchen was narrow and inconvenient, with taps that roared and knocked, and cracked linoleum counters that Nora set about briskly with a sponge, grumbling about the last tenants. The front porch was decorated with broken shells and dried-out geranium plants, and two elderly rocking-chairs, where Jam established himself with his bourbon to see who came down the road.

Most people went by in cars. Anyone who walked – children, dogs, old men in long-peaked caps, boys with huge feet balanced on skateboards, bubble-gum girls with shorts like brief knickers – was hailed by James.

Pretty soon, he was known at the post office down the street, where mail had to be collected. Talk about progress.

'When this drops on to your mat,' he wrote on picture post-cards of lobsters to favoured bar customers and to Jonesey in Wimbledon, 'give thanks for twice-a-day delivery in the dear old backward mother country.'

Business at the Cape Cod post office was so slow, they probably read all the postcards, going and coming.

James became a regular at the little corner drug store. Every day, if they weren't off on an expedition, he put on his new Boston hat, white cotton with little holes for sweat, a striped band and the brim turned up all round. Jam did not just put on a hat. He took it by the crown and dropped it on from a distance, at an insecure angle. Jaunty. He had found an old crooked cane on a hook behind the back door, and he rattled it along picket fences and aimed it at passing cars, as he walked down with his two granddaughters and Rose Mary to buy them ice-cream sodas at the drug store's soda-fountain.

He sat with them on a stool and chatted to the lorry drivers who turned off the road for coffee, or the plumbers and policemen who craved ice-cream as Englishmen craved beer.

The shapely woman who made coffee and pulled levers to put foam in the girls' sodas and bent upside down to scoop chocolate ice-cream from the bottom of the container, raising a nimble leg backwards, was called Dodo. She learned to call him Jam, and he carried home far more inside information about this neighbourhood than Lily or Paul had guessed at in their years of summer renting.

'It's lucky for us,' said Isobel, who was no dope, 'that you like to come down to the drug-store and make passes at Dodo.'

The first week, Paul took them to Martha's Vineyard, which was like the Isle of Wight, only less so, and drove them round to see folksy museums and gift shops where everything smelled of scented candles, and to eat fish dinners off oval plates that would have held a whole roast turkey. The second week, when Paul had to go to Boston every day to work, Lily and Nora and the children wanted to go to the beach every day. James sometimes preferred to stay behind in the shade of the porch, and listen to the commercials on the radio.

'The rocking-chair eases my lumbago,' he said, when Nora appeared in the square mauve beach-coat above sturdy bare legs that ran straight down into her new plastic sandals.

'You've not got lumbago.'

'I have now. Too much sitting on sand.'

One evening, James put his sporty hat on the front of his head against the low red searchlight of the sun, and walked with Lily down a sandy path to Hidden Harbor, the secret place she had discovered, with a shallow inlet behind, and a curve of clean sand and flimsy yellow shells, that was empty because it was private.

'We're not allowed here. But the shore ought to belong to everyone,' she said, in the democratic voice she had picked up at the college.

'But property is sacred.' James had thrown more cats and dogs and children out of the garden at 127 Granada Road than you could, as Dodo had taught him to say, shake a stick at. 'You got anarchy else.'

Jam was afraid of no man, but he respected the rights of Colonel Tilley and Sir Allen, who had the two big houses and what was left of the farmland around his village. Although he laughed about them with others in the bar, and imitated Sir Allen's twitch and stammer, he felt, as landlord of the Duke's Head, that he was correct in being tickled pink when they came into the pub.

'I'm too lucky, Jam,' Lily worried. 'I've got Paul and the girls and all this — well, I haven't got it, but it's here — and my nice house in Newton. And Paul.'

'You said him.'

'Not often enough. Paul! Paul! Paul!' She screamed at a flight of squabbling seagulls. 'He's my life. I'd die for him.'

'That wouldn't help.' James was skipping flat stones into the path of the red sun on the still water.

'I've got it all, and I don't know why, when I think of all the struggle and misery people have to go through. "Why me?" I think. Why not Ida?'

'Why indeed? Who's Ida?'

'My mate. You know, the one who had to come and take refuge with us last year, with all the children. She lives in squalor, Jam. I wanted her to come down here, but —'

'But you're lumbered with Yours Truly and Co.'

'Don't fish,' Lily said automatically. 'She wouldn't let herself come. But I don't think she's ever seen anything like this in the whole of her life.'

Lily's secret place was beautiful, but it was desolate, and the opposite shore only a faint line across the bay. James preferred the big public beach, where there were muscular male and female lifeguards, in case he swam too far out after beer and hot dogs.

There were also droves of girls in assorted shapes to chuckle about to Nora ('Not in front of the children'), and pretend to lust after, although he secretly feared he might be impotent before he was out of his fifties, and headed for a long and foolish old age, unless he could muster the nerve to shoot himself.

When he went down to the sea in his Hawaiian swimming-trunks, he sucked in his paunch and stuck out his chest, elbows out to show his biceps, which had been improved, since his Post Office days, by all those beer barrels.

If Cathy and Isobel each took a hand and walked into the sea with him, the muscle-man image gave way to the kindly grandfather, which meant he could let his stomach go, and flounder about with Cathy in the shallows, instead of having to strike out in a manful crawl, and try to look as if his feet were not on the bottom when he stopped for breath.

The best part of the beach was going home to coffee and jelly doughnuts and a shower in the downstairs bathroom, which was stuck on at the back of the house as if it had once been a woodshed.

'Let's put a shower in at the Dukerie, Nora.'

'If we're talking water pressure –' she liked all these new fad phrases, although they did not suit her face or voice, 'you're not on.'

'Why not? Why lie in your own dirty bathwater?'

'Speak for yourself. Because the tank's too low.'

When Paul came home, Jam would be on the porch in a clean T-shirt that said 'I luv Cape Cod' and plaid Bermuda shorts, with his first bourbon of the day. Before Paul's car had stopped by the side of the house, the screen door would bang open and Lily would fly out with the dog, an apron over the wet swimsuit she had not bothered to take off, thick hair bouncing, the bottom half of her face smiling, the top half frowning with the intensity of her emotion. Paul would get out of the car quickly to be ready for her onslaught.

She threw herself at him and they stood as one person, embracing as desperately as if they had been parted by six months and a war and a couple of mountain ranges. The dog sat back and waited for his turn, but if Cathy had followed Lily out, her fine hair still slicked down from the sea, she poked at her mother or father until they separated far enough to let her stand between them.

Isobel and Rose Mary would be down at the bottom of the back field with Tony, the dark boy who lived on the other side

169

of the fence with a jumbled family and too many barking dogs. He and Isobel were very thick, although he was five years older. They climbed trees and rode bikes and built a tree-house together. Tony's mother was part American Indian, and his father was part negro.

'You let the girls play with a black boy?' James asked Lily.

'Shut up, you can't talk like that over here,' Lily said. 'He's not black anyway. His grandfather came from the Cape Verde Islands, so he's Portuguese.'

'Don't confuse the issue.' James knew black when he saw it.

One evening, Paul came home early and Tony's big sister came up to stay with the children, while the grown-ups went to the local summer theatre. As they went in with the crowd, a glorious creature swam towards them through the men in coloured jackets and the women in flowered dresses, like a great angel fish among lesser fry.

'Poll – and my English lily!'

'Hullo Paige, how lovely you look. This is my mother and father. Paige Tucker.'

'Oh, my Gahd, isn't this the most delightful thrill to meet you lovely folks?'

She put her ringed hand into Jam's. It was like holding the crown jewels. 'Go on in, you beautiful people, I don't want you to miss a word of this fabulous show.' Her hair was a dawn cloud, her mermaid eyes were framed in glittering green paint. 'I'll see you in the interval. Can't wait. God bless!' She blew a kiss from lips that looked as if they would taste of raspberry ice-cream, and swam away.

'Puts it on a bit, doesn't she?' Nora said, as they went to their seats.

But James was wildly in love.

He sat at the end of the row and made two trips out to the gents for a glimpse of Paige Tucker, who ran the theatre and stayed out at the front by the bar or the box office. He could not risk a third time, because she might suspect prostate trouble, but there she was in the interval, asking him, in front of everyone, 'Don't you adore the show, my dear?'

James took her jewelled hand, raised it high, and found a place to drop a kiss, with pouting lips, the way it was done.

'It's a treat,' he said, although he had hardly been aware of the comedy. 'Congratulations.' He might have added, 'Dear lady,' if Nora hadn't been there.

'I haven't had my hand kissed for years. I shan't wash it. Poll, darling, bring the folks by for a drink at my table afterwards.'

At the big round table in the bar, Jam was so enslaved that he could not worry about what Nora thought. She and Lily were talking, about the children probably. They could go on endlessly about that, just as they used to do years ago about Nora's patients and Lily's cases. For a while, before more people joined them, James sat next to Paige.

He called her Pyge, putting it on a bit to make her laugh. 'I'm a good old cockney, in't I, Pyge?'

'Pyge,' she echoed him. 'Oh, I adore that. Poll, you do have the nicest fathers-in-law – oops, sorry. Rodney dear,' to one of the college-student waiters, 'bring Pyge a double J & B, you know the way I like it.' She winked at the golden lad, as if they were having it off after hours, damn her. 'And one for my new friend, James.'

'Jam, they call me. Jam Spooner, Jamspoon, get it?'

She got it. She loved it. She adored it when he talked about the pub. 'The Duke's Head – it's inspired. I can just *see* you with all those oak beams and pewter mugs. I tell you what, Jam, let's you and me start a pub here, a genuine, authentic British pub. The Pyge's Head. We'll make our fortune.'

She chatted and glittered to others, but always turned back to James. Once she took his hand, exclaimed at its size and strength and read his fortune from the palm.

'Journey overseas. Meet a fair lady.'

'Die in bed.' It was the best he could do. His wits were bemused and dazzled.

'Oh, Jamspoon, you are too much. Whose bed?'

Luckily she turned away to call to someone across the room. Nora was giving James one of her steady looks across the table. Lily and Paul were laughing together about something. Lily wore a white dress with a low square neck that showed a lot of smooth, sun-tanned flesh. How lovely she was, and my God, she looked fully mature, grown up at last at thirty-two. How can I be the father of a ripe woman almost half-way through her life?

When the pianist took a break, Paul went up to the piano and played at someone's request, 'They Try to Tell Us We're Too Young'.

'Thank God we're not.' Pyge leaned her head sideways, so that James was in a cloud of fine hair, like a scented Scotch mist. 'I wouldn't want to have to go through that agony again for anything, would you?'

'Not when it can be like this.' Jam was either drunk or insane. He felt about seventeen.

Next day, Pyge rang. She rang!

'For you, Gramps.' Isobel came in with her curled-lip face. 'Some old woman. She sounds kinda weird.'

'Cynthia Pigott.' An ex-neighbour in Granada Road, the reason he had to leave Wimbledon, he sometimes boasted. 'How could she track me down here?'

It was Pyge.

Tonight was the last night of the comedy. She knew how much he and his lovely wife had enjoyed it. It was sold out, but she would leave their name with the usher and they could drop in and stand at the back for that priceless last act, and stay for the farewell cast party.

'Bring Poll and that darling Lily, of course. See you, Jam-spoon!'

Lily did not want to go. 'You and Mum have fun without us. You can take my car.'

Jam's day went by in exaltation: at the soda-fountain, where Dodo was impressed that he had met Pyge, on the beach, on the porch, teaching the girls and Tony to play cricket in the field with a baseball bat and a rubber ball.

'I thought you had lumbago,' Nora called from one of the bedrooms where she was changing sheets.

'Instant cure. I am your young and sprightly bridegroom.'

While the children were looking for the ball in the long grass, James ran up the stairs and pushed Nora back on the bed for a passionate kiss. Better keep her sweet and unsuspecting, swine that he was. Impotent? Who said?

He could not take in much more of the comedy's last act than he had the first time round. Afterwards, in the bar, he did not get the chance to be next to Pyge, but sitting opposite, he talked and joked with the actors and kept up with their back-and-forth wisecracks in a way that would have left the dull-witted lot at the Duke standing. At the crowded, noisy table, he was playing to an audience of one, and Pyge knew it.

You could hardly blame Nora for wanting to go home. Back at the house, she undressed before James did, and climbed into bed and was asleep almost at once, the lines on her good, familiar face, which was getting to look quite old when she was tired, smoothed out under the window in the light from a million stars, many more than you ever saw at home.

Lily and Paul were asleep. Feeling like Lily's son, James crept past her door and went out and drove the few miles back to the theatre.

There was only a scattering of people at the tables in the bar. Pyge and the actors had gone on to a night spot.

'Where?' The barman did not know. 'Did she leave a message for me? I'm with Mrs Tucker. Where can I find them?'

'Who knows?' The barman's face, whose style of moustache had gone out with William Powell, indicated, 'If you were, you should know where she's gone.'

'*The joys of love*,' Jonesey used to sing at the George, when the mood of the bar was not too rowdy, '*are all too brief. The pain of love is a long, long grief.*'

James suffered all Sunday. Nora reported on how many J & Bs he had consumed the night before. They all thought he was hung over, so he went along with that, lest they should guess at the agonies of love that gnawed at his vitals.

He would not go to the beach. 'I ache all over.' The rocking-chair creaked like a dirge. 'Sick as a dog, Nora.'

'Spirits are six per cent stronger here, you know, and a single's like our double.'

'I may be sickening for something.'

'Keep away from the children, then, if you've got a little virus. We don't want to spoil their holiday.'

'I pray I may never get cancer, Nora. You'd pass it off as Jam's little lump.'

That evening, Tony Andrade, whose mother was part Wampanoag Indian, took Paul and his family to the pow-wow in the town of Mashpee. Tony's mother wore an Indian dress with a lot of beads and fringes and was called Princess Laughing Owl, instead of Betty Andrade. After the children had sung and danced in a more or less tribal way, Tony's father started the famous fireball game.

He brought out a huge ball of tightly packed rags which had been soaking for days in kerosene, lit it with a wild cry and hurled it on to the grass, where dozens of children kicked it about, shrieking with joy and fear. The ball flared as it rolled, and the skittering brown legs flickered and jumped in the flame and shadow, as if they were part of the fire.

Cathy clung with her arms around Paul's legs, and Rose Mary held Lily's hand, white-faced, but Isobel was out there with Tony, running and shouting and pushing small bodies out of her way. The only time she got near the fireball, she swerved away and Tony kicked it for her, and she grabbed his shirt and ran behind him into the zigzagging mass of dervish children.

A bigger boy scooped up the ball and threw it. A wild girl with flying plaits kicked it under a car.

A drawn-out, 'O-o-oh' from the crowd. The children fell back. What now? Paul saw the lumbering figure of James, who had tagged along to the pow-wow with no enthusiasm, suddenly stumble out from the line of watching grown-ups and throw himself flat to pull out the fireball and hurl it away before the car blew up.

'Who's that?'

'Who's the hero?'

'That's a junk car anyway. No gas in it.'

Poor Jam had burned his hand, and it had to be soaked in bicarbonate and bandaged by Nora. She treated him tenderly, although he winced and squealed and told her, 'Good thing you gave up nursing to pull pints.'

Poor old James was still a bit off-colour on Monday. When Paul left for work, he found his father-in-law up early and sitting on the swing in the maple tree, moodily drinking tea with the bag still in the mug.

'How's the hand?'

'Terrible.' He raised a bundle from his lap that was a scarf tied clumsily over Nora's neat bandage.

Before Paul reached the Bourne bridge, the traffic was clotting. Commuting from the Cape was dangerous in bad winters, and hell on wheels in the summer; but thousands of people did it now, and it was worth it to come back in the evening to the narrow land where Paul felt completely at home, as if he had been a fisherman or a saltmaker or an old Wampanoag Indian in a former life.

On a couple of evenings, Paige had lent him the nice little chestnut horse she kept at a stable near the theatre, and he had rented another quiet one for Lily, so that they could ride together.

She was learning well. She could ride a better horse. Paige's chestnut could 'walk a hole in the wind', but Lily's plain brown horse was used to pottering along yards behind with beginners who did not know how to use their legs. Lily talked all the time when they were walking, so that Paul had to sit turned in his saddle, holding the chestnut back, which made it jog fretfully.

'It's easier to make a slow horse walk fast than a fast horse walk slow. Kick him, Lily. Here, I'll pick you a stick. Whack him down the shoulder.'

Lily kicked and whacked. The brown horse was impervious.

Next time, he asked the stable for a better horse, and it ran away with Lily on the long stretch of grass that used to be an airstrip. Paul held the chestnut back with difficulty, so as not to race. He caught up with Lily as her horse slowed and swerved at the end of the field and stopped, and suddenly put its head down to tear at grass, although it was winded and blowing.

Lily fell off down its neck and leaned against the wet, heaving sides.

'My God, are you all right?' Watching someone else in trouble was much worse than being in trouble yourself. Paul had been in an agony of anxiety. 'Why couldn't you stop him? He must have a mouth like iron.'

'I wanted to gallop,' Lily lied. Her hair-clip had come out, and her thick front hair was over her face. 'I wanted to go fast.'

'In that case, you don't charge off without telling the other person.' Anxiety turned swiftly to anger. 'If you're going to learn to ride, you've got to do it properly, or I'll be damned if I'll bother to teach you.'

Immediately he wanted to say, 'Sorry, forget that,' but Lily said, 'I love it when you get severe with me. I want to do it right. I want to be the best at it.'

Paul left work early, and called in at his parents' house on his way to Cape Cod. He sat with them on the patio and drank Muriel's lemonade made from her grandmother's recipe in Indiana, and wished he did not have to join the Monday evening traffic of tourists starting their week.

'But you always say you want to live year-round on the Cape,' his mother said. 'The commuting would kill you.'

'I suppose.' Paul closed his eyes and thought of his boyhood bed upstairs. Once you were married, you couldn't come home for a night in your old room. 'What are you having for supper?'

'Baked scrod. Want to stay and eat? There's plenty.'

'No I'd better get back. I'll be glad when James and Nora go, and Lily and I are alone.'

'You don't care for her folk? I thought they were darling.'

'Oh, they are. But they're there.'

The Judge had had a cold, and Muriel worried at him.

'He takes on other people's work. They all take time off, and pretend to be sick when they want to play in a golf match, but your father won't call in sick even when he is.'

'I'm not. I'm never sick.'

'You are so, Steven. I've had some anxious times with you, over all these years. He'll pass away before me,' she told Paul, when the Judge went into the house, 'and that's the way it ought to be, because he'd be lost if I passed on first. I would manage all right. I wouldn't come and bother you.'

'I'd want you to.'

'No, I'd join a club, travel with some of the girls, take up reading or something. Go to Florida like Aunt Bessie. My family's full of widow women. I guess the men couldn't take it.'

Muriel stood at the edge of the patio and watched the red car until it was out of sight. There went a good man, her son, the best of the bunch, as far as her sisters and cousins had managed to produce, and their husbands certainly weren't a patch on Judge Steven. Right from the start, when she dated him at Anderson High in her pink and cream sweater she always loved, she had known he would go far.

How do I keep up with him? That had always been the point. People thought she was stupid, but she was smarter than most of them, because she had never tried to be what she was not, since Steven liked her the way she was, and that was all that counted. Maybe when he did go to his rest, she might branch out, if she wasn't too old and foolish by then, but not now.

She stepped off the flagstones on to the grass to turn off the sprinkler and pull some weeds while the ground was damp. Agh! I'm putting on weight. I get gas when I bend. Takes away your breath the way the pain goes right up into your teeth. The pain – oh no, please, oh no. A red car driven by Paul – she could see his darling good-natured face through the windshield – came at her and struck her in the chest and crashed her down.

When Paul got home at last, Lily came out of the screen door more slowly than usual.

His father had called. Paul's mother had been dead when the Judge came down from his study and found her.

'She can't be dead.' Paul was so tired, he could have fallen down at Lily's bare feet. 'I was just with her.' They were talking about someone else, not him, not Muriel.

The dog Arthur, distantly related to a large pale poodle, greeted Paul with his shy smile, lifting one side of his lip above his teeth, and waited with forelegs lowered and apart, to jump in whichever direction Paul would go. He went upstairs to get night things and a razor, and then back to the car.

'Stay and have something to eat, darling.'

'I'll get something with Dad. I must go to him.'

'You can't go alone. I'll just put on a skirt.'

'No, you stay with the kids.'

Arthur, who was everyone's dog but considered himself Paul's, stood with his ears down and his eyes wounded, as if he had seen suitcases packed. Paul knelt and put his face against the dog, wiping off tears on the rough coat. Then he got back in the car and drove fast on the empty side of the road, against the crawling cars piled with families and bags and bicycles and beach-chairs.

When Terry and Brian came down off the mountain, they walked along a road, not bothering to get on to the verge, making cars go round them, into a shabby Vermont town, with a dead car or the hulk of a trailer in every side yard.

Brian had wanted to stay up in the hills, but three nights of sleeping out was enough for Terry, and they had no more food. In the top apartment of a tall narrow house, they found a room which they could only reach by walking through two other bedrooms. Outside their room, a balcony sloped crazily, with part of the railing missing.

'Better not sleepwalk,' Brian said. The balcony was propped up by a slanting two-by-four in the backyard.

They left their back-packs, since the room had a lock and key, walked through a room full of odorous sleeping babies and another room with piles of dirty clothes on an unmade bed, and found a diner at the empty crossroads which was the heart of town. They ate in silence, taking turns to get up and put a quarter into the juke-box. They had nothing to say. They had not fought, but they were already fed up with each other.

Brian was a health freak. He had been jogging and doing long hikes for years, and he outwalked Terry, who was much smaller than him.

Terry had finished growing, too soon. Boys were always taller than their mothers, but his mother was only five foot four. He used to choose smaller friends, like Eddie Waite. He had seen Eddie the other day in the shopping plaza.

'Hi.'

'Hi.'

Eddie had dropped out of school two years ago, lucky swine.

'What's new?' Eddie had asked.

'Hunhnyah.'

'Want to go out some night?'

'Nah.'

At this stage of his life, Terry often did not let himself do things he wanted, to prove that he never got anything he wanted. One of the reasons he went with Brian, who was half a head taller, was to prove that he was too small.

When Brian enthused about the view, Terry sat with his back to it. Some of the time, the mountains and the freedom and the gallons of oxygen put Terry into a great spirit of excitement and nervous energy that made him run down the slopes when Brian kept his steady pace, and needle Brian about the things he set store by: his body, his girl, his uncle's ski lodge at Dixville Notch. But then Terry would be sitting on a rock, throwing orange peel into the trickle of ice-cold stream in which his feet were soaking, and the inert spongy mass that was his soul inside him would fill up with poured concrete and the weight would drop him down with it, and none of all this was any use, any use at all, and he could not dredge up words to speak to Brian.

There was a pay phone at the end of the diner.

'Gonna call your mother?' Brian asked.

Terry shook his head. His mother was the reason he was here. Since she married that zombie with the glossy beard and greedy white fangs, who hoped to revolutionize Terry's low-key life, he had kept out of the house as much as possible.

'My mother is a tramp,' he instructed Brian.

'Who says?' Brian had several big yellow teeth and a white one that had been put in after a football mishap, and one of those long noses that curl over and look as if they have a drip on the end, but it's a drip of cartilage.

'*I* say.'

All those years he had put up with her during her camel-blanket depressions, and stood up for her when Paul and Lily made snide digs, while pretending to be so decent and fair. All those years of her lovers, and himself as 'lover boy' when she was off men, and the last ghastly time when she had walked around the house in her underwear and then screamed about his filthy mind when he accused her of coming on to him. All those years, and then when things might have worked out, with the two of them at home and Terry getting some kind of dumb job when he graduated from high school, she went and married some guy he never even heard of. Drummond Blake, a tax accountant, a man with custody of a twelve-year-old daughter who looked like him, except she didn't have a beard yet.

Terry went to the wedding to be his usual sunny, devoted-son self. Afterwards, while he was staying with his North Shore grandparents, he sent his father a cartoon of Drummond Blake. Drum and Fife. He had him dressed as a revolutionary soldier, with a paunch and bandy legs and a gross head with legless things alive in the beard.

His cartoons were getting more cruel and far-out. He didn't do carefully drawn witty comic strips any more. He stabbed people on to the paper as grotesque caricatures. He had sent one of President Ford stumbling over a dead bag-lady to the *Washington Post*. He would make his fortune and give it all away to unworthy causes and live in embittered poverty.

Brian called home. His promise to do that had been one of the conditions for letting them come on this hike, although they would have come anyway.

'Your father called my folks,' Brian said when he came back to the booth. 'He wants you to call him.'

'What for?'

'How should I know? Just call him, is all.'

'All right, all right.' If they were going to have a decent night's sleep together in the back room of the railroad apartment, there was no sense in getting Brian mad. 'Lend me a dime.'

'Call him at your grandfather's in Dedham, right?'

'Why?'

'Because that's where he is, dope.'

Terry received the news from his father in silence. He did not believe it anyway. Gramma wasn't that old. She was ironing tablecloths somewhere and spraying polish on the leaves of her houseplants.

'I'm sorry,' his father said. 'I know how you must feel. I feel like hell, but your grandfather is amazing. The funeral is Wednesday. Eleven o'clock. Come to the house first and you can go with us to the funeral home.'

'I can't make it,' Terry said.

'What do you mean, you can't make it?' His father's voice rose so high it broke. 'Where are you, for God's sake? Get a bus, hitch, rent a car. I'll pay. Just be here.'

'Sorry, Dad.' Terry looked round at the two girls who were sitting near the pay phone, and looked away again, their smirking eyes on his back. 'I can't.'

Barbara turned up at the funeral home, without her new husband, thank God, although Paul was curious to see what he looked like, after getting Terry's caricature.

'Did you talk to Terry?' Paul asked her.

'I can't reach him.'

'I did. He said he couldn't be here.'

'Oh – bad.' Barbara curved up her mouth into her tight smile, with the lips sucked in. 'Your wife is very lovely.'

'Thank you,' Paul said stiffly. 'And thank you for coming.'

'I never had anything against your mother.'

Lily had no dark clothes on the Cape. She wore a grey dress with a lot of white on it. Barbara was in black, with the pearls her parents had given her when she married Paul. She looked very elegant. Her long manicured nails brought back to him the hysteria when one of them broke. Her hair was a lighter yellow, still short, but fluffier. It reminded Paul of how her usually sleek head had looked if she washed her hair at night and woke with it wild, and would not go down to bring up coffee for them, in case she saw the paper-boy.

Muriel would have been amused that she came. 'What in the world is she after?' she would have wanted to know.

Just before the service started, when everyone had been seated in the air-conditioned, flower-fragrant room where the casket was enthroned, Terry came in at the back.

Lily saw him and nudged Paul. Terry's brown curls were unwashed and uncut, and looked as if they might have bits of twig and leaves in them. Among the politely dressed mourners, he was insultingly ill-clad. But he was there, in hiking boots.

Paul put a hand on his father's arm.

'Terry made it.'

'Oh, good.' Even Steven smiled in a perfectly comfortable and natural way. He sat peacefully, with his knuckly brown-spotted hands in his lap, waiting for the service to begin, and prepared to give it his courteous attention.

The minister stepped up alongside the casket. He nodded to the Judge, and the Judge nodded back.

A service amid the textured wallpaper and thick grey carpet of a funeral home bore even less relationship to its subject than a service in a church. At other funerals, Paul had never been able to think about the dead person dutifully for a whole half hour, and he did not suppose all these people could either.

Some were known to him, some not. The Judge had greeted them all. Several colleagues were there, and people connected with the courts, including some defendants in whose favour he had found, after long hearings, and two of his greatest fans, a man and woman he had convicted two years ago, with an award of one of his humane Even Steven sentences.

This large insulated room with blinds drawn against the sun must be full of wandering private thoughts, drifts of other people's memories, a phrase of music, a commercial jingle, pictures behind the eyes, philosophies: We've all got to die, but not yet. One down means it's not me.

This time it's part of me, though. It's my childhood gone. Paul's father was his adolescence and manhood. His mother had taken with her his childhood, in which to her he could eternally do no wrong. I am always a grown man now, Paul realized, while they were standing to sing a hymn. I never did enough for you, and the last thing I could have done, I didn't do, because I drove away towards Route 128 and left you to die alone.

Years ago, his mother had taught him that when you die, you go up to the gates and they let you in, whoever you are, whatever you've done – because it wouldn't be worth dying if there were winners and losers up there, same as down here – and gave you a job to do, like making guests feel at home by letting them set the table. If that was what she believed, that was how it would be for her, if we create our own life after death, as before it. Except that by now she might have realized that no tables would need to be set with her briar-rose silver pattern, as she moved faster than light away from the contented personality and neat body she had discarded in favour of whatever came next.

It was Lily's first funeral since she came to the United States. She had no idea that she would see the body of her mother-in-law. When she went with Paul through the reception-room into the larger room, with the same reverent music coming out of the walls, she stopped and said, 'The coffin's open.'

'It usually is, in a place like this. Dad wanted it, and so did she.'

Muriel wore pale blue, the dress that was new this year and had been to two weddings and a few summer cocktail parties, and the dinner of the Norfolk County Bar Association.

'Come, darling. Come up to her.'

Lily had never seen anyone dead. After she made herself look at Muriel, she felt she still had not.

The line of people filing soberly past held back. Paul took

Lily's hand, and she peered over the edge of the coffin, like looking into the frozen-meat compartment at the supermarket. They had set Muriel's hair with tighter waves than she liked, and made up her face more elaborately than she had ever done. Her small domestic hands were crossed on her bosom, which they must have padded out, because didn't people go flat when they stopped breathing?

Did everyone who passed by to pay their respects have a look to see if the blue dress was moving, like the Sleeping Beauty at Madame Tussaud's? Muriel's eyes were closed, but she was wearing her glasses.

Thank God she had left the girls with Nora and James.

With Muriel exposed to view in this cheating fashion – was it fair to let people see you dead rather than just remember you alive? – it seemed rude to turn away. Lily went to Paul and his father and stood close to them. The Judge was very carefully dressed in his dark pin-stripe with a silver tie, every strand of grey hair in place, pinkly shaven, very gentlemanly. Paul's mouth was set in the way that told Lily that he was not as relaxed as he looked, and he was worried about Terry, but he was talking to people and helping them to find seats, in charge of himself and the occasion. He was the kind of man who was reassuring to have around at weddings and funerals.

After Lily sat down with him, she looked round her, because she could not sit up front there and stare at what was left of poor Muriel, and she saw Terry shuffle in like a small jeopardized alien, from another world.

Because he slid into a metal folding-chair at the back, Terry did not see that Gramma's casket was open until the service was over and his father beckoned him across the room to come up front.

Like this? Terry gestured at his jeans and dirty T-shirt and shrunk denim vest. His father nodded.

Terry put out his hand to his grandfather, who bent to kiss

him. He kissed his father. They had always kissed each other, and it was easier to go on than to make a big thing about stopping.

He never knew if he was supposed to kiss Lily or not, and she never knew what he wanted. She said, 'I'm so sorry. I know you must feel very sad about your grandmother.'

For some reason, Lily seemed to Terry like a kindred spirit in this unreal gathering. She looked like Cape Cod, brown from the sun, with the top of her hair lighter than the rest, fidgeting on her feet, as if she were ready to run out with him and go sailing, or roll in the dunes, or collapse into the surf. So when she leaned forward uncertainly, he kissed her on the golden fuzz at the bottom of her cheek.

Then he saw his mother watching him. Not mad. Coolly, as if he were an amusing child.

Then he saw his grandmother.

To cover his shock, he scoffed to himself about how conventional all this was, and how typical. Didn't his family have the guts not to let themselves be manipulated by a funeral parlour called Stanhope & Towle?

Two women turned away from the casket, and murmured to the Judge, 'She looks beautiful.'

'She looks dead,' Terry wanted to say. He edged closer, sideways, without it being obvious.

After the first shock of seeing his grandmother there at her own funeral, she did actually look sort of beautiful. Her fond, active face was smoothed out. The skin looked good enough to touch, if you wanted to touch a dead body. A sudden attack, his father had said, and Terry had imagined terror and pain; but this was only peace, masking the horror of death. All of this nonsense: the service, the minister who told them things about Gramma they already knew, the formally dressed people, the piped music, the quilted satin inside the open casket, maybe there was some point to it, because it was all so calm and normal in the face of the enemy of howling blackness.

'You okay?' His father put an arm around his shoulders.

'Sure.'

'Come back to the house with Grandpa and me.'

Terry looked at his mother.

'Go ahead.' She nodded. 'Give me a call later, and I'll come and collect you.'

Brian had gone back up another mountain. They had arranged where to meet. Maybe. Maybe not.

Inside his grandmother's house, he knew that he missed her. It wasn't comfortable here now, these three men of different ages sitting behind half-drawn blinds and sharing a bottle of wine and chicken-salad sandwiches with the chicken and celery cut too thick, so that they fell out of the bread.

'Can't we go sit outside?' Terry whined.

'It wouldn't be appropriate,' his grandfather answered.

He and Terry's father talked about who had been at the funeral service.

'She would have been pleased. She would have liked that,' the Judge comforted himself.

They told Terry he could stay here for the night if he liked, but if he did, they might expect him to go with them tomorrow to the cremation, where they would pretend not to know that the incendiarists would switch Gramma to a cheap casket after she rolled through the swishing curtain, and re-sell the expensive one with the carved bronze handles.

'Let's talk about your future, then,' the Judge said.

'Not now, Grandpa, don't you want to –'

'There's nothing I want to do.' The old man looked pretty bleak. 'You graduate next year. What are your plans?'

Mumble, mumble. Surely the Judge knew as well as everyone else in the family that Terry had been determinedly fending off plans.

'He's still got a bit of time to apply for college,' his father said, 'if he wants to.'

'Wants to? He's got to,' the Judge said with surprising energy for a man who had just said goodbye to his wife for ever. He talked about some universities he had in mind.

'I don't think –' Terry began.

'If you think you can't get accepted, you could always go to business school, like your father.'

'Might be a good idea?' Paul said, as a question. He was always careful not to push Terry. Too careful. Sometimes Terry wanted him to say, 'Okay, this is the way it is. This is what you do.' But the poor guy still seemed to feel guilty about the divorce, and marrying again.

'Do me a favour,' Terry sometimes wanted to say. 'I'm an independent being. What you do doesn't affect my life.'

'I thought, maybe, well, um – I might try art school.'

'You might, that's true, if you think you're good enough to make a career at it.' His father considered this seriously. 'Magazines, design.'

The Judge made a sort of 'Pfuh' noise, and went upstairs to his study with a bunch of letters.

'An advertising agency,' Paul said.

Terry felt very depressed. 'Or maybe I'll kill myself.'

'Don't be absurd.'

'No, honestly.' If you really did plan to kill yourself, would no one take you seriously?

'Are you on drugs?'

'No, Dad,' Terry said wearily. If I was, I wouldn't tell you, and grass doesn't count anyway. When they legalize it, everyone will get into something else, until they legalize *that*.

'Do your readers realize,' Terry had written to the *Boston Globe*, on his school's notepaper, 'that drugs could be legalized out of existence, if Washington was prepared to give up their share of the profits?' The *Globe* had not printed his letter.

'How about booze? I know that a lot of kids –'

'Don't, Dad.'

Terry meant, 'Don't feel you have to go through the litany,' but his father said, with more spirit, 'Leave you alone, is that it? Sit back and watch you mess up, so you can say, "No one wanted to help me".'

'Yeah.' Terry laughed. 'That's about it, I guess.'

'I love you,' his father said despondently.

'I do too. I'm sorry. I mean, I'm sorry about Gramma. I mean, she was your mother, and all.'

Terry thought about his own mother, tricked out in a fancy casket, in her pearl-cluster earrings. He had better give up the odd times when he wished her dead, in case she went and did it.

He and his father sat and looked at each other, with

Gramma's café-au-lait lace cloth between them, like their loneliness.

'Sure you don't want to spend the night here, Terry?'

'I guess not. I'd better call Mom.'

He turned on the television while he waited for his mother to fetch him. This house was clean, very tidy, no cooking smells. His father and grandfather were going out to dinner, which his grandmother had never wanted anyone to do, because for those prices, they couldn't get as good as she could serve them.

His father went outside to water her plants that were in pots and tubs on the patio. Unfamiliar in his dark suit, he looked less unhappy out of doors, with the hose in his hands, something to do.

When his mother's car stopped at the end of the front path, Drummond was driving it. 'Bye, Dad.' Terry hurried out, not wanting his father to see Drum and Fife.

'Where's your car?' he asked as he got in.

'I like your mother's better.' Scrounger. 'You okay, son?'

Terry nodded. He looked out of the window at the familiar streets and houses through which he had travelled since he was very small, with Mom and Dad a unit existing solely for him. Then he took the plug out of his mind to let it empty itself to a comfortable void.

Nora was very sweet with the children. She told them that their grandmother had gone to sleep and woken in a beautiful place where there was bright light and green grass and friendly people waiting on the other side of a sparkling stream to greet her.

'When my grandmother died,' Rose Mary said, 'they put her in a hole in the ground.'

'Yes, well,' Nora said brightly, 'but she has still gone to the beautiful place.'

'She was in the hole to stay. I helped throw some dirt on top.'

'Not dirt, dear, earth. Soil isn't dirty.'

'How come it's called soil, then?' Cathy looked up, strands of fine hair across her eyes.

'Bright as a button.' Nora hugged her.

'I want Gramma.'

Nora did not say, 'You've got me.' You could rely on her not even to think of things like that. She said, 'She'll always be near you to look after you. She loved you very, very much.'

'When I bow off the stage,' James said, 'will you say kind pretty things about me, Nor?'

'Oh, shut up, you.' Nora sat outside the house on what passed for a lawn, making daisy chains with the children. 'You always turn everything back to yourself.'

'Pardon me for living,' James said. 'You four girls have fun together. I think I'll call a taxi and go to town and see if I can get me one of those Boston Red Sox jackets to wear at home.' It would be, as they said over here, a conversation piece, the hit of the Duke's Head.

'I'm making hamburgers for lunch.'

'Don't wait for me. I may be a while.'

When Art came in Art's Taxi, Jam asked him to drive to the theatre. He went in, on tiptoe from holding his breath. Pyge was in her office, on the phone.

'Jamspoon! Excuse me,' to whoever was on the phone.

'We're going out to lunch,' Jam said masterfully.

'So we are.'

James paid off Art's Taxi and waited until she finished giving someone on the phone a piece of her mind about bit-part salaries, and then they went off in her car.

'Let's go where we'll be seen.'

She took him to a restaurant on the harbour, where she was greeted by several lunchers, to whom she said, 'May I present James Spooner,' in a way that made them think he was someone, from the theatre perhaps. She kissed the proprietor and fussed until he took a Reserved sign off a table by the water, where they could see the yachts going by, and the big power boats with fat men in dark glasses perched up high like emirs by the tall deep-sea fishing rods.

James ordered Bloody Marys, and told the waiter what should

go in them. They came with celery stalks as stirrers. He ate his crisply, to show his teeth were his own.

'I was afraid I wouldn't see you, Pyge.'

'You're not going?' She looked genuinely disappointed.

'Two days. I did come back to the theatre that night, you know, but you'd gone.'

'I left word for you. I'll kill that Alex. He's not reliable, and he mixes a lousy martini.'

Jam told her how he mixed his own Duke's Special, stirred in a pewter jug with a silver jamspoon. 'You'll have to come and try one.'

'And bring my own ice, I suppose.'

He laughed extravagantly, although at the pub, he was sick of American tourists and servicemen doing variations on that joke.

They had a wonderful time. They ate lobster salad, and Pyge kept saying things like, 'Ohmygahd, this is fun,' and, 'I'm having such a *great* time,' and laying her jewelled fingers on his arm, and tossing her head about with an eye on people at the other tables, who could not fail to notice her.

The ectoplasm hair was garnished with two micro-pigtails hanging beside either temple. She wore an orange caftan with huge violent beads: her office clothes, since she had not known she was being taken out to lunch.

She found Jam entertaining. He did his low-key imitation of Prince Philip teaching a girls' gym class, and sketched in Same-again Mabel, one of his bar creations: music-hall Yorkshire, puffing out his cheeks and waving an opinionated finger, with a napkin for a headscarf.

Pyge thought he was a riot. 'You have natural talent.' She dropped her voice to the throaty level she used for serious theatre talk. 'Too bad you're not staying on. I have all kinds of contacts in New York.'

'Oh, don't,' said James. 'I wish I could stay, I really do, but Nora would never hear of it. She's married to that pub.'

'And it could never do without you, obviously. You must be a big draw.'

'You think I'm wasting my talents?' James was in heaven. A

huge yacht crept past the window on engine power, and he raised his lager glass to a woman in a bikini on deck.

'*Quién sabe?*' Pyge smiled like a lighthouse in a storm. 'You are a gifted gentleman, Jamspoon, and a very rare soul.'

Back at the Duke's Head, he showed Pyge's photograph to some of the chaps in the bar, when Nora was not around. She leaned diagonally across the picture, with cleavage and those American teeth, and this cloud of amazing hair, like a dandelion puff-ball.

'*Yours always, Paige Tucker.*'

James boasted. He was entitled to. 'It was one of those things. We were soul-mates.'

'Har, har.'

'Knock it off, no, honestly. She says to me, "You ought to be on the stage, Jamspoon," she tells me. "On the styge, Pyge?" "A natural," she says, just like that. She has all kinds of contacts, of course, movies, T V. She could present Yours Truly, but I know where duty lies.' Sigh. 'One on the house, then, waddayasay fellas, to celebrate the Jamspoon's return.'

He talked American for a few days, then dropped it. There was a lot to do. Blanche and the others had managed well enough, but the stock was low, and bottles were in the wrong places on the shelves, and Martin had bought a case of flabby cut-price crisps from a vagrant salesman, and let his brass beer-pulls and drip pans become a disgrace. Nora was glad to be home, but after Boston and Cape Cod, James found it all rather boring and a big let-down. He began to plan when they could go back to the States again. He didn't call it America now. That was for tourists.

'It'll take us another five years till we can get the money together,' Nora said, happy in her flowered morning overall that covered the clean blouse with a bow at the front, and could be whipped off at opening time, 'and hope to keep ourselves above the red line. Let alone I'd never leave Muttonchop on his own again, now that Blanche knows it's twins. Duffy won't even be three when they're born.'

Calm, fertile Bianca, taking motherhood so placidly, not whirling about in a stew like Lily, always behind, always dropping one job for another and dropping everything to rush out and prove to the girls that she could still do hand-stands and somersaults.

Twins in the family. Skipped a generation from Jam's grandparents, just like they said. Twins were in Neil's family too, but the blood wasn't strong enough there to carry them on. It was amazing how he could knock them out, that runty little chap, James's second son-in-law, who couldn't poke a hole in a net curtain. Neil had some sort of dud job with a tractor firm, so that when one of the few local farmers, who had bought up everybody else, was in the pub, James could at least say, 'My son-in-law's in your line of business.'

Same old round. Same jobs to get through every day, same faces, same jokes. Always having to be up front, always sharp-witted, two shows a day, even when you felt like burying your head in the sand.

James put Pyge's picture under his thick Arran sweater in the bottom drawer. After a while, nobody wanted to hear about the States any more, although one evening when Jam was cutting up a bit behind the bar in an American sailor hat that said, 'Hello Cutie', Duggie Manderson did tease him, 'Ought to be on the stage, eh? Tell you what, though, you do look a bit like that loony chap in the beer commercial – "The Bitter End".'

That night, after Nora had gone through to the cottage, James spent some time making faces into the oval mirror behind the bar, framed by the arms of a naked lady, holding a glass of ruby-red on top.

He tried to analyse his funny old mug objectively. Some people suffer from superfluous hair. Superfluous skin was his trouble, but it made his face rubbery enough for exaggerated changes of expression. His big crooked nose could make his eyes look sad and triangular, when he dropped his head and turned the eyes upward. He could raise both eyebrows at the same end, for the quizzical look. He could suck in his mouth and be toothless, or stick out his bottom lip like a Hottentot, or flap his upper lip and lose his chin like one of the Hooray Henrys who stopped in here on race days.

When he stopped making faces and let everything go, he could look quite dreadfully old.

'Where am I going?' he asked the face between the fleshy arms of the mirror's frame. Man's age-old cry. 'What's it all about?'

He went up to London to buy Nora a birthday handbag from D. H. Evans, the kind she liked, with a thousand pockets and zips to carry all her worldly goods and letters from her sister in the Isle of Man. On the way home, he took a detour to Wimbledon to see Jonesey.

Jonesey was just home from work, with his shoes off, tie off, belt off, as always when he stepped through the door, diving into that dreadful old cardigan with the shawl collar, which he had rescued from the Oxfam shop twice when Sheila had condemned it.

'Want to go up to the George? Some of the old crowd's still there.'

'No.'

Not just to go back five years older, with nothing much to show for it. Being the landlord of a pub had seemed such a marvellous thing at first, the height of ambition and status. Now, like marriage or anything else in life, it was a matter of daily routine. Open, kick 'em out, open again next morning, close, open again before you'd barely had your tea, kick 'em out too late for the good programmes on the box. Who in the George would be impressed with just another pub keeper? They knew Nigel too well, and Nigel knew James and what he had let himself in for.

He and Jonesey drank some ale and sat by the electric fire while Sheila made ham and eggs. James had rung Nora to say he would be late.

'You said you'd be home by seven-thirty, so I could get to my meeting.'

'What meeting?'

'The church drama committee.'

'You don't go to church.'

'I'm talking about the play.'

'What play?'

'I told you. *Hiawatha*.'

'Oodle-oodle-oo!' His war cry choked into laughter. Nora had a fair singing voice, but she wouldn't be able to act her way out of a paper bag, in a black wig and chicken feathers.

'Do me a favour, James. You're wasting money. The phone company aren't in business for their health. If you start home now, I'll just get to my meeting. Please, James.'

'Sorry, kid. I've got a meeting too. Luck of the draw.'

His meeting with Jonesey in the warm sitting-room that drew the scents of the day from Jonesey's socks, was a comfortable time to talk about the States, and Lily and her girls, and Pyge.

'I love it over there. It felt right. I'd have stayed, given half a chance, made a new start, with a decent bathroom for once in my life, and a toilet you don't have to sit on backwards and take the lid off the tank to diddle the ball-cock to flush it.'

'Ah, I know.' Jonesey was contented with his lot, but he could still dream.

'Do you think I'm wasting my life?' Jam asked him. 'I have, like Noël Coward, if you know what I mean, I have this talent to what's it, a way of making people laugh. What the world needs.'

'The world needs love, the kids say.'

'That's a long way off. Meanwhile, a few laughs don't do no harm.'

Jam made one of his extreme faces and quacked at the cat, who got up and moved away under a table.

'You'd ought to meet my friend, Bill,' Jonesey said. 'He's got hisself into the business.'

'Street trade? I'm a bit old for that, seductive though I am.'

'No, being photographed, for an agency. He's on in years, like us, but there's a call for that. You may have seen him. He's the man who holds up the little tube of Hemerol and talks about what it'll do for your piles.'

Nora had been so huffy with James when he got back from Jonesey's, that the next time he went to London, he told her he was going to see his mother in Devizes, a satisfactory distance away. Nora could not ring her to check, because the nursing-home had no phone that wheelchair patients could use, and Ma could not talk sense into it anyway, since she was more or less permanently out to lunch, poor old dear.

The office of 'Faces' was in Kensington High Street. James walked nonchalantly up and down past the door a few times, then turned in and went up the stairs before he could change his mind. There was a waiting-room with a window in one wall behind which two women were working at desks, and a young man in a black turtleneck was on the phone, his chair tipped so far back, another half inch would put him in the lap of the tough-looking red-head. In case they had not noticed Jamspoon, he walked across his side of the window before he sat down.

Next to him sat Winston Churchill. Well, Winnie was dead, of course, but this chap . . . oh, Lord, was this only an agency for people who looked like other people?

The other person in the waiting-room looked like a dwarf. Because he was a dwarf. He had a good-sized head and tiny legs that dangled his feet miles away from the floor. He read a newspaper folded sideways to dwarf size, just two columns wide.

Winston Churchill and the dwarf went in for interviews with someone called Henrietta. The glass panel in the window never slid back to ask James to come through, or even to ask his name and business.

In for a penny, Jam. He stood up, neatened his sincere tweed jacket and tapped on the window. The blonde at the desk on the other side slid it open at once.

'Have you got an appointment?'

'No, but I was just passing, so I thought I'd drop in.'

'Are you registered with us? I'm not sure I −'

She seemed kind enough, so James said, 'Not yet, but I want to be. You're called "Faces". Well, I've got a face. Boy, have I got a face!' He struck a Jimmy Durante pose.

The blonde smiled charitably. 'Did you bring stills?'

'Come again?' James condensed his neck and pushed out his face like a tortoise.

'Still pictures. Come back with pictures, Mr −'

'Spooner.'

'Eight by eleven. There's one of our catalogues in the waiting-room, if you want to see the kind of thing we need. Bring in two poses, Mr Spooner, and you can fill out an application form.'

'Why can't I do that now? I'm up from the country.'

'Well, that can't be any problem if you're planning to work in London.'

She was polite and reasonable. She had a mid-Atlantic accent, with a short *a* in can't. He couldn't be disappointed in her.

'We'll look forward to seeing you here again.' Soft hiss of glass through metal slot. Gentle click of panel in window. She picked up the phone again, smiling and relaxed. James could not hear what she said.

While he was looking through the large intimidating catalogue of fascinating faces, far better qualified than James to advertise mail-order suits or a haemorrhoid cream, a nondescript-looking man bounded up the stairs.

Sorry, old cock, they'll never use you. The man tapped on the glass, made an 'Okay?' gesture with his head, and opened the magic door to go on through to Henrietta and the action.

He was neither short nor tall, fair nor dark, a middling sort of person you would use to shadow someone, because nobody would notice him. He must be the one who played Mr Ordinary Man-in-the-Street, the one who answers 'Don't know' to the pollster with the clipboard, someone with whom the dimmest customer could identify.

The younger men in the catalogue were good-looking according to fairly conventional types: slick, sporty, romantic, boyish, broody. Most of the middle-aged men were character types: pop-eyed comedians, fatties, skinnies, outdoor furrowed faces you could grow a crop of barley on. Some were in costume: a clergyman, a jovial bus conductor, a cook, a copper.

Next day, James drove into High Wycombe, which was far enough away for secrecy, and went into a photographer's, who had a nice line in gap-toothed brides and smirking children in the window.

'I need some publicity pictures,' he told the tubby young man with the loose mole, as if it were the sort of thing you needed every day.

'For – ?'

'Publicity.' Some people, you had to spell it out to.

'Sales promotion, that kind of thing?'

'No, more personal.' James dropped his voice. There were other people in the shop.

'A portrait, then? We have a process that will bring it up as if it was done in oils.'

James recoiled. I recoil from oils. 'Black and white,' he murmured. 'One normal – I mean, like you see me now, if you can call that normal, ha ha. In the other, I'll be wearing a character hat. Like a –' he sketched it around his head with his hands – 'a bowler or a policeman's helmet.'

'I don't quite think we –' The young man looked for help to where his mate was in conference with the bride's mother.

'Or a beret.'

When they had French bread at the end of the bar where Nora or Jenny set out the lunch snacks, Jam did a nice line as a café *patron* with a white apron and the bread under his arm and an old blue beret that Lily had left behind.

'I'm sorry.'

'Thank you.' James gave him a brisk nod and turned smartly to exit with his lips drawn up to whistle, as if his business had come to a satisfactory conclusion.

He rang up a woman he knew, whom he had seen a few times on the side, no funny business, just keeping his hand in.

'Didn't you say that son of yours was a photographer?'

'Ned? He's done a few freelance jobs. He's good, but he's got a long way to go.'

'I might be able to put something in his way.'

'That's good. He's having a hard time keeping up with his rent.'

Good. He wasn't living at home.

Ned took a whole afternoon to take three poses. He took dozens of shots, but that was his affair, since they had agreed on a basic price. Ned was eager and serious. He had once taken pictures of a visiting French singer, backstage, so James wore the beret as well as the bowler hat, and told him what it was for.

'It's sort of hush-hush at the moment, though,' he said. 'Top-secret campaign. The client doesn't want anything leaked, so better not tell your Ma I was here.'

'I didn't know you knew my mother. Are you a friend of Dad's?'

'Well, yes and no.'

James put Lily's beret into the bowler hat, which had been his father's, and hurried up out of the basement flat where Ned lived sparsely with his expensive camera and lenses and lights, and his cooker behind a curtain.

'These pictures are fine, but the bowler's out of date.' Henrietta's smooth brow drew into a severe frown.

'Don't I look like a banker?' Now that he had gained the fastness of Henrietta's office and she was taking him seriously, James was his bold self again.

'Brim too wide, crown too low. Won't do. The beret is good on you, though. The wink and the knowing leer may come in useful.'

'That's a smile, not a leer.' James reached familiarly across the desk to turn the picture towards him. Randy old goat. Maybe it was a leer.

'I could have used you last week, for a cheese promo.'

'You mean, you're going to take me on?'

It was easy. It was *dead easy*. He'd done it. Pyge was right. He had a lot to offer. He was *in*.

When he first saw Henrietta, on the phone when he went into her office, as they all always were, all the time, he had decided she was much too young to run an outfit like this. She was younger than either of the two women in the front office. But she had started this agency by herself when she gave up dancing, and, in spite of her fresh baby face and flat ballerina's shape, she was tough as old boot leather, and she knew her trade. She knew it all.

James could have fallen for her, but there wasn't time. He was too busy hearing what she had to say, as she assessed him swiftly and skilfully.

'You're a big fellow. Big hands too. They can be used in close up. Strong too, are you? I placed a couple of dustmen last week. Sometimes they need a load carrier.'

Jam's back cried out in fear. He shifted sideways in his chair and recrossed his legs and swung his foot, so that she would notice his new suede shoes.

'Pot belly we can always use, and balding is good. Dressed right, you could be a labourer or a businessman. There's a steady demand for executives. Let's see you with glasses.' She came round the desk and put dark-rimmed spectacles on him. 'Ah, yes, I like that.'

'I can't see.'

'You get a pair with plain lenses, idiot. At Woolworth's. You free tomorrow, James Spooner?'

'You bet.' His mind flew to Nora, cheerful and comfortable behind the bar, she'd be at this moment, sending the lunch-hour drinkers back to work in a good mood. How many excuses could he get away with? He would have to come clean sooner or later.

'There's a job for you, if you want it.'

'Lead me to it.'

'Get the glasses. Wear a business suit with a white shirt and club tie. The still should take a couple of hours in the studio.'

'What am I?'

'A balding executive who buys a little discreet toupee. Before and after.' Henrietta reached for the phone. 'Mr Arnold? Confirming your balding model . . .'

A model. I am a male model. Whoops, dearie.

'I am in show business,' he wrote to Pyge, enclosing one of the cards that Faces gave him with his name and description, and his pictures as they would be in the catalogue. 'Who'd have thought it? You would, I know, and what an inspiration. This is just the beginning, adverts, crowd work, TV background commercials. If I can get my Equity card, I hope to be featured.'

He took Pyge's picture out from under the sweater, and puckered his lips at it, like a kiss. 'Yours always, Paige Tucker.'

'Yours gratefully,' he wrote across one of the pictures on the lower part of his shirt, to hide the pot-belly. 'And with love. Jamspoon.'

In Ida's old home in Staple Street, Bernie slept in what had always been called the box room, although Ida's parents never went anywhere, and had no boxes or suitcases. It was a narrow space below the sloping slates, with a bed, but no door or window. Ida slept with Maggie in her old room next to it, whose low doorway was rounded at the top to fit under the pitch of the roof.

'Like a big staple, see.' She pointed it out to Maggie, as they lay in the bed together, because Maggie would not go to sleep in the strange house unless Ida lay down with her. 'When I was your age, I thought that was why our road was called Staple Street.'

'Wa' go pee,' Maggie said.

That meant going downstairs, through the kitchen and out to the toilet at the back. Ida waited outside to go back through the kitchen with Maggie, since Clara Lott, butchering a pale turnip at the chopping board, couldn't be trusted not to pounce on the child with a 'Twelve minus eight divided by two?' and point the knife at her for the answer.

When Ida had tried to explain Maggie, her mother's pumice-stone lips set firm. 'Never anything like that in this family.' She thought Maggie was faking, and tried to catch her out.

'Ny, Nan.' Innocent Maggie blew her a kiss as she plodded back through the kitchen in the pyjamas that were like a bolster cover on her stubby shape.

'Time you were in bed.' Her grandmother tossed chunks of turnip into furiously boiling water.

'She shouldn't have had the orange drink with her tea,' Ida explained.

'Well, goodness, she's old enough to know that.'

It was rum. Now Ida's mother was the one who would not see the child as she was. Since that terrible weekend when Maggie had wandered away with poor Adam, Ida had faced the truth, and it made life much easier.

'Kiss Gopher.' It was the nearest Maggie could get to Grandfather.

Gopher was in the front-room, reading brutal bits of the Old Testament aloud, while Bernie put a model plane together at the table. It was a chilly October day, but the fire had not been lighted until November since time began, or as long as Ida had known this house. The electric fire stood in the empty grate, with the orange bulb glowing, but not the heating bars.

George Lott sat in his grey shirt and a thick dun cardigan, swinging one foot in a backless leather slipper. He claimed he did not feel the cold, but his hands were always chill to the touch.

Ida could look at and even touch his hands now without revulsion. Those horrible years with him were all gone far behind, and done with. Marriage to Buddy had wiped out the power of those memories, at least.

Her father put one of the hands flat on the open page of the big Bible, and curved the other arm round Maggie to draw her close to him with a solemn look.

'Pay heed that thou respect thy elders,' he charged her, bringing shaggy grey eyebrows down like stern caterpillars; but the great thing about being Maggie was that she went her own way, regardless. She stood on tiptoe and reached up to plant a messy kiss right on those prim, tormented lips.

'Ny, Ber.' She made a dive at her brother.

'Night, Mags.' Bernie protected his model with his arms.

She scooted out, and up the dimly lit stairs. Before Ida turned to follow her, she saw George Lott pass his hand across his mouth, not the back of it, but the cupped palm, as if he were collecting nectar; then he wiped off Maggie's slobber down the side of the armchair.

It was weird being back at home. Ida looked up some of her old friends, and took her children to meet theirs, since trying to invite anyone to Staple Street wasn't worth the hassle.

'I'm afraid I can't fall in with your footloose American ways,' her mother said. Or, 'Linda Strong? The James girl that was? Her people and ours haven't spoken for years. Why does she want to come nosing round here?' Reminiscent of Verna Legge with her neighbours.

'I can't have any strangers here at this time,' her father said.

'These aren't strangers, Pa. This is Linda that I worked at the hotel with, and her husband who you used to know at the hospital. They've had me and the kids for two meals. I want to pay them back.'

So easy to do at 1009 Pershing, with the Commissary a few streets away, and the convenience store open until eleven at night if Buddy brought someone home, or anybody stopped by unexpectedly.

Ida had thought that England might have improved in the dozen years since she left, to her mother's farewell: 'You're a bigger fool than I thought.' True, there were pizza parlours and McDonald's, and a shopping centre and a multi-storey car park; but women with baskets still popped round to the baker's or grocer's every day. Swarms of raucous boys and shrieking girls owned the pavement, in a way that Ida and her lot could never have done, without being told off by the old duffers, who now stepped warily into the gutter; but there was still early closing, No Wet Fish, and 'Sorry, love, we don't stock that, there's no call for it.'

Nothing had changed at 39 Staple Street. Clara Lott was her same suspicious self, but with twelve added years of life which had lived down to her expectations. George was a nut case. Had he always been, or was he pottier now?

After a mysterious illness, he had retired from the hospital records department, from whose basement lair he used to issue forth pushing a trolley stacked with files and X-rays, which took up room in the lift when they wanted to get a body in; but he was still the nominal leader of the Church of the Completed Spirit. They had not rumbled him. Newer and younger members had taken over some of the organization, 'because my low blood pressure must be kept for higher affairs', George explained to Ida. He had been disfellowshipped from Healing, since that unpleasantness with the father of the terrified little deaf boy, but he was still called upon to preach to the faithful in the upstairs room of Winifred's mother's house, where the old lady lived in the downstairs front, and whacked her stick against the ceiling, like a morse message from the shades.

His doctrine convinced him of perfection. All life was his, and portions of it could belong to the small group in the back room that smelled of the fish the home-helper cooked for Gertrude's mother, if they would believe that their words and deeds were sanctified, and man could go no farther.

Maybe, just maybe — for every cloud has a silver lining — it wasn't Maggie's horrendous birth and 'minimal brain damage' that had retarded her, but her Lott inheritance. While Bernie looked around for escape, Maggie received Gopher's harangues with a serene blank smile, as if they were nursery rhymes.

Poor kid. But if she had got it from George, then Ida was off the hook and could drop the guilt that had been partly the reason she would have no more children.

A third child might have brought her and Buddy closer, as the dog Adam had done. Now that Buddy was so far away, in danger perhaps, afraid, in a foxhole crying for his Momma, Ida's anger had softened. Cora and Duane had sucked him into their game. He had been doing all right with the Elite Jewelry business until they started their fancy stuff. He didn't mean no harm.

'What's your Buddy really like?' Linda kept asking Ida. 'Are you close? I mean, I can't imagine me and Frank separate now. Is it like that for you?'

Ida could not answer. 'I'll tell you one thing,' she said. 'I feel better about him when he's not here.'

Linda was disappointed with Ida for being fat. She had expected her to come back from America a knock-out, but here she was in those sack dresses and straining slacks. Linda made her buy a dark knitted suit with a long loose jacket and a low-cut oyster blouse enriching her heavy breasts. She took her off to the hairdressing school to have the long straight hair styled by one of the students. Judy, whose instructor had once studied with Vidal Sassoon, took the scissors to her. Ida came out draughty, but delighted. The short bangs she had cut herself were now the longest part of her hair. What was left of the rest flew backwards in a wedge shape, as if she were going fast against the wind.

'Buddy will kill me.' He had liked to grab her horse tail of hair and swing her head round. 'My mother will have a fit.'

When Ida went home, Clara's narrow head with its knot of tired hair moved once from side to side. Her gritty grey lips said nothing, which said it all.

George, always up to scratch, proclaimed, 'But the shearing of the sheep shall not cast away evil with the unclean fleece.'

Ida felt years younger and pounds lighter. She began to use eye make-up again. She tried all Linda's lipsticks and settled on a blackberry frost, that her mother said looked like the plague.

One sunny morning, Ida took the children to the park, as much to parade her new agreeable self as to let Maggie play on the swings among smaller children, and Bernie visit the tatty little fake farmyard, where he talked to the calf and kid goat and the rabbits with the same serious concern he used to show to Adam.

A father had a reluctant three-year-old boy by the hand, impatient with him, frustrated in an 'I brought you here now bloody well enjoy yourself' way.

'Don't bust a gut,' Ida told him. 'He's too young for the chickens.' The spoiled bantams were pecking everywhere round the wailing child's feet and fluttering up against his legs.

The father turned to see this new annoyance. He was Jackson.

He did not recognize Ida at first, but he had not changed. He was still lean and hard, with that wiry light orange hair and conceited Irish mouth.

'Remember me?' Ida looked at him boldly.

'Christ,' he said. 'What's happened to you?'

'I had my hair cut.'

'I don't mean that. You're –' he let go of the child to sketch Ida's shape with his hands. The little boy moved closer to Jackson's leg and clutched it.

'That your kid?'

He nodded. 'I take him out a bit, weekends, so Diane can clean the flat.'

'You're married, then.'

'So are you. Or did you leave him?'

'Of course not. I'm here to see my folks.'

'You sound like a Yank.'

'Gimme a break, Jackson. I've been over there for twelve years.'

'Got out of here in time, didn't you?'

'In time for what?'

'Forget it.'

They said nothing much, but there was something risky in the way they talked: Jackson aggressive as always, Ida defensively jaunty.

She looked round for Bernie and called him to her. 'This is Mommy's friend.'

'Glad to meet you.' Bernie held out his hand. He was so damned polite. 'And that's my sister.' He pointed. Maggie was crouched like a toad on the low end of the see-saw, waiting for someone to sit on the other end and bump her up.

'What's wrong with her?' Jackson frowned. When his hair lifted in the breeze, it showed the box of his scalp. He seemed to have less hair, and his face was more battered, as if prison had aged him. Well, in twelve years, he would have aged, in gaol or out.

'Look, sonny.' Jackson gave Bernie his 'do me a favour' smile. 'Take Ricky over to your sister and give him a swing, eh?'

Ricky went happily with Bernie. Anyone would, children or old customers like Gopher, who went quite willingly on bus rides with his grandson all over the town.

'Sit down.' Jackson took Ida's arm and pushed her towards a bench.

'I don't know that I –'

'Siddown.' She sat. 'You're a fat old sow, but you're Ida underneath it, I know you.'

He did, that was the trouble.

'Why did you do it?' He sat a little apart from her, head down, twisting and squeezing one hand in the other, as if to test its strength.

'Do what?' Ida's mind raced over what she had told him about her interview with the CID, when she was still writing letters to the prison.

'You killed my baby.'

That was such a relief that Ida almost laughed. 'What else would I do, with you inside for at least five years?'

'It was my son.' Jackson bent to pick up a handful of dusty pebbles, and chucked them angrily one by one away from him.

'Could have been a girl. So what? You have a son now.'

'Ricky is Diane's, not mine. She can't have any more. She had the tubes tied.'

'Did you know that when you married her?' Ida did not know what else to say.

'Who says I married her?'

'Oh.'

He had stopped bristling. His hair was less electric, his hands were still, laid on his knee like an empty pair of gloves, his cocky, dangerous mouth was fallen in. He had lost some teeth in prison.

'Jackson.' Ida had to tell the lie now, because the children were wandering toward them. 'I never said nothing.'

He turned his light eyes sideways at her without moving his head.

'At first I thought I'd kill you. Especially when I heard you'd got rid of the child too, as well as me. I promised myself I'd kill you. But they give you stuff, you know, takes away your energy, and after a bit, you lose the anger. You lose even that.'

'You hate me?' Ida put a hand on his powerful slack hands.

'I'd ought to. It don't matter now. The past's gone. All of it. The whole thing was crazy, the guns and the drugs and the big money that was going to come so easy. All it got me was they took years off my life. I don't care any more. But they're not going to get me again. I've got my own business now. Junk car parts. I can live.' The children came up. 'I've got to take this bastard home. She'll think I've thrown him in the duck pond.'

'Goodbye,' Bernie said. 'Nice to have met you.'

'You too. Bye mate.'

Jackson stood up. He was behind the backless bench. Instead of getting up, Ida leaned back. He leaned against her. When she moved to stand up, he put his hands on her shoulders and held her down.

'Get rid of the kids tomorrow evening,' he muttered. 'I'll meet you.'

She stood up and faced him. 'I promised to go with my father to his church service. It's not a church, really, just a house.'

'Where?'

She told him.

'What time does it end?'

She told him.

'I'll meet you.'

'I'll have to go home with my father.'

'Make some excuse, don't be a fool. I'll meet you at the Lamb and Flag, opposite the garage.'

'I won't be there.'

Jackson picked up the little boy, and swung him, shrieking, on to his shoulder. He loped off, with his flat feet going out like duck's flippers.

'Who's that?' Bernie asked.

'No one.'

'Yeah, I figured. The kid was a real jerk. He made a huge great mess in his pants.'

'Oh, poor Jackson.'

At the thought of his shoulder, Ida began to laugh as she hadn't laughed for years, bending double, gasping in pain, sucking her breath back for another shriek of laughter. Maggie rolled on the ground. Bernie, who did not laugh hysterically, like a child, went 'Ha-ha-ha' and put a fist in his mouth. His brown eyes screwed up and disappeared.

When Ida stopped, he said, 'messed his pants!' to make her laugh again. The three of them ran to the gate, whooping and swerving in circles. To look at them, you'd have thought they were all drunk.

Ida got Maggie to go to sleep before she left for the church. Bernie was going to play cards with his grandmother. Clara did not go to the services with George any more.

'Afraid she might enjoy herself.' He made one of his rare jokes.

The small group of people on uncomfortable chairs in Winifred's mother's upstairs-room did not enjoy themselves a lot. It was completion contemplation night. After two or three people had told about successful healing, George Lott gave a brief rambling harangue. He stopped in the middle of a sentence and held up his hand like a traffic cop. They all closed their eyes. Jackson was imprinted on the inside of the lids. Damn him. She could even smell him. Would she never be free of him? She wouldn't meet him. She never wanted to see him again. If he came to her house, she would set her mother on him. He'd be at the pub, she knew that, so sure that she would come running when he snapped his fingers.

She would have liked to break the silence of the group. Her spirit moved her to say, 'Give me strength.' She took a deep breath, and just as she began, 'My spirit – asks –', George Lott snapped open his eyes and struck his hands together.

Mrs Rees and her daughter brought tea upstairs, with ginger-nuts. Everyone spoke to Ida, and said they were glad to see her back. They were decent people, George was the only dotty one, but Ida wanted to be gone and safe at home away from the Lamb and Flag, away from the chance of Jackson lurking in the street.

But when a small quarrel broke out among the faithful about whose turn it was to wash up and tidy, Ida heard herself say, 'I'll be glad to do it. You go on home, Pa. Give me the key and I'll lock up.'

'Good girl.' He put on his pouchy tweed cap. 'Use plenty of washing-up liquid.' He had a mania about germs. 'So shalt thou too be cleansed of all impurities.'

'Speak for yourself,' Ida risked, and the others enjoyed the laugh, now that they did not have to feel holy. George even laughed too. He honestly seemed to have lost sight of everything that had once happened in Ida's room under the roof, and with it, all guilt or blame.

A fearful excitement walked with Ida along the pavement and down Chester Street to the corner pub. She had escaped from Jackson once. What kind of fool was this who pushed open the frosted glass door, settled beside him on the stool at the bar and put her hand round the glass of shandy he had already ordered for her?

He was morose. She talked about the service, prattling on a bit to try and get him going. When she told him how she had sent her father home and tidied up the church house, he asked, 'You got the key?'

Ida put her hand into the pocket of her coat and showed him the key on her palm. He grabbed it before she could close her hand.

'Come on.' He got off the stool, and stared round belligerently at the few quiet drinkers. He turned up his collar, and Ida followed him out.

Winifred's mother called out to them as they went quietly into the house.

'Just some people from the church, dear.' Ida opened the door of her room. The old lady was settled for the night in a high bed with a lot of pillows and the radio reading her a story. She asked for a hot drink.

Jackson fussed and fumed while Ida heated the milk and took it in.

'Cup of tea?' she asked him hopefully because the automatic way she had followed him here was leading her toward panic.

He swore at her. They went upstairs. Behind the front-room with the uncomfortable chairs, there was a bedroom for Winifred's sister when she came from Weymouth. Ida lit the gas fire. The boiling radiators in Pershing Street had spoiled her for taking off her clothes in the cold.

'God, but you're fat,' Jackson said. 'Christ, look at all this, and this. You used to be a little skinny handful with nothing on you. I've got to get used to you like this. My God, you're so fat.'

'If that's how you feel –' Ida was going to say, 'Forget it,' and put on her clothes and march out and leave him to rape Winifred's mother. But by then it had started, and it all came back to her, what she had run away from, the old fear and fascination, the glory of the man.

'We were always meant for each other.' That soft, hot voice that ate through her defences to the core of her being and destroyed her into all body and no soul. 'There was always only you and me.'

Ida stayed in England longer than she had meant to. Shirley fetched her allowance from the Air Force and sent it over twice, but then there was no more.

At last, a letter came from Sis. 'Buddy is up here. With the war winding down, thank God, they're sending the men home. You'd better come back, Ida. He's in rough shape.'

Wounded? Gone off his rocker? Ida could hardly care. The whole focus of her existence was how often she could pretend to be going round to Linda's, after the children were in bed, and then sneak the church key off the hook on the back of the larder door and meet Jackson at the house.

Days when they could not be together, because of church meetings, or because of Diane, or Clara, or Ida's children, did not count. Buddy did not count. Her softened feelings toward him had disappeared into no feelings. That's it, she had told herself when he had shot the dog, and when he had hit Bernie. She had not known then quite what she meant. Now she did.

Sis wrote again. Buddy had been charged with receiving stolen goods. He was remanded on bail for a civilian trial, and living on the base. That was why Ida had no more housing allowance. A note from Buddy was inside Sis's letter, folded very small, since he was suspicious even of his own sister, who was helping him.

'When are you coming back? I need you. Their trying to frame me here after all I went through in the Nam war.' He had only been gone a few months, and never got farther than Australia.

Ida wrote that she and the children would not come back until he sent her some money. He sent a dollar draft. She changed it into pounds and gave it to her mother, so that she could stay longer.

When Ida discovered she was pregnant, she was thrown into confusion. At first, she wanted to run straight to the clinic where they had helped her before.

You killed my baby. Twice? Could she do that to Jackson? The next time they were to meet, she did not go, because she did not know what to say. She bought a kit and gave herself another test. No doubt. No doubt at all. At the church service again, she wanted to let out a biblical cry: 'God forgive me, I'm with child!' But George was there, and the others were so kind to each other, so peaceful tonight under the empty phrases that her lunatic father wafted over their heads like a drift of smoke from something burning in the kitchen. For the first time, she envied them. Maybe it was all delusion, but still, they had something she had not got.

'Pray,' George Lott intoned. 'Look into yourselves for the answers.'

Ida looked. She tried to see beyond the fear and confusion, to break out of the trap and find her way back to the commonsense that had helped her to survive this far. It all came to her. This baby was not her enemy. It was her friend.

Diane had had the good sense to have her tubes tied. Thank you, Diane. If Jackson wanted a baby, he would set Ida up in a place of her own, and leave Diane. They were not married. He liked Bernie, and if he had been willing to father Ricky, he would take on Maggie also, for the sake of living with his own child and his own Ida that he dwelt with in magic and obsession in the upstairs back room at Winifred's mother's house.

Dreaming, hoping, her voice airy-light so as not to threaten him, Ida said to Jackson quite simply, 'I'm going to have your baby.'

They were at the corner table in the Lamb and Flag, where they met so that they could arrive at the house together. Ida had her cropped head on one side and her chin down, smiling up at him.

Jackson had been watching the dart board. He kept his eyes there for a long moment before he took them away, very slowly, and looked down at her. His face was not pleased, not surprised, not angry, not sad. It was nothing, the mouth without expression, the eyes like dead fish.

'Get out of my life,' was all he said.

Ida got up and went out. As her new English shoes echoed along the pavement in this deserted part of town, she was bleakly conscious of the tiny foetus, flourishing within her like a parasite, a relentless invader.

Buddy had rented a house off base, a glorified shack that would never take them through the winter. It was a mean place, right on the main road, where Maggie could not go out on her own, and the furnace died if you turned the thermostat over sixty.

A place to fight in.

'Shut up!' Ida yelled at Buddy. 'The kids aren't asleep yet, and they can hear everything in this shoe box.'

'So what? They may as well know what's going on, since they're part of the problem. If we didn't have them, we might get by.'

'Shut your rotten mouth, you bastard.' Ida lowered her voice and hissed at him. 'If you think two kids is a problem, you don't know nothing. I'm having another baby.'

'Whose is it?'

'Yours, of course.'

'Like hell. I've been gone too long.'

'I'm four months gone.' She had calculated back to the night before he left for Viet Nam. Nearer the birth, she would tell him the baby was going to be late.

'Bitch.' He came toward her. He had lost weight while he was abroad, and being brought back to face the jewellery charges had given him a flabbier, shiftier look. After Ida came back, he had shaved off his moustache, to pay her back for cutting her hair.

'Watch it, Buddy. If you touch me, I'm sending Bernie next door to call the police. All you'd need, under the circumstances.'

He stood in front of her with his legs apart and his fists clenched, frustrated, his eyes, those soft brown eyes that had never grown up, looking from side to side in the cramped room.

'Whose is it?' he repeated stupidly.

'The night before you left – remember?'

'God damn. I was wearin' a rubber.'

'They can be torn.'

'I don't believe it.' But he did. He was so dumb, he was easier to fool than a child.

'You going to have another baby, Ma?' Bernie asked, next day, not curiously, but in a conversational tone.

'I reckon. Do you mind?'

'Okay by me. There won't be room for it in this dog kennel, though. Pop, kin we have another dog? A guy at school's got a litter of –'

'Cut that out.'

One of the hard things about being back with Buddy was that he had lost interest in Bernie. He no longer alternately spoiled and bullied the boy. He ignored him. Bernie tried everything in his repertoire to try to get his father back. It was pitiful.

Before the end of January, they all had colds or flu, and Ida's doctor said they must move to a warmer house. Buddy was frantic about having to pay more rent, with his future an unknown precipice. The longer his case was delayed, the worse it looked, and the legal officer on the base warned him that even if the court let him off with a fine, he was headed almost certainly for a dishonourable discharge.

Ida got the rest of the stuff out of storage. Since Buddy was still working at the base and being paid, she was able to buy herself a car, another clunking old gas-eater, the only kind she could afford.

She had arranged to meet Lily, but then she called it off,

because Buddy had hit her in the face, and Lily was too sharp to believe Ida had run into the edge of a door.

When the baby was born, things would be better. This one was a drag on Ida from start to finish. Her legs and back were killing her a lot of the time, and her fear that the birth would be as long and difficult as Maggie's weakened her strength and made her impatient with the children, and not able to keep Buddy on an even keel, as she had always managed to do.

She told the doctor that she wanted a Caesarean.

'Nonsense. You'll sail through it.' He did not know any of her history. Air Force doctors came and went all the time. They didn't care. Some of them had been in Viet Nam and were not yet fit for regular posting, and airmen's wives knocking out babies was not their idea of a thrilling career.

'If it's like the last one, it'll kill me, and maybe the baby as well.'

'You're hallucinating. You're in perfect shape. Small pelvic girdle, sure, but it looks like it's going to be a small baby.'

In which case, would Buddy still believe it was late?

The court case was now set for August. Through spring and early summer, Buddy went noticeably downhill. He would not see his lawyer: 'What's he pesterin' me for? Bump up the fees, is all.' He would not see his mother, or any of his family, although they were all ready to stand by him, and would swear to a man that evidence against him was false, if anyone asked them. He would not see any of his old friends, including Cora and Duane, which was just as well.

He had some new sleazy drinking buddies, one of whom was a tart named Allie, whom he might or might not be sleeping with. Ida didn't care.

Maggie was part of a programme to put handicapped children into normal classes with their own age group, which had made her more withdrawn. She said and did nothing in class, and got beaten up in the playground by a girl smaller and younger than herself, and lost a permanent front tooth. The dentist would only put in a temporary bridge until her mouth grew. Maggie quickly found out how to take the front tooth out, and wore it mostly in her pocket.

Bernie went into the jungle of junior high, and lost some of his sweetness and trust in order to survive.

'Better days are coming,' Ida told him, as she had promised him at every bad stage in his eleven years, because it was a belief that had kept her going through her thirty-three. 'Nowhere to go but up. After the baby is born, you and I will have fun together.'

Buddy still knocked Ida about if she did not get out of the way, or sometimes she hit him first. Somehow they stuck it out together. Buddy could not approach the precipice of his trial alone, and Ida had nowhere else to go. Maybe his lawyer would get him off in the end, in spite of himself. Ida still indulged in her optimistic dreams, all evidence to the contrary.

She was huge and slow-moving, with varicose veins that forced her to keep her legs up, when Buddy started to ask, 'Whose baby?' again.

'You know it's yours. If you can believe you had it in you.'

'Watch your mouth.' He knocked her feet off the chair and sat down. 'I can give you babies any time I want, but this time, I sure as hell didn't want, so come clean, you bitch.'

'Gimme a break. I'm not going through all that again.'

He lifted a foot as if he were going to kick at her sore legs.

When she refused to argue, it infuriated him almost as much as if she had told him the truth. So one morning at breakfast, she did tell him, crazy with the need to stop him nagging and tormenting.

The kids were there. That was the worst of it. Buddy pulled the kitchen chair out from underneath him, smashed it against the wall, and with Bernie hanging on to his shirt, his arm, his leg, anywhere he could try to get a slipping handhold, Buddy slammed one of the chair legs into Ida's stomach.

She went down. Buddy hurled the chair leg through the glass half of the door and went out after it.

'Oh, Ma.' Bernie and Maggie were on the floor with Ida, stroking her, mooing and whimpering. Maggie was white with mauve lips, gibbering with fright. Bernie was half out of his mind.

She had to get herself together. She sat up and leaned against the refrigerator with her legs stuck out beyond the huge mound of her stomach. The pain subsided. The baby kicked out sideways. It was all right. When Ida got her breath back, she stood up, with Bernie's help, and ran a hand through the hair she had kept short herself, raggedly, with Judy's style long gone.

'What'll I do?' Bernie was in anguish. 'The school bus will be at the corner in a few minutes.'

'Let it.' Ida felt like a giant. She commanded the universe. 'You're not going to school, neither one of you. Now listen. You go on up with Maggie and pack whatever you can get into those suitcases under my bed. Not just summer clothes, take your warm things, and find your boots. I can get my stuff into garbage bags. What I can't, the hell with it.'

Her saucepans, her favourite kitchen utensils, her ornaments, her picture of two children in sun hats walking hand in hand through an English meadow, the cushion cover she had been working on since her legs were so bad: she walked out on them all. She took her photograph album, and when she was ravaging through a drawer, she found the dead and dried carnation from her wedding, folded in the napkin with silver bells, where it had been ever since, and dropped it in the black plastic bag to remind her of her girlish folly.

They packed as much as they could into the old black car, which sagged on the back axle even with nothing in it, and tied Bernie's bike on the roof, because it would have dragged in the road if they had tied it on the back.

'Goin' Englin',' Maggie said comfortably.

'Don't be silly,' Bernie told her, sharply for him, perched on the edge of the front seat, his worried face almost against the shield. 'We can't drive to England.'

'To Englin',' Maggie said.

'It's all right, chick, we're going to Aunt Sis.'

But half an hour into the journey, Ida pulled into a rest area for a think, the baby pushing bits of itself against the steering wheel. Sis would take them in, but she lived too near Verna. The trouble would be colossal. It wouldn't be fair on Sis and Jeff.

'We'll find somewhere for tonight, a motel or something.'

She drove on, and ignored the start of a new inner disturbance, and then the first ominous pain.

'What's the matter, Ma?'

'I don't feel so good.'

Shirley had gone away, and she couldn't go back to any of the other women she had known at Watkins. Got to keep going. Where to? Where could she go?

'Feel okay, Ma?'

When the pain came again, she did not tell him. Stomach gas, maybe, or hunger cramps. She had eaten almost nothing since she got up. She swallowed air and made herself burp.

'Pardon me,' she said to Bernie.

'Are we nearly there?'

Where? The cramps again. She would have to pull off the highway and get them all something to eat.

But you don't go through two births and not know labour pains when they hit you. Regular. Must be about twenty minutes since the last one. God, she'd have to start timing them properly. She was going to have to go somewhere and have this god-damned, poor little, God-forsaken, father-forsaken, fighting baby that was in command now, in control of its useless mother.

The road on both sides was empty. Ida made a U-turn through a gap in the middle where it said 'Police and Highway Vehicles Only', and headed south again.

'Where are we going, Ma?'

'You'll see. We'll be okay.'

'Kin we stop and get something to eat?'

Ida shook her head. Got to keep going now.

'Where are you?' Ida's voice had not been urgent, but Lily's was. 'Where are you, for God's sake?'

'Somewhere near you, I don't know. Newton, Newton Centre, Newton Highlands, what's the difference? I asked at a gas station and he says this is Newton Centre.'

'What gas station? Where?'

'Near a big garden place.'

'Centre Street?'

'There's no names. I'm at a kind of shopping centre.'

'What stores?'

'Dry cleaners, liquors, paint store, nothing much.'

'I think I know. Hang on. I'll call an ambulance.'

'No, don't. I'm all right. But the kids are with me.'

'Stay there. Don't move, Ida. I'm coming. I'll be there in five minutes.'

It was fifteen minutes by the time Lily had explained to Paul, and taken pans off the stove and got Cathy out of the bath. Red lights went to war against her, one by one, changing just as she sped up to the crossing. She went through the last one, and passed a van by the skin of her teeth, as it was pulling out to go round a parked car.

The phone booth was in a far corner of the parking lot, outside the closed liquor store. Lily could see the heads of Bernie and Maggie hanging out of the windows of a big black car like a hearse. Ida was in the booth, talking to the maternity unit.

'Twelve minutes.' When Lily opened the glass door, Ida put out a hand to squeeze her arm. 'Twelve minutes now.' The hospital said something. 'I don't know . . . well, you're the boss.'

'Hi, Lil.'

'Hi, Eye.'

They looked at each other deadpan for a moment, like travellers meeting in the middle of a desert.

'"Plenty of time," she says.' Ida was huge, her general fat camouflaged by the specific bulk her short body could hardly carry.

'Not plenty of time. You should be in there now. Come on.' Lily opened the door of her car, but Ida went towards the hearse.

'I'm not going to leave my car. You know where the hospital is? We'll follow you.'

As Ida got into her car, her children got out and climbed in with Lily.

'We're hungry,' Bernie said. Maggie was grizzling.

'Haven't you had anything to eat?'

'Not all day,' he said, not pitifully, but as a statement of fact.

'Let's stop and pick up doughnuts somewhere on the way,' Lily called to Ida.

'I saw a place.'

Instead of stopping at a grocery, Ida led Lily at speed in the opposite direction from the hospital, and swung into the crowded parking lot of a McDonald's.

'Want a hamburger and fries, kids?'

'Ida – no.'

'Yeah, it's okay. I'm not scared now. This one's going to be a breeze, I know it.'

Whatever had happened, whatever she was doing here, there was a sort of unholy contentment on Ida's face under the funny cropped hair that made her look younger.

In McDonald's, Ida and the children ordered a full meal from the very young girl in the baseball cap, who shoved it over the counter without looking at them. They ate slowly, squeezing envelopes of ketchup and bright-green liquid pickles on to everything, while Lily fretted over her coffee and tried to re-member details of her brief student visit to Obstetrics, where the male students, stark white or green, were only allowed to watch from the doorway. Having a baby yourself was totally different from someone else having one.

'Let's hurry,' she kept urging, but Maggie was messing the food with her fingers and staring without drinking over the rim of the violent-coloured milkshake.

Ida ate a cheeseburger with a side order of french fries, and belched, without apologizing or putting her hand over her mouth. That much, at least, America had done for her.

'You okay, Ma?'

Ida groaned, and rolled her eyes at Bernie.

'How long?' Lily asked sternly.

Ida looked at the man's watch, clumsy on her narrow wrist. 'Five minutes.'

'Ida – *please* – let's go.'

'Maggie ain't done yet.'

'She can take it in the car.' If Lily had to deliver the baby on the floor of McDonald's, would the girl behind the counter look at them then?

At last, she got Ida going. A side trip to the ladies' room, more groans – 'Where were you born?' 'In the toilet at McDonald's' –

and then Bernie was in the back of Lily's car, Maggie beside her with the greasy food in a napkin, and she sped for the hospital. Ida drove so slowly that Lily kept losing her and having to wait.

'Maybe she's having it in the car,' Bernie said.

At the hospital, they all went up to Maternity, where Ida was told she might not deliver for another three hours – so much for the toilet at McDonald's. Lily would not leave her, but the children could not be in the waiting-room, so the three of them were put into the chaplain's office outside the Maternity unit.

Lily read Maggie bits from the Book of Common Prayer and drew pictures on the chaplain's note-pad, and took her to the ladies' room twice, because of the giant milkshake. Bernie took himself off on a tour of the hospital, with the purpose of going up and down in every elevator and stopping at every floor.

Maggie was greasily asleep on Lily's lap when a nurse came to tell her that Ida had a son. So much for three hours.

'Another boy, gee, that's good.' Bernie grinned. 'So it won't be just me and two women.'

'Have you –' Lily had not heard from Ida what was going on. 'Has your mother left your father, do you think?'

'Guess so. He hit her with a chair.'

'A *chair*?'

'Just the leg.'

Lily was allowed to see Ida before she went home. The children could come back to the hospital tomorrow.

'I told you,' Ida winked. 'It was a breeze. I don't know why I was scared. I could have had six more since Maggie.'

She looked drained, wrung out, heavy-eyed, the short fringe wet on her forehead, and so purely lovable that Lily went on her knees by the bed and laid her face against Ida's and cried a little into the pillow.

Did I look like that? I thought I must look like hell after Isobel and Cathy, but did I look miraculous like that? Was that why Paul couldn't speak?

'I'd better call Buddy,' Lily said into the pillow.

Ida moved her head sideways.

'He'll have to be told.'

'It's not his kid.'

Lily raised her head, and saw Ida fall asleep.

A nurse came in. 'Mrs Legge's boy says the little girl has wet her pants.'

'I'll take care of it.'

Six

*F*our years ago, after Ida's baby was born, that dumb kid Maggie had made the stain on the carpet in Isobel's room, and no power on earth had ever been able to get it out.

A small rug now covered the place where Maggie, crawling across the floor with Arthur in one of her dog games, had stopped, looked up at Isobel and then flung her big head forward to pitch its contents on to Isobel's blue carpet which she had chosen herself that year, when her room was done over for her birthday.

To open her bottom drawer to get the bag she needed now, four years later, for the plane trip to England, Isobel had to turn back the rug, and there it was, a ragged crab shape, turning the bright blue to pale brown, reminding her, as always, of Maggie.

'How did she manage to do that?' Isobel had asked at the time, when it was clear that carpet foam and scrubbing were not going to remove the stain.

'That's for her to know and you to guess.' Her mother sat back on her heels and quoted one of Granny's sayings. 'Must have been some kind of acid in her stomach.'

But normal people's throw-up didn't do that much damage. That nutty kid always had to be different, throwing up, or anything else. She wandered off and had to be whistled for, as if she were a dog, but she didn't know how to treat animals. She hurled herself on their dog Arthur and mauled him around as if he were a stuffed toy. If he hadn't been so gutless, he would have bitten off her face, and got blamed for it. The dope even came to Maggie when she called him, although she could not pronounce his name any better than 'Arth'. Daddy made that into a joke. Arthur's double bark when he was on the wrong side of a door, which he usually was: 'Arth! Arth!'

Maggie would have hurled herself on the baby, if her mother had left him within reach. If little Fred was on a counter, in the basket (Cathy's basket, it had been), Maggie would stand on tiptoe, trembling, her hands going everywhere, like butterflies;

her pink glasses slipped crooked, bottom lip wet with dribble from wanting to pick up the baby.

He was only a few days old, and red as raw meat, with a tuft of red hair. Maggie was eight, but she wasn't allowed to hold him on her own, in case she suddenly lost interest and dropped him.

Although Isobel was two years younger, she was allowed to hold Fred and help with his bath and diapers and bottles. It had been exciting at first, but it soon got to be a drag, with three of them and the baby crowded into the house, and Mum flat out all day, and telling Isobel, 'Not now,' and, 'I haven't got time.'

It had been neat having the TV on so much, because they all turned it on whether they were going to watch or not, which drove Daddy crazy. So did the bubble-gum. Bernie and Maggie chewed it all the time, blowing it out as big as their faces and cracking it back like a pistol shot. When they ate, they stuck it under the table. Ida would always give Isobel a stick of gum if Mum wasn't looking, but all the same, it was a relief when they all suddenly disappeared without a trace, taking with them the infant car-seat that had been Isobel's and then Cathy's.

Four years later, Isobel shut the bottom drawer, made a vomiting face at the stain on the carpet and turned the rug back over it. Downstairs, she played 'Chopsticks' on the piano with Terry. She took the base, because she liked thumping better than tinkling.

Terry was staying the night, and coming to England with them tomorrow. He was at college, but he hadn't gone grand and grown up. You had to leave him alone if he was in a bad mood; but he did funny things, like riding a bicycle backwards and leaving notes on parked cars, and he was teaching Isobel to draw horses facing right as well as left, and how to see monsters in clouds.

'My brother,' Isobel would tell everybody in England.

Ida's departure had been a relief to Paul too. If she had not taken off, with some of the baby things that Lily was saving, 'in case', he felt that he would have exploded, spattered over the walls and ceiling.

He was proud of Lily for rescuing Ida and her children and managing so cheerfully to fit them all into the Newton house; but after a few days, he had to grit his teeth to be that kind, tolerant Paul that everybody thought he was by nature, backing Lily up in all her warm-hearted spontaneous enterprises. The play group, the Golden Age picnic, the Fresh Air Kid, who had wanted to go back to the Bronx, the puppet show in the children's ward, the fruits of impulsive energy which didn't always ripen, but with which he went along, trying to keep the peace, and playing the piano where necessary.

Ida, who was as big as if she were still waiting to give birth, not recovering from it, had been given Cathy's room; but she spread the baby all over the house, even in the garden, since she insisted on drying its clothes on the line instead of in the dryer, and the trash cans overflowed with disposable diapers, and flies. She talked all the time, like a woman who has been cast away on a desert island, but she did not talk about that boor she had married, so nobody knew what her plans were, nor why she had been in labour in the phone booth outside Derry's Liquors.

She had stayed almost two weeks, but it seemed like months. The house was too small. The table was too small when they all ate together. The girls' bathroom was polluted.

Bernie slept on the sofa, and Paul fell over his model cars when he went through the darkened room to make his morning coffee. He was glad to go to work. He had always looked forward eagerly to coming home. Now he sometimes found himself dreading it.

Lily was exhausted. Isobel was snapping bubble-gum and reverting to tantrums to get attention. Cathy wanted to go back into diapers. Every time Paul got Lily alone for a moment, he asked, 'When are they going to go?'

'Ssh, I don't know. Thanks for being so nice about it.' That was how he always got trapped into being nice. 'Ida's not that strong yet Paul, and I think she's pretty desperate. I don't think she has anywhere to go.'

Desperate or not, Lily and Ida had some chummy times together. They talked and purred over the baby, and sometimes giggled about nothing, as they had in Iceland when he first knew them. Since Ida was manless, temporarily or permanently, Lily seemed a little less married.

After years of wearing her front hair fastened back, Lily had let Ida cut it in bangs, like her own. Her hair was now three sides of a square frame around her face. The bangs looked cute on her, although she agonized as soon as it was done. 'Disaster! It makes my face too broad. Where's my noble forehead? The back of my head's too flat.'

She cast away the collection of clips and combs that used to hold her thick swatch of brown hair, and Isobel took them all and fastened up bits of her strong curling hair in odd ways. Cathy fought for them, but they fell out of her fine hair.

Maggie took all the clips and combs out of Isobel's drawer and buried them in the garden, in the place where Arthur buried his bones.

'Do something, Daddy! Mummy, beat her up!' Isobel was scarlet, with brimming eyes and jutted bottom teeth. 'I wish she was dead.'

'Hush, Bella. Be nice.' Paul often found himself repeating things his mother had told him.

With Isobel lying on her stomach, beating the floor, Paul picked the wrong moment to tell Lily that they were invited for drinks and supper by the Jensens in Dover, who dated from his days with Barbara, and had remained friends.

'How can I? I can't leave the girls with Ida. She's got enough on her hands with the baby, and Mrs Dunn would never stand for the chaos here. You know what she's like.'

'Get someone else.'

'I can never get any of the teenagers at the last minute. Besides . . .'

'You don't want to go.'

The Jensens got along better with Lily than they had with Barbara, but Lily was still slightly insecure about Paul's past life She preferred the friends they had made together.

'Dammit, Lily.' Isobel stopped pounding her fists and looked up. Paul and Lily went out on to the porch. 'Do something for me for once, will you?'

'That's not fair. I do all the time.'

'Not this last week.'

'Don't be vile. It doesn't suit you, darling. You're always so good-tempered about everything.'

'I have to be. I like to feel calm and easy. Getting mad embroils you.'

'That's a cop-out.' Lily was trying to work up to a fight. They never fought. 'You're insulating yourself from the world out there.'

'I see more of the world than you do. You don't know what Turnbull's is like these days. The boss says, "Do it your way, Paul," and then breathes down my neck. Young Dennis says, "Great idea!" and then runs to Mr T. and gripes behind my back. Suppliers let me down. Customers want this, want that, want everything except to pay. I want to scream and shout and pull a whip off the rack and start laying about me, but I swallow a lot of oxygen and stay pretty calm, and everyone says, "Why do you stay so calm?"'

'Why do you?'

'Because it's the easy way out. Purely selfish. My father taught me long ago when I used to scream and yell, that controlling it is easier than letting it rip. He was right. So are we going to the Jensens', for God's sake, or does that bloody woman come first in our lives?'

'Don't shout. Why can't you stay calm about Ida?'

'That's it, I can't. Maybe I'm getting old.'

'Quiet.' She would never let him be ten years older than her.

'Aren't I allowed to be crabby at forty? She talks too much, and you'd think she had seven babies, the way it takes over the whole house. I don't trust her either, for some reason.'

'She's going to steal the spoons?'

'It's just a feeling. I think she exploits you.'

'She's my friend. I'd do anything for her.' Lily's noble look didn't come off so well now, with the bangs over her forehead.

'Would she for you?'

'Of course.'

'You said you wouldn't leave the girls with her.'

'Because it's too much. Why are you so suspicious?'

'Because I'm fed up. I want our nice cosy life back. We're going to the Cape in a couple of weeks. What if they're still here?'

'We could take them . . .'

'Then I'll stay here.'

'Oh God, oh God.' Lily burst into tears. 'This was never going to happen. We were never going to fight.'

'We're not fighting.'

'Men always say that, to make it look as if it wasn't their fault. No, you're right. I'm wrong. I'd love to go to the Jensens with you. I'll bribe Mrs Dunn to come. I'll pay her double.'

'You don't need to pay anyone,' Ida said, when they told her. 'I'll look after your kids.'

'You've got enough to do.'

'Don't you trust me?'

'Of course, Eye, but this is better.'

'Please yourself. But it's a waste of money.'

Mrs Dunn had come early, while they were dressing. When they came down, they found her standing uneasily in the living-room, because she could not find a place to sit down.

'Where are the girls?' Lily asked.

'Running around outside.' Mrs Dunn had glasses as thick as Coke-bottle bottoms. You could not see what she thought or felt. 'They seem kind of wild. The rascals.' She added an un-smiling afterthought.

Lily told her about the children's supper and bed time, and called them in to say goodnight. Isobel stamped in and flounced about. Maggie flopped in after her in a huge shirt of Ida's and grinned, 'Who you?', gap-toothed. Cathy would not take Mrs Dunn's hand to go into the kitchen.

Paul started the car, and the kitchen screen-door swung open. One arm and half of Cathy came out, the other arm held by Mrs Dunn.

Lily turned her face forward again. 'Let's go on,' she said tensely.

As they moved forward, they heard Cathy scream, 'I wish you dint never been borned!'

The party had been great, and Lily enjoyed it. She stayed close to Paul, and glowed under her thick, shining bangs, and flirted with him, and not with any of the other men, which she sometimes tried out mildly, to keep her hand in. Paul drove home fast in the rain, wanting to pay off Mrs Dunn and get up to the bedroom.

Something looked different about their road and front lawn. Ida's sagging car, obscene among the neat compacts and suburban station-wagons, was not parked outside.

'She's gone on a toot and left that woman with all the kids.'

Mrs Dunn was sitting in her jacket and plastic rain bonnet on a straight chair in the front hall.

'My friend gone out?' Lily spoke carefully to Mrs Dunn, who always looked as though she did not like what she could smell on your breath.

'Gone, Mrs Stephens. I sat upstairs with your little one; because she was fussy.' Pause to be told, 'Oh, thank you.' 'I heard them racketing around the other bedrooms. When I came down, they had fled like thieves in the night.'

After Mrs Dunn had been overpaid and gone down the street to her own house, Paul shouted, 'Hooray!' and poured drinks, but Lily was cast down.

'She'll get by, Lily darling. She'll go back and sort out that violent airman, or she'll make out on her own. She's tough, that one.'

'But after all we've done for her. That's what hurts.'

'Not as much as if we'd had to throw her out.'

'I wouldn't have.'

'I would.'

'Well, you didn't have to prove it.' Lily brightened up. 'She's saved you that. Good old Ida.'

They had drunk to her, and taken their glasses upstairs through the peaceful house.

Now, four years later, Lily took two weeks off from the Day-Nite answering service, to which she had returned now that Isobel and Cathy were nine and seven, and they took one of their trips to England, with Terry, who was in his second year at an art school in Boston.

Paul was going to the British Equestrian Trade Fair again. His Tack Rack had been a runner-up for the New Products award when he first showed it. It had continued to sell well in England, and now he was showing Tack Rack Junior, the same modular system, scaled down for children and ponies, which Turnbull's were claiming was their own idea, but they would still have to pay Paul the same percentages under his contract.

He would be travelling quite a bit on this trip. He hoped Terry might go round with him, because Lily was nervous about what her stepson would do with himself, and whether he would like her country, or despise it for all the bumbling oddities she could see with a clearer eye now that she had been in America for ten years.

Terry was grown up, but he was still as unpredictable at twenty as he had been when she first knew him at ten, and then as a teenager. When he was younger, Barbara had always managed a good reason why he could not go to England with Paul and Lily. He had never been out of the United States, except to Canada. He was excited about the trip, so it was fair enough that he did not want to sit with Lily and his father and the restless girls, but pretended he was travelling alone. The plane was not full, so after take-off he moved to an empty seat, like a seasoned traveller, clamped the headset over his ears and had two whiskies and some red wine, Paul observed by turning round cautiously, and was cross and rumpled when James Spooner met them at Heathrow.

Terry sat in the front, and Jam kept asking, much too soon, 'How do you like it, my lad? Never see anything as green as this where you come from, eh? Look now, these are the Chiltern hills, built up out of ancient history. Men have been here since 2000 B C. Bit of a time before Christopher Columbus and all that lot, eh?'

Terry was monosyllabic, hunched into the heavy jacket that he had brought because he had heard that England was always cold. But when he saw the brick and flint cottage with the wooded hills behind it and in front, the Duke's Head, white, with beams and curly red tiles, and the old inn sign of the laughing Duke, he said, 'Gee,' and got out of the car quickly.

Terry had seen this kind of thing in movies, and on calendars his step-grandmother sent, and he had heard about it from Lily and Paul, but he had no idea that England would be like this. He had expected to feel strange, and that people would see at once that he didn't fit into the scene, and would write him off as an American tourist.

It wasn't like that at all. No one noticed him, and at the airport the officials were totally relaxed. He had heard that students always got hassled in Europe, but he walked through British customs as if it wasn't there – just a few men in uniform lounging about on tables and not even looking at Terry and his hangover, let alone pulling him aside and saying, 'Excuse me, sir, where are the drugs?'

His grandfather, who had a loose lumpy face like a mobile potato, cried a little when he saw Lily and the kids, and wiped the end of his big nose on the back of one hand as he grabbed Terry's hand with the other, and said, quite emotionally, 'I'm *glad* you came.'

Maybe he was. Maybe he wasn't. He was quite a theatrical old buster.

As they crossed the road from the terminal building to the garage, the clouds were a low grey ceiling, and warm rain hung in the air like mist. Lily and Paul made the kind of ironic noises with which passengers in the plane had greeted the Captain's announcement that it was raining in London. But so what? Who would want to step out of Heathrow airport into the same crude blue skies and indiscriminate sun of New England?

Terry rolled down the front window of James's small sober car, and ingested the new traffic noises – huge double trailer trucks from France and Germany on these Mickey Mouse roads – and stared at the toy fields and the casual old houses and churches, any one of which would be a show piece in a neighbourhood in the States.

After they had turned on to side roads away from diesel fumes, he smelled pig manure and wet earth and an indefinable savour of new leaves and cut wood and sheep's wool on the vivid green turf of the hills that Lily's father was yattering on about.

Terry did not answer the old guy. He was too occupied with absorbing to be able to disgorge. They would think he was trying to be blasé, but he had grown used by now to being misinterpreted. If people couldn't guess what you thought or felt, too bad. It wasn't worth trying to make it easy for them.

They came over the brow of a hill and dropped into the wet fog which hid the bends of the hairpin road that Lily's father, like every other lunatic driver in this decadent country, took at death-defying speed. When the mist cleared at the bottom of the steep hill, there it was. It stood modestly by the side of an unimportant road, old as all get out, beamed, tiled, leaning slightly into the hill, a genuine English pub like dozens they had passed, but this one was in the family.

For a long time now, Terry had felt disgruntled and out of step with everything about him. Privately knowing that the unease was in yourself, not your surroundings, made no difference, if there was nothing you could do about it. You had to wear the appearance of a victim who never got a decent break. It didn't fool anybody, but it gave you the excuse to make no effort.

Here at the Duke's Head, in this small-time village which looked to Terry like it hadn't accomplished much of anything in hundreds of years, he felt at home. No need for defences. It wasn't long before he was admitting to his surprised father and Lily, who had both been dubious about bringing him, because he might not enjoy himself worth the price of the fare, 'This is my kind of place.'

'I know what you mean,' his father said. 'I feel like that when I come over here.'

'Why don't you move over, then?'

'That would spoil it.'

'Then this whole deal is an illusion, just because it's old and strange and foreign, and "there", the way we look at it, not "here"?'

'If so, I'll keep it that way.'

They were walking together up on the hills, along a sheep trail that took them through yellow gorse under the ridge, with the valley laid out below: tidy, cultivated villages no more than crossroads, farm clusters, towns like neat citadels, instead of octopus stains eating up the landscape.

One of the most remarkable things about this trip was that Terry was getting along pretty well with his father. The man could get along with anybody, but Terry had not been at ease with him for years. Now he was. Three thousand miles from his mother and sincere Drummond Blake. Was that it?

There was not room for all of them in the cottage behind the Duke's Head, where the faucets ran either hot or cold, but not both at once. Terry stayed with Lily's sister Blanche and her husband Neil, a bicycle ride away. James said Neil was a no-hoper, but Terry got on quite well with the shy, skinny man, no match for Blanche, who was as bossy as Lily in a quieter and more subtly smug way.

Neil collected snail shells, which was weird, but convenient, since there was a multitude of them colonizing this wet earth, where everybody grew vegetables. Terry made some sketches of the more colourful spiral shells, and Neil thought he would have them made up into a Christmas card.

'Not this year,' Blanche said. 'I promised the twins it should be them.' The twins were one year old.

Their house was fairly new and plain, but it stood next to an ancient farmyard, the top of whose front wall was as carefully thatched as if it had been a house, a glorious squandering of artistry, like an Italian Renaissance fresco on the wall of an out-house. Beyond Terry's window was a huge sagging barn with enormous doors that bulged like the side of a ship and had little doors in them, through which slow-moving men came and went in mossy pants and dark vests and collarless shirts. At one end, three horses looked out of shabby loose boxes, with crooked half doors and cobwebbed windows. When the horses came out to be ridden, or to go into the pasture at the side where Terry could watch them roll and shake themselves with legs stuck stiffly out like sawhorses, they were thoroughbreds, immaculate, elegant. They were like beautiful girls stepping out over garbage from a scarred door in a Boston back alley.

Besides the twins, Blanche had a fat small boy called Duffy. She also bred Jack Russell terriers, sexy little mutts who lived in kennels out back, and barked so continuously that you got used to them. Her favourites came indoors and lay on the rug on their tight rounded sides, with their short legs stuck out, but not reaching the floor. One villain sometimes sat up and let out a long red prick and took it in his mouth, and went round and round and round, damnedest thing you ever saw. Terry was shocked, but Blanche only said, 'Jack Russells are like that.' Terry tried to kick the rotating fiend when she wasn't looking.

Blanche gave him a great English breakfast, with slices of bacon as floppy as wash cloths, and bread fried in sausage grease, and tea that would have made his hair curl, if it had not been so hopelessly curly already that he had to keep it cut short when most of the other students wore theirs long. If he let it go, it grew out as well as down, and made his head look way too big on his body that was way too short and planted on feet that were way too small.

After breakfast and a few juicy burps to make Duffy laugh and the indoor Jack Russells bark, he did the dishes, because, 'Everyone does his bit in this house; Neil loves to hoover, don't you dear?' Terry would ride the bike to the Duke's Head, where he was allowed to help.

There was a public bar and a saloon bar, divided by a narrow passage from the front door where the jolly old Duke, the scourge of the land, so 'twas said, creaked in the wind. The public had benches and tables and a dart board and a cigarette machine and pictures of women advertising booze. The saloon had a carpet and small tables with wooden armchairs, and a fireplace large enough to have little seats in it on either side. Between the beams, the low walls were hung with pictures which looked as if they had been there since the first pint was drawn. Sporting prints too dark and damp-stained to see more than whiskered men in top hats leaning back on horses that galloped with all four legs out at the same time. Photographs of favourite dogs. Grooms in derbies holding short-tailed hunters. A woman in a hat like a cake, fixing ribbons on a champion bull that may have gored her the next minute. Lily said that her father sometimes claimed that this or that dog or horse or gent with a gun in the crook of his arm came from his family, although the regulars knew that the pictures had come with the pub.

James knew that they knew, of course, but it was all part of the character he had built for himself: funny, lovable, outrageous, gabby, faking voices, pulling his rubbery face about to make people laugh, giving them a verse or a chorus to make them protest, 'Knock it off, Jam. We come in here for a bit of peace and quiet.'

Terry loved it all. He usually stayed till closing time, serving drinks, collecting glasses, cutting sandwiches, exchanging a few words with strangers in a way he could never do at home.

There was a lot of work to do, especially when James was in London, having his picture taken for an advertisement. Terry washed glasses and sorted empties and brought up stock from the cellar, and Nora taught him how to pull pints of beer just the way people here wanted it, so close to the rim of a pint mug that one more drop would lose it. He could set it intact on the bar in front of a man who would square his elbow and lift it unspilled to sea-anemone lips.

The quantities of ale poured down was amazing, even by New England tavern standards. The stone passage to the bleak men's room out back was worn down by a constant weighty-bladdered tread.

Customers, tickled to see a Yank working with skill among the beer handles and optic measures, often offered him, 'One for yourself.' Terry's father did not monitor what he drank. Often he drank a bit too much and was amazed to find himself joining in the repartee of mild insult which was the coin of humour in the saloon bar of the Duke's Head. One evening when Paul and Lily were off somewhere, Nora let Terry help himself to as much

as he liked, so he got polluted and fell down in the acrid passage
to the gents. Nora drove him home with the bike on the back of
her car. When he rode groggily over next day, she gave him
something fizzy that took out his top sinuses, and said to him in
her wise, unflustered way, 'Better to know the enemy, eh?'

'Yes, ma'am. That stuff is dynamite.'

James was there most nights, and Terry helped him to shift the
barrels of real ale on to their sides in the racks in the cellar, so that
the beer would settle by opening time tomorrow, when the tap
would be piped up to the beer engine. The firkins and kils Terry
could roll about by himself. For the thirty-six gallon barrels, he
and James put their heads together and levered the weight between them.

'What do you do when Dad or I aren't here?' Terry asked.

James flexed his muscles. 'My strength is as the strength of ten,
because my heart is pure.'

'Because your wife helps you.' Nora made her composed, self-
satisfied face.

She let the old guy pretty much have his head. He liked Terry,
because he would listen to his stories, some true, some probably
not, of his new geriatric career. Terry called him Jamspoon and
loved to look at his album of clippings. Jam as a chef, licking
spaghetti sauce off a wooden spoon. Jam in sports jackets and
grandfatherly cardigans in a men's wear catalogue. Jam with a
hair-piece, before and after. The top half of Jam hanging out of a
wrecked car to illustrate a story in a magazine. Jam in a television
commercial as a background businessman in a derby, going
through a revolving door.

'Hey, Jamspoon, you're famous!'

Terry was suitably impressed.

He drew a quick charcoal caricature of Jam as the man with
the hat on the back of his head, looking at his retirement dream
house – a dog kennel in Terry's picture. It was pinned up in the
bar, until Bob Whittaker threw darts at it.

When his father came back from the trade fair, he took a walk
up in the hills with Terry before he had to start out again on a
sales trip for Turnbull's. Paul took off his jacket and put on one
of the blue sweaters Lily was always buying for him. Terry took

his big sketch pad under his arm. There was a particular view he wanted to get in this afternoon light, farther along to the west, where a grass path, wandering aimlessly among the broad grey trunks of ancient beech trees, suddenly disappeared down a chalky bank, with nothing in front of you but the rest of England, leading your eye away through mysterious changes of colour to a shadowy horizon that merged into the sky.

They took the car to the top of the road, and then followed the path round the corner of the first hill, and along the inner curve toward the next promontory. They walked among flat white and yellow flowers like poached eggs, and hoof prints in the spongy turf.

'What a place to ride,' Terry said.

'I can hardly bear to see the tracks of horses that don't have us on them, can you? You'd gone off horses last time you were on the Cape. I was sorry about that.'

'So was I, but that was why, I guess. Teen stuff.'

'Because you loved riding, or because I loved it?'

'Oh, Dad, don't try to analyse that kind of crazy stuff. Who knows? I couldn't let myself. Now I want to, and we can't.'

'Want me to try to get a couple of horses tomorrow?'

'Don't push it, Dad. My mind changes all the time. I never know how I'll feel.'

They were walking in single file along a sheep track on the edge of the slope, so they did not have to look at each other.

'You having some hard times?'

'Who isn't? Most people at school have some kind of problem. Capital P. It's a pretty weird place, you know.'

'I thought you liked it.'

'I do and I don't.'

There were a few classes that interested him, like life drawing and photography, but most of it was the pits. Second-rate students, and third-rate professors grinding out the same old ideas and stale techniques.

After his grandmother died and his grandfather was alone, the Judge had tried to help Terry grow up. He had taken him soberly to what had seemed like the right places: concerts, museums, good restaurants, a weekend with old friends in Maine who played word games. Terry had very little to say, although his head was so teeming with ideas and fantasies that he could have shouted round the courtyard of the Frick Museum, or dashed himself down on to the rocks of the wild northern coast.

To stop everybody asking him what he was going to do, he had chosen the art school. It was the only thing he could think of.

Last Christmas, he had planned to talk to his mother about dropping out until the fall semester; but she chose to be depressed – oh, but *depressed* – with pasty skin and the suspicious eyes, and that poor guy she married turning cartwheels to try to get her going.

The deadening stone formed and calcified within Terry, and unhinged him.

'Poor old Drummond Blake wanted to send me to a shrink.'

'Why, for God's sake?' Paul caught up with him as the ground flattened out.

'He thinks I act kind of bizarre sometimes.'

'Do you?'

'Hunhnyah.'

On Christmas Eve, Terry had taken money from his mother's purse and gone out and bought this huge frozen turkey that was marked down, and cranberry sauce and sweet potatoes and three different kinds of pie.

When he was unpacking it all, his mother had dragged into the kitchen in those decayed slippers and said in the drone she used, to make sure you knew how she felt, 'Who's going to cook that?'

'You, Mom. And I got what you need to make your famous stuffing.'

'Lover child, I'm sick.'

Terry and Drum were going to roast the turkey, but it wasn't thawed out by Christmas morning, and it didn't seem worth it anyway. It took up a lot of room in the refrigerator, and began to drip through a slit in the wrapping, so Terry threw it over the back fence of the house that had all those cats and dogs.

He went to a party and brought home a fortune-teller from Peru who did not speak any English. He went to the movies with some friends, wearing a robe and slippers in the snow. He drove his mother's car without gas and left it ten blocks away and pretended he could not find it. He went naked into the bedroom of Drum's daughter Wendy and pretended he thought it was the bathroom. He tried to make love to a flaky girl he met in a bar. He told her he was going to Katmandu and she said she would go with him. Next night, her boyfriend came and heaved a brick through what he thought was Terry's window. Poor old Wendy, with those earnest teeth. She wasn't having much luck.

Drummond called the police and Terry got out on the road with a back-pack and hitched up to his grandparents' house on the North Shore. He had spent the rest of the vacation with Uncle Robert, playing trains and sitting on a bench in the shopping mall, eating yoghurt and doing crossword puzzles.

'*Do* you?'

'Do I what?'

'Act bizarre.'

'Oh, well.'

They were into the trees by now, walking on centuries of dead leaves under the new green tracery that turned and glistened between the arching branches.

'This is the place, Dad.'

Where the trees ended, the sun lay along the edge of the bank, and then there was nothing more. Far below and beyond, the world of distance could never be reached.

Terry sat down in a hollow between two thick tree roots, and opened the sketch pad on his knees to the virgin page he was about to desecrate or transfigure. His soft pencil brought in the tree trunks, tilting here and there from the pull of their powerful roots, the path trodden into the leafmould, the dramatic shadow of the bank's edge under its rim of sun. He would touch it in with crayons at home and hint at the distance in overlapping colours, no detail, darkening as far as the gradual beginning of the sky.

The next time he looked up, his father was sitting on the bank, looking out over the sheer drop. His arms were on his knees and his shoulders relaxed forward. If you could see his face, it would be smiling peacefully. You would know him anywhere by the beautiful shape of his head.

The low sun along the ridge of the hills gilded the left side of his thick sandy hair and tipped it with thistledown, light and luminous. The other side of his head and the blue curve of his shoulder were in shadow.

When they got back, Terry worked quickly on the colours before his eye lost them. The muted distance, a blaze of green here and there on the leaves, spots of sunlight on the grey tree trunks, the gold light on the hair, the saxe-blue sweater.

'It's good,' Paul said.

'Don't be so amazed.' Terry put his arm over the picture.

Paul lifted the arm away. 'It's damn *good*!'

'Oh well.'

Terry had drawn it as a picture of this marvellous scenery with a man in the middle ground. It had emerged as a picture of his father, set in that scene.

'Come on the trip with me tomorrow,' Paul said impulsively.

'Dad, I –'

'I'll be going to an equestrian centre and some of the big stables. We could have a good time.'

Caught off guard, Terry did not know what to say. Why couldn't he say, 'I'd love to'?

He said, 'Maybe, but . . . it's the fête, you know. I promised Duggie I'd help with the dog show.' He made a face to show he too thought that was stupid.

In the morning, Blanche put down Terry's bangers and flabby bacon.

'You going with your Dad?'

'I don't know.'

'Because if you're not, I'll have Isobel and Cathy over here, so Lily can go.'

Paul and Lily came to fetch Terry in the rented car, because it was raining. When Blanche made her offer, they were overjoyed; you could see it.

'But are you sure you don't want to come, Terry? Come with us.'

'I guess not.' With the weight pulling him down, it was hard work to dredge up a voice.

He did not want to go shopping with them, or to go to the Duke's Head and help with the Young Farmers' meeting. He would stay at Blanche's and catch up on some reading.

Paul and Lily went out to the car. Terry watched them from the front window, his legs apart, because Duffy was pushing a wooden train back and forth between them. It was raining quite hard. His father and Lily turned up their collars and ran for the car. Paul opened the passenger door, but Lily did not get in at once. They both stood against the inside of the open door, their eyes eating each other up, their faces gleeful, like secret children, because they were going off together and they did not want anyone else.

They did not need to kiss. Maybe after ten years, you had progressed beyond the basic arousal of kissing.

The rain had darkened his father's hair. The expression on his face brought forth demons and red-hot fiends from Terry's soul to flail their arms about and gnash their teeth. Lily, eager and laughing, was simply a woman; not a mother, not anyone's daughter or sister, not a wife.

They were so in love, it was indecent.

Terry turned away, to a shriek from the floor as he splintered a car of Duffy's little train.

So in love.

It was still raining on the afternoon of the church fête. Well, of course. It always rained in England.

'The weather doesn't want to be kind to us,' Nora said.

The British always spoke of the weather as if it were a person with a mind of its own, whereas in the States, it was the property of The Weatherman.

'Won't they cancel it?' Terry asked Duggie Manderson.

'Cancel it, what for? If we cancelled things for a drop of rain, nothing would ever happen.'

Duggie was a large, bland, imperturbable fellow who was a regular at the Duke's Head, downing his half pints, not saying much. He had lived in the village since God began. Everyone knew him. Everyone asked him to help. Terry had seen him quietly dispose of a belligerent drunk for Nora one day when Jam wasn't there.

'Good thing I wasn't,' Jam had boasted, when he learned of it. 'If he'd said that to Nora in my hearing, he'd not have had a head left to pour booze into.'

By the time the fête had been opened by a local celebrity — 'Remember the church roof, friends. Spend your money today like water if you don't want to have water leaking down the back of your neck at matins' — the rain had lightened to that English speciality, a fine, penetrating drizzle. Sheets of plastic covered the food and gifts and used paperbacks on the stalls that stood about on Lady Somebody-Something's wet lawn.

Lady S-S, laughing on a brave high note, bending over the stalls to congratulate the peasants on their cakes and jellies and knitted junk, looked like a Boston bag-lady picking over the trash cans; but she was at least a genuine toffee-nosed Brit, the first Terry had seen, because that sort wouldn't be seen dead in the Head. Hooded girls led soggy ponies and donkeys around, with white-faced children clinging to the handle of the felt saddles. The barbecue was sheltered by a golf umbrella. Croquet, putting and hoop-la went peacefully on, as if the sun were shining. The fortune-teller's tent had a puddle on the roof and mud in the doorway.

Duggie's Dog Show was the *pièce de résistance*. Doggie's Dug Show. There were ten classes, and although the drizzle became rain, they went through every one of them.

Terry's job was to get the paid-up entries into the ring and see that they did what they were supposed to do, and did not go for each other's throats.

In the Fancy Dress class, Lady S-S led round a black Labrador wearing a frill on its collar and a limp ballet skirt. Blanche had made a tiny saddle for the terrier with the long prick, and fastened a jockey doll astride it. On the end of the leash, Blanch, always ready to enter into the spirit of things for the communal good, took off her raincoat to reveal herself also dressed as a jockey. Children had dogs they couldn't control in wet ribbons and melting paper hats.

The judge, who wore a sailing slicker with a hood and visor that prevented her or him seeing more than the tips of his/her green boots, wanted to give all the prizes to the smaller children, but the grown-ups wouldn't have it. The Comic Dog Show might be fun for the kids, but it was deadly serious for the adults.

'Choose on merit,' Terry heard Duggie mutter into the judge's hood. 'At least give a second to Lady S.'

'Fuck her,' Terry thought he heard the judge say.

Obedience was a farce. Dog Looking Most Like Owner was equally insulting to the dog and the owner. The classes thinned out. Gradually all the spectators disappeared.

'You're a brick, Terence,' Duggie said when it was over at last. 'Just take the shovel and clean up the dog mess from her Ladyship's lawn, will you, there's a good chap.'

Like hell, I will. Terry stuck the shovel into an impenetrable bush, where it would not be discovered until next winter, and went into the back of the great house.

Nora and various other women in aprons were handing out tea and cakes in a prehistoric stone-floored kitchen, where you might find one of Henry VIII's chewed drumsticks, or debauched serving wenches under a table.

'Sod this,' a hoarse voice said in Terry's ear, as he waited in line at the tea urn. 'Come on out to the van and have a drink.'

Terry turned to see who the voice spoke to, and found it spoke to him, out of the mouth of a youth in a heavy rain-beaded sweater with leather patches stuck all over it in unlikely places.

The van was up to its hub-caps in mud in the barnyard of the great house. In the back, on the carpeted floor, were another guy and two girls and some bottles and cans of beer.

What they were doing at the church fête was anyone's guess, unless they were picking pockets. They had Terry marked out, apparently.

'You're from the Duke's Head, in't you?'

'Uh-huh.' The Scotch tasted good. Terry was as soaked as a seal, seeing the world through wet lashes.

'We don't go to the 'ead. They grass for the pigs,' the girl with the snakes of hair said.

'How old are you?'

They were younger than Terry. Too young to drink legally, but they seemed to have plenty of practice at it, and no lack of supplies.

The weight lifted slowly up through the middle of Terry's vitals and out through the top of his head. The crushing picture of Lily and his father blew away in a wisp of smoke. His first joint since he left the States. How had he survived?

243

Terry was with these amazing kids for two or three days (he lost count), and screwed, or was screwed, twice – one success, one miserable failure – by Sue on the carpet in the back of the van. Or was it the one with the snakes?

They drove around the nastier parts of this tract of England, and sometimes went into pubs that were not so totalitarian as the Duke's Head, and got beer and pork pies. Terry was drunk or high most of the time. Once or twice, he surfaced to wonder if he ought to tell someone where he was (where was he?), but his father was off with the tight-crotch riding breeches set, and Blanche and Lily's parents were probably glad to have a break from him.

When James found him in the cold, grubby public bar of the Three Feathers, he didn't say 'Hello' or 'Where have you been?' He walked up to the bar and asked for a pint of Old Peculier, and did not turn around until he was half-way through it.

Terry was on a bench in the corner with Peter and Sue. Sue's face looked like empty paper. She had washed her hair in the ladies' room toilet tank because there was no water in the basin, and was drying it on her purple scarf.

'Ready?' Jam asked, as if the meeting were planned.

'Sure.' Terry got up and followed him out.

Jam did not take him to Blanche's house. He put him to bed at the cottage, and told Nora he had flu. All next day, he dosed him with some terrible oily stuff that got rid of everything inside Terry between his navel and his spine.

James Spooner's life had taken three turns for the better in the last two and a half years. First, he had fallen in love with Pyge – brief, but rejuvenating. Then he had signed up with Faces and begun to make up for fifty years of not being appreciated. Then he had met Evelina Rudd, and it was a good thing he'd already had that bit of a do with Pyge, or he might have thought he was past it.

It came about like this. For a year, he had been hoping to get his Equity card, so that he could do more than just background work in television commercials and films. But Equity wouldn't give you a card unless you could show a few contracts, and you couldn't get a contract without an Equity card.

Henrietta at Faces had told James that he might be able to squeeze through if he could develop the performances he had done in the George at Wimbledon 'by popular demand', i.e. when Nigel could get people to shut up and listen. He might get into Equity on the variety side, if he could get a few paid pub engagements.

Obviously the landlord of the Duke's Head couldn't go round singing 'The Parson's Lady' in other boozers, but why shouldn't he employ himself in his own pub?

'We'd ought to get a piano in the bar, Nora. Liven this place up a bit.'

'It's not that kind of pub.'

'But –'

'In any way, shape or form.'

'Why not? They loved it at the George.'

'Wimbledon is not South Oxfordshire. This old place is historic, James, in case you've not noticed. It's been like this since time in memoriam.'

'But with Paul coming over in a few months?' James suggested cunningly. 'You know how he loves to play.'

Nora adored Paul. He took more notice of her than most people, who had got used to her always working quietly and contentedly at something, in the house or in the pub.

'No piano.'

'No piano, Sergeant.' James saluted.

He had read in one of Nora's women's magazines that if you gave in over the little things, it was easier to get your own way when it counted. He used this as an excuse to himself for letting Nora have the last word.

For a while, he toyed with the idea of trying to buy an Equity ticket from the family of a member who had died. It had been done before, when no picture had been sent to the union. Then he met a black man at a stills session, where they were both photographed from the back, looking up at a hoarding. While they were getting cricks in their necks, waiting for the photographer to get his angles right, the other model told Jam he had got into Equity on the variety side by doing conjuring and ventriloquism for children's homes and private parties.

When James got home, he poured himself a glass of barley wine, 'builder of brainpower' – he often thought in advertising slogans now – took a packet of shrimp-flavoured crisps off the rack, and sat down in the empty public bar to have a think.

He wouldn't have the nerve to perform for kids. They could see through you, just like he always could when he was a boy.

'Too sharp by half.' His mother had clipped him when he spoiled the conjurer's act at a birthday party. 'Know it all, you do.' Then she had bought him a bag of sweets on the way home. 'At least you don't take after your father. You get it from me.'

Well, now she knew nothing, poor old dear, except her room at the old people's home, and a wet bed when the so-called nurses were busy. Shocking place.

Guilt. Hullo, my old unnecessary friend. James shoved it aside. He was too occupied with his career to go to Devizes just now. Poor old batty Ma, who used to do the crosswords and send in for newspaper competitions. 'Complete this limerick.' 'Put a caption to this picture.' Terrible to get so old that people forgot what you were really like. All those old folk, pushed away out of sight. Left to their own Devizes, ha ha.

Ha *ha*! Got it.

Nora was out shopping, so it was safe to use the bar phone. She went along with Jam's career, of course, but he didn't want funny looks and commonsense advice at this stage.

He rang Henrietta at Faces. She was always available. Lived and breathed the job, in the office at all hours, except when she was off bullying a film producer, hard as nails behind that baby face.

'What about me doing some concerts at old people's homes, to get my ticket?'

'If you think anyone would pay you.'

'Worth a try. Song and dance, monologues, the spoons, that style of thing.'

'They might pay you not to.' Henrietta's deep masculine laugh came out of her flat dancer's belly. 'It's no wonder I love you,

Jamspoon.' She was on that footing with almost everyone. It didn't mean a thing.

'Olde tyme numbers. Take 'em back, poor old dears. Puppet shows. I can do all the voices.'

'Just as well most of them will be deaf.'

James went to Soho and bought three hand puppets – old man and woman, young girl – with rather disgusting, crude caricature faces, but they were cheapish, and you couldn't be too subtle for this type of audience. The old-lady puppet looked like Edward Heath in drag.

The material he had used at the George would get him thrown out of the kind of places where his poor Ma lived out her unwanted days. He took a look at some song sheets and joke books, and found some old Stanley Holloway monologues and songs. Just the ticket. Just the ticket for the ticket. Clean, but comic. Saucy and sentimental. Music-hall stuff. The old dears would eat it up.

From the council offices, James got a list of geriatric warehouses in a wide area, not too close to home. It was hard to get anyone to talk about even a small fee, but he started out by going round gratis to test the waters and get his hand in, and soon they would be begging him to come back, and would tell their chums in the golden-age racket.

Testing the waters was about it, he thought to himself grimly, manipulating the old-gent puppet and singing, 'Champagne Charlie is my name, champagne drinking is my game, there's no drink as good as fizz! fizz! fizz!' to a semi-circle of bewildered old ducks, some of whom sat with their legs apart and their skirts ridden up to show the urine bags strapped to the unpromising inside of their scrawny thighs.

'You'd like to meet my missus,' he sang to them in an old man's voice.

But she can't get away,
She's working late tonight cos it's the other girl's 'arf day.
Nah, you wouldn't call her tall,
In fact, she's rather small,
But 'er 'eart is much bigger than 'er brain.

It was hard going, but he worked on his accents and droll voices, until some of the patter really came out comic. The nurses, glad of a break, shrieked with laughter and fell about. Some of the audience were asleep, or dead. Some were anxious about when tea would come. A few of the prize patients wagged their heads and cackled.

Why did people who had once been perfectly sensible take to cackling in old age? You heard them being interviewed on the radio. 'Oh, yes, I've seen it all, cackle, cackle. In my time, there weren't no lorries through here at all, just the trams, cackle.'

'Nora,' he begged, returning home, 'you won't let me cackle when I'm old, will you?'

'No, dear.' She was at the stove, her haunches square and familiar under the apron strings.

'I've had a hard day.' They had given him a cup of tea, but no biscuits. 'What's for my supper?'

He and Nora had to eat their evening meal separately, taking turns while the other was in the bar.

'That's for me to know, and you to guess.'

'Don't *say* that.'

'Would you rather I said, last night's shepherd's, hotting up?'

'Spare me. Here, I'll get things going in the bars. Do me a mixed grill, there's a love.' He advanced and put his arms round her warm waist. 'Got a kidney in the freezer?'

'Oh, *you*.' Stirring custard, she turned her face and leaned back to kiss him.

Irresistible, you see. She couldn't resist him. Cackle, cackle.

He put a scarf over the old-lady puppet's wild white hair and worked up a cackle routine – for the bar on Saturday night, not for the nursing homes.

The sight of all those old relics brought forth the lurking guilt about his mother that pounced out for an ell if he ever gave it an inch. He asked the manager of the home in Devizes whether he could come and entertain. Kill two birds.

'My usual fee –' he began on the phone.

'Oh, but I'm afraid we –' she countered.

These sentences seldom needed to be completed. So far the

only money he had got was from a rather posh place full of
vicars' widows, to whom he had rendered 'Get Me to the Church
on Time'.

Some of them were not too far gone to enjoy a little tap
dancing. Jam still had a few steps – ending with a cramp roll and
a couple of buffaloes off to the right, but he could hardly work
the clutch on the way home.

In Devizes, they got Ma up into a chair and wheeled her out,
to sit with her face hanging out of her head like a bulldog,
glowering and fumbling with the lap rug.

Oh, God, it was horrible. She was a lump in the chair, sliding
sideways like a blancmange, nothing to do with the strong, vigorous survivor who had been security and mate to James after his
father skipped. Not fair to the stocky, cocky girl in her wedding
picture, grinning up at her tall husband – look what I got! – to
obliterate that memory with this.

The clown with the breaking heart, James gave them:

I've been very poorly but I now feel prime,
I've been out today for the very first time.
I felt like a lad as I walk'd down the road,
Then I met old Jones and he said, 'Well, I'm blowed!
My word, you do look queer! My word, you do look queer!'

He wound up the show with his joke: 'I'm going to leave you to
your own Devizes,' which got a couple of titters, but no cackles.
Had everyone in the town been saying it for years?

'Who . . .' His mother was mumbling.

'That's your son!' A nurse bent over her. They had been telling
her that since James bounded out with the puppets.

'Silly fool,' she said quite clearly. It was the first thing she had
said for months.

At the home, some old people from outside had been brought
in a mini-bus to see the show. Their keeper asked James if he
would come to the council's day centre and perform for the
senior citizens.

He did not want to go back to Devizes, even for another
chance at making the joke, but he began to go round other senior

249

centres attached to sheltered housing, or sometimes to a hospital. There was always a piano, and he could work up a better act for them and ask for a fee, and sometimes get it. A couple of times, he was asked to perform at a town hall for a special group. Eventually he could send in some contracts to Equity, with a picture of himself in a Stanley Holloway bowler hat, so that Nora could not sell his ticket after he was dead.

The week after James got the tip from Jay Skinner at the Feathers and rescued Terry from those juvenile delinquents, his application was miraculously approved.

His card came through! In the nick of time to pull him out of the blues. After Lily and Paul and his granddaughters had left, he had felt as flat as a pancake. Ached all over. Nothing to get out of bed for.

Nora was her same old self, putting the cottage back to rights after the beloved invasion, carrying her little radio from room to room. She was always the same. Sometimes James felt he had outgrown her. Here he had soared into a new profession in his fifties, but Nora was content to potter along in the same old rut and let life happen to her, rather than make it happen. She was getting shockingly grey, and dropped in the front when she took off the hoists and let it all go. It must be worse for women. They had more to lose.

If little Duffy loved his Grandad, he concealed it. He and Bianca's ferret-faced twins, born with the misfortune to take after their father, were no substitutes for fairylike Cathy who doted on Zam, her baby name for him, and electric Isobel, inheritor of the energy of both Lily and Jam's mother.

James had not told Paul or Lily anything that Terry had said about his travels in the van with those gruesome drop-outs. He did not know how much Terry told them. There was a bit of a dust-up, and then it was time for them to fly back to Boston.

Terry hadn't wanted to leave. He got a bit tight with James in the bar after hours, and said he wanted to stay in England and get Jam to enrol him with Faces. In the morning, he went off to the airport with the others, looking washed up and childlike.

Jam would not have taken him to see Henrietta. Too young and awkward with himself. No confidence.

When his ticket finally came, James went confidently to the Faces office in Kensington High Street. Upstairs in the waiting-room, the window slid back for him at once.

'Well, look who's here!' Bunny leaned sideways from her desk for a kiss, keeping the phone against her other ear, into which someone excitable was talking. 'Want to see the boss? She's got someone with her right now, but it won't be long.'

Jam sat down and looked through the big catalogue of models. He never tired of seeing his two stills at the top of page 270, and reading his description.

'Height 6'1, chest 42, waist 38, inside leg 33, collar 17, hat 7 3/4, shoes 11. Hair: dark grey, balding. Eyes: brown. Character: sings, vocal impressionist/large hands/pot belly.' Next time it was re-printed, it would say 'Equity'.

A young woman with long black Hawaiian hair was also waiting. James was glad that she had heard his insider's conversation with Bunny, and he turned the book a little on the table, hoping that she would see his pictures.

When a man with a limp and a Groucho moustache came out of the inner door, James got up and went through it. The girl must envy him. Now he was one of the elite who went right on in.

Henrietta was talking on the phone. She was always on the phone. You sat down opposite her at the desk, and she chatted to you between, or during calls.

'A dwarf, you want? Two dwarfs. Can do. *Hullo, Jam love.* In running shorts. Okay. Men, you want. Oh – women? They'll have to wear tops . . . company T-shirts, you'll provide.'

When she put down the phone, Jam told her he had got his card, and she said, 'Fantastic!' before the phone light flashed again, which was nice of her, because Equity actors were in and out of here all the time.

'I'll ring Evvie for you. I know she's casting a TV film with Elliott Gould, and they need men ringside at a boxing match.'

Henrietta sent James out with an appointment for a casting audition. 'Don't shave before you go. Dress a bit rough. Stick your belly out. Good luck!'

'Thanks, Henry. It's a big chance. Wish me –'

'Get out of here. I'm busy. You people are all the same. A two-second character part and you want star treatment.'

James went back through the waiting-room, still wearing a grin. He gave some of it to the Hawaiian girl, and she sighed, and recrossed her legs. With underpinning like that, she would go much farther than James.

The audition was so-so. Evvie, who was a freelance casting person, was quite helpful and not unattractive in a fidgety, sharp-boned way, with a bush of dry brown hair round her head that stood out farther each time she ran her restless hands through it. There were dozens of men, all trying to look like the sort of men who went to fights. James smoked too many cigarettes, and when he was called into the room in front of Evvie and the producer and other people on the film, they told him at once, 'Light a fag,' and he started to cough.

'That's okay, Mr – er. Sit in that chair, hands on knees, lean forwards, stick your eyes out, you're looking at something incredible. Now jump up and wave your arms. Point at someone. The referee. You're mouthing. Good, okay, fine, thanks.'

James gave it his all and left, wrung out and coughing.

So when pub customers asked him, 'What are you up to these days, Jamspoon?', he could look at his nails and say modestly, 'Oh, nothing much. Little thing with Elliott Gould.'

It was bad luck to anticipate, but he did get called back for a second interview, which meant being paid for his time, at least. He got the job. Two days' work, in his old navy polo-neck and baggy back-legs-of-the-elephant trousers.

Evvie was there on one of the days, jittery, chain-smoking, hair like a thorn bush. James spoke to her. She answered, distracted, but friendly. He made sure she knew his name. The caster was your key to success.

Not long after, Bunny called him for a commercial that would be shot in a railway buffet. 'You're an old gent with a suitcase, travelling.'

No one ever said, 'You're supposed to be a so and so.' You *were* it.

The audition was in a video studio, with Evvie and an irritable cameraman called Kyle, who swore at her and bullied the group of men of about Jam's age, some better, some worse preserved. Evvie swore back. The candidates grew more nervous. They were friendly to each other, on the surface. Underneath, it was cut-throat.

'You're grandfather types,' the caster told them in her quick, creaky voice. 'All you do is drink a cup of tea at that little table, look at your watch, get up, put on your hat and rush out.'

'I haven't got a —'

'They didn't say we —'

'Anyone not got a hat?' Evvie raised her cracked voice above the complaints. 'Borrow.'

James had a hat. Faces always told you exactly what you had to have. It was a hat he had bought when he was demobbed after the war, and found again and resurrected when they moved. It had a crumpled top and a wide soft brim that could be pulled into a Trevor Howard angle to suit his crooked face.

'I'm sorry,' Evvie said from behind the camera and the lights. 'You're not a romantic old fart. You're a comic grandfather. Plant the hat straight on.'

Jam lifted and centred it, and made his face laughable.

'Get on with it,' the cameraman said. 'Action.'

Jam drank his cold tea, winced as if it were hot, raised an eyebrow at his watch, did a little panic routine – where's my bag? – and shambled out with his jacket flapping. He *was* a comic grandfather.

After an interview with the advertising agency, he got the part. His luck was running.

After the commercial was aired, he was famous. That is to say, once in a while, someone would say, in the pub or somewhere else, 'Saw you on the telly last night.' Even more than the small cheques coming in, that's when it was good, being in this game.

Nothing happened for weeks. That was part of the game too. James rang Faces almost every day, in case something had just come in, and they might not think of him. Often he rang from the phone box outside the post office, in case Nora got fed up with it.

She didn't understand that when James was called at the last minute, that was show business. That was the way it was done in that world, which was a universe away from this one-foot-in-front-of-the-other-it's-called-walking Chiltern village.

'Sorry, love, got to go. Last-minute call.' James would hurry puffing to find Nora.

'I need you here. Let them get someone else.'

'And have them never call me again because I turned it down? Nora – this is my career.'

He would get their weekend helper, Jack, to come in and give Nora and Jenny a hand, wheedle Nora to press a suit or shine his shoes, and dash off.

Jack needed the money. It wasn't a burden to him if Jam's engagement ran into overtime, and someone like Duggie would always pitch in, regulars who felt they belonged to the Duke, and the Duke to them.

Twice, Jam had a line to say. 'Let us pray,' as a plummy vicar about to say Grace, and, 'Give us a fag,' as a figure in an old army greatcoat, stumbling out of the dark.

Talk about drama.

One day when he was doing background in a commercial that Evvie was casting, she needed someone for a timed shot – crossing the street at the exact moment and angle to meet the star at a certain spot chalked on the pavement. She recognized James among the crowd, and asked him to do it.

He and the star had to nod and say something, in long shot, and then he bent to pat her dog. James did it right nine times. The star did it wrong. After the tenth time, when it worked, the star told James, 'Thanks.'

He went away, hazed about with the hot fragrance of her hair and skin and clothes, and leaned against a fence where Evvie was leaning, biting her nails and resting first on one thin foot, then the other, like a tired bird.

'Thanks,' James said.

'That's okay. It's useful to have people who won't make a hash of it.'

She sighed and dropped her cigarette and ground it out with a sharp heel. She did not use scent, or if she did, it didn't have a chance against the star's musky clouds that still invaded all Jam's passages.

'Tired, sweetie?' he asked.

She nodded. 'Fed up too.'

'So am I,' James lied. 'Like to come for a drink when this is over?'

She went with him, that was the amazing thing, this restless skimpy creature from the higher levels of power, hung about with scarves and beads. They had a drink at a tarted-up place near the film location. They had two drinks. She started to talk about the rotten state of her relationship with Kyle, the video camera-man, and by some miracle, James found the good sense to shut up and listen. Evvie was unhappy. James bought her dinner. She ate an amazing amount for someone whose figure looked as if it could hardly accommodate her internal organs, let alone an oval dish of steak and chips and a lump of Black Forest gâteau.

In his car, when he took her back to where hers was parked, Evvie sat for a moment and did not get out. James bent over in a chivalrous, sheltering way and gave her quite a gentle kiss. She tasted of French mustard and cigarettes. Her lips were dry. He wetted them for her, after the chaste kiss, licking them. Within the heavy mascara and painted green shadow, the whites of her eyes were not clear. Her skin felt hot.

'Got a temperature?' James asked.

She shook her head. 'Just tired and fed up.'

'That's why I asked you out, remember? You're supposed to feel better now.'

'Oh, I do. Thanks – er, Jamspoon. Do you really want me to call you that?'

'Not on the set.' He implied that they would meet on another job, one that she'd get for him.

'I must go. Kyle will be raving.'

'You live together?'

She nodded. She often used her bushy head instead of speaking, her narrow lips folded tight.

'Does he beat you?' James wanted to ask. He wanted her to be abused, so he could be the rescuer. Grandfather type? That was two other guys.

Kyle may have been raving. Nora wasn't. James had rung her from the restaurant to say they were shooting late, and she had accepted that, and kept his supper. He took it out to the back

255

and gave it to the Labrador that was always hanging round the dustbins. Taking sweets from a child, it was, fooling Nora. You rotter, Jamspoon. You glorious, regenerated, degenerate rotter.

Casters often asked for feature people by name when they got to know them, rather than just, 'Send me three bankers and a fireman and a saucy nurse.' So no one at Faces was surprised when Evvie asked for James Spooner to audition for the barman in an advertising campaign for fruit-flavoured cordials.

Jam was an oh-*ho* barman, pouring the vile-coloured syrups in a roguish, yet protective way for a young girl like a wood nymph. The idea was to reassure young girls who felt like wood nymphs that it was all right to go into pubs and bars, and that this low-alcohol poison was what you ordered if you wanted to be safe and sophisticated. What a hope.

Evvie was on the set, thin and pale, but full of fizz.

'Thanks for getting this for me.' During a break, James brought her a coffee.

'Well – thanks for the dinner. It helped just to be quiet and talk.'

'Want to repeat the therapy some time?'

'We'll see.'

'Just say the word.'

He saw her again not long after, at a stills session. Whether the TV was screened or not, they were going ahead with posters and magazines and point-of-sale. In a profession where more people starved than worked, it was a rare bit of luck for James.

He and Evvie met after that in a bar near her office. She told him about her divorce from the Iranian she had married when she was eighteen, and the child who was now at college. That put her within shouting distance of forty.

James told her nothing about his marriage, partly because that made him feel loyal to Nora, whatever he was up to (and he wasn't sure himself), partly because Evvie was not interested. James was attentive. He had brought her a pair of the black dangling earrings she favoured, and he drove her home to Finsbury Park, hoping and not hoping to be seen by Kyle.

The situation between them was this. James wanted to keep in with her to get work. Evvie liked an audience and she wanted to annoy Kyle, who was younger than her and believed she needed him more than he needed her.

They both knew the situation, but in a curious way, the lack of romance or lust led them very easily and unpossessively into bed in a second-rate hotel in the Midlands.

At first, James was nervous and hesitant.

'Just hold me, then,' Evvie whispered. Even her whisper had a creak in it. 'Just let's hold each other and pretend life is safe.'

But James could get the comforting routine from Nora. That wouldn't do. With a courageous cry, he threw himself at Evvie's bird body, and once she got the message, she responded with speed and skill.

By God, she knew her stuff! They did one thing that James had never done before, and didn't know you could do. In their younger days of good jolly straightforward sex, he and Nora would have been shocked to find that anyone did that.

No strings. That was how it was between Jam and Evvie. No obligations. I'm not ever going to leave Nora. Evvie's not leaving Kyle. Just thumbing her nose at him.

They saw each other at intervals, for a drink and a smoke, or a meal, and didn't go to bed, or did.

Wow! he sometimes thought to himself at odd moments during the day. Wow, Jamspoon. What are you up to, you old dog? He had a watertight alibi, with the uncertain hours of his profession. Nora could not possibly find out, and she would never be hurt.

One of Evvie's clients wanted small twins for an off-beat toddler-product advertisement.

'Get your daughter to bring her two along for audition.' Evvie rang James at home, and when Nora answered, said she was his agent, which she was. 'They look just right from their photograph. Not too bonny.'

'Thanks for those kind words.' Nora was in the room. James kept his voice impersonal.

'Don't tell your daughter that. Tell her she could pick up a nice little bit of cash. We could fudge them into the job under your Faces membership.'

'I can't promise.'

'Try it. For me, Jammie?'

How did she know his wife was not on an extension in another room? The thrill of danger crept up his chest and neck and into the nerves of his teeth.

'I'll let you know.' He would have like to have said, 'Forget it,' but Evvie was a powerful woman, in or out of bed. He never turned her down.

Nora would be proud to see the twins in an ad, even if it said, 'Which twin is wearing Bottidri?' Should he ask her to persuade Blanche? Instinct told him to leave Nora out of it. Anything to do with Evvie had got to be part of his guilty secret which, for some reason, gave him no guilt. During the last few weeks, James Spooner, full of fun, but at heart a conventional lad, had persuaded himself of the advantages of a bit on the side, for all concerned.

Blanche was furious. She did not often get angry, but when she did, her tranquil eyes bulged and cords stood out at the sides of her weather-browned neck, like tent-stays.

'It's bad enough to have you running about with that seedy theatrical crowd, and having people say, "Wasn't that your father I saw on telly, dressed as a policeman?"'

'You've got to accept, it's my career now.'

'Well, leave us out of it.'

'Why so bitter, Bianca?'

'You used to pull your weight in the pub, Daddy. Now you don't.'

'I bring in extra money.'

'How much, I wonder? A couple of thousand a year, perhaps, if you're lucky.'

'Who told you that? The sky's the limit. I'm beginning to get featured.'

'By the time you've paid Jack, and train fares or petrol to London, what's left? Let alone buying clothes. And that briefcase. And the tennis racket.'

'Child of my youthful passion, you want the parts, you've got to have the props.'

'Well, I think it's very hard on Mum.'

'She encourages me.'

Blanche moved backwards away from him, in her boots. They were having this nasty conversation in the yard by the kennels, with the terriers as Greek chorus. Her stiff retreat from him brought to James an overwhelming sense of the loss of his Lily, who always leaned forwards, who came at you with open arms, ready to agree or laugh or argue with equal enthusiasm. Her visit had been too short, and was long gone past. The thought of all that unfriendly grey water between them caused James to speak out of turn.

'Your mother would never hold me back,' he said roughly. 'She's not like you.'

There – gone and done it. Neil had been offered a job with better promotion prospects up north, but Blanche wouldn't go.

She pushed past him and went into her house. The dogs hurled their taut barrel bodies against the bars of their cages in protest, deafening him with their inane shrill barking.

'Shut up!' he shouted so fiercely that his voice skidded and rose as shrill as theirs. He picked up a metal bucket and threw it against the kennel bars.

Blanche opened the back door.

'I saw that,' she said.

On the way to Heathrow, Lily sat in front with her father, and Terry sat with Paul and the girls, hunched up in the corner of the back seat, like a sick chimpanzee. Beside Lily, Jam's profile had its crooked smile, the eyebrow nearest to her raised, trying to be ironic about his own sadness.

When they said goodbye, he clutched at Lily in a trembling sort of doddery way, which made her see ahead to her father as an old man.

'I need you,' he whispered from somewhere out of the depths of his reality. Not putting on an act, cracking a joke, smilin' through.

'You'll be all right, Daddy.'

Lily kissed him again, and they were gone through the gate with several people behind them, and it was too late to say what she should have said: 'I need you too.'

When the plane rose and banked above the piercing green, the reservoirs, the grids of tidy brick houses, she leaned the side of her face against the window, and felt English. Living in America with Paul and the children was all she wanted; but could I come back here . . . could we?

When she first went to America, everything was too big, distances too great, patches of scenery the same for hours and hours, stores too vast. Who needed ten different kinds of tuna fish?

Now that all this was normal, the bizarre was little potty English grocers with muddy potatoes, Nora's Mini, Blanche's small van for the dogs, rocking on its narrow tyres when they were all barking inside.

Two winters ago, she and Paul had bought rolls of cotton wool to stuff into the draughts round the cottage windows. The Duke's Head gents' froze up. The oven temperature dropped while she was baking a cake.

'Pair cuts,' Nora talked about. Lily had not understood at first what she said. Her own voice, basic Wimbledon, adaptable up or down, had become transatlantic: accused of sounding like a Yank in England, and, 'I love your British *accent*,' in the States.

Driving to Cape Cod to start their summer month in the old farmhouse, they stopped in Plymouth Harbor to visit the *Mayflower*, because Cathy had been doing the Pilgrims. Poor child, she would do them next year and the next and the next, obsessively, in her New England school.

They stood on the wharf and marvelled at the tiny rib cage of the hold where a hundred people had lived for a year, and had babies, and died.

'Did any of them ever go back home?' Cathy asked. 'I would have.' She liked England. She liked wherever she was.

'I wouldn't, you dope.' From Isobel, at ten, casual remarks often came out like insults. 'Would you, Mud?'

Since hearing Alan Sherman's summer camp song, 'Hello Mudder, Hello Farder', she called Lily Mudder, or Mud.

'We do go back. We just have.'

'I mean, to live.'

'Daddy's too American. I don't think he could take it. He likes plumbers and snow ploughs to come when he wants them. Remember when we bought the cotton, Paul, and Jam said we were decadent?'

'Suppose you got divorced.' When Isobel was working up to being difficult, she spoke without looking at you. 'Would *you* go, Mud?'

'What's this? We're never going to be divorced.'

'Daddy and Terry's mother did. He might have a taste for it.'

'Lay off me,' Paul told her mildly.

Isobel slid her eyes towards her father, and away. 'I'm only telling you what Terry said.'

'He wouldn't say that,' Lily said quickly. 'It doesn't sound like him.'

'All right, don't believe me. You never do.' Isobel threw her candy wrapper into the harbour.

'Hundred dollar fine,' Paul said.

'Want me to jump in and get it?' She started to climb the wooden railing.

'Get down, Isobel.'

'You want trash in the ocean, or dontcha?'

Isobel was going through the struggle of trying to fight her father at any opportunity. He gave her his 'stay calm' routine, but she would rather have a yelling match, or the drama of a punishment. When she could not make Paul angry, she would turn to her mother and goad her, until Lily obliged by shouting or whacking her. Once, when this happened in England, Nora had scolded Lily as if she were still a child, which had pleased Isobel tremendously.

Terry did not come to the Cape this summer. He had signed up for a course on the Impressionists at the Museum of Fine Arts, but instead he got a summer job on a fast-food counter at the airport. He wore a T-shirt that said 'Pie in the Sky' and a paper forage cap. He was growing his hair.

The shabby house was beginning to seem like theirs. As soon

as they arrived, Lily cleared out anything left by other tenants, except the battered books which were there from year to year: *Flora and Fauna of Martha's Vineyard, History of the Manamessett Yacht Club, The Outermost House, Byways of Old Cape Cod, Reader's Digest Condensed Books, 1956.*

They had only been there ten minutes before Tony appeared from the house beyond the field wall, grinning, teeth large and white in his dark face, giving them a chronicle of the tenants who had been in the house.

'Bottles – you should see the bottles that went out with the trash. One week, the lady asks me, "Where's the town dump?" She don't want to put them out by the end of the driveway no more.'

Tony was fifteen this year, working with his father on landscaping. He continued to spend a lot of time with Isobel. They still had the boards wedged into the crook of the big maple, that was their tree-house. In the curve of Tony's upper lip lay a shadow that was the prelude to a moustache. Isobel was only ten. Perhaps it ought not to be all right, but it was.

Tony was taking care of an absent neighbour's rough Western pony. Paul had brought down a bridle and was teaching Tony to ride it bareback. Isobel too. She was more civilized when Tony was around.

Cathy had made friends here, with the family who lived opposite, and other children who were there in the summer. Lily had got to know women on the beach and in the village. She and Paul got asked out. They gave a big chili supper on the grass. They were beginning to belong.

Lily loved the looks of Paul in the summer. His brown bare legs were straight and firm. His eyes were intensely blue. The sun put silvery streaks into the top of his fair hair. Not grey streaks. That was years away. He was only forty-four, an ageless age.

This year, he immersed himself in this place even more thankfully, because he had been having some hard times in Boston. Turnbull's were still trying to find a way to claim that Tack Rack Junior was theirs, not his. He suspected that they might be planning to design their own modular units and market them under another name, to cut him out. He had been successful on his last English trip. He had turned in an excellent report, but it had been criticized, and picked to pieces by people who did not know the British market.

When Edward Turnbull retired, it had always been assumed that Paul would succeed him as Managing Director. Dread Ed was pushing seventy, and would fuss himself into another heart attack if he wasn't careful. Paul was training a Turnbull nephew, one of a succession of family hangers-on who had come into the store, and passed on to what they thought were higher things. This one was digging himself in.

Turnbull thrived on its traditions. Bright, abrasive Leonard's unnecessary new ideas would not be adopted, but they were listened to and discussed, instead of being turned down, and the philosophy of the store's whole marketing programme explained to Leonard yet once more.

Paul got on with him all right, because life would be too unpleasant if he didn't.

'What are your plans?' he asked Leonard from time to time.

'Oh – I'll be moving on before too long, I guess. Pick up what I can here, and give you folks what I can. A very pleasant interlude. I'll always be grateful to you, Paul.' Patronizing jackass. Paul was not deceived. He bided his time.

Here on Cape Cod, he could forget it. He had a way of being able to put away worry and discouragement with his Boston clothes, and throw himself into happiness, taking Lily with him.

His friend Harry Sutton came down to stay. He had been married again and separated since Lily first met him. He had always behaved like a bachelor, even when he was with his second wife, and he was totally undomesticated. He strewed coffee mugs and beer glasses wherever he happened to be. He left dirty clothes in a pile in the corner of his room. He drove off without saying where he was going, just when you were going to put a meal on the table. He left Arthur shut in his car and forgot him. He dripped water and sand on cushions. He turned up, delighted with himself, with live lobsters and wine when Paul already had steaks on the barbecue. He was lovable and funny, tiring, argumentative. Lily and Paul and the children were very fond of him.

The three of them rented horses and rode through the small woods and moorland of the wildlife preservation area, where pheasants and deer were preserved to be shot at by men in plaid wool shirts in November.

Lily learned more about riding from Harry than from Paul, because she listened to Harry and didn't argue so much. She had ridden enough now to begin to understand Paul's horse passion. It wasn't just the ride. It was everything. When they got back to the stables, she liked going with the horse into the gloom of the barn where his box was, and taking off the tack and rubbing at the wet patch under the saddle, and exchanging casual horse talk with the young girls who were always around. If the horse was not going out again, she would take down his halter from the hook outside the box and lead him out to roll in the sandy patch at the corner of the field. She hung over the gate with Paul, chewing stalks of hay, to watch the horses moving quietly away in the evening light, and make fantasies of how it would be when they had horses of their own.

One evening when they had ridden far enough away from the stables, Harry pulled up, and told Lily to get up on the very good horse he was allowed to ride.

Paul wasn't sure. 'I don't think she's ready.'

'Don't cramp her, Paul. She's got to know what a good horse feels like.'

Harry was quite well known in the horse world, and the woman who ran the stables had given him one of her show horses, who needed the exercise.

He was a big bay. He felt better for Lily's height and long legs than the smaller brown mare she had been riding. You had to work quite hard to keep the mare going, but with Jacob, as soon as she picked up the reins and moved her leg back – 'Not too much leg, he'll take off with you!' from Harry – he stepped forwards eagerly, neck flexed, dropping his chin and playing with the bit. He was light and quick, and very responsive, but she could feel his strength, and spirit, and she wondered what would happen when he realized he knew more than her.

He outwalked the other horses.

'Try a trot!' Harry called.

Lily was perfectly happy walking, feeling the swing of Jacob's long stride, the muscle of his shoulder in front of her knee, the nod of his elegant head against her hands, but she thought, 'Trot,' obediently, and before she had gathered up her reins, this lovely horse was into his long springing stride, each neat hoof reaching rhythmically forwards to make its print accurately on the sandy grass.

'She's doing well,' Paul and Harry agreed with pride, as if they had invented her.

'She'll ride yet,' Harry said.

'I'm riding now.'

They were trotting abreast along a wide path, a low crimson sun at their backs and a soft fresh breeze off from the sea in their faces.

'We'll canter, then,' Harry said.

'You want to, Lily? He may take hold.' Paul never pushed her (she pushed herself). He never minded anyone being nervous. He had not forgotten it in himself, as most people do after they have learned to ride well.

Lily turned a happy smile to him, then sat down in the saddle and gave the horse a very gentle squeeze with her legs.

His trot had been magnificent. His canter was like flying, like flowing cream, like dancing.

They picked up speed. Harry was beside her, Paul behind. She was not aware of either of them. She was the horse, the horse was her. As she cantered on eternally between the trees with the clean wind washing her face and singing in her ears, she reached a state of exaltation where she felt, not only part of the powerful life that moved and breathed with her, but of the grass which flexed beneath his joyful feet, the moving air, turning leaves, all things growing, lingering small clouds ahead, flushed like shells in the reflection of the setting sun.

All living things are one, the horse displayed to her.

Then a bird exploded up out of the grass and the horse shied violently sideways. Lily lost a stirrup and lost her balance and jerked the reins, and Jacob threw up his head, and they were all at odds.

'Sit down,' Harry said. 'Sit back, don't lean forward. He'll come back to you. Well done. Good girl.'

'Are you all right?' Anxiety made Paul look older. His easily smiling mouth was pulled in.

'Sure she is.' Harry had taken over. 'You go ahead, Paul, if this one's going to be jumpy.'

They slowed to a walk. Lily and Harry rode behind Paul.

'You love it don't you,' Harry said. 'Your face back there – you're beautiful, you know that?'

'Oh, shut up,' Lily said in an English way. Harry was everybody's friend. He had better not look at her like that.

'Don't be scared.' He was still smiling at her, as if he knew something about her, and found it amusing.

She pushed the bay horse forwards to ride beside Paul.

After supper, the moon came up, full and staring. Cathy brought out a book she knew by heart, to prove she could read in the flat white light. There were glow worms in the bushes by the barn. The children stayed up late, because it was too beautiful to go indoors.

'We didn't get our evening swim,' Isobel complained, 'because you guys wanted to ride.'

'Well then, let's swim now.' Harry got up. He was not going to let her have a grievance. 'Come on, a moonlight swim.'

'It will be cold.' Cathy shivered.

'It won't, you dope. The sea will feel warmer because the air's cooler.'

'Let's go to Hidden Harbor,' Lily said. They couldn't go there in the daytime, because the family who owned it were usually there.

They left the car at the end of the sandy road that wound alongside the inlet to where the dredged sand had piled up a mounded beach. The group of lighted houses across the canal all faced away, towards the bay. If people were sitting out, they would be on that side, where they could not see this beach.

Cathy pulled off her shorts and top and went into the water naked, a silver fish, turning and plunging in shallow water.

'You can too, Iz,' Lily said. But Isobel kept on her swimsuit, and plunged in down the steep slope of the beach to where she could stand in the narrow opening of the canal with the water up to her nose and her thick dark hair floating backwards on the current coming in from the open sea.

'Shall *we*?' With his shirt off, Harry put his thumbs into the top of his swimming trunks to pull them down.

'We'd better not.' Lily looked towards the houses. The beach was in the full floodlight of the moon.

But Harry did, so Paul did, and then Lily did too. She ran into the deeper pool above the inlet, and swam away from the shore. Her fingers picked silver drops of phosphorescence out of the still, satin sea. The water welcomed her skin. Body and water were not divided by being solid and fluid. It was like that moment of exaltation with Jacob, when everything had shared life.

Paul swam up beside her. She put out a hand, and he took her arm. It was Harry. He held her, and moved his other hand slowly across her body.

Lily melted into the sea. She flung her face up to the moon, kicked out and ploughed fast back to the beach, where Paul was with the girls.

On the sand, she ran for her towel and put it round her.

'Cold, darling?'

'A bit.' She sat wrapped up, arms round her knees. She wanted to go home, but it was a long time before she could get the others to come out of the water.

Moon-struck and water-mad, they ambled back towards the car, Paul and Harry taking turns to carry Cathy on their shoulders. Her little water-rat's head nodded above the bundling towel. She was half asleep. Lily held hands with Isobel and sang, very quietly because they were not supposed to be here. She would not look at Harry.

When they got home, she went upstairs with the children, and then had a bath and went to bed herself.

She could hear the companionable talk in the living-room below, the sliding door of the cupboard where the bottles were, Harry's laugh and Paul's lighter one. Much later, while she was still reading, she smelled bacon cooking.

Paul came upstairs and opened her door. 'You want a BLT?'

'No thanks. Are you coming up soon?'

'Soon.'

She wanted him to be here, so that she could tell him about Harry. She told him everything. When he did come up, chattering peacefully about the room while he undressed, he told her what he and Harry had been talking about, and something surprising that Harry had said about his first marriage.

'It's good to be with him. He loves it here. Says it's his home life.'

Tell him.

But when Paul came to bed, she only reached for him in silence, to wipe out Harry's hands with Paul's.

She did not tell him the next day. Why not? She could give herself all sorts of reasons. It was too late, over now, irrelevant, meant nothing. Harry was Paul's good friend; no point in making trouble. Harry might not care, but it would hurt Paul.

She loved Paul totally. She would never do anything against him. Why drop the thought into his head that she might? Men were born jealous: little boys trying to get their mothers away from their fathers. Even secure, unpossessive men like Paul had primeval suspicions about what women were really like.

Those were easy reasons. There was another, which she looked at once and put away. Sex and the sea . . . for an interminable moment, she had hung still in the water under Harry's hand. She had melted.

The telephone rang while Lily was putting together the picnic to take to the Outer Beach.

'Damn them.' Paul came back into the kitchen. 'I'll have to go up to Boston tomorrow.'

'You can't. You're on holiday.'

'There's a small crisis. I'll have to go, because I'm the one who's had all the dealing with these people. Leonard says I can take an extra day. Leonard says! I'm his boss, not he mine.'

'Want me to drive up with you?' Harry asked.

'Thanks, but no. You stay.'

Harry looked at Lily. He caught her looking at him, and she looked away.

'You stay with Lily and the kids. You and Lily have fun.'

Trusting fool.

After the day on the Outer Beach, everyone was tired, so they didn't do much of anything when Isobel's father went to Boston. Isobel had not yet reached the point where she complained, 'There's nothing to do on Cape Cod; going to the beach is boring,' but she hung about aimlessly with her lip stuck out, because if Daddy were here, he would have taken her to fish off the bridge over the river that ran through Sandwich marsh.

Not Cathy. Not Mudder. Just Isobel. She loved him passionately. That was why she fought with him, because it scared her, how much she loved him. And he must be made to show that he loved her, no matter what. She couldn't make it easy for him.

Dumb happy kids like Cathy and Maggie thought that life was simple. It wasn't. Life was difficult and dangerous. Terry had told her that a long time ago.

'If you know that,' he had said, 'you got it licked.'

Nobody noticed that her lip was stuck out, so she went to the small local beach with a friend, and then did ball boy for Harry and Mudder at the tennis courts. Harry played well. Mud played rottenly, and laughed too much. Fifty cents was the going rate for being ball boy. Harry gave her a dollar, which was why she had agreed to do it. He also gave Cathy a dollar for hunting for balls that Mud hit over the wire fence, not being able to find them, and dashing across the court to pick up a ball just when he was going to serve. Not fair.

Later, Harry went into the barn to see how it could be made into stables for horses. He was crazy about horses, worse than Daddy. He looked at everything as a place where he could ride, or keep horses, or build a jump.

When Tony came back from work with his father, he came up to the house, and he and Isobel rode their bikes to the drug store for a soda. Cathy whined to come too, so they gave her a quarter not to.

'What good is that? I wanna come.'

'So now you have a quarter and the forty cents you'd have spent on the soda, that's sixty-five cents,' Isobel said. 'Plus the dollar Harry gave you for doing nothing except getting in the way, which is a dollar sixty-five which is more than I ever had at your age.'

'Gee, it must be great to be educated,' Tony said.

He was much cleverer than Isobel, and could measure and draw plans for carpentry, and do complicated things with figures, as well as drive a bulldozer and use a buzz saw; but they had this pretence about Isobel being so grand, to make a joke about the difference between their lives.

Isobel had climbed the rope ladder into the tree-house during the time that she was sticking out her lip. While she was up there, above the world which did not understand her, she had trodden on the end of a floor board, and the nails had pulled out and her whole leg had almost gone through and crippled her for life.

'And you could have said it was my fault,' Tony said.

'Serve you right.'

'What for?'

'Being a Cape Codder.'

They were sitting on the worn red stools at the drug-store counter.

'Being a Portugee, you mean. That's worse.'

'Oh, much worse,' Isobel agreed.

'I don't know.' Behind the counter, talking to a giant trucker whose rear end spilled over the stool, Dodo was also sharing their conversation. 'The Portugees run this town, is what I think.'

'You better believe it.' Tony's ancestors came from the Cape Verde Islands, off Africa, and he told Isobel that they were royal.

They went back to mend the floor of the tree-house. 'Better strengthen it if you're getting so fat and heavy,' Tony said. 'There's some short pieces of two-by-twos in your barn. Maybe I can use some of those.'

'Someone in there?' Tony heard a voice inside the barn.

'Harry went in there to play make-believe horses.'

It was beginning to rain. Tony stood on a block of granite that lay by the wall and looked through one of the small windows where the cow stalls used to be.

Isobel stepped up beside him. She stood on tiptoe, and then

270

Tony pushed her down and muttered, 'C'mon, let's get the wood from my yard.'

Isobel did not ask, 'Why?', because before he pushed her away from the window, she had seen Harry and her mother, half in shadow, half in dusty light.

Going across the back field, Isobel had to ask. 'Tony.' She coughed. It was hard to say. 'What were they doing?'

'I didn't see nothing.'

'You did. I did. What were they doing?'

'Oh.' Tony walked faster. 'Just kissin'.'

Grown-ups kissed and fooled around all the time, like a sort of game. 'But their faces weren't together. Harry looked stern, not like his usual self. She – why was my mother's face like that?'

'Forget it.' Tony's forehead was screwed up into ridges. 'You didn't see nothing.'

'I'm telling my father.'

'If you do,' Tony turned and looked at her, his dark face scowling, 'I'll break your little white neck.'

Then there *was* something to tell.

'Tell me.' Isobel ran up behind him.

'Do me a favour, will ya?' he brushed a hand backwards at her, as if she were a mosquito, or a child.

On the other side of the wall in Tony's yard, when he was turning over wood behind the open shed where his father kept the tractor, Isobel tried again.

He pulled out a couple of pieces of wood and threw them hard on the ground near her feet.

'Cut it out.'

She did. Tony was the only person she obeyed without arguing. He was her real friend. Different from friends at school who she bickered with back and forth, and strove to defeat.

'Tony!' Mrs Andrade shouted from the house. They could hear her from the farmhouse when she was in full cry.

'Yeah, Ma?'

'Bring Isobella inside. It's raining.'

When the tree-house was mended, Isobel went indoors and sat in the fascinating hot room, which had a carpet on the table and velvet chairs with lace pinned on the arms, and a gorgeously coloured bead curtain between the dining-room and living-room. If you went through it with your hands behind your back, it massaged your face like rain.

Mrs Andrade let Isobel sew some beads on the back of the fringed jacket she was going to wear when she went to the Martha's Vineyard pow-wow at Gay Head in September.

'I like it here.' The bead work was easy, big needle and big holes in the beads.

'We like you to come down here.' Sitting with Isobel at the table, working on the jacket sleeve, Mrs Andrade's face was folded in fat, comfortable creases. 'Tony always liked to be with kids younger than him. That's okay by me. Better than some of those girls at the high school.' She made a face, snarling as she bit off a thread.

In a while, she gave Isobel a root beer and sent Tony up to the farmhouse to ask if she could stay for supper.

Paul fretted at the traffic which held him up crossing the canal bridge. He badly wanted to talk to Lily.

When she ran out to him, bare feet on wet grass, he asked at once, 'Did you see the six o'clock news?'

'No. Why?'

'My Dad's in a bit of trouble.'

'On the *television*? What's he done?'

'Nothing, of course. It's what's being done to him. Come in the house and I'll tell you.'

Before Judge Stephens in Superior Court that morning, two young black men had been charged with assault and man-slaughter, after mugging an elderly white man, who died of a heart attack in the street.

Another white man, a witness, had refused to testify because he had broken a probation order which forbade him to leave New York state, and was afraid of bringing more trouble on him-self.

'Leave me out of it,' he had said in court. 'I'm not going to help the Law.'

Since Even Steven could not compel the man to testify without a court order from the District Attorney, he had to throw out the charges, accepting only a charge of endangerment and attempted robbery.

The black men were free on bail, and hiding from a storm of public protest. Paul's father was accused of being 'scared of the blacks'.

'Even Steven?' an angry white man had shouted to reporters outside the courthouse. 'It's Chicken Steven!'

That afternoon, a gang of white teenagers had set upon a black man in a parking lot and fractured his skull. He was in the hospital, 'fighting for his life', as they say when someone's body is trying to die. The Judge was accused of 'setting racial integration back twenty years'.

Paul had gone to Dedham to see his father, but a neighbour told him that the Judge was staying at his club in Boston.

Paul and Lily called him there.

'You heard about it?' The Judge sounded a bit anxious. 'Damnedest thing. I had no choice but to reduce the charges against those men, and now you'd think I was the criminal.'

'Are you all right?'

'I think so. I'm used to being attacked by people who don't understand anything about the law. I'm going to have some short ribs with old Callahan and get an early night.'

'Sleep well,' Lily said.

'I hope.' His voice was rather rocky.

How unfair, after all his years of scrupulous work. How damned unfair, when other men were taking bribes, peddling influence, keeping in with the boys. Paul ought to be up in Boston with him. The evening felt grey and drained of promise. The loose window over the sofa shook in a gust of rain.

'Let's have a fire.'

Harry had brought in some wood from the barn. Paul built a fire in the big stone fireplace, carefully, so that it wouldn't smoke, and sat by it, weary, in the only chair that was remotely the shape of a human being.

'You two have a good day?'

He had brought down an evening paper, and was reading what it said about his father. There would be a lot more tomorrow.

'Great.' Harry handed him a drink. 'I tried to put the make on your child bride in the barn, but she repulsed me.'

'Tough luck,' Paul said without looking up.

DEDHAM JUDGE IN COURT SCANDAL. RACIAL VIOLENCE INFLAMED. MANSLAUGHTER CHARGE THROWN OUT – 'DISGUSTING!'

Late news on television carried the story in some detail, going through the events in court, but skimming over the legal explanation. The black man who had been attacked in the parking lot was shown being lifted into an ambulance. A hospital spokesman said he was in critical condition. There was a five-year-old photograph of Judge Stephens, looking quizzical. There had been some minor racial incidents. Various citizens of all colours gave uninformed opinions.

Next day, Paul went early to Boston and drove his father to work. There was a small angry crowd outside the courthouse. The police cleared a way for the car, but a repulsive woman with hair like a scouring pad thrust her writhing face against the window and screamed, 'Nigger lover!'

When his father left the court, Paul had to fight to get him through a swarm of reporters. It was frightening, unreal. It was like scenes you saw, happening to someone else. Bystanders shouted ugly things. Paul thought they were encouraged by the television people, to provide better pictures.

More reporters waited outside the house, and a television crew. Before they went inside, Paul's father turned.

'Give us a statement, Judge!'

'Get out of my garden.'

That evening, a brick came through one of the front windows. When the phone rang, the Judge picked it up and stood for half a minute listening. His hand was trembling when he put the receiver down.

'Don't answer it any more,' Paul said.

When it rang again, he knew the kind of thing his father had listened to: filthy, crude. Shaming that anyone should choose words like that, should enjoy such mindless hate.

Newspapers and television stations kept calling. The doorbell rang while Paul was making coffee for his father.

'Go away.'

Two people took Paul's picture.

'What do you think about the rioting in Dorchester Avenue?'

'What rioting?'

'I guess you don't know. The black guy that the white kids beat up in the parking lot died in Intensive Care.'

'What do you think . . . how do you feel . . . do you think your father's decision . . .'

Questions were thrown at him. Paul went indoors.

His father had hardly slept. He was feeble and coughing this morning. Paul did not want to tell him about the man dying, but the Judge was watching the news in his bedroom. He looked old and drained enough to die himself.

'Paul.' He raised watery eyes in a doggy way, nothing like his usual straight look. 'God help me, I don't know that I can go to work today.'

'I wouldn't let you. We're getting out of here.'

They drove down to Cape Cod, where Lily had already repulsed two local reporters. At the end of the day, the Judge's clerk called to say that the District Attorney's Prosecutor was bringing forward the case to a grand jury, without the testimony of the cautious witness. The furore died down. Repulsive women and opinionated citizens found other things to raise Cain about, but the Judge had to spend a few days in bed, because his breathing was bad and the rhythm of his heart uneven.

'I guess this has hit me harder than I thought.' He apologized a dozen times a day. 'Must be getting old. Shocking weakness. Should know better.'

Each time he said he was going back to work, they persuaded him to stay one more day.

He was sitting with them on the porch, playing cards with Cathy, when the real estate agent came round.

'I thought I should tell you,' he said to Paul and Lily. 'You may not be able to rent this house next year.'

Paul's first thought was, 'I don't want to go anywhere else.' He loved this place. He had not thought farther than coming back here, year after year.

The owners had decided to sell the house and land. 'That's why I stopped by this evening.' The agent was a pleasant man, tanned and fit, more at home outdoors than in an office, working to support his racing yacht. 'I thought you might like to hear about it first, knowing how much you love this place.'

'Oh, *Paul*.' Lily turned to him an eager face that wanted to say, 'We'll buy it!' without a second's thought.

Paul's heart raced to match hers, but he said noncommittally, 'How much are they asking?'

It was far too much, out of sight for them. But the sudden dream did not retreat. It filled Paul's mind, although it had no connection with reality.

'That's a bit beyond us, I'm afraid.' He smiled, keeping his voice level.

'But we've always wanted to buy a summer place here,' Lily told the agent. 'I wish it could be this.'

'So do I. It's a steal, really, for what you'd be getting. These old houses just don't come on the market any more, and where are you going to find an acre and a half of land in the middle of a village?'

'Need a lot spent on it, though,' the Judge put in, looking judicial, in case the young man thought anyone was fooled by his sales pitch.

'Sure, but houses like this have been around so long, they can take their time about being done up.'

Paul and Lily did not say anything. They could not buy it. Someone else would. This was their last year here.

'Well, think about it.' The agent pushed himself upright from the porch rail, and put down his iced-coffee glass. 'It's not on the market yet. Incidentally,' he said before he left, 'because this house used to be in the Harper family, the rights to use the beach at Hidden Harbor go along with it.'

276

All evening, Paul and Lily talked about the house and the beach and what they would have done with the land and the barn, and went on half the night, lying awake for a long time. Cathy still came into their bed sometimes if she woke, so they incorporated her into the mound of their bodies, and went on talking.

In the morning, the Judge came down to breakfast before Lily could take his tray upstairs. He looked better.

'I'll tell you what I'm going to do,' he said in a slow, instructive voice. 'I'm going to help you with the down-payment, so that you can buy this house.'

He would not listen to objections. 'The money will be yours when I die anyway. Why not have some of it now, for your heart's desire?'

He had a way of occasionally using a sentimental phrase in a perfectly straight, serious way. As he looked at Paul and Lily across the table, his thin mauve lips moved in and out, releasing and then withdrawing a smile.

It took several months of surveyors and lawyers and banks and local officials before the purchase of the house went through, but since it had no proper heating system, they could not move into it for weekends before April or May.

Meanwhile, Lily continued to talk to all the unseen voices at the Day-Nite Answering Service.

'Dr Reed's line. No, not today. He's in Chicago at the APA. Day-Nite. Good morning, Elizabeth. Yes, a lot, and one you won't like. Letterman Clinic, one moment please. Vandermeer & Price, one moment please. Day-Nite. I'm on four lines, I'll call you back.'

She was quick and efficient and she had made a lot of invisible friends, but every week she vowed that she would look for something more enterprising. On a Monday in November, when she went into work determined to tell Gloria that she must leave,

Gloria was one jump ahead of her with an offer to manage the new branch that she was opening in Newton Centre. More money and responsibility. Less travel time.

Lily surprised Gloria by not accepting at once. The decision to move on, which she had talked about interminably to Paul over the weekend, had made her feel lighter. Jobless, but light and free. Gloria's offer was a good one. She would have eight or ten people under her, and the chance of supervising several branches later on. But the lightness was escaping. It felt like being dragged back, not pushed ahead.

'Let me think about it.' She would talk to Paul.

'I'll give you a week, but I want you to take it,' Gloria said. 'This business is growing, and the new branches will have to function a hundred per cent reliably. I really need you.'

Those magic words almost seduced Lily into accepting on the spot. But thank God she didn't, because something exciting and marvellous happened before the week was out.

Since Paul was always willing to look after the children, Lily was filling in at work one night when someone was sick. Mauro and Roger went home at eleven, and by one o'clock, the lines had quieted down. Then out of the silence a call exploded which shocked Lily wide awake from a doze in the armchair, with the lights set to 'ring' and her feet on the broad woolly back of Arthur, whom Paul had sent along to guard her.

'Dr Reed?' The woman's voice was breathless with anxiety.

'I'm afraid he's not on call tonight. This is the answering service. Can I –' Instead of finishing, 'take a message?', Lily instinctively asked, 'Can I help you?'

'Oh God, I hope so. Yes – help me! I don't know what to do.'

Lily was supposed to ask for the caller's number, so that whoever was covering the psychiatrist could contact her, but the woman was crying now, desperate, strangling sobs, and when she suddenly dragged in a great gasping breath and started to talk in a muddled rush, it would have been heartless to interrupt, and impossible anyway, since the tumble of anguished words never stopped.

Lily listened, and paraded her eyes across the long switchboard, forbidding any of the other lines to light up. It was three o'clock;

278

the time for drunken calls from people who had forgotten that it was not business hours, the time that Theodora Benz called on the office line just to hear a voice when she could not sleep, the time that calls sometimes came in from Europe, where it was early morning. Nora was up with the kettle on. Jamspoon was in bed with the radio, cursing politicans.

The switchboard, braided with plugs and wires, was dark and mute. There was only Lily and Louise, who was going to kill herself while her son slept.

She had sleeping pills and vodka. Her husband had left her two years ago after she tried to hang herself. Her parents were in Canada and she would not see or talk to them. She wanted to take all the pills, but she did not want to be dead. She knew she must kill herself, because she had known all her life that she must, and she was on the floor with the pills and the bottle, crouched between her bed and the wall, shivering in a cotton nightgown, terrified to die and terrified to go on living.

Her son – Damon?

'His father will take him. He's been trying to get him for months. I won't let him. But I must. I've got to make myself disappear. He'll be better off without me.'

'Why tonight?'

'I must.' The whisper was very faint.

'Talk to me instead. Remember, you did call your doctor. Doesn't that mean you were looking for help?'

'It means I was going to tell him I'd broken my contract with him. I was through.'

'And then he would have called the police and they'd have broken into your apartment.'

'But he can't because he's not there. He wouldn't talk to me because he doesn't care.'

'Dr Rosen is on call for him. Why not speak to her?'

'No!' Louise came to angry life. 'She's a hard bitch.'

'Talk to me, then.'

'I can't.' But she did, and the switchboard, benign tyrant, stayed quiet. Lily got Louise to go and put on a sweater, and then she got her to say what she might do tonight if she didn't kill herself.

'I can't sleep. I'm not going back to bed. It has nightmares in it.'

'What else could you do, then?'

'It's Damon's birthday tomorrow. He's having some friends in. I could make the spaghetti sauce, I suppose.'

'Do it.'

It was amazing how Louise could switch direction. 'When you've tried to kill yourself as many times as I have,' she told Lily, fairly calmly now, 'it's no big deal. You either do it, or you don't.'

Two jacks lit up. 'I've got to answer a couple of calls. Don't go away. I'll come back to you.'

'No, I'll be all right. Calm down, don't *worry*,' Louise said, as if Lily were the one in trouble, and hung up.

When the morning people came on at seven, Lily had her coat on to leave, when the office line rang for her. It was Martha Bradley, the director of the Crisis agency, with whom Lily had made friends in the days when Crisis still had to use the answering service at night. Louise, whom Crisis knew well, had called them after she had talked to Lily, to report that she had made a passable bolognese sauce, and would they please let Lily know, because she didn't want to bother her if the switchboard were busy.

'How can she be at the end of her rope one minute, and thinking about something else the next?'

'Oh, she can,' Martha said. 'She's amazing. Thanks for taking care of her. I guess you did a pretty good job. She said, "That woman at the answering service was more use to me than any of you guys that are supposed to be so well trained," which is a typical Louise remark.'

Lily wanted to get home before the girls left to catch their school bus on the corner. Arthur was whining and scratching to get out of the door, but she and Martha liked each other, so they exchanged brief news. Martha was in her normal state of chaos and frenzy.

'Only more so at the moment. I'm in despair, I'm in a crisis, I'm going to call my own service. As well as never having enough volunteers, my assistant's leaving. I've interviewed a dozen people, and they're all either too clever and efficient for me, or too stupid and slow, or too neurotic, or much too clinical. I wish I could find someone like you.'

Here it was. What she had been waiting for. Grab your chances, Dear Doctor Lily.

'I'm leaving this job,' she said quickly. 'Would you honestly ever think that I . . .'

'Why not? You had quite a bit of experience in London. But it's not that so much. It's whether you're right for the work, and I could teach you the rest. Want to come and talk about it now?'

'Let me just go home and get my children off to school and have a bath. Then I'll be there.'

Seven

*I*da's good friend Shirley from Watkins Air Force Base had separated from her husband and gone to live in the old fishing town of New Bedford, south of Boston. She had found rooms for Ida there, when she left Lily's house, and when Shirley took over her Aunt Gertrude's house after the old lady went off to the Sacred Heart Rest home, Ida and the children moved in with her.

Buddy was far in the past now – a dream, a nightmare. She had not heard of him since he wrote to her four years ago to say he'd been kicked out of the service with a dishonourable discharge, and would she come to New Hampshire and help him get his life together?

Ida had written back, 'No way, José,' and Buddy had disappeared out of her life. She had not given him her address, because she didn't want him coming after her. When she and Bernie wanted to talk nicely about him, they could say that this was the reason he never sent them any money.

Shirley was running a cleaning service – homes, offices, small motels – and Ida worked for her, on what they called the black economy, so she could still get her welfare cheque and family aid for the kids. She could pay her way in Aunt Gertrude's narrow green shingled house and run a car and get some things of her own together, to make up for what she had abandoned. Life was better than it had been for a long time.

Bernie was learning things at the high school which amazed Ida. He would go into computers and better himself so far beyond the Lotts in Staple Street and the Legges in New Hampshire and Ida herself, that it dazzled her to think what could happen to you in this country. She did not feel bitter about poor old Buddy, because that poisoned you, as Clara Lott had poisoned herself, and Ida could always remember that if it hadn't been for him getting hot and heavy at that drill hall dance, she never would be living in America.

Maggie was in special classes and learning to be of some small use in the world. She sometimes went with Ida to a weekend cleaning job, for which Shirley gave her spending money. Fred was in kindergarten, with his hair like copper wire and his chunky little body that he would gladly hurl into any fight that was going.

'Just like Puppa,' Bernie said, which made Ida laugh, because she was thinking, 'Just like Jackson.'

Ida had never got her figure back after Fred, but then she didn't have it before Fred. Men didn't seem to mind. She and Shirley both had guys off and on, in and out, come and go. Nothing serious. They were hard-working, independent women who had each been tied down to a bastard, and were never going to let themselves fall into the same trap again.

Mike was a bit different. He wasn't one of their fellas. In fact, he was a bit lacking in that department. He did not seem to have any girlfriends, and was too young for Ida or Shirley anyway.

He was a lonely guy who had been in the nut house, or it might have been gaol. Ida wasn't too sure. She told him about Jackson, so he would know it was all right with her if he'd been inside. But he stuck to his story of being in Bridgewater State hospital for some kind of breakdown. He said they had kept him there illegally, and his congressman had to fight to get him out.

Now he lived with his mother, and drove a taxi. He was a lovely young man really, with clean brown hair and brooding eyes and a pale romantic scar at the left side of his mouth to remind him of Bridgewater and the kitchen officer who didn't count the knives. Ida and Shirley had met him in a bar down by the wharf. He had gabbled to them for an hour, and then got so paralytic drunk that Shirley had to drive him home to Fairhaven in his own taxi.

His mother opened the door, wearing a wrapper, and he fell into the front hall. Could Ida and Shirley help? His mother shook her head and smiled at them politely. She moved to Mike's front end, dragged him forward by his arms until his feet were clear of the door, and then shut it.

After that, they kept seeing him around. He was quiet and pulled in to himself sometimes. Sometimes he couldn't get the words out fast enough. He pushed through the gate in the picket fence of Aunt Gertrude's house once in a while, and wanted food, or coffee, or a glass of wine, as if he didn't already have a mother in Fairhaven, doing a full-time job for him, it seemed.

Lily invited Ida to come to Cape Cod on a July Sunday to see the house she and Paul were so excited about. Mike was there when Ida got the call, and he said, 'I'll drive you and the kids down.'

'You've not been invited, pet.'

'Cab drivers don't get invited. They just drive.'

'Mike, I can't pay –'

'Don't insult me.'

'I can drive myself to the Cape.'

'In that heap?'

There was nothing wrong with Ida's Plymouth Horizon, but he wanted to drive her to the Cape, so she let him. He didn't look like a New Bedford cabbie. You could take him anywhere.

It was disappointing that he acted so strange at Lily's. He didn't want to go to the beach, or eat any of Lily's fine cold lunch, except some potato salad and most of the pickles. He wouldn't have a beer with Paul, or pay attention to any of the children, or even the friendly dog. He sat apart, wearing heavy boots that would give his mother stinking socks to wash, and would not take off his sweatshirt.

'Bit of an awkward cuss,' Lily said on the beach. 'Who is he, Eye? What are you up to, anyway?'

'Nothing, for once. He's a friend of me and Shirley.'

Ida closed her eyes. On the New Bedford public beaches, she always wore a man's shirt over her bathing suit, but on this empty shore, she could lie spread-eagled in her old-lady's flowered suit with the draped skirt, which was the only thing she could get in her size.

A few boats went past, and some of the family who owned the beach were at the far end, well away from this sheltered place under the breakwater rocks. Maggie and Bernie were swimming, and old Fred was messing about on a rubber raft, with Cathy pulling him around, and tipping him off, so that he had to dog paddle in the shallow water until he could climb on the raft again, screaming abuse at Cathy.

All aggressive males had deep, hysterical fears, in Ida's vast

287

and wearying experience. Swimming was one of old Fred's.

'Like it here?' Lily did not lift her head.

'Uh-huh.'

'It's our favourite place, mine and Paul's. I used to think no beaches should be private. Now that this is ours to use, that's different.'

'Snob.'

'Maybe.'

'You got it made.'

'I'm so lucky, Eye. Now that I've got this wonderful job in Boston, I've got everything.'

'That's what you said when you got Paul, when you got a baby, when you got a house in the suburbs, when you got a place on the Cape. So now what? A lover would be chic.' Ida pronounced it 'chick', which she knew was wrong, to stress the difference between them.

'Don't be duft.' Lily smacked the mound of Ida's meaty thigh. 'We ought to see each other more often.'

'No we didn't. We stay friends this way.'

The boy next door, Tony, who looked like thousands of dark young Portuguese in New Bedford, came to the beach with them, and was at the house for lunch. He and Bernie got along famous. While Isobel was giving Maggie and Fred rides on the pony, Horace, the boys went down to Tony's house. He let Bernie ride his trail bike, and they went off into the woods on the other side of the railroad with some other boys.

In the afternoon, Lily had a call from the place where she worked. A crisis at Crisis. She flew in when Paul called her, and made rather a big thing of shutting herself in her bedroom with the phone for ages, and then coming out, lifting her bangs away from her frowning forehead and shaking her head in a responsible kind of way, so they would all see she was a big wheel in the rescue business.

'Sorry about that.'

'We have to go,' Ida said, to show she wasn't impressed. She rounded up Maggie and Fred and got Bernie out of the barn, where he and Tony were on the trapeze. Mike was already in his taxi, listening to the radio.

'I'm so glad you came.' Paul said goodbye warmly. Maybe he'd been scared they were all going to move in again. 'So great for Lily.'

'Not for you?' Ida couldn't resist saying it.

'Stop that,' Lily said. 'He's on to you. You can't embarrass Paul.'

She made a joke of it in a way that had them all resuscitated as friends, and went some way toward tidying up the mess of that crazy time when Ida had squatted on them with newborn Fred, and had to clear off in the night, like a thief.

In the front seat of the uncomfortable Chevvy, Ida asked Mike, 'You like her?'

'She's okay. She didn't like me.'

Ida thought, 'No wonder,' but said, 'Sure she did. She likes everybody.'

'Doesn't make it worth much, then.'

'Fuck you,' Ida thought. 'You kids have a good time?' she called to the back seat.

'When can we come again?' Fred asked.

'Three or four years.' That was about the speed of her and Lily's get-togethers.

'Tony invited me to visit any time,' Bernie said. 'I could come out on the bus, he said, when his uncle cuts the hay.'

'You do that, son.'

Maggie said, 'I want a pony. I want a horse like Horrid.'

Isobel was quite good at riding now, and she had planned how she would show off a bit on Horace, jumping the small fences in the back field, to impress the kids from New Bedford, who probably had never seen a horse anyway.

She wanted Tony to ride too, but he was too big for the pony, and not allowed to ride Daddy's horse that he'd got for the summer, although he looked after him and Horace when Isobel's family wasn't here.

She went twice round the field, with no refusals, except nearly at the bottom fence; but with any luck, the watchers were too far away to see Horace stop dead and then leap straight up one side of the jump and down the other, with Isobel landing on his neck.

When she got back to the gate, Bernie and Tony had gone off somewhere. Isobel was wild. She slid off Horace and jerked his rein, poor pony, to get his head up from the grass.

'Gimme a ride,' Maggie was clamouring.

'He won't like it.'

'Oh, he doesn't care,' Cathy had to say. 'He let Sally and Brad ride yesterday. When he got sick of it, he just put his head down and they slid off.'

'Gimme a ride.'

Maggie had grown a bit more sensible since she had wrecked Isobel's bedroom, although her eyes still didn't both look at you at the same time.

'Do you mind, honey?' Maggie's mother asked. 'And Fred too, maybe? Gee, you ride so good, I can't believe it.'

But Ida's praise was no use to Isobel.

She gave Maggie a ride to show how nice she was, in spite of everything, and she let Cathy lead Fred around the top part of the field, but she had to run out and grab the pony, because he started to trot and Cathy let go and Fred screamed.

When she was taking Horace's tack off by the gate, the boys had still not come back. Isobel started to cry, with her face against the pony. Her mother saw, and came up and took the saddle, and they walked to the barn alone together.

Isobel let the reins trail on the ground, because she felt so draggy, and Mud said, 'Don't –', then thought better of it. They sat on a hay bale in the dusty feed corner, and Isobel had a good cry, while her mother held her tightly.

'Tony's almost grown up, you know,' she said. 'I know he's your best friend, but he's bound to have other friends too. You don't mind about Wayne and Ritchie and all that crowd he goes with?'

'No . . . no . . . I don't know.'

Isobel couldn't explain it. She didn't have to, because Mud

shut up after that and just held her, and they sat together and played with each other's fingers, and mixed their hair together.

'They'll be looking for us,' Isobel said, when she had dried her face.

'I don't care. I want to be here with you. I love you so much, Iz, I can hardly stand it. Why do I ever want anything else? Why not just be a mother?'

Isobel's heart was warm and spreading, like a cake expanding in the oven.

'But you love your job,' she said.

'I love you and Cathy a thousand times more.'

'But we do need the money,' Isobel said sensibly, 'if we're going to do all the things we want to around this place.'

'Lily! Lily! Telephone!'

'Oh, my God – I'm on call. Sorry, darling. Turn Horace out, would you, and check the water tub.'

Mud was gone.

Isobel looked past the open door to the small window where she had stood on the stone block last year and seen inside the barn. She looked at the rough, rubbed post at the end of the partition, where she had seen her leaning.

Once when she was mad with Mud for getting tied up at Crisis and sending Anita round to be there when they got home from school, Isobel had gone out to her father when she saw his car come home. In the garage, while he was checking on some seedlings on the bench under the window, Isobel said, 'You want to know something?'

'You bet.' When she didn't speak, he turned round. 'Well, what is it?'

Isobel turned her head away. She didn't want to look at him. She didn't want to tell him now, and spoil his smiling face, but he insisted, 'Tell me,' so it was his fault.

She told him about seeing her mother and Harry in the barn. She didn't quite know how to tell it, not really knowing what it was all about, but his smile did vanish, as expected.

'Why are you making up this story?' Her father caught hold of her arm, but she backed away.

'Because it's true.'

'Why do you have to lie so much, darling?' He wasn't even angry, because he didn't believe her.

'No one believes me when I do tell the truth, so what's the point?' No, wait a minute. That sounded as if what she had told him wasn't true either. He took his briefcase off the bench, and Isobel followed him to the door that led to the kitchen.

'But Daddy —'

'That's enough.'

He didn't believe it anyway. No point in going on.

When Lily told Ida about her work at Crisis, Ida had said, with the tougher, bolder laugh that was part of this new phase of her life, 'I was wondering why you hadn't told me what to do lately. Now you've got all these other sad-sack customers. That should keep you quiet.'

Quiet! That was what Lily's life had been when she thought it was hectic, having to fit in the comparatively peaceful answering service with the needs of Paul and the children. Crisis had turned her life into a maelstrom. She loved it.

Martha was energetic and effective and enthusiastic and without fear. She had a confident way of assuming that people would give her money and contacts and publicity, and they did. She expected a lot from the volunteers and the staff, and she got it. Sub-standard volunteers were ruthlessly disposed of. Those who made the grade did their utmost for the callers, and would do anything for Martha. So would Lily.

Her job involved helping to train the new volunteers who answered the phones, seeing clients who came in, following up their progress and sometimes arranging professional help. She took her share of the many phone calls, and bolstered up the volunteers when they were anxious about someone desperate, or fed up with the sex callers who used their number to ply their lonely trade.

Sometimes Lily went out to see somebody who couldn't or

wouldn't come to the centre. Richard Spence, failed businessman, was holed up in a cheap motel room, ashamed to go home, and afraid to go out. Lily had also been to see Louise, after talking to her on the phone many times, and found her a small frail person in shrunken jeans, with delicate features that could change expression in the flash of a thought.

When she was a little girl, Louise had invented a companion for herself, one long summer when her parents were abroad. He was an eight-year-old boy called Gerald, who was now a dominant part of her life and wouldn't leave her. The trouble was that while Louise was twenty-six, Gerald was still a ruthless and demanding eight. Her suicide attempts had usually been because Gerald ordered them. She could live quite normally for a while, with her son Damon, and then suddenly Gerald would take over and wreck everything.

Lily had seen him one winter afternoon. The Crisis centre was in a converted terrace house in a back street of Boston. Louise lived not far away, and she would often drop in for a chat. It tickled her that Lily was English, and she would bring in buns and want a pot of tea made.

This afternoon, she was fairly peaceful and ordinary. Then Lily said she had to leave her to make a phone call.

'Will you be all right for ten minutes?'

Louise did not answer, and Lily saw her face change in an instant from an animated young woman to a sulky, devious small boy, mouth obstinate, eyes sliding back and forth, looking for trouble. Even her body looked different. She sat with knees apart and small feet planted. She thrust her hands into the sleeves of her sweater, and hunched over.

'Louise?'

Louise-Gerald got up and went out of the small back-room, down the passage, knocking against someone with an armful of books, and banged through the door, out into the street.

Lily ran after her and found her standing stubbornly in the middle of the street, which luckily was not busy. Cars swerved round her. Students on bicycles wobbled, a van driver shouted, a car's brakes screamed.

'Pretty stupid way to get yourself killed.'

Lily pulled her out of the road. Louise stared at her as if she did not know her.

'Come in and get your coat.'

Indoors, Louise began to shudder and shake. Martha put her on a couch and wrapped a blanket round her. Louise, half herself, half still Gerald, wanted Martha to call Dr Reed, and then burrowed her head in a cushion and refused to talk to him.

Martha, who always knew what to do, talked to the psychiatrist, and then called Louise's saintly neighbour and asked her to fetch Damon from school, a favour she often had to do when Louise was disorganized.

Louise fell asleep. Lily sat by her and did some paperwork. When it was time for her to leave, to be back before Cathy and Isobel got home, Martha said, 'Damn,' and ran a hand roughly through her short stiff grey hair, still flecked with its original reddish-brown. 'I thought you could take Louise home.'

'I can't.'

'*I* know. The kids.' Martha was irritated, which wasn't fair, because these hours were agreed between them. 'I can't take her myself, because I've got a meeting. Andy's too new, and Fran is scared of Louise. I wish – oh well, off you go, little mother.'

Lily, who admired Martha, drove home too fast, upset, not with Martha, but with herself for having somehow failed, in a way she couldn't help.

She told the volunteers in training not to get too emotionally involved, but for herself, it was a bit different. She believed she could get close to people in trouble without losing her judgement or strength.

Paul was proud of what she was doing, and did not complain – much – about her preoccupation with people like Richard Spence, Louise and Peter and Rocky, and whoever was a current concern.

'Do you ever think you need these jokers more than they need you?' he asked reasonably, when she had spent two hours after dinner making calls to clients from home.

'Oh, God, do you feel neglected? Don't you know that you and the girls and our life together come first? Always. Remember that.'

'Oh, I will,' he said solemnly.

Before the Cape Cod house was bought, Lily had been able to give a large part of her weekdays to Crisis. When the house was theirs, she caught herself sometimes resenting its demands. There was a tremendous lot to do in planning and supervising repairs, painting the bathroom yellow, scrubbing out the kitchen accumulation of years, buying basic furniture and curtains and rugs and china and saucepans, taking stuff down that could be spared from Newton.

The Judge was still away from court on sick leave. Since he had made the house possible, Lily tried to get him to come to the Cape, but he came only once. He felt cold, although it was a warm weekend. The children and their friends thundered in and out on the bare wood floors. He couldn't risk eating lobster. When he went outside to see what Paul was doing on the fences, he fell over a rock. The fog horn sounded all night. It was too much for him.

The scandal over the two black youths and the man who died of a heart attack had been overlaid by many others, and forgotten by the public, but the hurt of it was not forgotten by Even Steven. His health did not pick up. He was seventy-two. He thought he might have to retire soon. Lily had found Mrs Meggs to be a live-in housekeeper, with a television set for her room that was half the width of one wall. The Judge hated her.

Every weekend, Paul worked outside with Tony, repairing fences, making a new gate, shoring up the barn, starting to do some rough work on the neglected land. Tony's father bulldozed out dead trees to be sawn into logs. He brought up his cultivator, and Paul started a vegetable garden and a few flower-beds near the house. Next year, they would tackle the tufted grass at the front and sides and start a proper lawn.

Paul came home from work early on Fridays, and they left the Cape late on Sunday nights. It was the best time of his life so far. In between weekends, he existed.

One weekend, Paul and Harry got a load of wood and partitioned off two loose boxes inside the barn. Harry lent Paul an old chestnut horse for the summer, and found a dependable bay pony for the girls, which was like a miniature horse, narrow and smooth going.

'Room for plenty more boxes,' Harry said. 'Tack room, feed shed, hay store. You could turn this place into a boarding stable and make enough money to keep your own horses. Run a tack shop, why not? Dump those robbers at Turnbull's, and use all your experience for yourself.'

'And live here all the time and be a doddery old saddlemaker.' Paul had already dreamed this dream.

'Lovable,' Harry added, 'with crooked eyeglasses and a stained white moustache.'

'And have horses and horses. Buy that bit of scrub land across the road from the Andrades, plough and seed it, put up more fences. Winterize the house. Knock the kitchen and living-room together to make one big room.'

In his office desk, Paul kept a drawer of plans and notes and catalogues that had nothing to do with Turnbull's.

Every night when they were here in the summer, he and Lily would walk out into the field before they went to bed. The horse and pony would come to them out of the darkness, slowly, because it wasn't feed time. Arthur ranged, nose down, on some serious night hunting. The grey cat that had moved in when oats in the barn brought rats and mice jumped to the top rail of the fence and did a tightrope walk. Paul leaned against the good old chestnut horse. He lifted its heavy head so that he could put his cheek against the soft pale velvet place just above the nostrils. He blew gently down his nose, mingling his breath with the horse's moist, grassy essence, which smelled of apples if Lily had brought some out, otherwise, curiously, of chicken soup.

When the horse and pony tired of it, they would wander off down the dip in the field and be lost in shadows, leading the secret life of domestic animals who sleep outdoors.

Then Paul and Lily would put damp horsy hands round each other, and wander back in silent content. Lucky, they told each other often. They were so lucky.

What Isobel had tried to say to Paul was totally absurd. How could a child of that age make up something like that? He put it out of his head, but the idea seeped back through treacherous cracks. When Harry was there, Paul occasionally caught himself watching him with Lily, but they were just as they had always been, loving and open, teasing, laughing.

Paul was forty-five. Lily was thirty-five. Harry was nearer her age. Paul shoved the unworthy thought down again and stamped on it. He was going to stay young, young with Lily; never be the jealous older husband – formula for disintegration.

Never be jealous of her job either. Or of superwoman Martha, whom she tried so hard to please. Or of the clients whom she talked about incessantly at home. There were times when Paul privately thought that Lily went a bit overboard. He remembered how she had been, years ago, over the man in the greenhouse whose little boy had died. Paul's father had warned her then: 'You can't take on everyone else's troubles,' and she had almost shouted at him across the table, 'But you've got to be involved!' with her face ablaze.

'I hear you're doing noble work,' Terry said to Lily when he came, after months, to see what they were doing with the house. 'Not bad for a young and irresponsible foreigner.'

'How *is* your mother?' Paul asked.

'I don't know. All right, I guess.'

Terry had left home last year, and stayed with different friends, moving around. When students left summer jobs to go back to college, Terry left the airport snack-bar and took three or four restaurant jobs and then one in the bar of a suburban motel. His girls were assorted, from black satin and high heels and squeals, to earth colours and long dusty skirts, and misfit people whom he described as 'older women'. He had dropped out of the art school.

The Judge was also going to drop out. With his doctor's encouragement, he had decided that he was not able to return to work. He seemed relieved.

'Only problem – how am I going to put up with Mrs Meggs all day? She's not bad in the kitchen, but she robs me blind at the market, and she's beginning to want to watch my television instead of hers. She's filtering down from her part of the house. She says we're two lonely people. I'm afraid she has designs on me.'

'No problem,' Terry said. 'We're three lonely people, counting me. Fire the Meggs and let me move in with Grandpa.'

'Lynette as well?' Paul asked.

'Who's she?'

Terry's girls came and went quite fast.

James had continued to see Evvie off and on, depending on whether a job from Faces took him up to London, and on the occasional television work Evvie got for him.

Kyle had moved out of her flat after a row, but she would never let James in there. So it was the odd hotel room, but not often. No strain. No sweat. It was there if they wanted it. They didn't usually want more than a chat and a meal together.

His best commercial had been for jogging shoes, in a sweater with vertical stripes to emphasize the old pot-belly. He made about £500 in repeats, and even Nora was pleased with him. He did a few days of crowd work: 'With Sir Larry – we're all in togas.'

'With your legs?' Nora got a laugh from the bar customers. 'That explains the fall of the Roman Empire.'

She had begun to see the value of what she still called 'Your fun and games in the wicked city'. (Could she know about Evvie? Not a chance.) They were going to take the plunge and go to America again to visit Lily and Paul. Nora had plodded round travel agents in her usual methodical way, and found the cheapest fare to Boston.

Blanche was willing to look after the Duke's Head. She was taking a bit more interest in the pub these days, which was good in a way, but upsetting in another, because she kept telling her parents what they ought to do. Once she brought in a friend who worked in an architect's office to discuss how alterations could be made to enlarge the kitchen and make room for a small restaurant.

'Very nice,' Nora and James said. They didn't argue. They just knew they weren't going to do it.

'You've got a little gold mine here.' Blanche's friend had bloodshot nostrils and huge round glasses like portholes.

They had made Blanche promise not to take an axe to any of the walls while they were in America.

'Why should I care?' was her answer. 'It's your pub. If you don't want to keep up with the changing type of trade, that's your privilege.'

'Watch her while we're gone,' James told Duggie Manderson. 'I don't trust her.'

'Telephone!' Nora, who was doing housework in the cottage, opened the back door of the pub and called to James, on lunchtime duty in the bar. He picked up the telephone, which was between the public and private bars.

It was Henrietta. 'Look,' he said quickly, with his back to the customers. 'I can't take the call here. Too much noise. Let me ring you back in a few minutes.'

'Don't muck about,' Henrietta said. 'I've got to call back with an answer for the magazine right away. The man's got a plane to catch.'

'Magazine, what magazine . . . what?' There were some farm workers in the public bar. They were making a racket.

'They asked for you.' Henrietta raised her deep voice. 'Remember the still you did for *True Tales*?'

Jam smiled, remembering himself. 'I was the alcoholic politician?'

'Something like that. This is another of their magazines. You may not have seen it . . . er, you may have. *Do It Yourself.*'

'So bring my overalls?'

'No, your executive suit, plus bowler, brolly, briefcase and that.'

'You mean, "Even a bank manager can build his own home"?'

'Not exactly. Look, you haven't got to do this if you don't want. It's soft porn.'

'Crikey!' James cupped his hand over the mouthpiece. 'I don't have to –'

'The girls do that. You have to be shocked.'

'I would be.' Jam was far more proper than he admitted to. 'But why is it called Do It Your – oh. Got it.'

'Seventy-five an hour. Yes or no?'

Good money. Go on, Jam. 'Of course I'll do it.'

'I knew you would.'

'Ho ho.'

'And ho ho to *you*.' One of the farm workers leered at him as he hung up the phone. 'Jam, you've gone all red. Was that your girlfriend?'

'That'll be the day,' Jam managed to say. He poured himself a shot of White Horse to steady his nerves. Better. What the hell. He was a pro. A trouper.

The next evening, he went down to the post office call-box to tell Evvie.

Kyle answered. 'You can't,' he said quite rudely. 'She's working late. What the hell do you want?'

James hung up. He could have said, 'What the hell are you doing there?' The man had moved out a few weeks ago.

There were three girls in the studio with him. The photographer was a jaded-looking man in a poncey yellow cardigan. His assistant was a bored fellow with dirty white jeans and shaved hair. They continued to look jaded and bored even when the girls came out of the dressing-room in tiny black bras, black stockings and black suspenders. No knickers.

The girls looked bored too, except when they rolled their eyes and grinned, or made 'oo' mouths for a take. James was the only one who was not bored.

He had to wear glasses, which was the only thing that saved his eyes from falling out of his head. The assistant arranged the girls in various rude poses. 'Wider, wider,' the photographer droned. 'Come on, you're here to show more than that.'

James was coming through the door marked 'Bank Manager', to be surprised by what, at a hideous stretch of the imagination, were supposed to be his bank clerks, cutting it up with spray cans of shaving foam. All he had to do was look startled, shocked, amazed, outraged.

The girls were called Doreen and Annabel and Holly. Annabel

had a very posh 'Mummy darling' accent. Holly was married to a company director. Doreen was a bit of a tart. James could not believe that he was mixed up in this. For the final still, the girls piled on to a sort of office cart like Nora's tea trolley, and he had to push them, bottoms up, through the doorway, looking back at the camera with the smirk he had been disguising when he was being astonished and outraged.

Afterwards, he took his briefcase and umbrella round to Evvie's office on the chance that she might be free. She was finishing up, so they went and had a drink, and James told her how he had earned his living that day.

Evvie didn't show whether she was amused, or shocked, or what. She was not excited, that was certain. James was.

'I think I'm getting delayed reaction,' he said. 'Have you got time to – you know – take a little trip to the Essex?'

'Could I spray foam on you?' Evvie giggled with a straight face.

In the hotel room, he asked her, 'What was Kyle doing at your place?'

'When?' Evvie called from the bathroom.

'I rang you a couple of days ago.'

'He came back to collect some film.'

'Hurry up.'

In that room, with the curtains drawn on the streets where people were going home from work, Jam felt something that was like love for Evvie. She had come to him in his hour of need. She was a totally different shape from Annabel and Doreen and Holly. She would starve to death rather than do something like that, and she'd never need to, because she was a sharp and successful business woman, and the fact that he was with her in the Hotel Essex was even more astonishing, when you thought about it, than being in that foam-spattered studio this afternoon.

He trailed home to the same old scene. Supper in the oven. Nora in the bar. Good old Nora. If she could even *guess* what he'd been up to, wouldn't she simply die? You rotter, Jamspoon.

Feeling mild pangs of guilt, he went through to the pub and told Nora to go and put her feet up. The bars were not busy. He was able to do most of the clearing up before closing time. When he went back to the cottage for a cup of tea, he gave Nora a hug. He felt mellow towards her. That was how guilt took him. Nora went to take the kettle off the stove. For an insane moment, he imagined her with those suspenders round her broad bottom, and depraved Doreen squirting foam on you-know-where.

Nora drank tea placidly, her eyes looking over the rim of the mug like a child.

'Slow tonight,' he said companionably.

'It was quite busy earlier.'

'That right? Who was in?' He didn't care, but the Duke was her life. She liked to talk about it.

She named a few boring names.

'Haven't seen old Duggie for a while. What's happened to him? He taken his trade to the Lion?'

Nora put down her mug. 'Since you brought it up.' She took a deep breath and told him. It didn't take long.

When she had finished, he stood up. 'Well,' he said, surprised to hear that his voice still worked, 'better go down and do those bloody barrels.'

'I'll help you.'

'Don't bother.' How dare she?

She got up. 'Jamie.'

Her pet name for him. He wanted to spit.

'Leave me alone.'

In the cellar, trundling a barrel across the floor, forcing the aching muscular effort to get it on the rack, he thought, 'Let me have a heart attack. Now, God. Let her come down in those pyjamas with the little prissy collar and find me here.'

But she would still go off with Duggie Manderson. 'Nothing will stop me,' she had said. Nora! *Nora* saying that. It was like a foreign language.

His heart didn't burst with the second barrel, so he sat on the stone step with an ache in his ribs, and pulled his face down to cry. How could she deceive him so cruelly? How could she go ahead and plan the trip to Boston, when all the time, she *knew*?

Tears fell into the folds at the corners of his mouth. 'Why? Why?' he asked the cellar. When he had asked Nora, she had said quietly, 'If you don't know why, Jamie, I can't tell you.'

'Hey, Lily.' Chuck, one of the Crisis volunteers, was on the intercom. 'I've got Louise on the line. She's in the bin.'

'Why?'

'The usual, I suppose. Can you talk to her?'

Louise was in South Side Hospital. She whispered to Lily, 'Can you come?'

'When?'

'Today. Oh, please. I'm scared.'

'Where's Damon?'

'He's all right. I've got to go. I'm only allowed –' A voice spoke to her. 'Leave me alone!' she gasped, and hung up. She sounded about two feet high, and fading.

'Want someone else to go?' Martha asked. 'She likes Chuck, and he's good with her.'

'No, I must.' Lily had made a good friendship with Louise. When the imaginary small boy Gerald left her alone, she could be funny and bright, playing intriguing games with her son, offering Lily love, which Lily also felt for her. But Louise was so unpredictable and self-destructive, and when something went wrong, she did not tell anyone until after it had happened.

'Shit, man, I'd like to go.' Chuck was a huge, bearded young man, with holes in peculiar places in his jeans.

'Shit, man, so would I.' Lily's language had deteriorated a bit to match the casual young students.

She called her good neighbour Alice, whose daughter came home on the same bus as Isobel and Cathy, and asked her if the girls could go to her house, finished up some letters, put away the confidential files, and drove to the psychiatric hospital on the outskirts of the city.

It was a state hospital, a Bedlam type of Victorian prison with heavy doors, steel bars across the lower windows, wire mesh for those above, a high brick wall round the yard.

South Side took up a whole city block among streets of what had once been decent narrow wooden houses, which were now sagging under the damp weight of poverty and squalor. Garbage and old iron fought the weeds in the tiny spaces between rotting front steps and the littered sidewalk.

Lily found Louise in the fourth-floor day room. It was a square bare room with a tattered sofa and a few lopsided armchairs, two lines of metal chairs facing each other down the middle, and a scarred table by the window where three men sat with their heads buried in their arms. There were more people than chairs. Some sat on the floor. Some paced. Some just stood. With their backs to the door through which Lily had been let in, two huge black female sentries sat with arms crossed over powerful chests.

Louise was sitting on a ledge by the wall with her feet drawn up under her. She was pale as milk, and her eyes looked dark and hectic. Beside her was the canvas satchel she took everywhere, with her journal and poems in it.

'What a ghastly place.'

'It's worse for you than for me,' Louise said considerately. 'I've been here before. You should see the Quiet Room.'

'What's that?'

'Solitary. No window. No door handle. No furniture. No light switch. No light, if the aide doesn't feel like turning it on.'

'Why are you in here?'

'Dr Reed's away. I wanted to be safe, so he got me into the psych unit at St Clement's.' This was a high-class downtown hospital. 'They threw me out,' Louise said with the glee her small alter ego, Gerald, might show.

'What for?'

'Setting fire to a wastebin?' Louise tried that out on Lily. Gerald was not far away.

'What else?'

'Oh, let's see – a little cutting?' Louise pulled up her sleeve. She always wore long sleeves, except when she was showing off, because her arms were scarred from wrist to shoulder with cuts and cigarette burns. A new dressing was on the inside of her forearm.

'And?'

'Well, I got a lamp cord and hung myself in the closet of my room. Something to do.'

'*Louise —*'

'Oh, I left the closet door open, and the door of the room. They found me, but they didn't like it. I'm glad you came. I knew you would.'

She put her arm round Lily. Patients kept wandering up to ask questions, or to show Lily something, or to stare. Louise was distressingly at ease in this uneasy room. She knew who to answer kindly, who to ignore, who to tell, 'Fuck off, Jack. I've told you before.'

When Lily left, one of the sentries heaved herself up to open the door. Instantly, a girl with long tangled hair made a bolt for it. The black woman shoved Louise and Lily back into the room with the flat of her hand, and locked the door. The elevator gates clanged. Bells rang in the hall.

'What excitement,' Lily said nervously.

Louise shrugged. 'Something to do. She's not going anywhere.'

When Lily collected her daughters at Alice's house, they were both watching television quite happily, lying on the floor among Alice's children with bowls of popcorn and soft-drink cans.

Cathy said, 'Hi,' without looking away from the screen, but Isobel jumped up and cried, 'Where have you been? I want to go home!'

She tugged her mother down the street, complaining about Alice's five-year-old, fussing about needing to call her best friend, asking what was for supper, when would it be?

In the house, she said, 'I'm going to call Jane,' and started for the living-room. The phone rang before she got to it.

'Gramps? Hi, how's England? I'm fine. At school, we're doing this really neat play, and it's with some of the parents and Daddy's going to play the piano and I'm going to sing. What? No, it's about a sailor who falls in love with a mermaid – well, she's not really a mermaid, you see, because this other sailor, not the one who's in love with her – what? Oh. Okay,' she said flatly, then shouted, 'Mudder! It's Gramps. He says it's urgent.'

'What's happened?' Lily grabbed the phone. 'Something wrong with Nora?'

'No. Well . . .' – hollow laugh – 'You could say that, I suppose.' Her father's voice was strange. The line was very clear, but he sounded as if he were shut in the cellar. 'Lily, I – Lily –' He was on the cracked edge of tears. 'She's left me.'

'What are you talking about, Jam?'

'She has. With Duggie.'

Dug Manderson – everybody's friend and asexual neighbour? 'This is madness, Jam. When?'

'She got packed up and went yesterday. She said a week ago she meant to go.'

'Why didn't you tell me?'

'I didn't believe it. I thought I could talk her round.'

'What about the pub?'

'Bianca is here. She's been a brick, I have to say it. Lily, you know about these things. How do people kill themselves?'

'Now, you stop that, Jam.'

'What is it, what's happening?' The shock and anxiety in Lily's voice had brought Cathy and Isobel clamouring round her.

'It's all right, darlings. Gramps has had a bit of bad luck.'

'I want to talk to him.'

'Listen, Daddy, you get on a plane and come out here. You've got tickets. Change the date.'

'I couldn't face the journey. I wouldn't have the heart for it. Lily, you couldn't, could you – my darling, I know you're so busy, but you're the only one who –'

'I'll come,' Lily said briskly. 'I'll make some plans and ring you back. It must be ten o'clock with you. What time are you going to bed?'

'You don't think I can *sleep*?'

'Lemme talk to Gramps.' Isobel took the phone. 'So when it's their wedding day, and the sailor carries her up the aisle in this beautiful white gown over her fish tail, and the organ plays "O Perfect Love" – that's Daddy – and the sailor, the good one, his perfect love turns her into a lady. Mud.' She held the phone away. 'Gramps is crying.'

★

Martha gave Lily a week off, and Paul's Aunt Bridget, a widowed good woman, would come and stay. One of the last-minute things was a quick visit to Louise.

She had managed to stay out of the Quiet Room, and was now a Trusty, free to meet Lily downstairs in the hospital lobby. They went to the cafeteria, and Louise took some papers out of her canvas satchel and spread them out on the greasy, coffee-ringed table. There were bits of her journal, unposted letters to her parents and to Damon, and to that love-hate child, Gerald.

'Has Gerald been in here with you?' Lily asked. She had got used to talking about him as if he existed. Louise was far beyond the point of understanding him as fantasy.

She shook her head. 'He put me in here,' she said, as matter of factly as if Gerald were a psychiatrist. 'He wrote these, look.'

She showed Lily some loose pages, disorganized cries of agony, stabbed on to the creased paper in big letters, a few words askew down the page.

'Psychotic writing.' She grinned sideways, to see if Lily was impressed.

As she displayed some of what she had written over the years of her illness, her eyes were alive, not hectic, but shining with genuine creative pleasure. She laughed a lot, and told shocking stories about the hospital staff. Silent people at other tables stared glumly. Louise nudged Lily, and giggled and whispered behind her hand. They were like two teenagers in a snack-bar: us and them.

'Don't go away, Lily.'

'You'll be all right.'

'Don't go.'

Lily flew to England to try to comfort her father, and bolster him up a bit to face the catastrophe of his life. At the back of her mind, she also hoped that in some way she might be a go-between. If her mother had done this in a fit of pique – although Nora had never done anything on impulse – Lily might be able to get her to go back home and start again.

That was what Jam hoped too. He was a wreck. Neil met Lily at the airport, because her father did not trust himself to drive.

She found him in a hot, stuffy room, sitting hunched into himself like an old man in front of the electric fire, as if in defiance of Nora, who would have marched in and switched it off and thrown open the window.

The first thing he said was, 'Get her back for me, Lily. I want her back.'

Lily was tired from the overnight flight, but she stayed up all day to be with him. He was a large, bulky man, but he looked smaller, because of this. He wouldn't stand up straight. He poked his big head like a tortoise. Even his paunch seemed to have shrunk, as if it were deflated.

They had supper at Blanche's house, with Duffy, which meant not much could be said. Afterwards, Neil played cribbage with Jam, while Lily went upstairs with Blanche, and they talked after they had put Duffy to bed.

'What are we going to do?' Lily had laid herself out on Blanche and Neil's neat double bed, exhausted.

'Nothing we *can* do.'

Because Lily had the wobbly indecision of jet lag, and Blanche had already been coping with their parents' problem, she seemed like the older sister, not the younger.

'Have you seen Nora?'

'I've been to see her, yes, but not him. He stayed out of the way, like the soul of tact he is, dear old Duggie, who wouldn't hurt a fly. They've moved out of this area, of course. He'll sell his house and they're going to start again in Essex, or somewhere.'

'Do people here know?'

'Not yet. They think Mum's gone to stay with Gran.'

'Will she come back? Blanche, she's got to come back.'

Blanche kicked off her shoes and lay down beside Lily on the bed. One of the terriers jumped up too.

'She won't.'

'But this isn't like her. She must be mad. It's the change of life.'

'She's had that.'

'But not *Mum*. I mean, she's always been the quiet, steady, hardworking one, never put a foot wrong, ever since we've known her. I mean, she would *never* –'

'She did.'

308

'I'm going to tell her what I think of her.'

'Don't.' Blanche lay like a stone queen on a tomb, with the dog at her feet. 'She's suffering. I know her. Don't make it more difficult.'

'She's suffering! Look at that poor old man down there.'

'You always take his side, don't you?' Blanche turned and put an arm round her sister. 'He had it coming to him.'

'Oh, *don't*.'

They held each other as they had not done since one or the other of them had been in love and was rejected.

Downstairs, Jam was asleep with his feet on a stool, splayed outwards. Lily left him there and went back upstairs to sleep on the other bunk bed in Duffy's room.

Nora and Duggie were living in a furnished flat over a promenade of shops in an indefinite place north of London. Duggie's firm was transferring him to the Chelmsford branch, and they would eventually buy a bungalow.

'In a village or in the town?' Lily sat on the edge of an uncomfortable settee like a railway-station bench, discussing practical domestic details with her mother in a calm and rational way that made her think they had all lost their reason.

She had started the visit by flinging herself at Nora and bursting into floods of tears, because her mother looked so normal and just like herself in her green crochet top and pleated tweed skirt. Her grey hair was done the same way, and she wore the same pendant round her neck which Lily and Paul had given her on her fiftieth birthday.

'Don't cry, pet.' Nora patted her, while Lily clung to those familiar fat, capable upper arms. 'It's all right.'

'It's not, it's not, you can't do this!'

Nora continued to murmur, 'Easy does it,' and 'It's all right,' so calmly that Lily pushed away from her and said crossly, 'It may be all right for you, but it's not for anyone else.'

'He's upset, isn't he? Oh dear, I am sorry,' Nora said, as if she had overcooked the beef.

'Upset? You've ruined his life, that's all.'

'Well, it was either that, or let him ruin mine,' said this mother, at once so familiar and so strange. 'Sit down, Lily dear, and I'll make some tea. Or would you rather have coffee, with your American ways?'

With the tea tray, she brought in Duggie, who had been skulking in the kitchen until he saw how the land lay. Lily had always got along perfectly well with him, as everyone did, and although she had come here prepared to hate and despise him, he was still the same polite, considerate, comfortable Dug Manderson, but there was a hint of smugness about him as he fussed over pouring second cups of tea that made Lily ask him harshly, 'Why did you do it?'

'Well,' he said equably, 'Nora and I are both fifty-five.' That was a lie. She was almost fifty-seven. 'We feel we're entitled to this last bit of happiness.'

'That's immoral.'

'Oh, I don't think so,' Duggie said, and Nora said, amazingly for one who had been a regular at the village church and helped Mrs French to deliver the parish newsletter, 'Morals has nothing to do with it.'

'You're a married woman.'

'Don't talk to me like that, Lily dear. I did my time with your father faithfully, and made a go of the Duke's Head. I brought up you two beautiful girls and saw you happily married, and I love my grandchildren. Now I'm going to do my own thing.' It was worse, to hear her using her inappropriate slang.

'You could have told us.'

'You might have tried to stop me.'

'Could we?'

'No, but I didn't want any unpleasantness.'

'What do you think you've got now?'

'That's enough, dear,' Nora said, as if Lily were a clamorous seven-year-old. 'I'm glad to see you, and looking so brown and well after your Cape Cod sun. I tell Duggie, "You can't beat a New England summer." It's wonderful to have you here, so let's not spoil it with water that's already gone under the bridge. Tell me about Paul and the girls. How are they? And the new house? I'm sorry I can't come this time, but we'll both be over to visit one of these days, if we may.'

'Why not?' Life must go on. Children need their only grand-mother. Lily showed Duggie her wallet photograph of the Cape Cod house, and he showed her some pictures of bungalows from estate agents.

'Why a bungalow, Mum?' was all that Lily could say. 'You've always gone upstairs to bed.'

Whoops. She expected at least one of them to blush, but they were serene, with placid mouths contemplating the various brick or stucco or concrete toadstools.

'Lately,' Nora said, 'I've been having that old trouble with my leg. My nursing veins, I call it.'

'I didn't realize that.'

'Well, I'm never one to complain, as you know.'

No, you just walk out.

'Any luck?'

When Lily returned to her father, he was hovering about, watching for her car in the garden behind the cottage, pretending to hoe the sprouts, which would go to waste now, since it was always Nora who had gone out to wrench those frozen grey-green balls off the ugly stalks.

Lily shook her head. 'She didn't say much, but she made it clear.'

'This is it, eh?'

'Are you going to get a divorce?' Lily asked him when they were indoors, having a drink. James had not gone back to work in the bar yet. Blanche and Jenny and Co. were keeping up the pretence that Nora's mother was ill and Jam had strained a rib muscle. It was the only thing he could think of, because he had done that before, over the barrels.

'She says she doesn't care. She and that man are content to live together. In sin, Lily. How do you like having a mother who's so up with the times?'

'I hate it.'

The sedative atmosphere in the furnished flat had stifled and choked Lily's distress. Coming home, angry thoughts had driven with her, and Jamspoon picked up enough energy from her to boil up some belated rage himself.

'I shall divorce her,' he told Lily, over his second whisky. 'Drag her through the courts. Who knows, I might want to marry again myself.'

'Oh, Daddy, come on.' Then Lily looked up quickly. 'Anyone in mind?'

'I wasn't going to tell you.'

Oh, my God, what kind of a mess was this?

Blustering and colouring up, her father told her a little about this woman friend, who seemed to be some kind of film agent. 'A colleague. We work closely together. Don't think badly of me, child. Try to understand.'

Take it with a grain of salt, Dear Doctor Lily. He's still sticking to his pathetic act of being a dashing philanderer.

But she asked, 'Did Mum know?'

'Of course not.'

If it were true, she must have. But he would not admit that to Lily; either because it wasn't true, or because he had to cling to his version of Nora's illogical mid-life madness.

'I'll divorce her and marry Evvie. That's what I'll do.' He perked up, and looked round for applause.

'How old is she?' Lily's heart sank.

'About forty.'

'Don't do it, Daddy.'

'I want you to meet my little Evvie. I've told her all about you. You'll like each other. She needs a decent man, poor wee bird, and Nora's lost her chance with me, serve her right. Yes, yes, that's it. Let's have a drink.' His eyes, which had been watery with tears since Lily arrived, were glittering now under Nora's crinoline lamp.

Jam tried several times to get his Evvie on the phone, but could never reach her. He left messages at her office, but she did not ring him back.

'That's show business. Here and there, all over the place. She flies to Germany. She's going to get me work there.'

Lily went home, still not sure whether he was really having an affair with this unlikely-sounding woman: 'Brilliant. Built up her own business. Highly respected. Stunning looker. Knows all the stars.'

Her father . . . her mother. The background of Lily's life had reeled and turned upside down with a hollow lurch. She could not depend on her parents any more. They had gone off the rails. She was the parent now, and they were the children.

Usually, when she first got back to Boston, it was too fast, too crowded, too shifting, too American, and she felt one of her pangs for the dependability of England. Now England was like a loose tooth, a conquered country, an island adrift and sliding into the sea.

'This is security,' she told Paul, as they manoeuvred with a throng of other cars to get into the needle's eye of the harbour tunnel mouth. 'I've never been so glad to get home.'

Next day, after Isobel and Cathy had gone to school in their new British sneakers and the sweaters with sheep and lambs spiralling round them, Lily went straight to Crisis before she had finished unpacking, or cleaning out the army of tiny left-overs that Aunt Bridget had arrayed so thriftily in the refrigerator.

'Hi, Lily,' Chuck said, when she went into the telephone room to greet the volunteers. 'You heard about it, then?'

'About what?'

'Shit, man.' Chuck put his hand with the bitten nails over his bearded mouth. 'Better let Martha tell you.'

'What's *happened*?' Lily ran upstairs into the office.

Martha spun her chair round from the desk. 'I didn't know you were back yet. Now listen. I don't want to hear you say, "I shouldn't have gone."'

'It's Louise.'

Martha nodded.

'Where is she?'

'Nowhere. She's dead.'

Lily sat down on the hard chair by the door, and began to cry. Her eyes were sick of it. She had cried with Jam, with Nora, with Blanche, and with Paul at the airport, because she was so glad to see the dearly beloved safeness of him.

Louise had done so well at South Side that Dr Reed had transferred her, not to St Clement's, who would not take her back, but to the psychiatric unit of another Boston hospital. Because of her history, she was on suicide precautions until she settled down. She was supposed to have a nurse with her all the time, or to be checked every fifteen minutes when she was asleep, to make sure she had not cut herself or taken pills.

On the third evening, she told the young nurse she wanted to sleep.

'You don't have to sit there,' she said. 'It upsets me. I'm all right. Please leave me alone for a bit.'

The nurse went away for fifteen minutes, was called to do something, then something else, got involved and did not come back for two hours. She found Louise hanging in the closet with a lamp cord round the clothes rail. She had not left the door of the room open, as she had at St Clement's, presumably because she felt certain the nurse would come back.

'But who knows?' Martha said sadly. 'After so many attempts, flirting with death like she did, maybe the time came for her to say, "This is it." '

'But she was so much better the last time I saw her,' Lily agonized.

'Dr Reed showed me a page from her journal they found in the drawer by the bed,' Martha said. 'Here, I copied it.'

A week ago, Louise had written neatly, 'Suicide is an angry, panicky, uncontrollable gesture which appears forced upon you. There is no alternative – it must be done.'

'And I thought she was all right. God, I'm stupid.'

'Do you feel responsible?' Lily did not look up. 'How arrogant can you get? Take a hold of yourself, Lily.'

'I feel so rotten.'

'For Louise? Or for yourself?'

'Isn't it always for yourself, when someone dies?'

'You know what I mean.'

She didn't want me to go away. The thought drummed heavily through Lily's head. She saw Louise, laughing, alive, her hair in skimpy braids, in the shoddy cafeteria. *Don't go, Lily.*

Lily had encouraged James to go back into the Duke's Head bar with her before she went home to America. He had a drink to steady him before opening time. No one came in until after six, and by that time he'd had another, and was ready to accept the jokes and teasing from old friends, and the civility of strangers who treated him like the landlord, which always gave him strength.

'Place isn't the same without Nora, though,' people said. 'When's she coming back?'

'Soon, I hope.'

'Gone to visit her mother?' George's wife asked. 'I always understood she was dead.'

'No, worse luck.'

Eventually, the news would be all over the neighbourhood, but by that time, James would have seen a solicitor and got something started.

At last, he managed to get hold of Evvie. She had been away. She had been ill with flu. She had moved to a different flat.

'Why didn't you give me your new number? My daughter's been over here, and I wanted her to meet you.'

'Oh, I think not.'

'But you don't understand. Things are different now. Me and Nora aren't together any more.'

'You've separated?'

'You could call it that.'

Evvie coughed, and sucked in a breath, as if she had whooping cough. 'Are you all right, Jamspoon?'

'In the pink. You know me. Are *you* all right?'

'Just the fag end of flu. Things are different with me too.'

'We have our ups and downs, you and me.'

'I'm back with Kyle again.'

She was off her rocker. 'Why?'

'We need each other, I suppose, in a sick sort of way.' Evvie gave one of her rasping laughs, and coughed again. 'So –'

'So sod off, Jamspoon?'

'Oh *no*. I'll see you soon. There's a job coming up at Shepperton next week that you might do.'

'I'll be away,' James said shortly. He wouldn't, but he might as well bugger up his career too. He had wrecked everything else.

A few weeks later, when he was at a very low ebb – drama and crisis over, loneliness and boredom here to stay, the dubious comfort of self-pity ousted by self-hate – George Dunn leaned across the bar and began the head-wagging and winking routine that would get him certified one of these days.

He put up his hand and said behind it, 'Picked up a copy of *Do It Yourself* the other day.'

'Going to build Sheila's greenhouse at last?'

'Come off it. You know what I mean. Couldn't believe my eyes when I seen you in that dirty book. Bit of fun, eh? Lucky old lad.'

'Get your eyes examined,' Jam said. 'It wasn't me.'

'I could have sworn – well, bad luck. But I'll bring it in. See what the lads think.'

'You do that,' James said pleasantly, 'and I'll carve my initials in your face with a beer bottle.'

Eight

*W*hen Mike lost his job with the New Bedford taxi firm, after he wrapped the cab around a pole at the bottom of Union Street, Momma was not so good to him as she had been when he was out of the house most of the day.

'Get out and get work,' she would say, hitting his feet down off the furniture, or banging both kitchen chairs tightly under the table just as he was going to sit down and ask for coffee.

'Can I find anything?'

'Your father always did. Time and again, he always found a job.'

'What were they? On the roads, cleaning up at the bus station. What kind of jobs for a man who'd been a teacher?'

'He had the work ethic.'

'He needed to get away from you.'

'He was a good man. That terrible winter, rather than see us go short of food and fuel, didn't he go out with the storm crews?'

'And didn't it kill him?'

She could not deny it. 'You'll never die of work, Michael Baxlee.'

'Aren't I on my way to the Manpower office? Why have I got my jacket on?'

They talked to each other in thrown questions.

'What am I – a mind reader?'

One night Mike met a man called Laurence who wanted him to go home with him, and got him pretty drunk. Mike got away through the men's room window, and stumbled across the bridge and through the prim hostile streets to his mother's house, which had lace curtains in front that went up in an arch, so that she could peer out from the darkened room where she sat waiting for him.

When she opened the door, he pushed in past her, lurched to the end of the hall, and threw up in the kitchen.

She went out back and got the shovel and cleared up the mess, with her elbows squared and her mouth set like an *H*, a thin line with two deep bars from cheeks to chin. It was very annoying to him, leaning against the wall, to see her going at it, as she had gone at it for his father without a word, tough little pioneer woman, doing her job, martyr to the beast in man.

He gave her his unemployment cheque, and she gave him a miserly allowance, cutting it down, week by week, to just a few dollars.

Corrigan was in town, and came looking for him. Mike pretended everything was fine, because Corrigan was in a delivery business in Hanover, south of Boston, and fat, with a decent car. They went out drinking. Before he left the house, Mike went into his mother's bedroom and took the small amount of money that was in her old sewing box. It played 'Annie Laurie' when you lifted the lid, so he opened it, quick and neat, when she flushed the toilet.

When Corrigan dropped Mike off at home hours later, all his clothes were out on the porch in black plastic trash bags. Only two bags was all it took.

Corrigan leaned on the bell. The curtains moved infinitesimally – or did they? The bell shrilled through a house as empty as an old conch shell. Under the door knocker was a note.

'You're out,' it said. 'Yours truly, Grace Baxlee.'

Mike slept in Corrigan's motel room, and after Corrie left next morning, he walked down the hill towards the docks and spent the last of Yours truly, Grace Baxlee's money on a cut-throat deal for pills with the guy behind the bar at Henry's Lounge and Deli.

Ida and Shirley were watching television with Bernie. The other kids were in bed. They let Mike in and gave him a beer.

'Long time no see,' Ida said. 'You look rough. What's wrong?'

'Tired and hungry, that's all.'

'Go make yourself a sandwich,' Shirley said. 'We want to see this programme.'

He was out of the room quite a long time. When he came back, with another can of beer, he looked worse. His hair was like brown seaweed. The knife scar was livid in his white face. He slumped in a chair facing away from the television, and fell asleep. Bernie caught the beer can just before it tipped on to the floor.

Mike slept heavily. His mouth fell open. He snored. His head tipped back over the top of the chair, then fell forward on his chest.

'Shut up, Mike,' Shirley called to him. 'Wake up, you'll crack the light bulbs.'

'He's dead to the world,' Ida said.

Bernie got up and went to the kitchen. He came back with an empty pill bottle and what was left of Shirley's half pint of vodka.

They had some ipecacuanha in the house from the time that Maggie drank furniture polish by mistake for cough syrup. They woke Mike up and dosed him with that to make him throw up, and forced him to stand and walk, the two women holding him upright and dragging him up and down the hall. Good old Bernie, expert from the bad old Buddy days, was on the floor with the bowl and sponge and roll of paper towels.

When he could speak, Mike begged them not to take him to the Emergency Room, because he would be sent back to Bridge-water. They let him stay for the rest of the night, taking turns to keep him awake, and in the morning, he was well enough to call his friend Corrigan in Hanover, to see if he could help.

Corrigan said that Mike could stay at his place for a while, and he would give him a job driving a van.

'But if things are this bad,' Ida told Mike severely before she put him on the bus, 'you've got to do something about it. It's all right to be messed up for a while – we've all been – but you can't make a lifestyle of it. You've got to get some help.'

'Not the hospital, Ida, you promised.'

'Don't be so paranoid. I'll make some calls. Somebody's got to be able to do something for you.'

'Let me stay with you and Shirl.' In a last gasp, Mike turned back to the car, although his bus was panting to leave, and the driver had slung his trash bags into the baggage compartment underneath.

'No way. Shirley and me has our lives to lead. You've got yours.'

Childish men. Ida rolled up the window and put the car in gear. No thanks. No more of that for me.

'Hey, Lil! How you doing!'

'Hey, Eye! How are you?'

'Listen, girl. I've got a friend who needs help. You know all about people who screw up. Could you talk to this guy?'

'Well, he could talk to anyone at Crisis. I'll give you our number.'

'He'd never call. He needs an appointment to see someone. Why not you? It's Mike actually, my friend that I brought to the Cape.'

'Oh.' Lily paused. Then she said cautiously, 'I might not be the best person to help.'

'You didn't like him,' Ida said quickly. 'Some crisis worker! Choose who you help and who you don't.'

But I'd rather he saw Martha, or one of the counsellors. If I get him an appointment, will he keep it?'

'He will, or else.'

'Good girl, Ida. When am I going to see you? I'll be on the Cape all the time soon. We're going to sell the Newton house and winterize the Cape one. How are you, Eye? Bernie gave me all the news when he came to see Tony last summer. He told me about the contract with the new office building and you and Shirley taking on more cleaners. Sounds as if things are going really well for you.'

'Never better.' Ida flexed the muscles of her personality. 'My life amazes me.'

After Terry had gone to live with his grandfather, life looked up a bit, and he was peaceful and fairly content.

Pursuing his brilliant career in the catering business, which he pretended – though not to himself – was going to lead him one day into hotel or restaurant management, he had a job in the high-school kitchen, and was also doing a small weekly cartoon for a local paper.

The Judge had let him take up a big table to put by the window in his room, and Terry had invented a sarcastic character called Tiffin, who wore baggy pants and a shrunk sweater, and commented on neighbourhood events and people.

The drawings were good, although the humour was feeble and the pay even feebler, but working to a deadline was surprisingly satisfying. Terry began work on some designs he was going to submit to a greeting card company. He was getting alarmingly square. He left lunch ready for his grandfather before he went to the school kitchen, and cooked supper in the evening for both of them, and often for Amy, the dearest and simplest of his girls who was the only one he saw now. Visitors dropped in to visit quite often, and sometimes a legal friend to consult, and the old man was writing an article on 'Evidentiary Problems in Child Abuse Cases' for the *Massachusetts Law Quarterly*.

After the first heavy snowfall of the winter, the fire station hooter sounded, 'No School'. Terry, who had hated and despised shovelling snow at home, spent a contented, sparkling blue and white morning making a beautiful job of the paths and driveway. He was ridiculously proud of it. That was probably why, when it snowed again two days later while he was at work, the Judge went out with a shovel and broom to restore the perfection of Terry's front path.

Terry found him collapsed in his leather chair by the unlit fire, breathing painfully and shaking, his faded eyes flat with panic.

Nothing lasts. I lose everything.

Terry stayed on in the house for a while after his grandfather died in hospital.

'What are your plans?' his father asked. People seemed to have been asking him that since he was born. If you were content with no plans, they were not. If you had plans, it took the edge off to disclose them.

'I'll be okay.'

'Do you want to go back to college?'

'God no. I'm too old.'

'At twenty-two?'

'I feel forty. Missed out and past it.'

'You haven't even begun.' Sometimes his father lost patience with him. 'I hope you stick with Amy, at least.'

Amy had come often to the hospital, bringing tiny gifts, gentle, loving to the old man, unobtrusive. 'Better be good to her. She's a darling girl.'

'Too good for me?'

'Oh for God's sake. Don't be such a bore.'

When his father got angry, his fair face flushed and his eyes narrowed and concentrated to an intense blue within the white corner wrinkles that had been folded away from the sun.

'Sorry, Dad,' Terry said, because poor guy, he was an orphan now, which must be hard, not being anybody's child any more.

While Amy was helping Terry to sort and pack books at the Dedham house, she sat back on the floor with her wide Peruvian skirt in coloured circles around her and asked sensibly, 'Why don't you and I get married?'

'And do what?'

'I'm working. We could live at my place till we could get somewhere bigger. You could paint while I'm out. I'd love you.'

I'd love you too. He didn't say anything.

Nothing lasts. I lose everything. Yes, because you let it go.

'Well, all right.' Amy knelt up and began dusting books again. 'It was just a thought.'

After the furniture was moved out, Terry went to Europe with a friend called Oliver who was researching folk music. They parted company in Scotland. Terry wandered about, coming south in spirals, and ended up without any money, staying with Jamspoon at the flint and brick cottage, and helping out at the Duke's Head.

Besides the Dedham property, there was more money in Paul's father's estate after taxes than he had expected. He invested something for Terry, sold the house in Newton, paid off the mortgage on the Cape Cod house and put in proper heating and plumbing, got free of Turnbull's at last, and set up his own business at one end of the big barn, converted for a tack shop. Eventually, he would improve the stabling and fence the new piece of land he had bought, and board horses for other people.

In the old farmhouse, he and Lily did the things they had planned for its future in the days when they had loved it just as it was. They knocked down the wall between the kitchen and the dining-table end of the living-room and made it all one long room, with the big fireplace at one end, and the piano, and a wood stove and comfortable chairs at the other, with the round oak table half in the living-room, half in the kitchen.

When they were packing, and Lily was laughing at Paul for rolling sweaters, as if he were still packing a navy duffle bag, she found at the back of a drawer the plastic spoon that she had kept, unwashed, from the Air Force coffee machines at Flekjavik almost twenty years ago.

Lily hung it on a nail near the wood stove, where she could see it from the deep wide chair Paul had bought her, to match his own old shabby one, over which he and Barbara had fought when he first set up house with Lily.

'What's that?' Isobel asked. 'It looks tacky.'

'It is the spoon that stirred my heart.'

Lily had framed the crayon sketch that Terry had done of his father in the wooded hills above the Duke's Head. Now she hung it on the nail with the plastic spoon. On late summer afternoons, the low sun came through a small western window opposite and swept across the picture and the side of the man's light hair, just as a different sun, in England, had done when Terry had drawn it.

'Best portrait I ever saw,' Harry told Paul.

'The back of my head?'

'A speaking likeness.'

Terry had said he was doing some caricatures in England, but it would be sad if he wasted his talent on things like Tiffin cartoons and greeting cards. Very rarely, he would dash off an extraordinary sketch like this, and then do nothing more for ages.

When Paul was alone, and not self-conscious about looking at the back of himself in the blue sweater, he would occasionally stand and stare at it, until the man with the light in his hair blurred outward into the guessed-at distance below and beyond, inward into the heart of the picture.

Isobel was almost fourteen when the new school year started. Everyone told her it would be traumatic to change schools, but apart from her two soul-mates, who would come to the Cape often for weekends, it was quite a relief to shake free of the assorted come-and-go Newton friends, and the hangers-on who had nothing better to do than call her up to talk about nothing when she wanted to be left alone.

At the new junior high school, she was not as far ahead as she had expected. Her class had the same lump of neanderthals, who didn't count, and didn't know they didn't count, and the same percentage of stars and leaders. Isobel had thought she would be more sophisticated than them, and it was a shock to find that some of these people who lived on the wrong side of the Cape Cod canal were ahead of her.

But she had Tony, and he was eighteen. These girls who took an hour to dress and do their hair before school were fooling around with fourteen- and fifteen-year-old hairless zombies, cratered with acne.

Tony had a soft line of moustache and a tiny clump of apprentice beard in the cleft of his chin. He was up at the house a lot, working for Isobel's father. Although they were free and easy with each other in the old way, she no longer thought of him as a childhood friend. Pretty soon, he noticed that. He scolded, 'Bella, don't do that. Don't look like that.'

'Why not?'

'You're – listen, you're too young, that's why.'

'I won't always be,' Isobel warned.

Tony had a motor-bike. He took Cheryl and Dana and others out on the back, girls who were dark like him, related, many of them, within the Portuguese community.

Isobel was not allowed to go on the bike, but she was Tony's only white girlfriend. Her time would come.

It had been harder for Cathy to leave the chattering sunshiny crowd of friends who had flocked in and out of the Newton house, and 'slept over' in each other's bedrooms where every wall and door was papered with posters of harmless rock stars whose only groupies were little children. On Cape Cod, Cathy cried every morning at first, before the school bus came, because she was not tough, like Isobel. But she quickly made new chattering, whispering friends, and one of them gave her a black cat with an extra toe on each paw.

Now that they lived in the country all the time, Arthur was not enough, because he would only stay with Cathy when her father was not about, so she was working on her mother to let her get a dog from the SPCA kennels. She would get it. Both of them could handle Mud pretty well these days, each in their own fashion: Cathy quietly persistent, like drops of water on stone, Isobel threatening to build up to a scene. Mud was busy and often distracted, with getting the house into shape and going to and from Boston to her job at Crisis. Either method worked.

Lily knew that Paul had hoped she might give up her job after they moved seventy miles south of Boston. He did not talk about it, and since she did not want to leave Crisis, she did not talk about it either.

Three days a week, she left home early, and struggled to be back by the time Isobel and Cathy came home, if Paul was not going to be there. She was always home in time to cook supper.

Martha needed Lily, and Lily needed Crisis. She could not pretend to herself or anyone that she wore herself out with the long drive and the traffic and the urgent pressures of the agency out of a sense of duty. She loved the volunteers. Many of them were young students. Lily trained them and backed them up and gave them praise and solved their problems, and delighted in their enthusiasm and laughter and the serious kindness with which they responded to callers, who might be two or three times their age, but often benefited unexpectedly by finding that they could unload their fears and anxieties to someone of a different generation.

With the clients, she tried not to become as involved as she had with poor Louise, but her style was to go overboard, and she hoped that she could energize depressed and defeated people, and rekindle dying self-esteem by the strength of her own hope.

Timid Gloria, hanging on to old guilts. Veronica, whose child was killed. Selina and Joe and their grisly marriage. Dennis, the congregational minister with a drinking problem, abandoned by his wife, kicked out by his congregation.

'I must go and see him,' Lily said, when Dennis had finally agreed to go into an alcoholism unit.

'I know. He needs you.' Martha sighed. 'And you need him. You try to show him that he matters to you, and without knowing it, he makes you feel that you matter.'

'Is that so dreadful? Everyone's got to have some justification for taking up space.'

'Don't lay your dependency on these people,' Martha said. 'It isn't fair.'

But sometimes in the street, or on the subway, or in a crowd anywhere, Lily imagined the strangers round her into people who might need her help. What's wrong with *her*? Is *he* all right, with his pale face and loose collar and suit that hangs on him as if he'd lost weight? Why is that boy standing so near the edge of the platform?

One day towards the end of winter, when Lily went down from the office to the telephone room to clear up some things before she went home, she saw that friend of Ida's sitting in the waiting-room. He had been seeing Martha off and on for quite some time. He could never seem to get his life straightened out. Martha knew he needed more help than she could give, but there was no way she could get him to see a doctor.

'Hello, Mike.' Lily went into the waiting-room. 'How are you?'

'Not too hot.'

'Have you come to see Martha? I'm afraid she –'

'Yeah, I know. She said come yesterday, but I got the day wrong. I'll stick around and see if she comes in.'

'She's gone for the day. Didn't they tell you?'

'Yeah, but I thought they were trying to put me off.'

'They wouldn't do that. Did someone give you coffee?'

'Sure. They always give you *coffee*.' Mike jerked his head at the untouched mug on the table beside him. He had the same disgruntled air that he had worn at Lily's house, with Ida and the children.

'Would you like to talk to someone? Elaine's upstairs, one of the counsellors. I'll get her to –'

'I'd like to talk to *you*.' Often, Mike looked down or sideways when he spoke. When he turned his head to look at you, he gave you a full, flat stare, dark eyes sombre, unblinking. 'But I suppose you haven't got the time.'

'Let me get Elaine.'

When Lily had originally turned down Ida's request to see this man herself, it was soon after Louise had hanged herself in the hospital. Lily had been feeling useless. She was not going to go sailing into Ida's friend's problems as if she were the only one who could help.

'You know who I am, don't you?' Mike continued to stare at her. The face was boyish and vulnerable, in spite of the battle scar, but the eyes were ageless.

'Of course. You came to my house with Ida. I didn't mention that when you came here to see Martha because –'

'You knew you didn't like me.' Mike was quick to cut you short.

'Don't play games,' Lily said. 'I'd like to talk to you, but actually, I'm on my way out. I've got to get some papers over to City Hall.'

'I'm going that way myself.' Mike stood up. His hair was clean and neatly cut. He wore decent boots and a heavy white sweater and had kept on his padded jacket, although the waiting-room was warm. 'Were you going to walk?'

Lily was going to drive, but she did not want to be in her car with him, so she said, 'Yes, let's walk across the common, then, and we can talk on the way.'

A light snow was falling, and the muffled air was warmer. Mike was quite tall. He walked with his head down and his hands in his pockets, talking steadily without looking at Lily, and occasionally stopping on the path, so that she had to stop too, and giving her the brooding stare.

He had quarrelled with his friend in Hanover, and moved out of his house and given up that driving job, and lost two others. He was living in a rooming house where the heating system froze or fried you. He had been picked up by the police with some other men after a fight in a bar. He had been selling cocaine. He had a stomach ulcer. His mother wanted him home again, 'But if I ever go back, it'll be to kill her.'

He was angry with her, and with the whole world. He nursed his anger across the whitening common, and showed it off to Lily like a valuable attribute. He told her some of the stupid things he had done lately, and explained them as inevitable, 'Because I was so mad.'

'Come back and see Martha tomorrow,' she told Mike when she left him on the snow-swept brick plaza to go up the steps to City Hall.

'What good will that do?'

'You've got to find some way to help yourself.'

'Why doesn't someone do something to help *me*?'

When Lily came out again and headed for the subway entrance, he fell into step beside her.

'I thought you were on your way somewhere, Mike.'

'I changed my mind.'

He put money into the turnstile for both of them and went with her without talking on to the platform and into the crowded train, where they stood side by side and swayed together as the

330

antediluvian car rocked round the perilous curves. His anger had left him. He was silent and rather meek, smiling nervously if she looked at him, widening his smile when she smiled. If he followed her to the parking lot, he might expect her to take him back to Hanover on her way home. While she was wondering what to do about him, he got off the train at a stop before hers, and turned to wave dejectedly and was gone.

Walking across the common had made Lily late. This would be the second time this week she was not home for her children. They did not mind, but she thought Paul did, although he never said so. She always left a note somewhere for him to find during the day, and he always put a note into her briefcase for her to find in Boston.

She rang Paul at the tack shop to make sure he was at home.

'Don't rush,' he said. 'The roads will be bad.'

'It's not snowing much.'

'I said, don't rush.'

'I heard you. Thanks. I'll be back by six. Take some frying chicken out of the freezer.'

The main road was crowded with homing cars and buses throwing up slushy snow against each other's windshields.

Nearer to the canal, the snow became rain. Lily was late. She speeded up, worrying, and had a near miss, pulling out to pass a car when another was already passing her. The other car's horn shocked her like a pistol shot. Farther on, she passed him too, to serve him right.

She was driving too fast for the wet road, taking chances, in that idiotic delirium when you risk your neck to get somewhere on time, too strung up to admit any sobering thought like, 'What's the good of getting there dead?'

The state trooper came up behind her and flashed his blue light for her to stop. He took a long time getting out of his car and a longer time going back to it with her licence, and writing up Lily's warning notice.

'Next time, it'll be a ticket.'

'Oh, thank you!' Lily was too effusive. They didn't like that.

'Keep that thing down,' he said impassively. He had not looked at her.

331

He was chubby and pink. Not naturally a stern man. Did his family ask him to make this face sometimes, for a joke?

He followed Lily for a while, and then, in her rear mirror, she saw him turn across the grass in the middle of the highway and go back the other way. Lily speeded up again.

She was over an hour late. She left the car outside the garage and ran breathlessly into the house. Paul kissed her and held her tightly.

'I'm dreadfully sorry I'm so late. And it was my turn to feed the horses and muck out, wasn't it?'

'We and Daddy did it.'

Isobel was frying chicken. Paul and Cathy were cutting vegetables minutely for Chinese stir-fry. When Lily went to help them, they sent her away.

She went up to the bedroom and called the centre to tell them, 'If someone named Mike calls in the night . . .'

She did not tell Paul about the state trooper.

Best thing that's happened to me in a bad world, Mike thought. She might be able to help me, that Lily. She understands, a bit. Not all of it. No one can. But she's honest and when she smiles, there's hope for the world.

Martha's tough. She's not really like a woman, and I can't fool her any more than any of these other tough dames like Connie, or Ogre Momma, or Ida or Shirley. I can't fool Lily, either, but would I need to?

She's kind, he said to himself, sitting in a bar. She likes me.

'Have a drink.' He went over to a woman sitting on her own with a beer and a pack of cigarettes, getting through the smokes faster than the beer.

'Fuck off,' she said, and added, 'Kid,' as if she knew his fears.

Paul had a lot of good news to tell Lily. He started, but she interrupted with, 'I saw that friend of Ida's today. The taxi driver – do you remember?'

'A surly fellow. *I* saw Pyge Tucker today. She's building a new barn at her house here and going to bring two horses down, for the local shows. She's getting all the stable equipment through me, and she's got me orders for at least half a dozen Tack Racks from friends here, and given me a whole lot more names for the mailing list. I'm going to get some dressage saddles for her to try too. She says she'll never buy anything more from Turnbull's.'

'Sucks to them,' Lily said. 'You're a wild success. Listen, Ida's poor friend is in a mess. I can't tell you about it, because it's confidential. I shouldn't even tell you I saw him, but I know you're safe.'

She could never resist bringing back to Paul her excitements and her problems. Some were fascinating. Some bored him. Now that he was plunged up to the neck in his own business, he often wanted equal time to tell her about the tack shop, but a rise in the wholesale price of New Zealand rugs and orders from new customers for Tack Rack 'seconds', which Turnbull's had agreed to let him distribute, were pale stuff compared to Lily's visit to the Charles Street gaol, or her confrontation with a battered client's husband, who pushed in front of her face a fist that wore a gold ring, out of which sprang a tiny curved knife.

Paul's first expansion had been printing and mailing hundreds of brochures, designed by a young woman whom Terry had known at the art college. Lily had resented Jeanette's frequent visits to the shop, because she was petite and freshly beautiful, and took herself too seriously and said things like, 'I'm not comfortable with the impulse image, quote, unquote,' waggling two fingers of each hand in the air. 'Do you know what I'm saying?'

Lily did not like the look of her forties coming up, which made Paul smile, since he was looking at fifty. Lily wanted to feel young. That was one of the reasons why she was so absorbed by the student volunteers. Some days she went to work in blue jeans and one of Paul's shirts worn outside. Four-letter Americanisms had crept into her English vocabulary. Paul had to stop her saying, 'Shit, man' in front of the children. They heard enough of that at school.

Fooling around with Harry probably also made her feel young, Paul thought. When the stables were finished, Harry had helped Paul to find a wonderful bay horse for himself, half thoroughbred, half quarter horse, and a fine safe but lively brown horse for Lily, and a larger pony for Isobel, who wavered between loving horses more than people, and not riding for days, because losing interest in it was a sign of growing up.

Harry had continued with Lily's training, so that she could now do almost everything with her springy, compact brown horse.

The two of them were very thick.

'Harry may be just a good friend to you,' Paul said once, 'but what does he imagine you are to him? You come on pretty strong.'

'Oh well,' Lily said airily. Caught, she was bluffing it out – Paul knew her so well. 'I've got to keep my hand in.'

'At what?'

'Men.'

'Why?'

'Oh – I don't know. To prove something to myself? No, that's awful, darling. I'm sorry. Hate me.'

'I am consumed with love for you.'

'And I for you.'

They were. They told and showed each other this often, in many ways.

In May, Harry brought down one of his horses in a trailer. He wanted to take it over to ride at Sandy Neck, the long beach between Sandwich and Barnstable on the north coast of Cape Cod.

'What do you say, Lil? Do you want to bring John along and ride with me?'

'I'd love to. But I don't know that I –' Lily looked at Harry and not at Paul. Her face was alive, eyes eager, that lovely mobile mouth open, chin forward, as if to grab at the treat.

'You go ahead,' Paul said. 'You've always wanted to ride on that beach.'

'You wouldn't mind? I was going to start typing up addresses for you from that new list you brought.'

'That can wait. You go, love.'

'All right then, Harry.'

Harry looked past her at Paul. Paul looked at Harry. The look held years of friendship.

'No, Lil,' Harry said, as if he were years older than her. 'You go with Paul.' Lily reddened and closed her mouth up tight and looked down, as if she had been chided. 'Paul can drive my truck and I'll mind the store and watch out for the girls.'

'But you came —'

'I'll take Dorado over there on Sunday. You two have fun.'

It was a glorious day. Not a soft spring watercolour day, like May in England, but crisp and vivid, with intense new green, and clouds furling and tumbling high up in a piercingly blue sky. Paul parked the truck and trailer in the sand at the landward side of the low dunes, and they backed the horses out and saddled them, and set off along the sand track that wound along the edge of the great salt marsh.

The bay horse Robin stepped out strongly, neck flexed at just the right angle behind the leaf curve of his ears, black mane sailing out toward the marsh when the sea wind came through gaps in the dunes. Half-way to the end of the Sandy Neck promontory, they passed a cluster of little shacks, facing the marsh, their backs silted up by dune sand. They were all still boarded up, except one which was hung about with coloured floats. The door and shutters were open, and a man and a woman were inside with buckets and brooms, cleaning.

Paul and Lily slowed to a walk.

'Let's make them sell it to us, and live here always,' Lily said. 'You and me.'

'You'd get sick of me.'

'Stop that fake just-an-ordinary-guy stuff. You'd get sick of me first.'

What would it be like to live without the world? Paul wondered. The dream was that it would be easier. Nothing to interfere with love. The reality might be a suffocating strain, the two of you needing people and life and challenge and children to give purpose to your alliance.

Cathy, Isobel, Terry. Three completely different beings who were on earth because of Paul, but following the course of their natures independently, growing the way their genes dictated. His, but miraculously themselves.

The dream vision of him and Lily selfishly marooned gave way to another, in which Terry came wandering along the edge of the marsh in those great hiking boots that were two sizes too big, turning up unexpectedly at a meal time. 'Oh, hi.' He sat down and picked up a fork, as if he had just been outside for two minutes.

Isobel was reading under yellow lamplight, her swatch of dark hair swung forward over her flawless cheek. 'This is a great story, Dad. Sit down, I'll read to you.' She read to him now, as he used to love to read to her, in her Massachusetts version of her mother's clear, vivacious voice.

'Daddy, Daddy!' Cathy flew into the shack like a moth, bare feet pattering like wings. 'Daddy, c'mere, I found you a sand dollar!', carrying the fragile gritty disc to him unbroken.

The man in the shack stepped suddenly into the doorway and flapped a duster cheerily at them. John jumped sideways, dropped a hind leg down the bank of the bog and only just managed to pull it up and recover himself.

They turned across the end of the dunes where the flat tops of stunted pine trees were blown toward the land, and got off to have something to eat. Lily was already hungry.

'I guess I was wrong about Harry,' Paul said.

'No, I was.'

'Did you really want to come here with him?' It was easier to ask this sitting in a hollow on the coarse dune grass, holding the reins while his horse nipped new leaves off a little bush.

'Well, he slapped me down, didn't he? I asked for that.' Loading the horses into the trailer this morning, Lily had been silent with Harry, following his instructions, instead of kidding him and laughing. 'Whatever it was – and it was nothing, honest – it's over now.'

Paul risked telling her what Isobel said she had seen in the barn.

'Physical excitement.' Lily was leaning against her horse, eating a sandwich. '*Playing with fire,*' she declaimed dramatically. 'I'm sorry, darling. Harry played the game for fun, but then, as you see, he dropped me on my face. Oh dear, now you won't have any excuse to have old Jeanette down again, to make *me* jealous.'

Paul groaned. 'Don't bring her name into this lovely place. She finally sent me a bill for the work she did on the brochures.'

'Too much?'

'Fifteen hundred bucks.'

'That rat. Why didn't you tell me?'

'It was my fault for not making a written contract with her.'

'Bemused by all that oily fawn hair?'

'Wretchedly unbusinesslike.'

'You think I'd criticize? It's me that makes a mess every time. Me, me, me.'

'Let's not beat our breasts.' Paul got up and pulled Robin's head out of the bush. 'What am I going to do about Jeanette?'

'Leave her to me,' Lily said aggressively.

'It's my business.'

'Mine too. I'll see her off. Listen, darling.' She held Paul's arm and looked at him seriously. 'Nothing comes between us.'

With one of her quick switches between solemnness and excitement, Lily got quickly into the saddle and turned John toward the ocean.

'Ready to gallop?'

As they left the stunted trees and turned to the gap in the higher dunes, the wind from the sea hit them in the face like a shout.

The tide was out. Beyond the deep soft sand, ridged flats and shallow pools glistened in the hard bright light. The sea was far away, breaking in overlapping ranks of small surf.

The horses were wild with excitement, trampling, and grabbing their heads down, eyes agog. Lily could not hold John, so she shouted, 'Let's go!' and they went.

They had miles of hard sand before the cottages started, and a scattering of hazily glimpsed tiny people on the beach. All you had to do was lean forward and let your horse go until he was ready to slow down, and if he never was, you could turn him up into the soft sand to stop him.

The quarter-horse part of Robin sent him into a flat-out sprint for a quarter of a mile. Then his head and back came up a bit and his stride slowed and lengthened, and he settled into a steady powerful gallop, drumming the hard sand, splat, splatter through the pools and channels. The wind tore past, shrieking. Lily and John came alongside. She and Paul could only look toward each other with joy and open their mouths on a wordless shout that streamed away behind them with the streaming tails and storm of kicked-up sand.

For a long time, the beach was endless. The houses and people did not seem to come any nearer. They galloped for ever, out of time and out of life. Suspended in the ecstasy of power and speed.

At last, John slowed. His dark, chunky head was down. People became distinguishable; a woman with children, men jogging along a sand bank, still figures on the edge of the surf with fishing poles stuck at an angle into the sand. Lily turned John toward the dunes and stopped. Ahead of her, Paul pulled Robin in. He trotted a few paces and then stopped, wet and heaving.

Paul's hair and face and shirt were soaked with spray. He turned in his saddle to look at Lily. She had got off. She stood with the red shirt clinging to her, her hair tossed back wildly from her wet face, holding the reins of the brown horse. John stood with his legs apart, head up, nostrils squared to the salt wind.

Paul's body was relaxed in exhaustion. His mind was swept clear of everything but serenity. Lily. The horses. The sea. Freedom. Peace. His lovely children. He thought: I have everything I want.

When they got home, Harry came out to help them unload the horses. Lily seemed at ease with him again. In the house, she went straight to the phone in the kitchen, and she talked loudly to Jeanette, so that Paul and Harry could hear.

'That bill you sent us. It's far too much.' Some fast talk from the other end of the phone. 'Agreed? No, it wasn't. You've got nothing in writing ... What? Oh, about five hundred at the most. I don't even think the work was all that good, but we'll send you a cheque.' Splutter. 'Well, if you don't like it, come down and we'll give you a saddle or something ... a second-hand one.' Quack, quack. 'Okay. So sue already.'

'Power!' Harry threw out his long monkey arms, with the fists clenched.

Lily threw her arms out and backwards, sticking out her glorious chest, which had lost nothing in fifteen years of marriage and motherhood.

'Oh, Harry, we had such a wonderful day! I ... love ... my ... life!' She flung her arms round Paul.

Joy. Almost too intense to bear.

Mike called Lily several times on the Crisis number. Sometimes she talked to him. Sometimes one of the volunteers told him, 'I'll see if she's in here,' as if it wasn't obvious that they would have known whether Lily was there.

Mike was working again now. Indestructible Corrigan had taken him back, to load and drive, though not to live, because Corrigan, famous lone wolf, had let a domineering female move in, and was on a diet and in danger of becoming domesticated.

Occasionally, when Mike was delivering near the south end of Boston, he would drive behind the Crisis centre, and if Lily's white car was there, he would park the van and go in to see her. Sometimes she would sit with him for a while, whether he chose talk or silence. Sometimes Martha came down to see him, and tried to find out how long he was prepared to live on the edge of a precipice.

Lily would be upstairs. On his way out, Mike kept Martha

talking in the hall and sent his senses up the stairs to where Lily sat or stood or moved about. In an odd way, he could feel closer to her in his imagination than if they were actually in a room together, when he often could not look at her, and could not speak.

Last summer, Lily had employed a girl to be with Isobel and Cathy, so that she could go to Boston to work. This year, she had asked Martha to find a temporary assistant. Lily went into the office only about once a week, and supervised from home the volunteers in the outreach programme, with which Crisis helped people who could not come in to the centre.

Martha would take her back in the office any time. Meanwhile, Paul's shop was doing well. It might take two or three more years to show a profit, but customers were beginning to come to him from a wide area. Turnbull's wasn't the same now, some of them said. They would rather come here, because they knew Paul, and although he did not have a huge stock, he could always get them what they wanted.

More people were coming to live on Cape Cod. Some of them brought their own horses, although too many of the places to ride were being bulldozed up and built over, and sold to people who would not let riders skirt round the edge of their property to reach a trail that had been a bridle path for years.

Paul had two extra horses now, as boarders. Tony helped and Lily worked in the stable and in the shop, and went to horse shows with Paul to follow up the right contacts. They were very happy.

She had given her father the fare to Boston for his sixtieth birthday, and he came for two weeks and talked his heart out to Lily and Paul and Isobel and Cathy and Tony and Dodo at the drug store, and anyone else who would listen. Although he lived in a pub world where people came in morning and evening, and he had to chat to them, he was lonely, and hungry for his own kind of talk: showbiz tales of photographers and film studios, past days, the old gang in Wimbledon, the post office talent shows. Nora, Nora, Nora.

'She's lost so much.' He ruminated in his favourite wicker chair on the porch with the same brand of bourbon that Paul had remembered to get for him. 'What I can't see is how she could chuck it all away. Marvellous woman, Nora. I'm not saying a word against her, mind, but the change of life makes some women go dotty, and that's all about it.'

Cathy and Isobel were both teenagers now, busy with many friends, and with tennis and horses and boats and ballet, and Isobel had a morning job, taking a toddler to the beach. Lily had been afraid that their grandfather would be disappointed to find them no longer children who wanted to go to the drug store for sodas, but he was enchanted with them because they were beautiful – dark and vivid, fair and graceful – and they told him jokes and gave him a lot of loving attention.

'I've got something *she* hasn't,' he said, after Lily had used half a roll of film taking pictures of him clowning and hamming with the girls, and wearing a hallowe'en wig to support Cathy in a ballet pose.

'She's coming over to see us.' Cathy sat on the grass, where he had let her fall. 'She said she would.'

'But I came first.'

He would not go to the theatre, nor make any move to see Pyge Tucker.

'She'd love to hear about your success,' Lily urged him. 'You could tell her about the doctor commercial, and going to Germany for the tourist advertisements. She'd be so impressed.'

'Success isn't everything,' James said weightily. 'Pyge, glorious Pyge, God bless her, she knew me in my halcyon days when my ego was intact. Now I am but a hollow man.'

They all told him they were sad when he left. So he sprang it on them jauntily at the airport.

'You think I'm only going back to the pub, to see if Terry and Blanche have killed each other yet. You don't know about Pixie.'

'Who's Pixie?' If he had made her up, wouldn't he have invented a more convincing name?

'Aha!' Finger to large nose, more bony now, because he had lost weight with losing Nora, and Faces threatened to take the speciality 'pot-belly' off his page in the next catalogue. 'She shall be nameless. Soul of discretion, that's Jamspoon. Wish me luck.'

Ida's friend Mike was working again and in better shape, although he often seemed to guess when Lily was in Boston, and called her there, or came in to see her.

'Watch out,' Martha said. 'He has a yen for you.'

'I don't think so. He's scared of women.'

Lily still felt she could help him. Once, when he panicked on the phone and told her that he was losing his mind and his grip on any kind of reality, she was able to reassure him and get him slowly calmed down. She did not know what was wrong with him. Nor did Martha. 'Except he's pretty sick. If he goes on running away from help, he'll run into real trouble and get picked up and put back into Bridgewater again.'

One evening in October, Mike called Lily at home. He had been in an accident, and was in trouble with Corrigan and with the police, because of his record. He was hysterical. She had to talk to him for quite a long time. Paul was used to that. She often made calls to clients she had been to see. But when Mike called her again, when she had just put dinner on the table, Paul said, 'Tell him not to call you here. I thought you weren't allowed to give clients your home number.'

'I don't. But he knows it, because he was here.'

Once Mike called her in the night. She made him hang up, and got a volunteer on duty at Crisis to call him back. An hour later, he called Lily again and was angry at first, and then wept.

He knew where she lived.

One morning when she was in bed with flu, he turned up at the house in one of Corrigan's brown and white vans. From upstairs, Lily heard Paul talking to him, and Mike arguing.

'I've told you.' Paul raised his voice. 'You'd better go.'

Lily got up and put on jeans and a loose old sweater and banged at her hair with a brush, and went down.

'What's the matter, Mike?' His hair was greasy and ragged.

His clothes were dirty. He had a stubble of beard. He was haggard.

'Let me talk to you,' he said hoarsely, and coughed like a derelict.

'What's wrong?'

'No, Lily,' Paul ordered her. 'You go back up.'

'I'm all right. I feel better. Come and sit in the kitchen, Mike, while I make some coffee.'

She felt she could not turn him away without some kindness, but Paul was furious. He said, 'For God's sake!' and banged out of the house.

'Don't come here again,' Lily told Mike. 'I can only help you through the centre. Don't call me here. I can't talk to you.'

Of course. That confirmed what Mike knew. She wanted to see him, but her husband wouldn't allow it. Paul Stephens. Mike knew all about him. 'Too good to be true,' Ida had told him long ago in the New Bedford days, which had semed so lousy and hopeless, but looked like a paradise of security compared to the way he lived now.

'I've told you.' Driving away, Mike imitated the level, snotty voice to himself. 'You'd better go.'

Too good to be true. Too good for Mike, but Mike had the edge of him. He knew Paul wasn't good enough for Lily. Ordering her upstairs like a child. 'Oh, for God's sake!' and banging out of the house. Well, she didn't go up, did she?

Mike had the edge on him, because Paul Stephens didn't know who Lily was. Mike's precious, his dear, his love. Lily knew, pale and pitiful in that sloppy grey sweater. One day, she would get sick of being treated so badly, and turn to Mike and ask him to be kind.

Driving over the high bridge put the Cape Cod canal between him and her. The water ran swiftly, choppy, swirling into smoothness under the middle of the bridge, as the tide dragged it out to sea. The road ahead was a flat and empty future. Grey sky of November, hauling winter behind it like a funeral train.

Nothing good ever happened to Mike in November. With winter coming, his mother had always stirred him up, goading him, reciting everything about him she couldn't stand, before the unnerving plunge into Thanksgiving and Christmas, when he must be her spoiled baby.

It must have been November when he took the pills at Ida's house. To make it the last November. Someone should have kept Bernie out of the kitchen.

Only Lily could shatter the curse of November. And the treacherous month was not even half done.

Mike did not take the van back to Corrigan's depot. He went west on the turnpike and drove around the Worcester and Springfield area for days, sleeping in the van, drinking, buying some dope. He called Lily from different pay phones. At first she said, 'I'm sorry. Tell me where you are, and I'll get someone to call you back.' Then she hung up on him. Then her husband answered the phone and hung up on him. Then they left the phone off the hook, so that he could not get through.

Mike was angry. He smashed up a few pay phones, because if anyone got him angry, they deserved what they got.

Corrigan would have reported the van by now. A police car spotted him and came after him. Mike pulled the van off the road, grabbed a bottle, jumped out and ran into the woods.

A wanted man. Liquor and amphetamines kept him going. The wind hunted him through the trees and across cold open fields to the lights of a small town. He took a beat-up old Volkswagen from the yard of a dark house and drove east through a storm of rain, sucking at the bottle, crying sometimes, and wiping his nose and sore eyes with bits of dirty paper towels that were on the floor of the car. The November skies wept across the streaming windshield.

Because Crisis had to be able to reach Lily, she could not go on leaving the phone off the hook at night, so Paul had changed the house phones over to the number of the shop, until they could be sure that Mike had given up.

They were still up at midnight when Chuck called from the centre.

'The Sandwich police just called. They've got a man on the bridge who needs talking down, and they want us to send someone. In haste, man. Life or death. Who lives closest to the Sagamore bridge?'

'Me.' Lily looked round at Paul, who was rubbing oil into an old saddle on the back of a kitchen chair.

'Looks like you, then, kid.'

It was a black night of wind and rain. The bridge was blocked off and traffic diverted, but the policeman let Lily through, and she got out of her car in the middle of the span, among the police cars and lights. The man had climbed over the railing and crawled along a girder below the bridge, under the middle of the roadway.

Various people were trying to shout at him over the rails on either side, but the wind shouted louder. A Coastguard boat was below, pushing against the tide, to keep a spotlight trained on the man on the girder. Would someone like to go under the bridge in another boat and try to talk to him through a megaphone?

No one offered. 'I'll go,' Lily said quickly.

A police car took her to the Coastguard dock farther along the canal. One of the men on the boat gave her a big orange waterproof jacket, and she stood with the hood over her head by the bow rail of the small boat, staring to see the man under the bridge. When they were almost underneath the soaring span, the pilot shouted, 'There he is – see him?'

In the beam of light from the other boat, he was miles above them, sitting on the girder. He looked like a fly.

'Go ahead.' The other man gave Lily the megaphone.

'Don't *you* want to?'

'I wouldn't know what to say.'

'Nor would I.'

Lily began to yell through the megaphone. What did she say? What could she say? She did not afterwards remember, but whatever it was, the whole of south-eastern Massachusetts heard it.

'Please! Climb back up – you're safe, I'll help, don't be afraid!'

Something like that, something about a friend, about love. How could she compete with the magnetic pull of the dark water swirling below the tiny man to sweep him out to the peace of the sea?

'I love you!' she probably said desperately. It didn't matter what the men in the boat thought. It didn't matter what south-eastern Massachusetts thought. Anything to get him up off that girder.

If he responded at all, she could not see or hear. At one point, he let something fall.

'A bottle,' one of the men said. It took a long time to reach the water.

'I'll die if he jumps.' Lily was shivering, soaked, frozen, hopeless, useless.

He jumped. With a long trailing yell, he threw himself outwards, sprawling, clutching at the air. After an eternity, he hit the water feet first, and disappeared. The body came up, slumped over, face in the water, held up by the air in the humped jacket.

The other boat was there. They fished him over the side and shouted, 'He's alive!' and the two boats churned back to the dock.

He was lying in a well at the stern of the other boat. When Lily knelt beside him, he raised his plastered eyelashes and looked at her. His skin was ashen, drawn back against the skull, his teeth chattering, his body shaking and rigid under the blankets.

It was Mike.

The ambulance men, doing the necessary things as they drove to the hospital, made feeble jokes like, 'Thought you'd take a late swim, hey, feller?' Lily sat in a blanket on the seat opposite, envying them for having a job to do and for being able to be jolly.

In the hospital, they found that, amazingly, he had no injuries except heavy bruising on his chest and the soles of his feet.

'The alcohol in him must have saved him,' the doctor said.

Lily rang Paul, and stayed to watch Mike for the rest of the night, because the nurses were busy. Asleep, he looked dead. When he woke, he half raised himself on his elbow to look at her. She tried talking to him, but he did not say anything before he fell back into sleep again, his lower teeth uncovered, like a skeleton's jaw.

When Lily got home, everyone was up early, wildly excited.

'It was on the radio! It was on the TV early news!'

'The whole story,' Isobel said. 'Not your name, thank God. They'd have had a fit at school. Bloody heroine, Mud.'

'I didn't do anything. He jumped anyway.'

'But you were brave. It said so. On TV.'

'Who was it?' Paul asked. 'They didn't give his name.'

'One guess.' Lily looked up at him over her coffee mug.

'Mike. Oh, my God.'

Did it go through Paul's head that they had been almost freed from him by the dark water? Did he think those ghastly selfish things, like everybody else?

Lily asked him.

He only smiled. 'Did you?'

While Mike was in the hospital having X-rays and tests recovering from shock, which to him meant the shock of being alive, his mother came.

She had on a new winter coat and a little pair of red boots. She did not come into the room shyly, as the visitors to the other two men did, carefully not looking at anyone who did not belong to them. She bustled in as though she were going to give everybody a bed bath, nodded at Ginger and Matt and said, 'How are *you*?' took off her coat and stood over Mike with her arms folded and said, '*Now* then.'

'It's now then, is it?' Michael had been listening to the radio that Lily had brought in. He leaned over to turn it off, wincing at the pain in his chest.

'They didn't say anything about broken ribs.'

'Why would they? It's called contusions.'

'Show me, son.'

He pulled open the hospital jacket. She gasped. He had not looked properly at his mother's face since she came in. Now he looked and saw that it was soft like jelly, the determined little lower lip sucked in, the eyes sentimental behind the round glasses, roofed by furry grey brows.

'Michael.' She sat down on a chair by the bed and took his hand in her warm paws. 'You should come home now.'

'Didn't you kick me out?'

'Can you blame me? I've come to tell you, son. You can come home. But you didn't jump off the bridge, remember. We'll tell people you were leaning over the rail and you fell.'

'All right.'

But she banished him again. She let them take him off to a rehabilitation centre too far away from New Bedford for her to visit, since her eyes were too bad for her to drive now.

In the rehab, memory slowly returned. In sleeping or waking dreams, the concrete floor of the roadway pressed over his head. He could feel the cold steel girder under his thighs. His feet hung over space. He could not see anything, because they were shining that brilliant light into his eyes. How did they expect him to jump when he could not see the water?

He jumped, and the wind came shrieking past and carried all the breath away out of his body. He fell for ever, and came out of it gasping and clutching his throat and screaming soundlessly.

'Cut it out,' Robbie grumbled. 'You can only die once. You don't have to do it every night.'

'Okay, Rob.' They lit cigarettes and talked for a while in the dark, and the bridge retreated to where it belonged, humping its back over the Cape Cod canal.

Awake, he began to remember the voices. People shouting at him faintly from above, then suddenly her voice exploding out of the heart of the dazzling light.

In the early months at the rehab, through the boring therapy sessions, the quarrelsome groups, the gym, the workshop where they were teaching him to be a carpenter and 'start life again', Mike could turn on the sound of her voice, metallic, booming, larger than life. A garbled bellow of vowels that sometimes sounded like, 'I love you!'

If she did not come, he would find a way to sneak a chisel out of the workshop and kill himself quickly and cleanly in the third-floor broom closet.

It was fun, having a day out with Lil again. Now that poor Mike was safely out of her hair, Ida did feel she owed him a visit. After all, she and Shirley had let him come in and out of their house in the days when he had only his mother to fear, and was lonely for their sort of household, with the kids around.

When Ida read in the paper about his antics at the bridge, she knew he must be crazy, but when he wrote to her from the funny farm, she could not turn him down. Shirley wouldn't go with her, but Lily's social conscience was nagging her to go and see Mike. Paul and her boss had said, 'Forget it,' so she used the excuse of taking Ida.

'I could never have gone in here alone.' Ida bit her nails as they drove through the guarded entrance gate and approached the large innocent white building along a driveway bordered by neatly kept lawns and shrubs. It was a warm spring day. Men and women sat outside on garden chairs. Three old stagers played croquet, their legs bowed out at a wider angle than the hoops. On the grass, a group sat in a circle round a demented young woman who must be staff, nodding her bushy head and gesticulating with her fingers as if they were deaf.

'Why don't they cut and run?' Ida rolled up the car window.

'They could. But if they're here under a pink paper, like Mike, they could be picked up by the police and brought back.'

'They look as if they don't even want to make a run for it,' Ida complained.

'Perhaps for some of them, it's better than where they were before.'

Ida was glad to see Mike. She really was. He looked older. He had put on weight and his hair was short, and he had a small neat moustache and beard close round his mouth, so that you couldn't see those stormy boyish lips. His eyes still looked at you as if they saw your soul and wouldn't give you a nickel for it. Ida had thought he might look drugged. She had heard that they controlled the inmates by knock-out drops, but he actually looked less drugged than in the days when he was on the stuff off and on in New Bedford.

He was in the day room upstairs, writing something at a table.

'Michael,' the orderly said. 'Someone for you.'

He kept his head down, annoyed to be disturbed. He went on writing, and then shut the exercise book with a sigh. When he saw Lily, his eyes lightened. Then he saw Ida and frowned.

Hey, wait a minute, Michael Baxlee. Lily may have tried to stop you jumping off the bridge, but who was it that emptied you out of all that demarol with vodka gravy, and wore a hole in the carpet walking you up and down the whole night?

He pushed himself up from the table. 'Oh, hi,' he said. 'I thought it was my mother.'

'Sorry to disappoint you,' Ida said.

'No. I mean. I'm glad you came.'

There were very few people in the big room, but he could not decide where they should sit. When Ida and Lily headed for an empty corner and sat down, he couldn't decide whether to go and get coffee for them, or to take them into the kitchen.

He was fumbling around so, perhaps he was thrown off by them seeing him in this place. But when he came back – coffee hot and the right colour, no spills, plate of cookies, not bad for a man whose mother had not even taught him to boil water – he talked a lot about the rehab, and what they did and how it had helped him.

Ida had been afraid she would be nervous too, but he made her feel easy by saying candidly, 'Maybe I'm still crazy. Chronic condition. But it's a crazy world out there, so they think I ought to fit right back into it pretty comfortably.'

'You bet,' Ida said. 'They got the wrong people in here, hunh?'

He was bluffing, so she played along with the standard joke. But Lily, who had been quiet for a while, observing him with her face non-committal, leaned forward and said, 'Mike, you're not crazy. You're all right. You're going to be all right.'

'Oh sure. Everyone jumps off a bridge once in a while,' he said quite nastily. 'Don't give it a thought.'

'That night.' Lily moved her eyes away from his face and looked down at her hands, clasped in the lap of the faded jeans she had worn so as to look old shoe. 'When you – when you jumped, did you want to drown?'

'I was full of pills and booze,' he said. 'How do I know what I wanted?'

'What do you want now?' Lily plugged on as if Ida wasn't there observing her ironically as she pursued her duty.

'If they ever let me out of here' – Mike decided to give her a break – 'I'm going to give life one more chance, before I try the other thing again.'

'That's great.' Lily sat back. 'I know you'll make it.'

Ida changed the subject, and started to tell him about her children, and show him pictures. She knew Mike well enough to realize that somewhere inside himself, he was standing apart, seeing right through Lily's earnest attempts to help him, and Ida was not going to have good old Lil made fun of by the devious secret soul of a weirdo like this who would never let you win.

When it was time for them to go, Mike walked with them to the parking lot and stood with his hands in his pockets, looking boyish again, and disappointed.

'Thanks for coming,' he said. 'It's meant a lot. Will you come again?'

'Maybe,' Ida said. 'If I can find the way.'

'I'll see,' Lily said. 'You're doing so well, you may not be in here very much longer, after all.'

'Decent of us,' Ida said as they drove away, 'to leave the poor guy guessing.'

'It's worse to promise and then not go.'

'Dear Doctor Lily.' Ida patted her arm. 'You haven't lost your touch.'

Lily's bridge-jumper did not leave the rehabilitation hospital until the end of the summer, when Lily heard that he had got a job with a builder in Vermont.

Too far away to call her, with any luck.

She had worked at Crisis most of last winter, and had started going to Boston again when the summer vacation ended.

'I liked it better when you were here all the time,' Paul told her.

'So did I.'

'Then why. . . .? Don't tell me. I know. Martha needs you and the clients need you and the new student volunteers need you to train them. And you love it.'

'Do you mind? I mean, honestly, darling, if you mind –'

When she gave him these generous openings, he always missed his chance of telling the truth. But he would never hold her back. He needed her to help with his business, but how could he compare the importance of his work with hers?

Another winter boarder was in the stable, a fancy horse that would need a lot of care. Tony was off on a motel swimming-pool project with his father in Sandwich, and could help only on Sundays. The land Paul had bought between the back road and the railroad needed a lot more work before the winter. When Lily could be in the tack shop, Paul was out there clearing brush and levelling a place for an open shelter. He got a lot done. He was strong and fit at almost fifty. Then she would be gone to Boston the next day, and Paul had to choose between leaving the land, or closing the shop and missing customers and calls.

In October, he had to make trips to see suppliers in New York and Florida, because if he didn't keep up a certain amount of orders with them every year, he could not keep their dealership for special lines, and get their wholesale prices.

Paul had to change his dates to suit the man in New York, who was his friend from the old Turnbull days. When he told this to Lily, who was going to run the shop and the stable while he was away, it turned out that she was committed to speak at a two-day conference in Rhode Island.

'I told you, Paul. They booked this months ago.'

'Can't they get someone else?' It was complicated enough already to fit in his dates and appointments. The Florida situation was still uncertain. He was worried about budgets, and a bit fussed about the trip, without this difficulty at home.

'I hate to say it, but they did ask for me, because of the seminars I did last spring. This lot are social workers too. I'll be speaking on how agencies can use volunteers.'

'Why can't Martha do it?'

'They did specially ask for me. Remember, you were pleased too, when I told you.'

'And now I'm not. Oh, hell, don't make me get angry. You know how I hate to get angry.' He could hear himself sounding childish. He felt it.

'Then don't. Have you got your tickets? Can't you change the date again?'

'No, God dammit, Lily, I can't.'

'Well, nor can I.'

They glared at each other. It was horrible. They were outside on the terrace, everything brilliantly edged by the low, intense October sun. Mrs Dawson, coming to ride her horse, rolled down the driveway in her bloated white car, and waved to them.

Paul turned away to go to the stable. Then he turned back and said, 'Look, I know how important your work is to you. I hate you being in Boston so much, and I hate you being out in the traffic on that highway, but I wouldn't try to stop you doing it. But look, I know that you're dealing a lot of the time with quite desperate people. But right now — I have to say it — I am pretty desperate too.'

Lily did not say anything. She looked stricken. Paul went out to help Mrs Dawson, reassembling his usual serene face in front of his thoughts. He shouldn't have said that. Pretty underhand. Not fair to play on her so easily aroused emotions.

'Hullo, Mrs D! Good to see you. Hey, are those the new breeches? They look great. Felix looks great too. He's doing very well on those new pellets.'

In the morning, when Paul came in from the stable where the horses, executing their daily innocent expressions of eagerness for breakfast always made him feel that his world was a well-ordered place, he was ready to tell Lily that he would make new arrangements.

'That's all right.' She beamed at him. 'I've already called Martha and asked her to wriggle me out of the conference. Of course I'll stay here, darling. I must have been mad to think I couldn't.'

And being his darling unneurotic Lily, she was totally cheerful and ungrudging about it, and enjoyed going over with him everything that was likely to come up with the tack shop or the horses. So after the trip, when the hapless bastard Michael Baxlee was found sitting on the wall of the stable yard when they came back from shopping, Paul felt obliged to be more helpful than he felt.

Mike's job had lasted three weeks. The carpentry skills he had learned at the rehab centre were not advanced enough for the needs of the builder.

'It's rotten bad luck,' Lily said.

Mike had helped to carry in the grocery bags, and they were all three sitting round the kitchen table, discussing his future.

'I don't know. Must have been my fault.'

Probably was, but it was bad luck too, the kind of inherent luck that dogs a loser like this, even when he tries to get his life together. He had liked the work, and seemed to have tried his best, and when his employer brought in another carpenter without warning him, Mike had gone round some local builders in Vermont, vainly trying to find at least a low-paid job where he could learn.

He had gone back to New Bedford. One man who might have given him a job remembered about the bridge, and said, 'Whoa – wait a minute. Aren't you the guy who – ?'

Ida and Shirley were away visiting Shirley's family in New Haven. If Mike could not find work, he would have to go back to the rehab and ask for a psychiatrist's letter to get Social Security special payments.

'I walked out of that place proud,' he told Paul and Lily. 'A good job and a new life. "Don't come back," they said, like a kind of joke. So it would be tough.'

'It would be a step back,' Lily said. 'Perhaps we can help you to find something.'

'My record's bad.'

'You can't have that hanging round your neck for ever.'

'Hard to get rid of, though,' Paul said more realistically.

'But how's he ever going to make something of his life if no one will give him a chance?'

'That's true.' Paul's resentment against Mike's intrusions last year was forgotten. That didn't matter now. He was sorry for the man, and he wanted to show Lily that he could be part of her work, because she was part of his.

'Let's see, maybe I have an idea that could tide you over.'

Here was a way to thank her properly for giving up so gracefully the excitement and acclaim of her conference.

Isobel knew that Tony wasn't too pleased when Ida's taxi driver turned up, one of Mud's lame dogs, who was going to clear brush and thin saplings in the new field, and finish the fences and the horse shelter: things that would have been Tony's jobs. He had no time to do them himself now, but he wasn't happy about someone else moving in.

'You stay clear of him, Bella,' he warned.

'Why? He's quite nice, for a nut case.'

'That's it. He *is* a nut case.'

They knew, although no one had told them, that this Mike was the man who had jumped off the bridge that night when Mud was a heroine. Not that wanting to kill yourself was all that far out. It was talked about a lot at school, and a few of the kids had even overdosed, or cut themselves.

'Anyway, I hardly ever see him,' Isobel told Tony. 'He's down in the back field beyond your house all the time.'

He was up at her house occasionally, because he had helped to bring Cathy's little blue sailfish up from Hidden Harbor, and he was scraping and repainting it with her in his own time. It was Isobel's sailfish as well, but she had lost interest in it, because Tony, born and brought up near the ocean, thought boats were toys of the rich, unless they were fishing boats, or the Martha's Vineyard and Nantucket ferries, on which he was going to start crewing next year when his younger brother graduated from school and took over the bulldozer and back hoe.

Everyone had always thought that Isobel would grow out of Tony, if you can grow out of someone five years older than you. But at fifteen, she needed and wanted him more than ever. He had grown into a man, good looking and muscular, with thick curling black hair and a wide white smile. She did not mind too much about his other girls. They would never be special to him, like Isobel. They were just practice for him, while he was waiting for her.

Now she could not see the sense of waiting any longer.

Megan and Josie Phillips and Mary-Anne had all had sex. 'I really want to,' Isobel said.

'No you don't, Bella. You're too young. Your Dad would kill me.'

'He wouldn't. He wouldn't know anyway, but even if he did, what difference if we do it now? We'll be doing it when we're married.'

'You're not going to marry me, Bella.'

'I *am*. Why not?'

'Girls like you don't marry Portugees.'

'Shut up. You talk about racism. It's you guys who perpetuate it.'

'What if I married someone like Tony?' she asked her father.

'Well – he's too old for you.'

'You're too old for Mudder.'

'Yes. I knew you'd say that.'

'Wouldn't you care that he was black?'

'No, of course not. I hope not.'

A lot of people talked liberally like that, but could not pass the test of, 'But would you let your daughter . . .?' Dad would, she honestly believed.

Mike had acquired a dog since he came to Cape Cod, a heavy young black dog, a Labrador, like half the dogs on the Cape, that some man had sold to him for ten dollars in a bar. He was rather quarrelsome, for a Lab. The people who rented a room to Mike didn't want him to keep it there, so he offered the dog to Cathy, and of course she took it.

'We don't need another dog,' Lily told Mike when she found out about it. They were only just free of one of Cathy's strays, a terrier who had started chasing horses and had to be sent away.

'I didn't know what else to do with Hector.' Sometimes Mike talked to Mud in a very dumb way, mumbling and not looking at her, and fumbling his hands as if they belonged to somebody else.

'We always need another dog,' Cathy said. 'I wish we had six. Dad's always bringing in more horses. Why can't I –'

'Arthur won't like it.'

'Arthur doesn't care. They've met and Hector was a lamb. He just wants to get along with everybody and be a good dog and I'll feed him and take care of him, and –'

'And he'll be no trouble and everyone will grow to love him.' Isobel finished for her. Like all the dogs and cats and rabbits and guinea pigs and tortoises that Cathy had introduced. The latest before Hector was a dwarf donkey, who lived in the loose box with her pony.

'Oh dear,' Mudder said. But she could not turn away Hector and his thick pushy shoulders and destructive tail.

The woolly dog Arthur, who was twelve now, and getting a bit set in his limbs, as he was in his ways, growled and lifted his lip if the new dog came too near. Otherwise there was no trouble.

For some time, Isobel had known that there were a lot of beer cans and a few half pints thrown among the trees beyond the fence where Mike was working. She didn't say anything, it wasn't her business, and it didn't matter, as long as the guy was doing the work. Then one evening when Isobel was in the yard outside Tony's house, helping him to clean his car, they heard shouting from the end of the new field, and pretty soon, her father came across the road with a furious face.

'What's all the yelling, Dad?'

'Mike, of course. I haven't checked on him for a couple of days. He did pretty well on the shed, but he's done a perfectly lousy job on a section of fence. Rails all crooked, ends of nails sticking through on the pasture side, and he wants me to advance his next week's money because –' He took a deep breath and puffed out his cheeks and recovered himself. 'Oh well.'

'Want me to go up and straighten some of it out after supper?' Tony asked sweetly, not sorry to hear that the intruder was no good. 'There'll still be just enough light.'

'No, it's all right. He'll have to do it over again tomorrow. I'll just have to keep an eye on him.'

The next day, it rained. The day after, and another day, Mike wasn't there to keep an eye on. At the end of the week, Isobel came home from school, and found a big fight going on in the kitchen. Mudder, who never did only one thing at a time, was making pastry and putting in her opinion indiscriminately on either side to the argument between Paul and Mike.

'Give you another chance? I've given you chance after chance.'

'That's right, you know, Mike, he has.' Mudder, flouring her hair to get it out of her eyes.

'I've done the work. It's not my fault if it isn't good enough for you. Nothing is.'

'Listen, Mike, be reasonable. A job's a job. You turn up on time, and you don't walk off till quitting time. If you're not coming, you let me know.'

'How could I know it was going to rain? Give me a break.'

'It didn't rain yesterday and the day before. Why should I make allowances? How are you ever going to get back into life in competition with everyone else?'

'Maybe I don't want to. Maybe I don't like being a slave.'

'If you don't like the job, you're welcome to quit.'

'Wait a minute, Paul.' Lily turned round, and put flour on his sleeve.

'All right, I'll quit. That's what you want, isn't it, you bastard?'

Mike began to shout and Lily shouted at him, 'Don't talk to Paul like that!' Cathy came dreamily through the door with Hector, just as Arthur got up from under the table to go out, and the two of them were into a hideous dog fight.

Lily threw a pan of water at their heads. Cathy and Isobel shrieked at both dogs, and Dad shouted orders. Everyone was telling each other what to do, and picking up chairs and trying to keep their legs out of the way of the ferocious, snarling mass of fur and teeth. Cathy was in a frenzy that Arthur would be killed.

At the height of it, the cushiony grey cat, who had lived with Arthur for six years, jumped from somewhere like a flying bat into the fight, and was immediately thrown out of it, her small brave body flung out of the turmoil like a rag.

Blood was being thrown out too.

'Do something!'

Cathy screamed, 'Arth! Arth! Hector! They'll kill each other!'

Paul put down a chair and waded in and tried to grab one of their collars. He got Charlie and pulled him back, and kicked out hard at Hector. Dad's hand was bleeding. He put it in his mouth. When Lily pulled it out to look at it, there was a puncture wound at the base of the thumb. She held it under the cold tap. Isobel flew for the first-aid box. She was good in emergencies. Years ago, her English Granny had taught her how to bandage and take temperatures, and she was always the one who nursed people, when they were hurt or sick.

Lily took Paul off to the Emergency Room at the hospital. Cathy went with them because it might have been her black dog who had bitten him. Isobel went too, because it was her father.

All the excitement had taken the tormenting attention away from Mike.

'You're welcome to quit.' That cold politeness. You couldn't fight it.

'All right, I will.'

When the turmoil died down, it would probably turn out that he was fired anyway, so he would quit before Paul could give himself the satisfaction of firing him. He would walk down now and get his stuff from his room, and then hitch a ride into town and get a bus to New Bedford. In the little movie theatre of his mind, Mike saw with some pleasure the blood pouring from the man's hand, and after she washed it clean, before the blood welled up again, the nasty little tooth hole, and the pad of the thumb already beginning to swell and change colour.

Serve him right. Smug bastard.

'Don't speak to Paul like that!' Lily was too much in Paul's power. It was wicked. She was the queen. For ten days, Mike had been part of her kingdom. He had not been able to see much of her, but she was *there*. That was the magic.

November. It would be November – you could trust November to take everything away and give him nothing. What was there for him in New Bedford? His mother acted now as if she had never said to him in the hospital, in the first shock of having her son pulled out of the canal like a dead cat, 'You can come home.'

He couldn't anyway. If he once got him into the pinched Fairhaven house, he would never get out.

He imagined Bernie painting the picket fence at Ida and Shirley's house, and saw himself pushing open the gate and going to the door with white paint on the palm of his hand. But Ida was pretty thick with Lily. She would be mad at him for quitting. Everybody would be. Dr Theale at the rehab would be. Mike was supposed to do what all of them wanted, and be grateful.

Cathy would not be mad, but sad, because her boat wasn't finished. And God damn. In the bus, Mike remembered that he had promised her he'd go down to the beach and drive in the stake that had pulled loose and let her boat drag over to the other side of the inlet the day before they brought it up to the house.

When he got off the bus, Mike went to get something to eat in a place where they didn't know him. He stayed in the bar and grill until they threw him out, and then went back to the bus station and slept on one of the benches among the winos and derelicts. At first light, he put his stuff in a locker and walked over the Coggeshall Street bridge and out on to the highway, where a truck stopped for him.

'What are you going to do on the Cape this time of year?' The trucker had the radio on very loud, so there was no need for much talk.

'Got a job to do.'

'I wouldn't work on no Cape,' the trucker said. 'They can have it.'

He let Mike off at Buzzard's Bay. Mike did not want to walk across the bridge, although this one had a high suicide barrier on it to stop people being in charge of their own destiny, which was why he had had to go to Sagamore that night. He got a ride in a car that was going to catch the early ferry to the Vineyard, then walked by the back road into the village, avoiding Tony's house and going quickly through the field to get to the toolshed without being seen.

The barn door was shut, and there were no lights in the house. A horse banged a hoof against the side of the stall. A dog barked. Mike waited, but it did not bark again, so he opened the shed door quietly, and found the sledge-hammer in the shadows.

Carrying it over his shoulder, he walked to Hidden Harbor by a roundabout route, turning down a dirt road and cutting through fir trees. He came out at the end of the inlet where the stone breakwater ran out between the open beach and the sheltered place where they tied up the boats. Behind him, the sun was coming up, laying a carpet of colour on the calm cold sea.

Mike clambered out over the big boulders until he had water on either side of him. He sat for a long while looking at a small green lobster boat chugging slowly out to its pots, and watching the hovering mirage of the New Bedford shore set down its feet and begin to look real. At last he climbed down and walked over the wet gritty sand to where the stake for Cathy's boat would be lying somewhere among the long grass and beach-plum bushes. Gulls wheeled and called above him, making plans for the day. Back toward the road, a blue-jay squawked, announcing the distant thud of a horse's hoofs on sand. They came nearer, travelling quite fast. Were here.

Paul on his bay horse, looking healthy.

He called to Mike, 'What are you doing here?' and Mike asked at the same time, 'How come you're riding with that bad hand?'

The dog Arthur came through the long grass to Mike and wagged his tail, and then went down into the water to scrape about for clams.

'How's the thumb?' Mike kept his head down, searching for the stake.

'Fine.' Paul was holding the reins in one hand, the other bandaged. 'Only a small puncture, but I had to have a tetanus shot.'

'I'm sorry, if it was Hector.'

'That's all right. But Cathy's upset.'

'I didn't want her to be upset with me. When the stake for her boat pulled loose, I promised her I'd knock it in, so she'd have it here for next season.'

'Don't worry. I'll do it.'

'No, *I'll* do it.'

'I thought you'd left the Cape.'

'I came back to do this. When I can find it.'

'Here, I'll help you.'

Paul got off the horse and put the reins over his arm. 'Was this all you came back for? Or did you think you could persuade me to give you your job back?' He was not angry, but smiling, which infuriated Mike.

'Don't kid yourself,' Mike said. 'You can stuff the job.'

'And you might like to stuff this,' Paul said. 'You whine a lot about bad luck, but it seems to me that most of the time, you make it for yourself. Have you ever thought about that?'

'I think a lot about how people who've had some luck go around telling everybody else what to do.'

'Oh, grow up,' Paul said wearily, sick of Mike.

'Damn you!' Heat rushed up through Mike and his anger exploded. He jumped back and grabbed the sledge-hammer, and swung it hard. In the instant, he saw Paul with his arms up, frozen, the bandaged hand against the sky, his mouth open on a shout, saw the horse rear and pull back, and saw the dog leaping at him with its teeth bared, water spattering off its coat.

The thud of the sledge-hammer was sickening. Paul made a strange choking sound, and fell. As the dog's weight hit Mike, he kicked it into the sea. He hurled the sledge-hammer far out into the deep part of the water, and ran for the trees.

Lily woke to a staccato of hoofs outside. She sat up. Paul's side of the bed was empty. Gone out for an early ride? But he wouldn't be clattering fast like that. One of the horses had got out. She went to the window and saw Robin swerve round the corner of the drive, reins dangling and stirrups flying.

Paul must have fallen off and let go of the reins. Or a branch took off his cap and he got down for it, and the horse pulled free.

When she ran downstairs, Robin was eating the lawn, a front foot through his reins.

'Where did you leave him, you faithless brute?'

Paul had probably gone down to the beach. He had an early appointment and would not have gone for a long ride. Lily got on Robin and trotted down the road and cantered along the sandy track to Hidden Harbor, expecting to see Paul at every turn, walking home. She was cantering over the fresh prints of Robin's hoofs, where he had gone down to the beach, and come back.

She saw Arthur first, on the edge of the sea. His back end was lying with the legs straight out sideways, his front end sitting propped up. His head hung and his jaws were open, strings of saliva hanging down. Then she saw beyond a thorny bush something blue, almost hidden in the long grass and reeds.

She jumped off. Robin would not be led forwards, so she

slung his reins quickly round a branch of the bush and ran to where Paul was lying on his back, a wound on the side of his head, eyes closed, mouth open, arms flung out and up, like a gesture of surrender.

He's dead. She knew and accepted it, for a cold suspended moment. Then she came to life and started to call his name, touching his face and telling him, 'You're not dead, you're not dead!' over and over again. Kneeling, she raised her head and shouted across the inlet to the empty, shuttered houses.

He had a faint pulse, and his skin was cold and clammy. His breathing was harsh and laboured. Grasping his thick blue sweater and the back of his riding breeches, she managed to turn him on his side. He groaned, a horrible throaty noise, and stopped breathing. She shouted at him and shook his arm. She did not know which part of him she could touch. His lips were turning blue, but as she leaned over him to try mouth-to-mouth, he gasped, and the struggling, rattling breaths began again.

There was an enormous swelling on the side of his forehead. The skin was torn and shattered. Blood from his scalp and from his ear had run down his neck, and was beginning to congeal. His breathing was still hoarse and irregular, with agonizing pauses, but she had to leave him to get help.

She shouted again, and screamed. No one. No workmen in the summer houses. No boats on the sea.

'Arthur – I'm sorry. I can't help you. I'll be back. Hang on, guard him, I'll – oh God, let it be all right – it'll be all right!' she told them wildly.

She forced herself away from Paul, freed the horse's reins and galloped back like a maniac out on to the road. A car just missed her, swerved and stopped in the loose sand.

'What the –'

'Call the rescue squad. My husband's badly hurt. Down there on the beach. Call the vet too – *please*. There's a smashed-up dog.'

'Will do.' The man had a shiny bald head and a firm mouth. Thick black sides to his glasses. Dependable.

'Hurry – I'll go back there.'

Soon after she reached Paul, the ambulance came, careering

down the curving path in a cloud of dusty sand. Two people jumped out, a short man with bristly grey hair, a young woman, strong, with a high colour. They knelt and stood and got equipment out of the ambulance, and knew what they were doing, swiftly, and communicated briefly. Lily's mind kept on registering details normally by itself, while she stood by, frantically doing nothing, her whole being concentrated on Paul.

Inside the ambulance, he was breathing oxygen through a tracheal tube, the wound covered with a loose pad, the bandaged hand lying on his chest over the blanket, where the man had put it carefully, as if the thumb still mattered.

'What happened?' he asked Lily.

'I don't *know*. I wasn't with him. He was riding.'

'Thrown off? Hit his head on a rock, I guess.'

'But the dog – someone attacked them.'

The man looked out of the back door of the ambulance at the peaceful seaside scene, sparkling in the early sun. 'Anything's possible.'

The young woman finished talking into the radio. 'Right. We're to take him to Boston. Massachusetts General neurosurgery unit.'

'Can I come – oh, God, what will I do with the horse?'

'Leave your husband to us.' The woman put her arm round Lily and rubbed the side of her face against hers in a friendly, animal way. 'You follow in your car.' She did not add a futile, 'Don't worry.' Lily liked and trusted her for that.

They were gone. Now Arthur. 'Oh, my poor Arthur, my good dog.'

He had dragged himself farther away from the sea, and was lying flat, panting, his tongue and gums too pale, one eye rolled up at her with his funny china-eyed look, a lot of the white showing. Lily could see that his back leg was broken. She sat by him in the wet sand. Stroking him and telling him he was brave and good, while her mind was with Paul, speeding head first unknowingly up the highway, scattering the early rush-hour traffic with sirens and flashing lights.

The vet came. God bless the bald man with the dependable

365

glasses. The vet put on a splint and laid Arthur in the back of his car, and put two rugs over him.

'I can set the leg. I think he'll be all right.'

That meant that Paul would be all right, of course it did. Signs and portents. Omens and charms. Her breath rasping her throat, Lily chanted voicelessly to the beat of Robin's hoofs racing home on the sand and on the hard road. He's all right he's not he's dead he's all right . . . Cars pulled out of her way. A woman ran out of a door, shouting. A bicyclist wobbled and stopped and put down a foot.

Cathy ran out of the house, hair tied back, dressed for school. Lily flung herself off the horse and told her. Blood drained from Cathy's delicate skin. Her light blue eyes overflowed. She cried without noise, trembling.

'Where's Isobel?'

'Gone. Her bus comes before mine.'

'How can you and I go off to Boston, Cath, and leave her at school, not knowing?'

'Go and get her?'

'Take too long. Should I call the school, or is that worse?'

Cathy shook her head wretchedly, standing with her toes turned in and her arms hanging helplessly forwards.

Lily dithered. A car came fast into the drive. Lily's friend Nina had seen her galloping back down the road. Oh – *friends*. Thank God. Nina took it in swiftly.

'You and Cathy go. I'll feed the horses and put them out. Then I'll go and get Isobel from school and bring her up to the hospital.'

'Paul may be dying.' Lily looked into her eyes. Cathy had gone into the house for jackets.

'Yes.' Nina looked back steadily. Like the rescue squad woman, she did not say, 'You mustn't think that,' or, 'He's going to be all right,' or any of the cowardly talisman efforts to ward off disaster.

In the Boston hospital, Paul went through a long operation to raise the depressed fracture of his skull, tie off damaged vessels and remove a deep blood clot. While he was in the operating room, Nina arrived with Isobel and found Lily and Cathy in a hot and airless waiting-room that clung to its aftertastes of anxiety and overflowing metal ashtrays. When Nina went to get coffee, Isobel fell upon Cathy in fury, because she had gone to Boston without her.

'We had to get here – don't!' Cathy pushed her away. 'Daddy was *dying*.'

'Why should you be there and not me?'

'Go ahead – go on only thinking about yourself!' Cathy turned on Isobel in a way she never did.

While Lily could only sit and watch them dully, they hit each other, and then cried.

After that, they were both marvellous. They listened, one on each side of their mother, propping her up, while the surgeon talked. A square man, ruddy-faced from some autumn vacation, pink hands clasped: the hands that had been inside Paul's brain, folded over the secret of the terrible injury.

Deep haematoma . . . bruising and lacerations to the brain.

'Brain damage?' Lily whispered.

'Not necessarily permanent, no. No, you don't have to expect that, Mrs Stephens. See how he does . . . very serious blow . . . brutal force. Mrs Stephens, have you any idea who did it?'

Lily shook her head. Cathy and Isobel continued to stare at the doctor in silence, their sweet young mouths pulled down, their clear eyes stricken with terror.

Lily opened her mouth, shut it, licked her lips, swallowed, and heard herself ask, 'Will he die?'

'Always the chance of another haemorrhage. But no, I don't see why, Mrs Stephens.'

He was one of those people who tell you your name all the time, in case you don't know it.

After Paul became hazily conscious, in Intensive Care, he seemed to have no memory of what had happened. He hardly spoke. He drifted in and out of a sleep that was like a coma. The police were there from time to time, but he did not see or hear them. Lily and her daughters were there all the time, for as long as they were allowed. Nina went home and came back again to be with Isobel and Cathy while Lily slept, and to wait with Lily while they slept. The motel room had brown zigzag bedspreads, and a roaring bathroom fan that came on with the light, so you could sob and howl in there.

Tony came and sat dumbly with Isobel in the cafeteria, staring at her dulled, colourless face and holding her hand under the table. Harry and other friends came and went as in a dream.

Once, when Cathy was close to her father's head, he opened his swollen eyes as far as he could, below the white turban of bandage, and said thickly, 'Arth.'

'He's all right, Daddy.' Cathy's small hand went on stroking his arm above the intravenous needle. 'He broke a leg.'

'Flew into the fray ... like your grey ... your bray ...'

'My brave grey cat.'

Paul smiled and shut his bruised, watery blue eyes, and Cathy dripped tears and soft pale hair on him as he drifted away from them again.

Jamspoon had not been able to find Terry for several days. He had wandered away from the Duke's Head months ago, because he got fed up with Blanche bossing him around and making him serve the lunches that were spoiling the old pub by becoming grander and more elaborate.

He had drifted away from James, because he got tired of going with the crazy old guy to spend hours of agonizing boredom hanging around on movie locations, after Jam had got him to sign up for crowd work. He removed himself completely after Jam's grisly old girlfriend Pixie, who was also a film extra, specializing in spangled evening dresses, had told her daughter Button that Terry needed a woman as much as Button needed a man.

Yikes! Get me out of here! Terry was working in the kitchen of a hotel in Aberdeen when James finally tracked him down and told him what had happened to his father.

'A week ago! My God, I should be there. Why didn't you —'

'Why didn't *you*? I had the devil's own time finding you, and Lily says they haven't heard from you for months. So much for this great love you've got for your father.'

'I'll kill you, Jamspoon.' Terry was standing at the wall telephone in the stone passage between the kitchen and store-rooms, shivering.

'You do that, my dear. But get your lazy bum over to Boston first. And – Terry!' He called out to stop him hanging up. 'Tell Lily I – tell my Lily, if she wants me, I'll come.' His voice broke, hammily.

Jamspoon was let off the hook, because Lily did not want him. Paul was going to be all right. He was not going to die. She couldn't be distracted from her effort to get him well enough to go home from the hospital. She did not want her mother yet either.

'Later,' she told Nora. 'Come later when I've got him at home and I'll need help.'

'Will you, Lily?' Terry asked. 'Will he be in bed all the time?' Was his father going to be a paralysed invalid? 'Will he need a lot of nursing?'

'I don't suppose so, but if Nora wants to come, she may as well feel needed.'

'Why don't you think about yourself?' Terry asked.

'I do, all the time. But it's not much fun.'

'Why?'

'There's Isobel at the end of the hall. It's your turn to be in the room now.'

Sometimes his father wanted to talk, half sensibly, half vaguely. Sometimes he just wanted to sit in the chair by the window, and frown and fall asleep while Terry talked to him. He did not remember that Terry had been in Europe for two years. He was unnecessarily polite, from habit, but he could not be interested in hearing about any of it.

The police, who were still looking for this Michael Baxlee character, whom Terry would torture and strangle when they found him, had told them all to keep asking, to try to help Paul to remember.

369

'Who, Dad? Who was it? Who came at you? The vet said Arthur's leg was probably broken by a kick. You saw him jump out of the sea, didn't you? Who did Arthur jump at? Who did it?'

'Who did what?'

'Who hit you?'

'What who?'

'Try and see it, Dad. Try to remember.'

When his father first left his room, to go to the sun lounge in a wheelchair, it was Terry who pushed him. Lily wanted it to be her, but she let Terry do it, because it would be 'good for him', as it would be good for wanton old Nora to leave Duggie to feed budgies in the bungalow and come over to help.

When Mike turned up with his hair long and greasy and someone else's jacket that was yards too big for him, Ida had not seen him for a long time. She had thought he was still working for a builder in Vermont. Now he was going to fly to Toronto to see his old rehab roommate Robbie.

Ida and Shirley did not want Mike around, because the police had been to their house looking for him, for some undisclosed reason. So they lent him some money, and Ida took an afternoon off to drive him to the airport. She was upstairs getting changed when the police arrived. She had to come down in her wrapper to open the door. Mike was in the kitchen with a bowl of soup and a boloney sandwich. They put the handcuffs on him first, then talked.

Assault? Who? What did Mike do?

Aggravated assault.

Paul Stephens.

Ida's stomach caved in as if she had been kicked by a horse. She backed to the sink and leaned over the draining board. The contents of her head had dropped into her stomach. She was going to faint or throw up, or both.

The same prints of his boots on the beach and in the field where he had worked. Why had that crazy Lily ever taken him on?

Mike went into one of his show-piece rages. A cop had him by each arm. His wrists were locked behind his back. Ida could have told him that language like that would get him nowhere.

The very blond cop with the sinister white eyelashes told him, 'You can tell that to the judge.' He made the corny joke seriously.

Ida and Shirley went to the courthouse, because Mrs Baxlee would not go, and there was no one else. Mike did not tell anything to the judge. The albino policeman read out the statement he had made at the station, and the judge ordered him to gaol, awaiting trial.

Nine

*A*fter Paul had been home for about a month, Ida came to see Lily. Paul was asleep when she arrived. 'But he wouldn't want to see me anyway.'

Lily did not tell her politely, 'Of course he would.' Even when he was free from headaches, Paul only wanted to see his family and close friends for a very short time.

'It's you I came to see anyway, me old Lil, dear old pal.'

'That was nice of you, Eye. I'm glad. People have all been so great. Americans are very kind, kinder than English people, don't you think?'

'I don't know. I feel American, don't you?'

Lily shook her head. 'I love it here, but I don't think I'll ever completely belong. I still feel English.'

Lily sat on the floor by the fire, wrapping a few Christmas presents with no enthusiasm. Ida sat in a chair. At forty-three, her fat was a solid structure, anchored to floor or furniture. She had lost her light balloonlike movements, although her breathy voice was still weightless.

'I'm sorry, Lil.'

'Yes. It was a ghastly thing to happen.'

'No, I mean, I have to say, I'm sorry for what I did.'

'What?'

'Bringing you together with Mike.'

'It's not your fault. It's mine.' Lily had not said this to anyone, and no one had said it to her. Yet. 'Dear Doctor Lily – you know me, Eye. I had to wade in with both feet.'

'Why did you give him the job here?'

Lily stared into the pulsing red hollow of the logs on the wide hearth, and leaned against Ida's short strong legs.

'Paul did it to please me, and that's the terrible truth of it.'

Ida put her hand into Lily's hair and stroked her scalp. It felt good.

'I had tried so hard with Mike,' Lily said. 'Too hard. Thinking I could straighten him out, ignoring how sick he was, I suppose.

375

After the attack, it was a long time before Paul finally re-membered what had happened. He suddenly said one day, when we'd been talking about something else and he was looking blank and not listening, "My God, you're right. It was that damned madman. It was Mike," he said, and looked at me like a sword. It was as if he had said to me, "It was you!"'

Paul never blamed Lily for getting too involved with Mike, but since she blamed herself bitterly, it did not make any difference.

At first, while he was still very weak and not able to move about much, he was his same old sweet self; but as he began to creep back into life and be more active, the cycles of headaches and depression began, and he was not so much himself, as his sick self. A new sick self who had bursts of temper and said un-characteristically irritable things to Lily and the girls, even to the animals. Arthur was the only one who could never annoy him. The dog kept close to Paul, moving his back leg stiffly, next to the leg on which Paul limped.

The sledge-hammer blow had ruptured his ear drum, and he was still rather deaf on that side. Cathy's voice was quiet, and he would snap at her, 'What? Don't mumble.'

Obligingly, she moved round to his good side. 'That better, Daddy?'

'Oh, God, don't be so nice to me. Why don't you all walk out? Let me rot. I'm no use to you.'

When one of them offered help, he might say peevishly, 'I'm all *right*. Don't fuss.'

'Don't *you* fuss, then,' Lily was driven to retort.

'What?'

'Calm down, darling. Remember how you were the one who was always so calm?'

'How can I be calm when things are in such a mess?'

He fussed about nothing, or panicked, because he could not remember, or could not understand. Harry had found a young couple to run the tack shop and the stable, and Paul was often on their necks, criticizing and agitating and wanting to take charge of things himself, when it was almost all he could do to walk with his stick over the uneven ground down to the barn.

Once Lily found him in Robin's loose box, a fork in his hand, leaning against the wall with his eyes shut. He had been trying to muck out. The wheelbarrow was in the doorway, with some of the dirty bedding in it.

'Paul – darling, you –' No. Mustn't say, 'You shouldn't.' 'Let me help you,' she said.

He opened his eyes and looked at her without seeing. Then he jerked his face away, tipped his head up, and slid down the wall to lie in the shavings, jerking and shaking. Lily pulled the barrow out of the way and knelt down to hold him, until the brief seizure was over, and he went limp, and opened his eyes and smiled innocently up at her.

Afterwards, with the doctor, he couldn't remember the fit, nor being able to walk from the stable to the car. Dr Monroe thought it was part of a cycle of pain and headaches, caused probably by scar tissue.

'Could it happen to me again?' Paul was recovered, but sleepy.

'Not likely.' Dr Monroe always gave you the best news. He believed in the possibility that you could make things happen by believing that they would. 'But it means you won't be able to drive.'

'Oh, *God*.' Paul slumped and sulked like a child unfairly chastised. He actually had not driven his car yet, but the news that it was forbidden made him feel trapped.

'I've got to get going again,' he grumbled restlessly to Lily. 'Why do you all hold me back?'

But the next day, he told her, 'I feel lousy. I don't want to get up,' and would not let her even open the curtains.

'Bad headache?'

'Not even that excuse. I just feel, kind of . . . undone.'

Once when he didn't come in for dinner, he was in the office behind the shop, with papers and bills muddled all over the desk and file drawers open. He sat with his head in his hands. Lily thought he was crying, but when she spoke to him and he raised his head, his face was dry.

He had lost weight in the last weeks. It was very painful to see the lovely triangular shape of his broad-cheeked, smiling face narrowed and bonier, the skin looser, dry and colourless. Sometimes now his blue eyes which had always been so hopeful looked haunted by troubles that Lily could not know or comfort.

'Come on in for dinner.'

'I've got to get these orders straight. But I can't, Lily, I can't. What's happened to me?'

'You're not ready for this yet. Your head has got to heal.' Lily bent and picked up off the floor the glasses that he had to wear now. 'Anthea will straighten it out in the morning.'

'I want to do it. She doesn't know what she's doing. Her experience has been in a different kind of business. She can't understand the way I've built this up.'

Anthea came to Lily and said, 'I know he's not well yet, but it is hard to do things right for him. You know that Frank and I will have to leave in the spring anyway. Maybe it would be better if we —'

'Wait. Hang on. It will be all right.'

'You should make a tape of that, Mud,' Isobel told her. 'You say it all the time.'

'Well, it will be all right. We've just all got to hang on. One day soon, things will be back to where they were.'

Dr Monroe, fatherly and reassuring in his British-style tweeds and old rowing-club ties, continued to be hopeful. Medication had controlled the seizures. Paul had only had one more. Isobel, alone with him in the house, had heard him call out, and found him shaking and scared in the bath, teeth chattering, his hands trying to hold on to the sides, water sloshing.

She had held him and calmed him and found the right pills, and helped him out and dried him and got him into his bathrobe and into bed.

She and Cathy had always wandered in and out of their parents' bathroom when they were children. 'It's a bit different when your daughter is sixteen,' Paul said afterwards.

'Were you shy?' Cathy asked.

'We didn't have time for that,' Paul said. 'It was a crisis we were in together.'

Since Paul's moods had made him more difficult, the stormy scenes of Isobel's childhood had recurred a few times. Lily was happy to see them so close.

The neurologist in Boston was hopeful too. The cycles of pain and depression were still intense, but they seemed to be further apart.

When Nora came over, on the heels of a blizzard, which caused her to observe, 'It's a white world,' five times during the drive from the airport, she was helpful to Lily, and comfortable to have around. Paul was fond of her. She had always adored him, and she showed her love and sympathy in the busy, practical ways which she had perfected all through her life. With her mother taking some of the load, Lily realized how exhausted she was, far more tired than when she used to drive seventy miles each way and put in a day's work in Boston, and shop and clean the house, and go chasing off after emergency clients in her spare time.

Away from Duggie, Nora was her old self, which was comforting and peaceful for this household where so much had changed. Her grey hair was still set in the same neat, old-fashioned way. She had brought the old fur-coat which had seen her through many Oxfordshire winters, and a new pair of her usual broad fawn suede boots, which made her look like a cart pony. Her red-veined cheeks were smooth and round. Her hands were plump and soft, after nearly five years of Duggie doing the washing-up and the heavy cleaning.

Isobel and Cathy, who had been mystified by the improbable exploits of their staid, cosy grandmother, wanted to talk openly about the break up of her marriage to James.

'Old devil, he is,' Isobel said. 'Remember when he fell in love with Paige at the theatre? He even told Dodo about it at the drug store, when we were having our raspberry sodas. Even when I was little, I used to wonder sometimes how you put up with him.'

'Oh, it was quite all right, my dear,' Nora said, ironing in the living-room, so she could watch the television soaps. 'Froth and bubble. Marriage is a lottery, as you'll find out one day. Swings and roundabouts, *I* say.'

'You probably shouldn't have walked out though, Gran.' Cathy was very moral. 'But perhaps if you hadn't, *he* might have.'

379

'Grandpa? Oh, no, dear.' Nora would not criticize James, especially to her granddaughters, who were still children to her, although they had always talked about everything with Paul and Lily and had both become very mature and responsible since that ghastly early morning of November 7th, when Mike split their world asunder, like Vulcan parting the clouds with thunder.

With Nora there, Lily was able to drive up to Boston to see Martha and to collect the books and papers that she had left in the office at Crisis.

She had sent in her resignation, but Martha was irritatingly persistent in telling her, 'You're on leave, not resigned. Take as much time as you need, and come back to us when Paul is better.'

'I won't want to. I don't want to do anything like this any more.'

'Do you think calamity will make you change your ways? Look at some of our customers.'

'No, I'd be no use. I couldn't help anybody now.'

How could Martha even ask her? With her candid, weathered face and her chopped brindle hair, and her sneakers and the faded jeans too tight across the womanly bottom she tried to ignore, Martha was so totally wrapped up in Crisis that she was impervious to what was going on in the world outside.

As Lily had been. Sometimes when she looked at her battered Paul, in the dark glasses he had to wear when the headaches messed up his eyes, and saw the beloved face, that used to be so serene and smiling, drawn and puzzled and in pain, she thought about the Judge on that long-ago Easter at the ham lunch, 'with all the fixin's'. Lily in her red dress ranting so earnestly about involvement, and the Judge with his mixed metaphor about not plunging in up to the neck: 'It could sow the seeds of ruin.'

She tortured herself, going back and back to that.

In bed with Paul, their bodies could occasionally reach each other. Often he was frustrated and distressed. Lily's instinct was to hold him close, fiercely close, force it to be the way it used to be, not let him turn away to the edge of the bed.

She and Nora came back from the supermarket with the car filled with bags of all the stupid things that seemed necessary to keep life rolling along; more of them with Nora here, since she could not pass any new displays or special offers.

As they came up the road, a car was turning out of their drive. Paul was in the stable yard with Arthur, cleaning one of the horses, tied up to a ring outside the barn.

'Who was that?'

'Summer people. They're going to board two horses and two ponies.'

Oh, *no*. With Peter and Anthea leaving, even if we have to close the tack shop for a while, how will we manage? Paul can't possibly do the work.

He was happy, out here with the horse, working slowly and thoroughly, holding Robin's thick tail in one hand and brushing it out in strands.

'I think I'll go for a short ride.'

'I'll come,' Lily said.

'No, you unpack the groceries, or Nora will put them away in a new system.'

Lily did not want him to go out alone, but she could not stop him. Arthur, who could not run with the horses now, sat at the end of the drive and waited. Paul came back quite soon, thank God.

'How did it go?'

'Fine.'

Paul looked a bit shaky. 'I had to come back because I want to start moving hay out of the end boxes,' he said as an excuse.

Four extra horses – how was she going to stop this? Could she call the owners and explain?

'Who are these people? They had a New Jersey licence plate. Where do they live?'

'Don't worry. I'll be dealing with them. It's not going to make extra work for you.'

'I didn't *mean* that.' Lily took John's reins, to lead him in, but Paul took the reins from her.

Frank had left everything ready for Paul to bring the horses in and feed them, but he stayed out there for a long time, as darkness fell and it grew cold. Lily's normal self would have barged out and said, 'Let me help,' not bothering about what Paul wanted. Now she had to be contained and careful, not knowing if he wanted her out there or not, not even able to go and ask him.

She stood by the glass of the back door, looking out at the light in the barn. When Nora came and put an arm round her, she began to cry.

'What's happened to us all? Our lives were so secure and unchanging, and now your life and Daddy's is turned upside down, and Paul and I – my poor safe Paul – we had everything we wanted. He was so happy! Mum, it's not fair. He was so happy.'

She slumped at the kitchen table and sobbed rendingly, out of control. She had not cried much, because it made her feel too ravaged, and she could not let Paul see. When the stable lights went out, Nora took her upstairs to weep.

'What's happened to us, Mum? It wasn't meant to be like this.'

Soon after, Lily let herself get angry with Paul, because she thought he was unfair to Cathy. Cathy was taking a music exam, and she had to practise the piano, but it never seemed to be the right time when the noise would not bother Paul.

She was starting a dog obedience class for some of the children in the village. When he went outside, he was upset because they were all out there in the field with their assorted mutts and mongrels, calling and whistling and shrieking hysterically at stubborn rebels and threatened dog fights.

'Come and help judge, Daddy,' Cathy called. 'We're doing tests.'

He turned and went back into the house.

'Why take it out on her?' Lily heard herself grumble, quite nastily.

I'm glad Lily chewed me out. Better than knocking herself out to be so patient all the time. Like poor little Cathy. When I told her not to play the piano, she said, so damned amiably, 'You play, then, Daddy.'

I can't. My fingers slip off the keys. I blur the bass. Terry used to show me new chords on his guitar, but now I can't follow. I hear it wrong. When the sledge-hammer hits me again and the pain and nausea start, I'm deaf and blind. When the pain goes, sometimes everything else goes. They all fade away from me. I can't reach them. I can't feel. I'm lost.

I'm fifty. I think I'm impotent. 'It will be all right,' Lily says. 'Lie with me, like this, like when we were in Iceland and you wouldn't do it.' She was a fat baby, and desperate, and I was so smug and paternal.

I can't always remember much of last month, last week, but everything about the golden past. When you love only the past, you're getting old. I'm old. I look at the back of my head in Terry's picture, and then I look in the mirror that Lily hung next to it, 'So you can see the front of you as well as the back,' and I see this old grey sick man, and new lines are being drawn in every day.

Terry says I look glamorously consumptive. 'Keep the limp,' he says. 'It's romantic.' I wish he'd stayed here and not gone dodging off to Boston. 'If you're okay, Dad, I'll go and see some friends.'

'And your mother.'

'I guess.'

Would Barbara also nag at Terry about getting into a proper career? Why doesn't he come back, so we can talk? Because he doesn't want to hear what I want to say.

'Lily, how about calling Terry and see if he'll come down next weekend?'

'Of course, darling.'

If he won't, she'll make up an excuse that won't hurt my feelings.

The elm trees are hazed with green. The pines have pushed out bright new fingertips. Blossom foams and there are tiny violets scattered along the paths where we used to ride so joyfully in the spring. The horses were shedding lumps of winter hair from their hot stomachs, and were wild to gallop when the wind swung sweetly round to the west and rushed into their faces.

I can't ride. My balance has gone. When I got on Robin yesterday, the ground tilted up. Tony reached up to help me off.

'Don't!' I yelled at him. 'Leave me alone.' I don't want him around here so much. Isobel isn't a child now.

Isobel's father grumbled to her, 'Why don't you have any white boyfriends?'

Daddy, of all people. He was the most unprejudiced person Isobel knew. Everybody was racist in varying degrees, even if they didn't admit it or even realize it; but her father genuinely wasn't. Or wasn't *then*. Since November, life for all of them was divided into then and now.

He had loved Tony. He had taken an interest in him since they first came here, and helped him to grow up, and taught him about horses.

'There's your mate,' Mud would say to Daddy when she saw Tony coming up through the field. They were always working on projects together.

'It's his injury.' Tony was amazingly forgiving about Paul's new attitude. 'It isn't him talking, see. It's still that old hammer. It's that frigging Mike, it's all his fault. I hope they put him away for ever.'

Now that Tony was working as crew on the island ferries, Isobel saw less of him. If he was on the late boat to Nantucket, he would stay over there and do the early-morning run next day. He would be on the boats long hours for several days, and then have a few days off, but he often spent them on Nantucket, where he had friends.

When he was twenty-one, he had moved out of his parents' house, as a sort of coming-of-age ritual, to a pad of his own in Mashpee, where most of his cousins lived. He had taken Isobel there a few times. It was a tiny little place, like a hut in the woods, with a sofa-bed in the one room and a lean-to kitchen and shower at the back. Isobel cleaned it for him, and helped him to clear away enough scrub oaks to dig and plant a vegetable garden. The blinds were old, so she made curtains for the windows.

'What are you making?' Her father came into her bedroom when he heard the sewing-machine.

In the old days, he would have been pleased to hear her say, 'Curtains and a tablecloth for Tony's house.' Now she had to say, 'Curtains for a girl at school's room.'

'Bit jazzy.' Her father picked up a piece of the bright patterned fabric and blinked.

'He likes it. She does, I mean, and her boyfriend does.'

Now that the crisis had settled down into part of family life, they all coped with it day by day, and it sometimes seemed as if it had always been with them. But once in a while, when Daddy's migraine was bad and he couldn't talk or eat or sleep, and threw up all night in the bathroom, it hit Isobel with such an overwhelming sorrow that she could hardly stand it. Friends noticed a difference in her at school. She couldn't study. She dropped out of the class play. There were days when she dreaded getting home to find out what was going on.

When Tony had three days off, her friend Linda, who had her licence and the use of one of her parents' cars, took Isobel over to Mashpee.

She cooked some fish and vegetables and she and Tony drank some wine, and she begged him not to take her home. Their kisses and petting had become more intense lately, as Tony's caution dissolved. Tonight, the despair that had been building up in her for weeks exploded in a fury of tears that engulfed them both. Then they were on the floor, and away from the world, and out of their minds with a passion that carried Isobel beyond the pain and the moment of fear into a soaring triumph.

It was done. At last it was done. She wasn't a child. She could do this just as well as anyone else. Better, because Tony kept saying, 'It was never like this, I swear. Never with anybody. Only you, Bella.'

'Better than the Indian girl on Nantucket?'

'What Indian girl?' She was a joke between them, whether she existed or not. Isobel had invented that she had a gold tooth and long black greasy braids. 'I don't know no Indian girl on Nantucket.'

Isobel got up and drank some wine and called her mother and told her she was staying the night with Linda, and called Linda to warn her, in case Paul was in trouble and her mother needed her. She pulled out the sofa-bed and straightened the bedding and plumped up the pillows in a domesticated way, and turned on the small lamp and switched off the ceiling light. Then she took off what was left of her clothes and got into Tony's bed, and he started to teach her some of the things she needed to know to further the progress of her sex life.

Linda owed her something, because Isobel had helped her when she was depressed after she had to have an abortion, so she went along with being used as an alibi. Once, when Isobel was with Tony, her mother did call Linda, and Linda came over to Tony's and beat on the door, and they shouted, 'Get lost!' because they thought it was one of Tony's cousins playing tricks.

Linda took Isobel home, very fast through the night, swerving round corners because she had a right to, in an emergency. Cathy was sick, with a fever, and Daddy was very restless and jumpy. Mum needed to go to the hospital for his pills, which she had forgotten to pick up during the day.

He had not told her the bottle ,was almost empty. She should have looked. Poor Mud. She stuffed her nightgown into a pair of slacks and pulled on a sweater, and roared off without combing her hair.

Cathy was asleep, flushed and damp, with her arms flung out and her feet kicked out of the bedclothes. Isobel covered her up and went to sit with her father.

'Good girl,' he told her. 'I can always count on you. You'll always be there for me, won't you, Iz?'

While her mother was gone, Isobel brought the backgammon board upstairs, and he played distractedly, wanting to win, but not wanting her to let him win, which was how she herself had felt, as a child.

'Who taught you to play so cunningly?' he complained when she won.

'You did.'

'Good for me. Good for you. Good girl.'

Isobel did not feel strange or guilty that she had got up from Tony's tumbled bed to come to him. She felt proud and adventurous. She was a grown-up. She could love her father even more, as an equal. She had something of her own now.

Terry was amazed that his father and Lily were not bitter or angry against the man who had attacked him. Mike seemed irrelevant to their present situation, as if the assault were an act of God.

Isobel and Cathy were encouraged not to feel hatred.

'What good would it do?' Lily said sadly. 'It wouldn't hurt Mike, and it would only poison you.'

Terry thought he was the only one who openly hated Mike's guts. If the man had not been locked up, he would have stalked him and shot or knifed him on a dark night. He tried to go and visit him in the county gaol, but Mike refused to see him.

'If I was you,' Terry told his father, 'I'd think about him every day. I'd blast him with evil vibes and damn his soul to hell for what he did.'

'I've got enough to do coping with the results of that.' His father smiled in his old equable way that showed more teeth, now that his face was thinner.

'You'll have to give evidence at the trial. How will you like standing up there looking at him?'

'I think they usually let you sit,' his father said. 'Especially if you've been ill.'

In some ways, he was like himself. In others, the brain injury had changed him. He had never nagged at Terry before about what he was going to do with his life. He had understood when he dropped out of art college, and been glad of Terry's ability to get jobs. Now he harped on his inability to keep them. Terry had got to have a career. He must reapply to the art college. Or go to business college. Or get in on the ground floor of some big firm.

Terry did not want to be at the Cape Cod house all the time. He had nowhere to stay in Boston, so he went to Amy's apartment and asked her if he could have a bed. She was cooking pasta and vegetables for herself when he turned up, but she added chicken and all kinds of other things and gave him a most marvellous meal, with subtle hints of herbs, unlike Lily, who either threw in too many, or forgot. All or nothing.

She was touchingly glad to see him. Amy never played games

to make you guess how she felt. Terry stayed for a week or two, but it was awkward for Amy, because she was involved with another man, and could not have him at the apartment while Terry was there.

'If you would stay for keeps,' she told Terry candidly, 'I'd find some way to get rid of Bennett.'

'I wish I could.'

'Why can't you?'

'Don't let's go into that again. I'm years away from committing myself, you know that.'

'Since you left, I've had another guy like you who ducked out to save his skin. So what are women supposed to do until you all grow up?'

'That's not like you, Amy.' She had sounded fierce.

'I know, but I'm fed up. That's why I'm tempted by Bennett. He actually wants to buy a house and marry me.'

'Go ahead.' Terry laughed. He and Amy had always laughed at people who got sucked into marriage.

'I just might.' She hung her long mole-coloured hair down and then swept it back in the way she had, which did not stop it falling forward again.

What with that, and his father fussing at him about a career, and his mother's lack of interest in anything he might do (which was almost as bad), Terry thought he might as well go back to the hotel in Aberdeen, as long as Dad was doing all right.

Paul seemed sorry when Terry left, although pleased that he had not thought it necessary to wait around and watch his father die.

'You can all get used to the idea,' Paul told Lily. 'I'm going to be all right. I'll have the tack shop open again by the middle of summer, and maybe some other boarders besides the New Jersey people.'

'Do you really think you can manage?'

'No.' He screwed up his eyes as he did when they hurt, and

opened them wide to look searchingly at her. 'But I'll have a damn good try.'

'I know you will. I knew you could beat this.'

'You didn't. You thought I was dying. I could see that. I thought so myself. I didn't care. It's interesting. When you're so out of it, you're half dead already, and it would be no trouble just to let yourself go the whole way. But when you're alive and well, it looks as if dying would be very harsh and difficult. That's the fear. Dying. Not being dead.'

They had taken Arthur with Cathy's two dogs for a walk down to Hidden Harbor, along the inlet where the mussels clung to the sticky bank, and out on to the beach, their favourite place to be.

'Let's go on the bay side.' Lily followed the dogs, who were running on to the crescent of sand where the cormorants kept watch on the rock, gowned in their black wigs like mouldy clergy. This was Paul's first time to be here since the attack. She did not want him to see the place where it had happened.

'What? No, come on. Down here in the reeds. I thought that was why you brought me here, to exorcize the demons. I thought Donna's self-help group had told you to do that.'

'Paul – I don't think I want to.' He did not hear her, so she came across to him. It was all still much too clear. The blue sweater half hidden in the grey sea grass. His fair hair dark and matted into the hideous wound. The noise of his breathing, and the worse silence when it stopped. Arthur's back legs lying in the water.

The other two dogs had stayed on the open beach. Arthur had turned to follow them to the inlet and was nosing about in the same place where Lily had found him, trying to hook up shells with a clumsy front paw.

'I've remembered something else.' Paul was down there with him at the edge of the water. 'This is where Cathy ties up her boat. The stake had pulled loose and Mike had brought the sledge-hammer down to knock it in for her.'

'I thought you knew that.'

'No. I thought he'd carried the hammer down here to do me in.' Paul found the stake and pounded it in as well as he could with a rock.

'I'll have to bring the sledge down to get it firm enough.'

'You'll need to buy another one, then. The one which – the one that was ours is being held by the court.'

They stayed on the beach a long time, walking slowly beside the subdued hush, hush of the small breaking waves, picking up wet pebbles and looking for a butterfly shell that had not been broken by the winter.

'When we do die,' Paul said, 'let's come back as something that lives here all the time. A rock, I wouldn't mind, or a hermit crab living in one of those black snail shells. Waiting for the tide to come up and wash over me, waiting for the tide to recede and let me feel the sun.'

'How do you know we'll be together?'

'I don't know anything. No point in going through this life if you knew all the answers. But if we've been together before, that explains why we knew each other, at the coffee machine.'

'I knew you in the plane,' Lily said. 'When you looked at me with those eyes that turned my stomach to water, and said, "I don't want you to be scared."'

'Did I? I was nicer then. I'm a pain in the neck now.'

'It's not *your* fault.'

'You're supposed to say, "No, you're not." Oh, God!' He put a hand to his scarred head where the hair was growing fuzzily in again. 'Flashing lights. I shouldn't have bent down.'

'Pain?'

'Threatening.' His eyes were shut, his front teeth clamped over his bottom lip. 'Help me up to the path, my darling. I don't want to fall.'

Donna had encouraged Lily to come to her women's group, to get some support in the long ordeal of Paul's illness. It was a group of ordinary women, most of them married, some dumb, some quick and perceptive, which had started out in the sixties days of Consciousness Raising. Now it was all right to call themselves simply a women's group, and be more practical and less self-conscious.

They had taken up, rather belatedly, the therapeutic vogue for 'letting the anger out', as a blanket solution to all ills. Lily must be angry about the gross wrong done to Paul, and what it had done to her life.

'Talk about it, tell us,' they urged, these kind, sincere, perennially tanned women, with their Cape Cod sneakers and their glasses in expensive Nantucket baskets, decorated with a scrimshaw whale. 'Swear. Yell if you want. It will be such a release for you to let the anger out.'

Lily shook her head. 'I'm not angry.'

'Say it. Tell it. Rage away. Say anything you want. You're safe with us.'

The only thing she wanted to say was, 'It was my fault,' but she couldn't. To disguise the guilt, dutifully she fell on her knees and punched a cushion, feeling absurd, but glad that they were pleased with her for doing it. They were all so sympathetic and encouraging, it was enough just to be with them.

With all the effort she had put in at Crisis, trying to find answers for other people, and plan the next step, and trying to ginger up defeated clients to lift themselves out of their mess, the most useful thing was probably just being with them. I thought I was Dear Doctor Lily, giver of counsel, but it wasn't much I did at all.

One day in the town, a woman stopped her outside the cleaners and said, 'Lily?'

'Yes. Do I – ?' She did not remember having seen the woman before. She was too vague, these days.

'We only met once, briefly. Margaret Spence. You got to know my husband pretty well. You helped him so much.'

Richard Spence! My God, a name from the past which had been part of her life for weeks after the failure of his business, and his despairing intent to escape the people he had let down, by shooting himself.

'How is he?'

'He's all right. After he decided to go on living, he was able to start again. We're living here now, running a motel.'

'That's wonderful. I'm so glad I met you.'

'So am I. I wanted to tell you.' Margaret looked down, then at the traffic, then up at Lily. 'How do you thank someone for giving you back your husband?'

Lily went on, smiling, into the cleaner's, feeling better. Much better than punching pillows.

One night, Lily woke up because Paul was thrashing about in the bed.

'What's the matter, darling?'

'God-awful headache. The pills don't touch it.'

He was sitting up, rubbing his neck. She turned on the light.

'Turn it off. I – oh, God, Lily –' He turned away and vomited into the pillow.

Lily called Dr Monroe. 'He's really bad. I don't know what to do.'

'I'll call the ambulance. Better get him to Boston, to be safe.'

At the hospital, after a CAT scan and a spinal tap that showed blood in the spinal fluid, they told Lily that Paul had suffered another haemorrhage, undoubtedly from the original damage.

'We'd like to operate, but he's not in any shape for it.'

'And if you don't?' Feeling like a lost child, Lily was surprised at how grown up and sensible she sounded.

'He may die, he may not. An operation would almost certainly kill him.'

Wordless and disbelieving, Lily and her daughters watched Paul slip slowly from unconsciousness into death. His agreeable face and his poor violated head, his gentle hands, his compact, agile body, from one moment to the next were no more than an abandoned, empty casing.

Lily and Isobel and Cathy had never seen anybody die. Instinctively, they all looked towards the open window, where bright specks of dust drifted out into the sunlight.

In the county gaol, Mike wore dark green cotton pants and a green T-shirt, because the gaol was very hot, winter and summer. The clothes had no pockets, so he carried his cigarette pack twisted up into his left sleeve, like a freak biceps.

Most of the time, there was nothing to do but smoke and gossip. When the weather improved and the ground thawed, there was some work to do outside. There were tattered paperbacks in the library, and AA meetings, which Mike attended from time to time, because there was coffee, and there was nothing else to do.

Like the time before, in another gaol, it was degrading and noisy and raw and relentlessly boring. No one seemed to know when his trial date would be. He wanted it and dreaded it. His lawyer seemed to have no idea how it would go. Conviction could mean a few months or a few years in the House of Correction. It could mean Bridgewater again, which inmates called 'The Ranch'. Sometimes a guy would fake being crazy, because there was a myth that life was easier there, but Mike told anyone who was not too bored with the subject to listen to him, 'If they send me back to The Ranch, I'll hang it up.'

One Monday of black thoughts, he went before the gaol master and was told that his trial date would be next month. That evening before they were locked into the cells, Phil Hogan said, 'You know that guy.'

'What guy?'

'The guy whose head you pulverized.'

'He asked for it.'

'Oh, sure, you got your reasons. We all do.'

'That's why they don't listen to us.'

'That guy's dead.'

'Cut it out.'

People like Phil plucked news out of the air, and it was all around the gaol with the speed of light, sometimes right, sometimes wrong.

'He's okay,' Mike said. 'That kind always are.'

'Not this baby. I heard he died. You got given your trial date today, huh?'

'Uh-huh.'

'Forget it. They got to have time to change the charge. You're in the big league now, fella.'

Mike hated Phil Hogan, who was fat and white, with tits like a woman under his T-shirt. 'Lay off me, will ya?'

'They'll try you for murder now.'

The Sheriff boasted that men did not commit suicide in his gaol, but there were many ways to hang it up, and they had all been tried. A sheet could be soaked or twisted to make it harder to loosen. People had drunk bleach or swallowed razor blades. They had put their heads in plastic bags and their fingers into light sockets, overdosed on water, stuffed socks down their throats or banged their skulls against the floor.

After Mike found out from one of the officers that Phil was telling the truth, he hanged himself by his bootlaces from the heating grille in his cell.

Ten

'**W**here have you gone? Where are you?'

Lily wandered from room to room of the house, and all over the land that was theirs. She walked on the haunted beach with her weeping face raised to the sky.

'Where are you?'

Long ago, she had faced the truth that he might die. All through his slow recovery, through the hopes and the anxieties, she had made herself remember the possibility of his dying, and what she would do. Now, any strength or sense that she thought she had built up was wiped out by the shock of the dizzying emptiness.

He wasn't there.

She realized that when she had imagined how it would be if he died, it was with a vague notion that he would be dead and somehow still there at the same time.

'Where have you gone? What are you doing? Paul! Paul!'

The seagulls mocked her cries.

For days that became weeks, her whole being was flooded with water. Tears poured out of her without sobs. Her eyes were sore and swollen in her drowned face. She brushed her hair without looking at herself in the mirror, and occasionally dabbed on useless make-up that would be washed off quite soon.

Cathy slept with her. They talked and cried and were sorry for themselves, as they could not be in front of other people. When Cathy began to sigh deeply, and then fell asleep, with the smaller dog behind her bent knees, Lily lay stiffly on her back and stared through the dark ceiling, which was the nearest she could get to Paul. The hot night tears stung her tortured eyes and ran down the sides of her face into her neck.

After Lily and Isobel and Cathy had come home from the hospital alone, and Lily's friend Nina was getting them something to eat, a barking outside announced a rather grand truck coming down the drive. It was Paul's famous people from New Jersey, bringing their horses and ponies for the summer.

Nina's husband, Sam, went out to deal with them. They stood around for a bit, looking nonplussed, and then they turned the truck and left.

The tack shop was closed and the two other boarding horses had been taken away, but Lily was glad to have the care of John and Robin and the pony: familiar physical work among the good smells and textures, the horses absorbed in their unchanging daily routines, Arthur lying in the sun across the barn doorway. He was not visibly pining for Paul, but he had attached himself very closely to Lily.

Isobel found her in Robin's loose box, crying while she forked manure out of the shavings. Her daughters were more help to her than she was able to be to them. She could not feel their pain separately, only as a component of her own anguish.

'Dr Monroe called to see how we were doing.' Isobel had tied back her strong curling hair challengingly from her exhausted face, while Cathy let her cobweb hair float forward in a misty curtain. 'I said okay. He didn't want me to bring you up from the barn. He said he'd call again.'

'Did he talk to you?'

'Yes. He said if Daddy had lived, he could have got much worse, physically and mentally. "He's been spared that," he said, "and so have all of you."'

'I don't care!' Lily flung the fork into the wheelbarrow and covered her face with her hands. 'I want him here. I want him back – sick, crazy, helpless, crippled – I want him here on any terms. I'd nurse him and take care of him for the rest of my life. I don't want my life – I want him back!'

Isobel put her arms round her mother and let Lily cry into her hair. She didn't say anything. There was nothing to say. She knew that too well herself.

Paul had died before Terry could get there. His resentment about that simmered at the front of his gloom and silences until the rage beneath it inevitably surfaced and boiled over.

He stayed in the house longer than Lily expected, longer than he ever had before. He ate and drank a lot, but would not help with anything about the place. He whispered in corners with

398

Isobel, and was quite rude to Lily in a way that reminded her of their struggles when he was ten years old and she was first married to his father. He would not share his grief with her. Engrossed in her own, she could not make the effort to reach him.

One night, when he had been drinking quite a lot, Lily asked him what his plans were. He was sitting low down in Paul's deep chair with his feet on a stool. His hair, which had been long and bushy when he came over, had been chopped raggedly by himself, after Cathy threatened to cut it. He wore Paul's shirts, un-laundered. At twenty-six, he was old enough to put them in Lily's machine by himself, but he hardly ever did. His bare feet were dirty, the toe nails broken.

'So tell me, Terry.' When the June evening cooled, Lily came in from outside. She had been lying in the long chair under a bright half moon, trying to sail with it through small silver clouds. Such an evening that used to take her and Paul out to the field where the horses grazed, and the grey cat balanced along the top rail of the fence. 'What are your plans?'

'What plans? I guess I'll just stay here for a while in my father's house.'

'Pity you never stayed as long when he was here.' She knew, even as she started, that she shouldn't say it.

'You force me to remind you.' Terry looked up at her with his eyes narrowed spitefully. 'That it was a pity you didn't give up charging around Boston pretending to save the world, while he was alive.'

'Oh, God.' Lily stepped back against the wall as if he had punched her.

Isobel, who was sitting on the floor in front of the television, looked round over her shoulder. She had been drinking too. Her glass of wine was on the carpet. Lily thought she would attack Terry, but she said, 'I used to tell you, Mud. Daddy was fed up with it.'

'He wasn't. You didn't.'

'You didn't want to hear. You thought he thought everything you did was wonderful.' Isobel turned all the way round, the television screen blabbering and rioting behind her. 'So you got away with it.'

'Isobel, don't, I —'

'You know what you did.' Terry suddenly swung down his feet and leaped up, knocking over Isobel's wine-glass.

'Look, please — stop this. I'm going to bed.'

'No.' Terry kicked a small chair out of the way and came to stand in front of Lily, moving his clenched fists as if he would hit her. 'You know what you did. It was your fault — that crazy, fucked-up Mike. I'm glad he killed himself. Best thing he ever did.'

'Terry, don't. What good will that do now?'

'Oh, yeah, of course. One of your beloved underdogs. Still in love with the no-hopers, and look what it did to us all!'

Isobel scrambled up, shots and shrieking tyres behind her.

Terry jutted his anguished face forwards and screamed, 'You killed my father!'

'Don't, don't,' Lily moaned. 'Don't you know I think that all the time? You're right, it was my fault. I wondered when you'd say that. Thanks very much, Terry. I hope you feel better.'

Surprised, Terry opened his fists. He raised his arms sideways helplessly and let them fall. Lily still stood backed away from him, rolling her head from side to side against the wall.

'Don't, Mud.' Isobel pushed Terry aside and took her mother's hand. 'You didn't know . . . How could you know?'

'I should have.' Lily went away from them, to lift her feet with difficulty up the stairs, hanging on to the rail like an old woman. Nothing could relieve the heaviness of her guilt, which had a life of its own, apart from her.

At the top of the stairs, she leaned on the windowsill and looked out at the whitened lawn and the dark mass of the old barn, riding like a high ship below the stars.

Guilt couldn't help Paul. It could not help her children, or Terry, and if she let it increase its stranglehold, it would ruin her.

The seeds of ruin. Well, she had sown them, and this was the harvest.

One night after Cathy had moved back to her own room, Lily's exhaustion played its game of dropping her into sleep over a book and then bringing her wide awake as soon as she turned out the light and laid down her head. Arthur snored on his bed in the corner. The night was endless. When she could not stand her circular sick thoughts any longer, she got up and went into Isobel's room.

The bed was neatly made. Isobel's purse was not there. In the kitchen, the keys of Paul's car, which she had been driving since she got her licence, were gone from the hook.

When Lily went back upstairs, the dog in Cathy's room barked, and Cathy woke.

'Where's Isobel?' Lily went in to her.

'Gone to Linda's?'

'Not in the middle of the night. She didn't go to bed till after twelve. Do you think she's all right?'

'Don't worry.' Cathy pulled the sheet up to her chin protectively and said in a small voice, 'She's probably with Tony.'

'At his place?'

'Mm.'

'Does she go there often?'

'I thought you'd guessed.'

'I suppose I did, but I didn't really want to know, because I couldn't say anything to Daddy.'

The extravagantly beautiful Cape Cod summer was wasting its time. Day after day of intense blue skies and tireless sun. It might as well be cold and grey and raining.

Visitors came and went. The phone seemed to ring all the time; Boston friends, people in the village, friends Lily and Paul had made during nearly ten years on the Cape, all so kind and considerate. They invited her to their houses for supper. She did not want to go anywhere, but she must, so that they could feel pleased that they had done something for her.

Weeds grew among her flowers. Crab grass crept over the lawn. Spiders' webs in ceiling corners were larders of dead flies. Slats fell out of the shutters. In the barn, the feed-room was unswept. Straw from hay bales was not hanging on a nail, but tangled on the floor.

Lily put off and put off deciding what to do with the stock in the tack shop. She hardly ever rode, or went to the beach to swim. She went into rooms for a purpose she forgot, and stood looking round vaguely, touching things, putting out a hand to pick something up, drawing the hand back, wandering out.

At one point, she turned Paul's picture to the wall, because it seemed that she stood trapped in the shadows under the English beech trees, watching helplessly while Paul would get up with his hair full of light and move into the distance away from her.

Terry turned the picture back the right way.

She thought she might be going insane. The idea of escape preoccupied her more and more. She could not stay here like this.

When she went to Donna's women's group, wearing a bright flowered shirt that Paul had bought in Hawaii, the women explained to her that she was trying to escape from the pain.

'Wait a year,' they said. 'Don't do anything in a hurry. You need your home.'

'No, no, I can't stand it. There's no reason for me to be here now. It doesn't feel like my home. It's not my house any more. It was *ours*.'

One Friday, she went to the city to talk to the lawyer. Isobel had a summer job as a waitress. Cathy was a counsellor at a small children's day-camp in the village. Tony had helped Terry to get work at Woods Hole, parking cars for the ferries. Lily went to Boston alone.

Each year, the traffic was worse. She fretted and stewed on the way home, as she used to when she drove home late from Crisis and she was afraid Paul would be upset and ask, 'Where have you *been*?'

He never said that, but he always came out of the house as soon as he heard her car, looking anxious.

At the place where the cooler air from Cape Cod Bay began to mingle with the inland heat and then gradually took over, her mind cleared.

I don't need to fret and push and hurry and take risks to pass. The girls will get their supper if they want it, if they're home. I'm free.

I don't want freedom.

Use it, said the strong sane part of her that had been lying dormant under the flooded wallowing and dithering and guilt and craziness.

Experimenting with the freedom, she went back another day to Newton and stayed with her friend Josephine who was now divorced, and went to the theatre with Harry and saw a few other people.

Harry did not want to talk about Paul, because it made him unhappy, and he wanted to enjoy his evening. Lily still needed to bring Paul into the conversation whenever possible, although she had already sensed that this made some people uncomfortable. When she said yet again, 'Paul used to say . . .' or 'Paul and I went there . . .', she felt them thinking, 'Why does she keep on?', but she had to keep his name alive.

Being social again in town clothes was an effort. Lily wanted it to end so that she could go home; but when she got back to her house, which was empty, it did not close round her as she had expected. It had stepped a pace back. It did not want her.

'Shan't we ever be happy again?'

If she had not had Tony, Isobel could not have borne this terrible time. Her love for him was nourished by her desperate need. He could not say the right things to her, but he was there. He held her close and made love to her, and their love-making eased the weight of her sorrow.

She had got a prescription for birth control pills from a woman doctor, but Tony had to remind her and urge her to take them.

'I want to have a baby,' she told him. 'Everything's ruined and different. I can't go on with my life as it was before.'

'What do you want to do then?' Tony took the lead in some things, and was quite strict and demanding with her. Sometimes he was at sea, and looked to her for answers, as if she were older than him.

And now Isobel's mother was talking about moving. There were people who wanted to buy the house and take over the stable and the tack shop. Her house, sure, she had a right to do what she liked. 'But it's our house too,' Isobel protested. 'You haven't asked us yet.'

'Oh, God, I'm sorry. I'm so selfish now, I'm all tied up in myself in knots and I don't think about anyone else. What do you think? We can't run this place on our own.'

'And you want to go. That's okay. I just wanted to be asked.'

Later, when Isobel came home one night from working at the Pine Tree restaurant, Lily called her into her room, where she was sitting up in bed in Daddy's blue pyjamas, with tea and bread and butter, a sign that she had tried to sleep, and couldn't.

'Darling.' She patted the bed for Isobel to sit down. 'What would you think if we went to England?' Isobel looked down and said nothing, picking at the frill on the edge of her short white apron. 'I don't think I can bear to stay on the Cape, and it's getting so crowded and spoiled anyway. But where else would I go in this country? I don't belong here, without Daddy. Cathy seems to quite like the idea, as long as she can take the dogs. Would it be very hard for you? You could do a year in sixth form there. What do you think?'

Isobel let her finish talking, then waited a moment before she got up in her silly green and white pixie uniform and said, 'You go ahead and do what you like. I won't be coming.'

Poor old Mudder. She had disintegrated a bit in these last months. In the old days, she would have come back sharply with, 'What do you mean, you're not coming?' Now she just said, 'Oh,' and looked crushed. Then she said, 'But you've got another year before you graduate. You can't live alone. Where would you live?'

'With Tony.'

Isobel watched her mother. She said, 'Oh,' again, and you could see her mind working and struggling and then shrugging its shoulders and giving up.

'In that shack?' was all she said, bleakly.

'I'm making it nice. I've bought some stuff. When school starts, I can keep working at the Pine Tree, evenings and weekends, and pretty soon, we'll get a bigger place.'

'Do you want to marry Tony?'

'Maybe one day. Go on, say it. I'll have dark-skinned children.'

'No, Isobel, don't be silly.'

'You'll have black grandchildren.'

'*Good.*' Lily smiled in a 'Take that!' way.

'Then you don't mind?' The woman was amazing. A weeping widow dithering around the place in her dead mate's plumage, but she could still struggle up to a challenge and be Lily-isn't-she-marvellous.

'I mind about you being so young.'

'I've aged a lot since November.'

'So have I. Look at me.'

'You look good, Mud. Much less than forty. You need to put on a bit of weight again, that's all.'

'Funny, when you think how hard I tried to lose it.'

'Not all that hard.' Isobel waited, wondering how to say this. 'Do you think Daddy – I mean, do you think Daddy will mind about me and Tony?'

'Shit, man, he's not up there on the roof like an Old Testament patriarch.'

'If he were, you couldn't say, "Shit, man".'

'I've got to learn to do the things I couldn't do when he was alive,' Lily said slowly and instructively, to herself as well as to Isobel.

'Good old Mud.' Isobel looked down at her with approval. 'I think you're going to make it.'

'I'm scared, though.'

'So am I.'

But they were two strong women. They admired each other.

Pixie was a good old gal, but there were times when Jamspoon decided he was sick of her, and might have written her off if he had anyone else for company. In a rash close moment by her wide gas fire, a delightful furnace, Jam had told her his age, believing that she was older than him. She wasn't. She only looked it. She was five years younger, and the discovery had encouraged her natural tendency to boastfulness.

Pixie had been in crowd and stand-in work for years, and fancied herself the darling of Central Casting. She knew all the assistant directors of all the film and television companies.

'Oh, yes, they always ask for me.' Jam was getting fewer jobs these days, and he did not want to hear from Pixie that she was still on the crest of the wave, dear heart. 'Wedding guest, restaurant, audience at the opera, stand-in for a difficult artiste – "Call Pixie Lamont," they say. They know they can depend on me.'

'I'll tell you what,' James said to Lily, when she was in England looking for a house, 'I wish Nora hadn't left.' He gave it out as new information, because during the five years since his wife had gone off with Duggie, he had persuaded himself that it had been a mutual separation. 'Sometimes, you know, I day-dream that she'll come back.'

'I don't think she will now.'

'You can't tell with women.'

But if she did, it could be awkward, because James had a much better dream that he kept shrouded and in waiting, while Lily went round to estate agents, and looked at totally unsuitable houses all over the Chilterns and the Thames valley.

He had more or less given up films and commercials, because of the early calls and all the standing about, which was murder to his varicose veins. There was also the risk of running into Evvie. He was still getting a bit of advertising work from Faces, although the products tended to be things like pensioners' rail cards and laxatives and denture stickem and last-ditch life insurance. He had even done a charity appeal for an old folks' home, with a sagging cardigan and a walking frame for props, because none of the resident old codgers could do it right.

'Next step will be a coffin ad,' he joked, and consoled himself with old slogans like, 'Pour me a Porsons' and 'A little luv, a little Lux-u-rest' from the days of his glory.

Before Lily even came over, he had laid his plans. Poor dear girl, who could she turn to if not her old father? He began to talk to Blanche about selling the Duke's Head to her and Neil, although his son-in-law would have to sharpen up his act if he were going to keep the bar customers happy.

Blanche would immediately sacrifice the public bar and the

dart board and fruit machine to make a proper restaurant. *Tant pee*, as they said, and James would feel like a conservationist who has held out against a motorway through the swampy meadows and finally gone under to the juggernauts of progress.

Lily had tutted at the state of the cottage and the random quality of Jam's life, but she did not try to straighten him out. She would not go into the pub, because it was as hard for her to be confronted with people who had known her as part of a couple as it had been for Jam when Nora scarpered. He told Lily he knew just how she felt. She looked at him blankly, as if she had no idea what he was talking about.

She was out most of the day, came back to cook supper for James on the crusted stove which would have given Nora a terminal stroke, and went to bed early, but was often still awake when James closed the bar and shifted the barrels and came upstairs.

'You're overdoing it,' he told her. 'Take it easy.' The only way he knew how to treat a bereaved person was like an invalid.

'I've got to keep going,' she said. 'I don't want time to think. My only hope is to start a new life. Find a little house to be a hermit in. Get a dull job. What's it matter?'

'You've got the girls,' James ventured, as a preliminary to one day saying, 'You've got me.'

'Yes, thank God, but not really "got" them. Isobel will stay in the States, I'm sure.'

'Doing what?'

'Well ... she plans to live with Tony. Remember Tony Andrade, who used to work with Paul so much? I haven't told you before, because I hadn't the strength to hear you say, "He's black." He's a decent young man, and she –'

'She can't. He's black.'

'Thank you, Jam. He isn't, incidentally. My little Cathy will be gone off to college before I can turn round, then gone away from me, like they do.'

'You could take a refresher course,' Blanche said when Lily talked about a job, 'and finish your exams. Go back to being a social worker. They're crying out for them.'

'They'll have to manage without me. I'll never do anything like that again.'

'But you're good at it, I thought.'

'Shut up. I don't want to hear about it.'

'My lips are sealed.' Blanche, in her mid thirties – good God, how had he acquired children of thirty-four and forty? – sometimes sounded like her mother.

When Lily finally found a cottage, she decided on it immediately, without taking time to think about it, because she was afraid she would lose courage. Blanche went over with her to take some measurements and help her talk to the estate agents, and she did not take James there until everything was settled.

The cottage was on the Berkshire downs, where she had no associations or friends. After leaving the security of the motorway, James found himself winding through narrow lanes and up and down hills, until they turned off at an unmarked lane that was hardly more than a cart track, and came to a gate in a thick box hedge labelled 'Daisy Cottage'. It was low and white and thatched, too typical for James's taste, like a greetings card. Beyond an over-run garden that would take years to clear, pastures and stubble and new ploughed land folded down into an unseen valley and folded up over the opposite hills, with not a house in sight.

The village was some distance away from Pie Lane, only a few straggling houses and farm buildings, with no shop or pub.

'It's pretty lonely here,' James said.

'That's what I want.'

There were three small bedrooms and two downstairs rooms that had been knocked into one long room, with a fireplace at each end and ceiling beams that were much lower than at the Duke's Head. It was not bad. Old places that had been done up with radiators and the decencies of life were hard to come by. It was a nice cottage, if you wanted to live like Peter Rabbit.

As James stood in the doorway to scan the lonely view for a sign of life, even one man on a tractor, the sun came out and flooded past him into the house. He stepped back inside. He could learn to duck his head. Perhaps those old red tiles on the floor would not draw the damp up into his bones.

'Well, what do you think, Jam?'

'Pretty fair.' They could invite people to stay – join local clubs

– get a video. 'You could put a bed for me in that little downstairs room at the end. Otherwise we wouldn't have a spare bedroom.'

'Jamspoon – oh, my God, you didn't think . . .'

'No, no, of course not.' No fool Jam. He knew when to bluff. 'Just joking. But when you invite me for dinner, I might have to stay the night because of the dreaded breathalyser ha ha.'

But why, 'Of course not'? Why wouldn't a daughter want to live with her old Dad who loved her and had stuck by her, unlike some parents he could mention?

After Lily finished her business and had gone back to America, Blanche started talking to a solicitor, and an architect visited the Duke's Head.

James began to panic. Pixie baked him a lovely cake for his sixty-second birthday, with no candles on it, for tact. Her daughter Button had gone to the Isle of Man with a woman friend who was an obvious dyke. Pixie wore the gold lamé that she had worn for the 1930s ballroom scene in *The Woman I Love Beside Me*. The front of it dipped very low in a U-shape, but her bosoms dipped lower.

It was candlelight and wine all the way, and poached eggs on a slice of gammon for breakfast, and spiced tomato juice for his hangover, which he had not had since Nora flew the coop. I might do worse, Jam thought, resilient as ever, so used to having his dreams shattered that he was a dab hand at building new ones. I might do worse.

Wearing the Japanese peignoir with the friendly dragon clinging to her broad comfortable back, Pixie rang Central Casting.

'David? Hullo, dear heart. Anyone want Pixie Lamont . . .? Tuesday? Smart rural? Lovely.'

James rang Faces, not to be left behind. The new young man in the outer office, brisker than Jam's old pals, who themselves were not as thrilled to see him as in days of yore when he was a hot number, said, 'May be something. Not sure. Call you back.'

'Wait, Eddie. I'll give you another number. Put it in my file. If you can't reach me at home, try here.'

'Oh ho,' Eddie said.

'Yes, as a matter of fact, oh *ho*.'

Lily was away two months. When she got back, the autumn leaves were flooded with spectacular colour. As she drove home from Boston, she looked for the huge maple tree before the Plymouth exit. It was a spreading burst of orange, tipped with fire from the setting sun, in its full glory, displaying itself to her with, 'Look what you'll be missing!'

As an antidote to the reproof of the blazing maple, Lily thought possessively of Pie Lane on the Berkshire downs, its blowsy hedges nearly meeting, and of herself standing by the fence between the pasture and the small garden, trying to absorb the strange new view that kept its distance, leaving it up to her future eyes whether it became closer and familiar.

At the house, Brad and Allie Miller, who had stayed with Cathy, had left everything in good shape. It had usually been Tony's sister and her husband who stayed in the house when Paul and Lily went away, but it had not seemed right to ask them under the circumstances, since the Andrade family were less relaxed than Lily about Isobel moving in with Tony.

Terry had said, 'We won't need anyone in the house. The girls and I will cope.' But he was still not coping with anything very well, and often going to work with a hangover.

He was gone before Lily returned. A friend from England had turned up. 'A very strange guy,' Isobel said. 'What's Terry been up to over there?' Brendan had stayed two nights, and they had left together.

Arrangements for the sale of the house went ahead. Lily and her daughters started to sort out what she would take to England and what Isobel could use, and what should be sold or given away. Lily kept some of Paul's shirts and sweaters, and the old faded gold Turnbull pullover, which still smelled quite strongly of him.

Arthur's eyes and ears and limbs were deteriorating, and he was a bit old for the plane journey and six months in quarantine kennels, but Lily could not go to England without him. She sent him off ahead with the black and white sheepdog that Cathy had rescued on one of her obsessive visits to the animal shelter. Driving back from leaving them in their cages at the airport, she thought, 'That's done it. Now I'll have to go.'

The pony had gone to one of Cathy's friends who had younger sisters. The Grossmans, who were buying the house, wanted to keep John. Mrs Dawson's spoiled fat horse and another boarder had already come back, and the stable and yard were busy again. Lily did not often go to see the horses, but when she saw the younger Grossman boy fooling about with John in the field, she wanted to storm down to the tack shop and tell Mr Grossman, 'John doesn't like being messed about by children.' But as she watched, she saw that he did.

The boy was riding bareback, his thin legs hanging straight down, hands high, turning the horse with the reins against his neck, and all John's Western memories of his youth in Kansas were coming back to him. Paul had wanted him to look like an Eastern hack: extended trot, head and neck up to the right point of flexion behind the ears. Now he looked contentedly like a cow pony, over-flexed, feet sliding into a flat singlefoot jog.

Harry, who had found Robin for Paul, was going to have the bay horse in his stable. He came down with the trailer to fetch Robin, and Lily gave him lunch and enjoyed being with him, able to talk about Paul or about other things quite easily. None of the strain that she often felt with people who were not close friends – either quiet and abstracted and losing the thread of the conversation, or trying too hard to chatter and be lively, to show she was all right.

When Lily left the table to put a log into the stove, Harry got up too and went to stand by her.

'I want to put my hands on you. Would that be all right?'

'No, Harry.' She straightened up.

'We could go up to bed?'

She smiled and shook her head at him.

'We might have once,' he said, 'if it hadn't been for Paul. I still want to. Do you?'

'I want someone to put their arms round me. That's all. That's one of the things you take for granted, and then miss dreadfully.' She wrapped her arms round herself. 'I find myself embracing people like the minister and that nice man in the drug store who was so helpful with all the pills.'

Harry moved her arms aside and put his arms round her. He tightened them, and as his funny creased, boyish face with the long tilted eyes came close, she felt the nerves in her body responding, and pulled away in horror.

'Just testing, lady.' Harry laughed, protecting himself from being hurt. '*Kaput*. Too bad. Doesn't work.'

When Lily was packing clothes for the movers, she found herself not folding the sweaters, but rolling them tightly, in Paul's naval style. She had already noticed that she was keeping her accounts more neatly. She had run the Crisis office efficiently, but her own affairs had always been slapdash. Paul was methodical and tried to teach her a system, but she had only half listened, restlessly, because there were better things in life.

Now she was doing what he wanted, although he wasn't here to see. Who was doing it? Dead people are too busy to come back and roll a sweater or balance a cheque book.

In a drawer, she found one of the notes from early in their marriage that he had left for her every day before he went to work at Turnbull's. In the desk in the study downstairs, she found that he had kept every one of the love notes she had left for him on scrappy bits of paper, on the kitchen table, in the tackshop office, on his pillow if she were going away, in his suitcase when he went off without her.

The loss was not so much not getting his notes now, as not writing hers.

After the movers came, Lily and Cathy and Isobel cleaned the house and lived for a week with a card table and garden chairs in front of the fire, and sleeping bags on old mattresses that were going to the dump.

The morning that Isobel was going to leave with the big grey cat for Tony's shack, now known as Our Cottage, Lily sat helplessly at the card table, stricken by what was actually happening. 'How can I leave you?'

Cathy went tactfully away, so that Lily did not have to add dutifully, 'But I've got Cathy.'

Isobel sat down again and put her hands over her mother's on the table. 'I'll be okay,' she said perkily.

'*I* won't. I need you.'

'I need you too.' Isobel's lip dropped and stuck out as if she were still a small child, and a tear fell into it.

'I'll come back, lots, and send you money to come over to me.'

'Yeah, I know.'

They looked at each other across the small rickety table.

If she had cried, at any time, 'Don't go, Mud!', would Lily have stayed? But Isobel was starting her own new life for herself, and making the shack a place for Tony. For Lily to have hung about on the edge of it (waiting for black grandchildren) would have been madness.

When she went to New Bedford to say goodbye, Ida said, 'Hang on a sec, I'll come with you.'

'I wish you could. Would you ever go back to England?'

'I'd be daft to go. Bernie's doing so well at the community college. Myaggie's Myaggie, and old Fred's in trouble all the time, but so he would be in England. Lying? He has the gift, and a terrible temper, just like his father. If I ever think I want to go to England, it's because I imagine that all the things I hate here — crooked pols and violence and bullshit and rip-offs — aren't the same over there. Which they are. Like I say, I'd be daft to go. *You're* daft.'

The Grossmans started to move into the house, and Lily and Cathy spent their last few days with Nina and Sam. On a freak warm early April morning, Mrs Grossman called.

'It's such a great day. Come and have a last ride.'

Lily wavered. 'Go Mud,' Cathy said.

'Go,' Nina ordered. 'Take my car.'

In borrowed jeans and oversize boots, Lily rode John down the track towards Hidden Harbor. Not to the beach. She would only go half-way, then turn through the woods and ride round the sandy roads among the deserted summer cottages where she and Paul and Terry had stayed by the marsh. When they came to the turn-off through the trees, John resisted. He wanted to go down to the water, so she let him go ahead.

He was not being Western, but moving strongly and collected, head up to the bit, in his old way for her. He was doing beautifully and she was riding well. She hadn't lost it. At the mouth of the

413

inlet, she let him walk out through the seaweed in the shallow low-tide water.

Not so long ago, she had dragged her feet through the sand here with Arthur, crying out to the seagulls, crying for Paul. Now that madness seemed far behind. She had moved a long way ahead from despair.

Paul was here. Not as a fallen ghost among the cold winter grasses. He rode with her. If she had seen him physically, sitting easily on Robin and turning back to smile at her, she would not have been totally surprised.

John put down his broad black head and started to slap at the water with a front hoof, a threat of sagging down to roll. Lily pulled up his head and he stood stock still and stared across the inner bay to where a yellow bulldozer moved like a toy among the rocks.

'I'm going, Paul,' Lily said. 'Is that all right?'

Her mind knew the answer in his dear remembered voice.

'I'm coming too.'

Without warning, John suddenly buckled his knees and went down into the sea. Lily stepped off just in time. He thrashed and floundered about. Her borrowed clothes were soaked. The wide boots filled with very cold water. She laughed aloud. She had thought you couldn't laugh alone. You could.

Back on the beach, she hung John's reins down to the ground so that he would stay, like a Western-trained horse, and stood on her head in the sand to let the water run out of her boots.

Eleven

*F*irst there was mud and sticky ploughed land which clung to your boots and the underside of your dogs from January to April. Then imperceptibly the landscape greened. Points of life pricked through the heavy brown earth, and it gradually dried, giving up its moisture to what grew above it.

The corn was an inch high. Then, suddenly it seemed, between one rampaging spring storm and the next, the fields were upholstered in lush green velvet. Ankle high. Calf high. The trees puffed out, round and rich. The hedge lines looping up and down the contours of the gentle hills blurred and spread.

The hectic patch of rape-seed flower in the middle of Lily's view was constant sunlight, enhancing the subtler pastels of the changing greens and the pale-washed sky. Lambs, kids, calves, foals came forth as rapidly as the growing grass and grains, and celebrated. In May, cow parsley foamed from the banks, and wet days turned Pie Lane into a car wash. The hay beyond the garden fence would soon be ready to cut. Silvery waves shivered through the green wheat. Already a light brown haze was on the curving slope of barley, as if the whole field had been put under a grill and lightly toasted.

Last year, Lily had walked on the hills, along riding tracks that made her sick with nostalgia as she sloshed through the puddles of other horses' hoofs, without really seeing the countryside. She had leaned on her post-and-rail fence and looked over the stunning view without being able to absorb it, or to comprehend that it was *her* view, which would eventually become as familiar in all its changing aspects as her own face in the mirror.

A year later, she realized that she must be walking with her head higher, because she stumbled over ruts and craggy flints that she had avoided when her eyes were on the ground. She saw much more, and what she saw began to mean something.

'I think I've turned a corner,' she told Susan, who lived in the village, comfortable, casual, doing two part-time jobs and

bringing up three children and making allowance for an immature, variable husband who came and went.

'Hope for you yet? Then who will I have to be sorry for?'

'Was I so dreary?'

'No, brave, you and Cathy. You've got guts.'

That was what Lily wanted to hear. They had survived the
upheaval of departure. They had got through the first year,
learning not to be strangers. She had thought she knew England,
but it had changed, or she had forgotten. Everything was slower
than in America, and appliances and gadgets fell apart more
quickly. The workmen who did up her kitchen and bathroom
were lovely men with sturdy jokes, but they worked like snails
and kept disappearing for two weeks at a time. Once when she
had been to London, she found two of them on the floor, asleep
by the fire with woollen hats pulled over their eyes.

In the bad storm last winter, the snow shrieked across the open
fields and piled up in impassable drifts at both ends of Pie Lane. In
New England, the snow ploughs would be out all night, but here
you waited for a humanitarian farmer. People of the village
struggled back and forth in a friendly way, borrowing milk and
yeast and baked beans from each other, and playing cards and
looking for a book to read. Lily could not get her car out for a
week.

Later, odd little cranky Eric Pigeon dropped in once at midnight, when he was walking his matted mongrel down Pie Lane
and saw that Lily still had a light on.

She was wearing Paul's winter dressing-gown. 'Sorry about
this.' She knew she looked frumpy.

'Moronic woman,' Eric said. 'Don't try to flatter me that it
matters.'

She poured him a whisky, but he only stayed two minutes
before his dog whined, tied up outside, and he jumped up and
went away, with the whisky and Lily's glass.

The village was calmly friendly. Lily and Cathy were assim-
ilated effortlessly, no big social deal, just allowed to start be-
longing here whenever they got around to it.

Some of the women still talked in funny trumpeting voices
(which sounded funnier after you had been living in the States),

as if they had not heard about the revolution. Their children or grandchildren talked cockney or Berkshire, an accent whose stressed r's were pleasantly not unlike American.

The B BC was riddled with rare dialects. A Scots newsreader talked of Aggravated Buggery. The House of Commons sounded like the Battle of Hastings. Punks were creatures from European outer space, unknown in Boston, Massachusetts. Punks in Newbury? Lily had visited it when it was a little backwater country town. She stared, because it seemed more insulting to ignore them.

In the main street, where people milled up and down with pushchairs all day and every day, as if the shops would close for ever tomorrow, a boy had bleached his hair a dry, hard gold and tortured and spiked it into a horrendous crown of thorns, which he carried, stiff-necked, past Marks & Spencer. No one paid any attention to him. Lily stared, and felt quite old.

Cathy made some friends quickly at school and in the village, and rode with them long distances on her bicycle. In the first few months, she and Lily had to break their hearts every week, visiting the dogs in the kennels. Young Sheila was undaunted, a key member of the deafening chorus that barked and yelped when anyone came within smelling distance of their yard, but Arthur was muted and lost. When Lily and Cathy had to walk away, Sheila would be up on her hind legs at the wire, tossing out shouts of protest, but Arthur stood foursquare in the middle of the run, down at the front as he had become with age, and moved his grizzled head uncertainly. What . . .? Where?

'Don't look back, Mud. He'll be all right when he comes out.'

Cathy could not wait for that, but acquired a small furred beige dog from the postman, for whom she made tea every morning, because she was up early to catch her bus. A postman bringing letters at six forty-five! But Lily had to quell a treacherous self-indulgent nostalgia for the old walk along the abandoned railroad track to the post office on Cape Cod, to turn the knob of her mailbox to its combination.

Two times right to H. Once left to B. Reverse and stop between K and L. Or was it J and K? My God, she had forgotten it already, and she chose to let herself become distressed over this unimportant symbol of her lost past, which led to others, and others, and wasted half a day.

Daisy Cottage did not accept her for some time. The Cape Cod house had withdrawn as she prepared to leave, and now this solid old thatched cottage held itself back to see what she would do. Her chairs and tables were not quite at home either. Not enough people had sat yet in this place. The air was empty of voices and laughter.

In the garden, Lily did enough weeding and tidying to save the plants that were already there, but she did not make changes or plant anything new. She did not know how long she was going to stay. Parts of the white cottage walls needed painting. The roof needed re-thatching. That could wait.

She did not hang up Terry's picture of Paul on the hill for a long time. Her bedroom walls were too low, because of the sloping ceiling under the thatch. Neither end of the long living-room was the right place. The picture either dominated the white walls, or was submerged by the open beams. Eventually Lily hung it, with the plastic spoon, in the front hall, where the western sun struck across it from the side, as the sun along the top of the hills had irradiated Paul's hair while Terry sat on a tree root behind him and quickly made the sketch.

When the dogs came out of quarantine at last, Sheila was ecstatic and unchanged, but Arthur seemed blinder and deafer and vaguer. He was upset to find the bossy small dog there. A striped cat had turned up too, as cats did for Cathy. It stared uncharitably at Arthur, and he moved shiftily away, and waited his chance to steal its food.

There had been no rabbits or hares on their Cape Cod land. Here the fields were full of them. When small bold rabbits came under the fence to sit on the lawn in the early morning and evening, the dogs shrieked at the glass door and burst out, all three of them, always too late. In August, a hare got up in the stubble and Arthur was gone, faster than he had run for years, almost as he used to run behind galloping horses.

He did not come home. Lily found him collapsed under a hedge, and he died on Cathy's lap on the way to the vet.

He had been everybody's dog, but as he got older, he had

depended more on Paul, and when Paul was ill, the dog was by his chair, on his bed, following him where he limped, his stick on one side, Arthur on the other. When good dog Arthur left them quietly, he took with him one more visible part of Paul.

During their first winter, Cathy had changed to a weekly boarding school to be with two of her close friends, and Lily got a job at a country hotel outside Newbury. It had recently been re-opened by an energetic and ambitious couple in their thirties, who had tried a lot of other things they didn't like, and finally put money into what they loved. With him, it was cooking, with her, doing domestic things beautifully, and making people comfortable and happy.

As Round Hill Rectory began to be discovered, they needed more than the odd chambermaid and weekend waitress. They took on Lily, who did a bit of everything for an unsensational salary, because she liked the odd hours, and the optimistic courage of Gerry and Janet and their cheery approach to disasters, real and threatened.

They also loved each other, and showed it. Lily found she could not be with couples who fought or hurt each other. Once, invited to the big house of Mrs Colonel Dodgson – 'When we were ee-nindia' – a woman craftily insulted her husband across the table, and Lily had cried impulsively, 'Oh, be nice to him, for God's sake, or he'll die and it will be too late!' and disgraced herself by bursting into tears.

For quite long periods, she felt strong and content, and could enjoy her new friends and even look ahead with some pleasure. Then – bingo – she would be awake all night in a cocoon of guilt and regrets, remembering, sorrowing, reminding herself deliberately of all the things with which she could chastise herself.

Selfish. Arrogantly sure of his love and admiration. Impatient when he was ill. Consumed by the work at Crisis. Always home late, talking about her day, not Paul's. 'I'm desperate too,' she had to hear him say, again and again, and at three o'clock in the morning, all her mistakes with Mike were jostling and crowding in. The spectre of Paul's anxious, sick face and his limp and silent tears of pain was obliterated by Mike up there like a fly, under the canal bridge in the Coastguard spotlight.

'I love you!' Silly fool. The men in the boat and up on the bridge must have had a riot with that afterwards.

She saw him jump and fall feet first through the black swirling water into the dark image of his unloved young body hanging like a puppet from the ventilator grille in the bare prison cell.

When Cathy at the weekend asked her how she had been, as she always did, Lily told her.

'What's the point of all that?' Cathy asked sensibly. 'You think you owe it to Daddy, or something? The way I see it, that kind of carry-on must push him farther away, not bring him closer.'

She was beautiful and healthy, with milky whites to her steady light blue eyes. In the States, she had been rather neat: bouncy sneakers, plain bright clothes fitting her tidy narrow shape. Now she wore sloppy disconnected garments, black and earth colours, shuffling happily in loose flat shoes, like the other girls.

In the summer, she hiked in groups along the ridge of the hills above the Vale of the White Horse, learned to play tennis well, bicycled to Kate's swimming pool, adored Kate's brother, who never spoke to her.

On the first very hot day, Lily was going to garden and paint the outdoor chairs and clean the windows . . . until she let herself be seduced into thinking about Hidden Harbor, on such a day as this. Sick with longing for the sea, she lay for hours in the hammock and did nothing but nag at the aching memory of all the lovely summer places – Nauset Outer Beach, the Vineyard, Sandy Neck and the wild drumming gallop over the hard sand and through the splattering tide pools.

She fell heavily asleep and woke when the little dog jumped into the hammock. The Judge's grandfather clock was striking five. Dogs' dinner time. Detached from earth, unreal, she held the warm, quickly pulsing heart of the dog to her chest, swinging gently under the sky, and was at peace.

'The widow Stephens,' Eric Pigeon said to her in his insolent fashion. 'This place is crawling with widows. They come out from under mossy stones and embroider hassocks for the church, and expect me to be an extra man at dinners, to pour the wine.'

'I don't,' Lily said.

'You don't give dinner parties.'

'Should I?'

'God, no. Disaster.' He was opinionated and quite rude. 'A fortyish widow. Who would come?'

'You would.'

'I'm safe. I'm a eunuch, I think.'

'I never knew one of those.'

'And you shouldn't now, darling.' He stood on tiptoe to embrace her outside the village shop. He could be spasmodically warm and quite loving. 'You've got to devote attention now to the serious man hunt.'

Lily stepped back, furious. 'Don't dare say anything like that to me!'

'Don't snarl at me like a bitch over its dead mate. I'll cut your tongue out.' He said things like that.

Eric was a balding, slight, retired fellow in baggy trousers, who lived alone with his smelly dog and a few chickens and goats. He had been in marketing for something like margarine and cooking oil, writing promotion and packaging copy.

'Words are my slaves, damn you, don't criticize,' he had said before Lily ever opened her mouth. He was writing a book. 'Who isn't?' When people smirked at him, 'I suppose you're writing about all of us in this village?' he snarled savagely, 'Readers want to be entertained, not bored to death.'

He had insulted almost everybody, but because this was England, they tolerated him for being batty.

Cathy wanted to go to the village church, because she liked the school services, and Kate's brother could occasionally be viewed here. Lily liked the vicar, a large cheery man who rode a big roan mare with a rump the same shape as his. The minister on Cape Cod had said to her, 'You'll be all right, my dear. You're British. Stiff upper lip, okay? Okay.'

This vicar had said, 'What a terrible time for you, and how hard it must be to struggle to create a better one.'

It was all right for admirable Susan in the village to tell her she was brave, because Lily wanted Susan to admire her; but she had been pleased that this vigorous ruddy man had let her pull a sad face and indulge in, 'Poor me!'

She and Cathy stopped on the way into church to watch the smooth arms-up-arms-down of the bell ringers: two sweet serious women and a young boy with his tongue between his teeth and Thomas who was a thatcher, from one of the villages on the opposite hill, across the valley.

When Thomas said, 'Stand,' and the organ swelled to accompany the vicar and robed choir up the aisle, the ringers left the bells up and went to their seats. Lily, sitting in a back pew, heard Eric come in late and bang the heavy door, saw him look at the vicar's broad praying back and the congregation bent painfully forwards, and saw him turn and look again at the bell ropes. Then he leaped and grabbed the coloured woollen sally of the tenor bell and was carried up to the roof with a high curdling scream. That was the kind of thing he did.

Lily and Cathy quite liked him.

'That's because you're foreigners,' Eric said, calling in on them with his wrist in plaster from the fall in church. 'Youm doan't unnerstand our ways.'

He tied his goats out along the grassy path where Cathy walked the dogs, and the billy butted Sheila in the ribs and knocked her into the hedge.

When Cathy complained, he glared his myopic eyes almost to bursting through his thick spectacles and shouted, 'I'll shoot your dog!' That was the way he was.

He was wispy and delicate, always injuring himself, and knocked off his feet by coughs and flu. When last winter's storm cut off the village, he had slipped on the ice and opened up his forehead, hurrying to take a thermos of bloody Marys to an old lady before any good woman could get there with her home-made soup.

'Listen, will you, for once in your life,' he told Lily, sitting up when he had been told to lie flat. 'You must keep an eye on Ma Eccles. She likes rum in her tea. And there's trouble with her granddaughter. The probation officer's got to be talked to, so you must see to that, and ring up her cretinous son and tell him you'll drain all the blood out of his liver if he doesn't get up here with the electric blanket.'

'Lie down, Eric. Don't drag me into it.'

'You've got to help. What's the use of you?'

'Leave me out of it.'

Lily could not explain why. Nobody over here knew the true story of what had happened on Cape Cod, although she was sure they all told each other versions of it. She made Eric's coffee and left him. She could just imagine herself intrusively involved with the village, trapped again by needs and wants, trying to run people's lives. One of Mrs Colonel Dodgson's 'splendeed weemeen', knocking herself out to please the disgruntled old bags at the Silver Threads teas, chasing Ma Eccles's son over half the home counties, and going to the juvenile court with his delinquent daughter.

The job was enough. It kept her busy, and most of the time, it kept her from pain and nostalgia. At the hotel, she did whatever was needed: cleaning, flowers, kitchen, serving meals, making drinks, reception, phone, talking about the States with American visitors who detected the transatlantic leftovers in her speech.

She often stayed later at Round Hill Rectory than she had meant to or was paid for – as at Crisis. But when Cathy was not there, she did not have anybody to come home for.

The bitter loneliness of this gradually lost its sharpness. Although she was still often homesick for many places and people in America, she knew she had been right to make this tremendous change. Going home to nobody at the Cape Cod house would have meant continually missing Paul, looking for him, remembering him in his old places – the piano, his chair, walking up from the barn when he heard her car. Coming home to Daisy Cottage was a lonesome business sometimes, but he had never been here. She did not look for him.

The dogs' welcome never failed. After she had fed them and made herself tea or a drink, there began to be tired times when she caught herself feeling glad that she did not have to cook anyone's supper.

Jamspoon came from London once in a while, looking better fed, wearing coloured waistcoats, fancying himself as a Londoner, not interested in the garden, cracking the old jokes about the silence keeping him awake after lunch. He was always going to bring Pixie. She adored the country. She was a peasant girl at heart, you could tell it by her pastry. She and Lily would hit it off something astonishing. Lily found him very tiresome, and was glad that Pixie never came.

Nora had gone back to nursing, but she made the long journey from Essex occasionally and moved the furniture about and uprooted weeds, with or without Duggie, who might as well not have come for all he said or did, unless you let him go to the kitchen sink, or tell you what route he had taken from Chelmsford.

Blanche came over with the children. Duffy was eleven. He had a lovely voice and was taken up with his choir, but the eight-year-old twins were out of hand. The Duke's Head took up a lot of Blanche's time and energy and she and Neil could hardly ever be at home in the evenings, because of the bar and restaurant.

With the sun brilliant on a blowy day, the twins did not want to walk with the dogs up to the White Horse at Uffington. They wanted to watch television. Cathy unplugged the set. Gordie flew into a rage.

'Be nice,' Blanche pleaded. Gordie attacked her with blind violence.

'I think I'm losing my grip.' Blanche sent him outside, to throw clods of earth at the cows in the paddock. 'Stop that!'

'Not you,' Lily said. 'I've always envied the way you cope with everything so calmly.'

'I envied *you*,' Blanche said, unexpectedly shy. 'You came and went, you and Paul, like – sort of – creatures from another world. You came home to dazzle us.'

'Did you think that? How odd.'

'Gordie, come inside! Helen go out and stop him doing that to the tree.'

'I hate him.' Helen ran up the steep little stair that went up like a loft ladder to the spare room.

'I was jealous of you, Lily.'

'Who wouldn't be, when I had Paul?' Lily said. 'And look at me now.'

'Yes. Look at you.'

Anyone else would have said something like 'You're doing well.' Blanche simply mirrored the situation as it was, and it was oddly comforting.

When Lily's car failed her, she could not miss work, so Eric drove her to the hotel and promised to come back after she had finished lunches.

He did, but not as planned. He always had a better idea. He came back early and had lunch at the hotel himself. Spying on her? Out for trouble? He wore his droopiest dark-green trousers which looked as if they were tied at the waist with string, and a flashy black and white check jacket with a red bow tie.

He was courtly with Janet. 'But listen,' Lily told him privately. 'No funny business.'

'Why can't I lunch here the same as anyone else?' Eric raised his voice. A man and a woman at the bar looked round.

'I'm warning you.' Lily picked up glasses from the next table and spoke without moving her lips.

'I'll slit your gizzard,' he hissed, smiling and nodding at the couple by the bar.

Lily was in the kitchen. Janet and Val were in the dining-room.

'Who is that dreadful little man?' Janet pushed through the swing door in a fluster. 'He's complaining about everything and annoying the other guests, and Val is a nervous wreck. Why did he have to come *here*?'

'To fetch me, I'm afraid.'

'When will your car be fixed?'

'Two more days.'

Angrily, Janet rearranged the meat and vegetables on Eric's plate, shoved it into the microwave to heat it, and took the same food back to him.

'Fabulous lunch.' Eric raved about the hotel on the way home. Lily would not talk to him. As they came into Newbury, the traffic was very heavy. It was a race meeting day and it was raining. Racegoers were going home.

Eric, who became infuriated in crawling traffic, and was at risk of getting out and thumping the lids of other cars, yanked his wheel and dived down a side street on one of his complicated, time-wasting short cuts. He slammed on the brakes at a roadworks barrier blocking a narrow back alley. Ahead of them, a boy with a shaved blue head and another with a Roman helmet of stiff orange hair fell out of a doorway, dragging something with them. It was a girl in black tights and a torn top, hair like a bushman. She broke away and darted round the boys, slapping and kicking at them.

They pushed her up against the wall. She was screaming and struggling, and they were hitting her.

'Sod's teeth!' Eric was struggling with his seat belt. 'Wait till I get at those swine.'

'No, Eric, stay in the car.' Lily leaned across him to try to hold his door shut. 'She probably asked for it. Leave them alone.'

'She's younger than Cathy. Come on – help me!'

He was out in the street, all five foot two of him, flailing his thin arms.

'Let's go for 'em, Lily!'

'No – it's not our business. Stay out of it. You haven't got a chance.'

Terrified, she got out of the car and could only stand and watch as he climbed over the barrier and tore down the alley, shouting at the tangled confusion of the boys and their victim. Shrieking a sort of war cry, puny Eric, tiresome little man, waded in. He was as brave as a lion.

Lily, bigger and stronger, stood paralysed, with her hands over her mouth. She thought he would be killed.

As quickly as he had gone into the fight, he was thrown out of it, flung against a dustbin, like Cathy's brave grey cat being thrown out of the dog fight. As Lily ran towards him, the girl stood up from the wall, ran her hands through her wild hair and bent double. She was not hurt or sobbing. She was laughing.

Out of the doorway, furtively, came Lily's punk with the golden crown of thorns, pinch-faced, peering up and down the alley like King Rat coming out of his hole. The four of them jeered at Eric and ran off down the street, hooting and zigzagging from side to side.

Lily helped Eric to his feet and he kicked the dustbin. He had been hit in the face. A bruise was swelling and darkening over his right cheekbone, and the eye was closing. Lily drove his car to the hospital.

'You think I'm an ass,' he said, through the paper towel he was holding to his face.

'I think you're incredibly brave. I was a drivelling coward. I'm sorry.'

'Moronic woman. It was man's work.'

As they went into the hospital, Thomas the bellringer was coming out of the lift with some other visitors.

'What's it this time?' he asked Eric. 'Been fighting?'

'I'm accident-prone. Can you take Lily to work tomorrow?'

After Terry was fired from the Regent Street store, he stayed on with Brendan in the Balham apartment until he could neither pay his share any more, nor tolerate Brendan's innocent chatter about the management training course and what a fool Terry had been to chuck up his chances of a fine advanced career in retailing.

Terry had stayed at the department store longer than in any other job, nearly two years, which almost constituted a career. When Brendan had turned up at the Cape and persuaded him that signing on for the Christmas shopping rush in London was money for old rope, Terry had gone with him like a zombie. He had been wretched in his father's house. No point to anything. He might as well be wretched in Regent Street.

Brendan came from Belfast, but would never go back. The Provos had shot his brother, for whom nothing had ever worked out right, by mistake for an informer. Nothing would ever work out for Brendan either if he stayed in the decaying furniture shop with his demoralized family. By working hard and making his way in London, he could somehow make up for his brother's thrown-away life.

After three weeks as temporary sales staff, he had signed on for full training.

'I'm doing it for Billy,' he said, 'and you should think what you're doing too, Terence.' He was a great moralizer, was Brendan. 'Wasn't your Dad always after you to settle down? Here's your chance. Settle.'

'Too late.'

'Don't give me that. Heaven is not a far country. Make him proud of you.'

'A-a-ah.' Terry shoved that away, but he was so confused and without direction that he did hang on to the thought. He knocked himself out in Toys all through the Christmas pandemonium and the January sales, and, needing more money to move with Brendan out of their bed-sitter and into an apartment, he took extra tests and training and found himself wearing a plasticized label that said, 'Mr Stephens Second Asst. Mgr' in Men's Knit-wear.

He had finally got it together for his father, and the great emptiness began to fill up a little, from the bottom, like new tissue growing in a wound. He did not go to visit Lily. She might be still raw with pain, or she might be ready to talk sentimentally about his father and the past. Either way, he was afraid of being dragged back.

He was drinking less. He liked London, and he liked the people he worked with and most of the customers. He kept a note pad in the drawer with his order book, and did some quick sketches of features and clothes and attitudes, and the faces people made in front of a mirror when they tried something on, to blow up for the sensational composite magazine illustration, 'Menswear, 1985' which he would accomplish some day.

Brendan had the girl Kitty in Ireland who would come over eventually. Terry got to know a few girls at the store, nifty with their long black British legs and black and white striped shirts, and a few outside, who would never apply here, or get taken on. One of them was a pudgy girl with rounded edges, but a very sharp nature. She got disgusted when Terry would not take days out to go off on a tear somewhere with her, because he was being tried out as Assistant Manager and that was more important to him – just, by a big effort of will – than Denise.

Denise took up again with her property-developer friend.

'You'll lose me,' she had told Terry when he would not do what she wanted.

'I'll take that chance,' he had said, knowing that they had something strong between them, that she wouldn't ditch him, not now when they were still in a fever for each other. But she did. Brendan was quite relieved. Terry agonized over Denise. He could hardly manage to fake a sane appearance at work. He took two days off to walk the streets round about the east London neighbourhood where he thought the property man lived.

His department manager warned him. Terry was back at work, performing niggling tedious tasks and talking to customers through a blur of depression. When the pain of Denise faded, the depression stayed. If he made a sale, okay. If he didn't, so what? The order books went to seed. He clocked in late. He was rude to a man who swore that a red pullover was bought here, although he brought it back in the bag of a rival store.

The manager warned him again. Ronnie, the very young Second Assistant, toadied around hopefully. The old black pit opened up inside Terry. He fell into it, and from its depths, he told the manager what he could do with the job.

Once more. Once more into the breach, dear Dad. Blown it once more.

When he was in steady work, God help him, he had bought a small silver car like a rusted biscuit tin. He put his clothes and books and stuff into it, left a note and some money for Brendan, and drove out west to find Lily's house.

He got lost. Natch. He had gone uphill on the right road, according to the map, but nobody in the village had heard of Lily. That was not like her. She usually made enough noise. So much for the boast of, 'Cathy and I are beginning to feel we really belong,' that she had written to him. But no one had heard of Pie Lane either. He was in the wrong village.

Why did she have to hide herself in a place like this? The narrow lanes wound back upon themselves purposelessly. Any one of a dozen side roads might turn out to be a cart track ending in the middle of a field, or it might be Pie Lane.

Who needed it? She probably wouldn't want to see him anyway. Terry was ready to give up the whole idea, when he passed a cottage with a small grey truck outside and recognized it from the picture that Lily had sent him.

He backed up. A man was on the thatched roof – thatching, what else? He had steel spectacles hooked round his pointed ears and leather pads on his knees, like a horse.

'Mrs Stephens here?'

The man had taken off most of the old thatch at one end of the house and was laying in sheaves of straw with the wheat heads still on them, packing them tight.

'At work,' he said.

'What time does she come back?'

'Early, late. You never know with her.'

Terry could not tell one English country accent from another. This was pleasant, vowels soft and slow, a blur of r's.

'Oh. Well, I – I'm her stepson.'

The thatcher nodded down at him civilly. 'The house is open. You can go in if you want to make the tea,' he said familiarly, as if he had been working here for some time, which presumably he had, since all but one end of the roof was covered with a thick new thatch.

The cottage was really nice. White walls and beams, and wide windows low enough to see the whole garden and the view. Pieces of furniture from Terry's past made the rooms familiar. Healthy plants on the windowsills and hanging from beams looked more like his father than Lily. In the kitchen, he found a bottle of Scotch and had a quick drink, because he was nervous of meeting her here, on what was completely her own ground. He made strong tea and took two mugs and a cake out to the garden table.

The thatcher did not introduce himself. He drank his tea, looking peacefully at the view, and pointed out where his house was hidden behind the hill on the other side of the valley. He let Terry fetch him another mug of tea. His hands were brown and square, criss-crossed with scratches from the straw. Without his glasses, his brown eyes were inward-looking. He was a composed, deliberate man. Terry had been in a stew driving down, but it was comfortable, sitting here with him in the late afternoon sun.

When the thatcher went back to work, he tied some of the

loose bundles of straw on the lawn into tight sheaves, and after Terry had watched him climb the ladder with half a dozen, then down again to fetch some more, he started to pass them himself, climbing half-way up the ladder and reaching up past the man's heavy boots.

Lily hurried through the garden gate, breathless, dropping things, more like her old self than the drained, dry-skinned woman he had fought with on Cape Cod.

'I couldn't think whose car it could be, and then I saw your guitar. Terry, this is wonderful. Hullo, Thomas. I see you found an assistant at last.'

'Sometimes I wonder if I want one, after that last young man took off with the money.'

'And your jacket and the radio, don't forget.' It was evidently an oft-told story.

Cathy would be home from school at the weekend. Terry must stay. He did not tell Lily yet that he had nowhere else to go, and she said nothing as she helped him to unload his worldly goods from the car.

Thomas had swept up straw and orange string like a tidy housewife, and left. The sun had gone down in a blaze of autumn splendour on the other side of Pie Lane. Opposite the sunset, the stubble fields of Lily's view were golden-pink in the afterglow. Painted clouds hung above the valley. The whole sky was a rose-coloured bowl. As Lily and Terry stood with their backs to the fence to look at the cottage, the amazing light suffused the new thatch like a blush on a dusky skin.

'Pretty nice, huh?' Lily had talked English to the thatcher, but she dropped into easy old American with Terry. He was afraid she was going to say, 'I only wish your father could see it,' so he said, 'Your lawn wants mowing. Want me to do it for you tomorrow?'

'I'll let it go for a bit. You can see how the cottage got its name. I hate to cut those daisies.'

'They'll grow again.'

'Like you and me. How *are* you, Terry? You've done well in London, haven't you? How's the job going?'

'Oh, that. I packed it in.'

'Then what –'

Don't start on me. 'Can we have a drink?'

Lily told him that Isobel was going to have a baby. That *Kid*? My God, she had grown up ahead of Terry in the end. She was going to become a Roman Catholic, and she and Tony were getting married. Lily and Cathy were going over next month for the wedding.

A crazy little runt called Eric stopped by that evening, and poured his own drink and was very familiar with Lily, and rather caustic with Terry. A couple of Scotches and some wine had made Terry feel more morose – as usual. He might have given the guy a poke if he'd had the energy, and the little jerk had not been smaller than him.

'What a wimp,' he said, when Eric had gone off, singing in a high voice down the lane, because half a bright moon and all the stars were out.

'Not really.' Lily told him a story about a fight with some punks.

'Stupid with it too,' Terry scoffed. 'You can't marry *him*.'

'I'm not going to marry anyone. You know that.'

'You're only – what? – forty-one, forty-two.'

'I'm married to your father.'

'To a ghost? Come back to haunt you, that weird stuff?'

Lily laughed. 'Wherever Paul is, he's got better things to do than that. It's not that he's come back. He's gone, but sometimes he's here, not all the time, just now and again, in some strange way I never expected.'

'How, here?'

'It's very odd. I say things he used to say. I do things he used to do. Unconsciously. Things that aren't like me. I check the oil in the car sometimes.'

'You're copying him. That's not so odd, because he's not here to do it for you.'

'It's more than that. I do it without thinking. Remember how he used to lay those wonderful fires with tight rolls of newspaper?'

Terry nodded. He had seen how the fire was laid here before she lit it when the evening grew cold.

'Look at the house plants. I could never touch them at home. I was the kiss of death. I screw in screws. I coil the hose instead of leaving it all over the lawn. I – oh, a lot of little things. I clean the sink. Remember how I was such a slob, and he'd come and scour it out, whistling like a sailor scrubbing the decks? I'll tell you a funny thing, though. I forgot Paul's death day this year. May the tenth. It came and went.'

'Not for me. It hit me hard. I called you, but you were out.' Part of this was true. The day had sunk him, but he had not called. 'You're lucky you forgot it. You're tough, aren't you, Lily?'

'No.'

'You've been better than me,' Terry said. 'But then, I wasn't doing so well before he was killed.'

'He wasn't killed,' Lily said patiently. 'Poor Mike attacked him. Paul died later.'

'He killed him.' It infuriated Terry that she had said, 'Poor Mike'. 'But you can't live with that?'

She smiled. She looked younger and more colourful again, in the deep striped chair that Paul had given her, at home, not just passing through.

'For a long time, I had to torture and almost destroy myself with, "It was my fault." Crazy. Fault doesn't come into it. Fault's always irrelevant. He died. I'm alive. I miss him all the time, but look, Terry, if it *was* my fault, I suppose I can live with it.'

Eric was having a dinner party. He had invited seven people, but after he got himself thrown off next year's fête committee for telling the secretary that he would ruin her before the whole of Berkshire and that part of Oxfordshire that Edward Heath took away from Berks. in 1974, she and her husband would not come and nor would the committee chairman, so Eric invited Lily, and told her why. He always told you if you were a stop gap.

He cooked a superb Beef Wellington, and harped on how long it had taken him, so that no appreciation could be enough. In every discussion, he waited until he saw what everyone was against, and then took that line, which did at least force people to defend their opinions.

When the other guests left, he wanted Lily to stay and help him wash up. He tied a greasy apron round her, but she took it off.

'I've been at the sink all day at the Rectory. The kitchen man's got mumps. Let me go home. You can do all this tomorrow.'

'Don't boss me about. Did you boss your wretched husband?'

To test her new growing strength, Lily said, 'Sometimes', quite honestly, and wished she hadn't, because Eric asked, 'Did he lie down and say, "Kick me"?'

'I'm off.'

'No, you're not. Forget the sink. We're going to have a drink and play backgammon.' Lily had not played since she had played with Paul. 'Don't leave me. I get nervous.'

'All right, but only so that I can beat you. The British don't know how to play this game,' she said as they set out the pieces.

'You're British.'

'When I'm with you, I feel American.'

They were in the front-room, playing and insulting each other quite harmoniously, when they heard some small noises at the back of the house. Eric's grubby dog jumped up from its deplorable bed, releasing a miasma of different smells, and let off some shrill, ugly barks without leaving the room.

'There – there it is again. Hear it? Go, Sherman, go and see what it is.'

The dog would not go, so Eric went. He opened a small drawer in the dresser and took out a pistol.

'No, Eric – don't be a fool.'

He shook off Lily's hand and nipped down the passage to the dark kitchen. She followed him, keeping out of his way. Eric without a gun was dangerous enough.

'Come back!' she called, and heard him open the back door in the scullery.

There was a confusion of noise and shouts and then a shot. Going cautiously to the door, Lily saw that someone was in her car. The engine started and the car jerked backwards.

'Hey!' She had stood back when Eric went after the punks, but now she ran out, shouting. There was a man in her car, a clownish, large contorted face, lank hair stranded on a bulging forehead. He looked at Lily aghast, then crashed the car backwards into Eric's hen house.

Chickens squawked out of the loosened door. The car engine stopped. The man got out with difficulty, because he was big and blubbery, and stood in front of Lily with his fat bottom lip and his fat hands hanging and said, 'I'm sorry.'

She grabbed his arm as if she were a policeman, and looked round for Eric.

'Lily.' His voice came creakily from low down by the wall of the house. He was hunched up under the scullery window. 'I hate to say this, but I've shot myself in the foot.'

Once again, she drove Eric to the hospital in his car. This time they had blubbery Roger in the back. Time enough to take him to the police station after she had got Eric's foot to Casualty, wrapped in towels. Roger was passive and willing. He had only tried to take Lily's car because he needed to go and see his wife, and was too tired to walk any farther.

She did not take him to the police.

While Eric was in hospital for a few days, Lily brought him his letters, cleaned up the dinner things and tidied the house, fed the dog and let it out three times a day, and found a capable child in the village who would feed the chickens and goats and milk the two nannies. It was the least she could do for a neighbour, but she also found herself embroiled with Roger and his myriad problems.

She tried to resist. 'Don't tell me,' she wanted to beg him. 'I don't want to know, I don't want to get involved,' but he was such a great blockheaded baby and he had got himself into such a mess that she could not abandon him. She did not really want to. Dear Doctor Lily, a charger scenting battle, galumphed into the fray.

Roger had a council flat, no job, which did not worry him, and no wife, which did. He and the misguided woman who had married him fifteen years ago had been separated for a long time, but he still mooned over her and wanted her back. She was quite contentedly settled down with a man by whom she now had three children, but that made no difference to Roger. The only thing on his mind was getting into their house to see his wife.

Under siege, she and Mack had been surprisingly patient. They turned the television up louder when Roger banged on all the doors, front, back, front, side, back, front. When he prowled outside at night, calling her name, they would open a window and throw water on him.

'Not hot water,' Roger explained, 'and never any muck or like that. If I could just get to talk to her. I know we could make a go of it again.'

'But Roger, she doesn't want to see you.' Lily had been to talk to Roger's wife, at his request. She did not add, 'They laugh about you. They just wish you would go away.'

She had also talked to Roger's probation officer, who had been part and parcel of his life since he had breached a court order not to go within a quarter of a mile of Number 14 Elsmere Road, and done a little minor criminal damage when he was upset. Lily did not mention the attempted theft of her car. Roger had troubles enough. Eric's hen house had suffered more than the car, and Roger was sorry, and had brought wood and long nails and tacked it together again.

The probation officer was a sensible harried woman with too many clients, who would like to get Roger off her books.

'If you could just get it out of your mind,' she and Lily told him when the three of them met in her office, 'you could go ahead with your life.'

'Okay,' Roger said cheerfully. He was a likeable lump of dough. He never got aggressive or cantankerous. He always agreed with you, and raised his fat curved eyebrows and smiled his loose smile and tipped his large head on one side hopefully.

'Perhaps if he had a job to go to,' Lily said. 'If you had a job that you were interested in,' she amended quickly to Roger, ashamed of having talked about him over his head, as if he were in a wheelchair. 'You've got too much free time, and you start brooding. You need to be busy.'

'That's right,' Roger agreed.

Lily knew he had done kitchen jobs in hotels and restaurants. The mumpsy man was not coming back to Round Hill Rectory. Gerry and Janet needed more help. Sidetracked from his obsession, Roger might be all right.

438

Am I going out of my mind? Yes, but she could not stop herself.

'I'd like to ask around a bit and see what I can do. If that's all right with you?' she asked the probation officer. 'Is that all right, Roger?'

'Oh, yes, that's right. Yes.'

'You want to work again?'

'Yes, please.'

'You take it easy for a bit, and we'll see what we can do. Stay away from Elsmere Road, all right?'

'Oh –' he pushed his lips forwards like a trumpet – '*Yes.*'

Three days later, he went to Elsmere Road and let the air out of the tyres of Mack's car. Then he threw the dustbin – full, but he was a strong man – through the lounge window. Patient or not, they had to call the police.

With all that was going on with Roger, Lily was not very receptive when her father turned up with his tale of woe.

'A wand'ring minstrel, I.' Pixie was ill. She could not work any more. 'I think it's the big C, but they won't say. She looks dreadful and it's made her shockingly crabby. I tell you, Lily, it's been very hard for me, living in that house of sickness these last few months.'

'Hard for *you*?' However well you knew him, James could always take you by surprise with the depth and breadth of his selfishness.

'I've been an angel of mercy, but it's clear that the time has come for me to fold my tents.'

'You mean, you're walking out on her?'

'Well, there's always old Button, when she comes back from Greece, and so I thought, if I could hole up here for a bit, you and I could be cosy together and catch up on old times, and I can pop in and out of London as ness, to flog the odd laxative, although the profession is falling on evil times, and jobs are few and far between.'

'You are a swine,' Lily told him.

'That's a thought that hadn't occurred to me. I'm supposed to be a lovable old rogue.'

439

'Not to me. I see through you, Jamspoon.'

'Since when?'

'Since always, I suppose.'

'But you loved your poor old procreator.'

'I still do. But you're not going to live here.'

Grown a bit hard, his darling Lily, but then, she had suffered much. James was a big enough man to make allowances. He had covered his retreat anyway. Before he came to Lily, he had been to see Nora, because she owed him something, for old times' sake.

She was still nice to him. Exasperated but kindly, in her old way, and she gave him a bacon sandwich and a brown ale and seemed quite glad to sit and talk to him. Getting a bit pissed off with deadhead Duggie, no doubt.

One of her nursing pals had just killed off a private patient, in her own home. Easier to do there than in a hospital. The rich patient's house could not be sold until the solicitors and the government got their cut. A caretaker was needed, small salary and all found.

Near Nora?

'*No*,' she had said in her prim bossy way – you could always see where Lily got it from – but with luck he could keep his car on the road and keep his driving licence out of the hands of those eager breath-testers in green Day-glo jackets who swarmed on the edge of the motorways like maggots on a rotting corpse. They'd not get James Spooner. Too canny, Jamspoon.

When Roger went before the magistrates on a charge of breaching the court order and the terms of his probation, Lily went with him. She drove him to the court, because he seemed to be uncertain whether he would turn up or not.

They sat on a bench at the back of the court and listened to short stories about driving without a licence, or over the legal alcohol limit, or failing to stop for a police officer.

Some of the men were rough customers, but when they stood behind the high ledge of the dock, they were diminished, their public masquerade stripped away, crumpled up and thrown into a corner. The man who had spent the night in custody had a hangover clamped round his brow. They were substandard now, but when they had paid their fine or done their time, what would they care? Most of them had already paid visits to this court from time to time, like going to the dentist.

But the magistrates on the bench carried patiently on, fair, well-mannered, mild keepers of the gate against total anarchy: a clean-faced woman with a brisk bronze tassel of hair, a bald man like an accountant, a large chairman with brindled hair and beard all in one, like a pelt. All three of them wore half-spectacles. Looking over them at the defendant, pallid in the dock, they were quite magisterial and intimidating.

When it was Roger's turn, he had nothing to say. He put his fat hands on the edge of the dock like a dog begging, and looked hopefully for a bone from the bench.

The chairman told him he might have to face a custodial sentence. Lily wondered if Roger knew what that meant. She began to feel nervous. Now she was about to be something more than just a spectator in this drama.

Roger's probation officer, who had painted her eyes hyacinth blue for the court, which made them look more tired, was telling Their Worships about this person Mrs Lily Stephens, who was helping the defendant.

'Is Mrs Stephens here?'

'Sir, she is.'

The usher, who was no more than a young woman with a pony-tail and a sleeveless black gown over her pink angora sweater, ushered Lily to the witness box. There she stood, on trial for her life, the gallant little widow in decent black, twisting a lace handkerchief in her slender fingers. Pay attention, Lily. The chairman was asking her if she would answer a few questions.

'Sir, I'd be glad to.' That was how you said it.

'You have been taking an interest in the defendant?' The magistrates looked at her over their spectacles. Were they thinking, 'Hullo, here's this widow. What kind of an interest, eh?'

But she had the letter from Gerry and Janet. It was passed up to the bench and the magistrates put their bronze and bald and pelted heads together and muttered and whispered like the three bears, and nodded at her, and looked a little less inscrutably at Roger with his silly childish grin and hopeful eyebrows.

'Are you willing to take this job at the – let's see – at the Round Hill Rectory Hotel?'

Roger nodded. Too hard.

'Do you consider that he can perform it satisfactorily, Mrs Stephens?'

Lily nodded too hard also, and launched into an enthusiastic sales pitch for Roger and his future. The court must be impressed. 'I work at the hotel and I'll undertake to keep an eye on him and see that he works properly.'

Here's this amazing woman, they were thinking, willing to rescue this poor hapless fellow. Lily had already written the chairman's speech of gratitude.

He didn't know his lines. 'We thank you for the help you've given, Mrs Stephens.' He lowered the spectacles a bit farther down his leonine nose. 'But don't go too far. We would advise you not to take the principal role in this man's welfare. That will be best left to the probation service.'

But I know him best. And the probation officer has got too many customers already, without old Rodge. She would love to unload him.

'If we give him another chance by allowing his probation to run on, it will be up to him, you know, not you, whether he takes it or not.'

Ticked off.

'You may stand down.' The three bears were quiet and patient. Paul would have made a good magistrate. If he and Lily had bought a house in the English countryside, as they always said one day they might, he could have gone on the bench.

'Keep trying,' he would have said to Roger. 'You can make it.'

He would not have said to Lily, 'Don't go too far.' No don'ts, except, 'Don't be stifled. Keep on being yourself.'

Up on the barn roof, Terry looked over the farmyard and the wide ploughed field to the thin line of trees on the curving horizon, and felt at the same time on a level with the sky and at one with the turning earth. Since he had been with Thomas, he had realized that this was the only honest-to-God work he had ever done in his life. He was learning something that men had been doing in this country for six hundred years. He was going to be good at it. For the first time that he could remember, he felt a part of the life of the world.

Thomas was at the end of the long roof, laying wadds of straw against the barge board and tying them in with tarred cord. They hardly talked when they were working, and not much at other times. When they took their breaks, it was mostly brief un-sensational bits of information that Thomas had picked up since he started hanging straw with his father when he was a boy.

After he left Lily and Cathy, Terry had stayed with Blanche for a while, helping in the pub, which he had always enjoyed, and which reminded him of the happy old time with Dad before Terry had got mad with him and Lily for being so exclusively in love, and gone off in that carpeted van with Sue and the girl with the snaky hair.

He was beginning to be able to think rationally about good times lost. Lily was right. For a long while you had to shut the dead person out, for fear of the pain that came with them. But when you finally began to risk opening the door and letting them back in, they came familiarly to reassure you that the past was now, and was not lost.

When Blanche began to ask, 'How long are you planning to stay?', Terry packed his stuff into the biscuit tin and came back to the Berkshire downs to find Thomas. He knew that Lily's thatch would be finished. He drove around the lanes over a wide area, staying away from Daisy Cottage, until he saw the small grey truck outside a cottage with a ridge of Thomas's own pattern of scallops and points, having one end of its thatch repaired.

How did he ever get the nerve to ask a solid citizen like Thomas, a guy who had got it all together, to take on a short square person of twenty-seven with a forgettable face, who had screwed up pretty well everything he had ever laid his hand to?

Thomas's wife had gone off with a greyhound slipper three years ago, taking their teenage son with her. After Terry had worked with him for a month, Thomas suggested diffidently that he might like to leave his lodgings with Mrs Rambert and her beehives and move into his house.

Terry went down the ladder to make some more 'bottles' from the split bundles of wheat straw. He knocked the butt ends of the straw on a board to level them and tied them tightly enough to satisfy Thomas. He carried several up in a curved iron holder and hooked it into the old thatch, then banged in some spars for Thomas with the mallet.

'Let's see that hand.'

Terry turned over his hand, blistered and sore and chapped with the cold. The straw wrecked your hands, but when it had become thatch, end over end over end to lead water off the roof, it looked as smooth as a velvet cushion, graciously rounded. There was a healing split in his palm where he had tried to knock in hazel spars with his hand, like Thomas.

Thomas looked at it and nodded. 'Rub in some of that oil and make me some more spars,' he said. 'We're running short.'

Sitting on the tailboard of the truck, splitting the tough lengths of hazel with a billhook, Terry remembered too late to keep his fist on his knee as a buffer, and the knife slipped and cut the front of his knee.

Damn, damn, damn. A woman at the farmhouse bandaged it up tightly, and Thomas told him to take the rest of the day off.

'I'm all right.' Terry was furious with himself. He knew his job too well to make a stupid-ass mistake like that.

'Go home and put your foot up. Go on.'

'I told you. I'm all right.'

The cold light was waning. They only had an hour or so to

444

work. Terry's knee was throbbing and he had started to shiver, but he sharpened his cut spars and twisted them with his sore hands to show how tough he was. When he shifted the ladder along and went up on the roof again, he could hardly drag his stiffly bandaged knee up the ladder.

He did not have to drag it down again. He stepped down with one foot, and as he put his weight on that rung to bring the bad leg down, suddenly there was nothing there, and he and the ladder fell on to the hard ground outside the barn.

Roger was working out fairly well at Round Hill Rectory. He was slow and stodgy and unenterprising, but as long as you told him what to do, he usually stuck with the work until it was finished, and then went padding off with his gorilla walk to hoot at someone through his adenoids, 'What you want me to do next?'

Lily kept a sharp eye on him. Three bears or no three bears, she reminded him every day that the extension of his probation depended on him turning up at work on time and keeping away from Elsmere Road.

'Elsmere Road, where's that?' He arched up his eyebrows like furred caterpillars to make Lily laugh at his innocence.

'Man to see you.' He came one morning into the office where she was making up bills.

'Where?' There was no one in the entrance hall beyond the office window.

'Service door.'

'Well, Mr Blair is in the kitchen. He can deal with it.'

'He wants *you*.' Roger made his trumpet lips.

Now what? In a hotel, you could never do anything without an interruption.

Thomas was standing on the back drive. Lily took the harried look off her face.

'I don't want to bother you,' Thomas said, 'but I thought you'd want to know about Terry.'

'*Terry?*' What on earth had Terry got to do with Thomas? What now? She had got Eric back on his feet, and pretty much straightened out poor old Rodge. What kind of trouble was Terry in now?

Thomas did not want to come into the hotel, because he was in his working clothes, but Lily took him into the small library lounge and brought him coffee. Terry had cut his knee and then fallen off a barn roof.

'He set the ladder against some metal at the eaves, and it slipped. Bit shocked after the cut, I daresay. He's all right,' Thomas said in his calm way. 'Bit knocked about, poor chap, but he's young and tough and the doctor says he'll do, if he stays off the roof a few days. Terry said not to tell you, but I thought you should know.'

'Why didn't he tell me he was back here?'

'He didn't want you to feel responsible for him.'

'You mean, he was afraid I'd try to run his life?'

'Well –' Thomas looked up and laughed – 'that too. He thought you might feel you had to take him in.'

'I wouldn't have.'

'You might. You're a bit of a one for lame dogs, aren't you?'

As the hotel got busier before Easter, Roger started to turn up late, and once he missed a whole day.

When Lily tackled him, he shifted the blocks of his feet and confided, 'I don't really like getting up in the morning.'

'But you know your probation depends on you sticking to the job. If you don't keep the conditions, you could get a really heavy fine. They could even send you to prison.'

'I don't think I'd like that.'

'Well, if you want to work here, and I know you do, you must come in on time. You make it too difficult for everyone else, don't you see?'

'Oh, I wouldn't want to do that.'

'Good. Then we'll see you tomorrow at eight thirty.'

'I don't know. I mean, it's nice getting the money from you or Mrs Blair, but perhaps it would be better if I got it from Social Security.'

'Oh, *Roger!*' Lily was furious, but she turned away from him to restrain herself and put her face back together. 'I'll take you home after work.' She sighed. 'And we'll talk about it.'

'All right.' Roger went back to the kitchen.

No one could force him to stay here. No one could force him to stay out of prison, or to pull his amorphous life into shape. Whatever he chose to do, with or without the help of Doctor Lily, he had got to do it his own way, not hers.

All right, I can accept that. He's allowed not to change his ways unless he wants to. So am I.

In early April, it was still frosty in the mornings. Lily always went outside as soon as she was up, because it reminded her of going out early on Cape Cod to feed the horses. She went to the fence, and the dogs hared off. Cathy was already out in the field, with soft apples for the young Jersey heifers who were out again after being penned in for three months, making fertilizer. One day perhaps, she would be feeding a horse out here. Her hair was like thistledown.

Under a pearly sky, the bright young wheat was frosted to a pastel green, like lichen. The cows were pale as cream. Their breath steamed gently over the grey grass. Everything was muted. Tree skeletons were softened and the hills opposite were blurred behind low wisps of cloud that trailed idly along the valley.

Now that Terry had settled into his life with Thomas, and was at peace with Lily, he had painted a picture of her like this, with her arms on the top rail of the fence, looking out into a disappearing view. Her hair and skirt were blowing sideways, and Terry had made her neck more slender and her waist smaller than it really was.

The new picture hung beside the one he had painted of his father. Lily was no longer troubled by the idea that Paul was walking away from her into his own mysterious landscape. Side by side, the two of them looked calmly out together upon a universal horizon.

Together, but myself. The sound of bells came faintly from behind the opposite hill. Thomas and the sweet serious women and the boy were ringing for early service.

. . . each hung bell's
Bow swung finds tongue to fling out broad its name;
Each mortal thing does one thing and the same;
Deals out that being indoors each one dwells;
Selves — goes itself; myself it speaks and spells,
Crying What I do is me: for that I came.